IN ~~T~~
OF THE ~~BEHOLD~~

The model, still shaken from her encounter with the prowler, arrived early. She had spent the night in a hotel, but she was not able to sleep. There were dark circles under her eyes, and after she cleared a space in front of one of the makeup mirrors, she attempted to cover them . . .

Then she remembered her eyedrops. She wondered if they were still there or if some model had filched them again. To her relief, the bottle was where she had left it. She unscrewed the lid, put a drop in each eye and started to screw the lid back on when she dropped it.

The pain was instantaneous, so excruciating that it felt as if someone had driven white-hot pokers into her eyes . . .

SKIN DEEP

----

*A Terrifying Novel of
Beauty, Jealousy, and Murder*

SKIN DEEP

Kae McCullough

B

BERKLEY BOOKS, NEW YORK

The characters in this book are fictional. Any similarity to real persons, either living or dead, is purely coincidental and not intended by the author.

SKIN DEEP

A Berkley Book / published by arrangement with the author

PRINTING HISTORY
Berkley edition / December 1993

ISBN: 0-425-14009-1

BERKLEY®
Berkley Books are published by
The Berkley Publishing Group,
200 Madison Avenue,
New York, New York 10016.
BERKLEY and the "B" design are trademarks of
Berkley Publishing Corporation.

PRINTED IN THE UNITED STATES OF AMERICA

10 9 8 7 6 5 4 3 2 1

In memory:

SY LOEWEN
1952–1992

At unexpected times,
I smile at the memories of you.

Prologue

She quietly made her way down the darkened hallway to Alan's bedroom, a glass of Bacardi in her hand. Behind her she could hear Alan ushering his guests out, bidding them a good night. Soon they would be alone, she thought, and a little shiver of anticipation ran through her. Silently she slipped through the double doors, quickly reclosing them after her, and looked around in surprise.

Alan's living room was one of understated contemporary elegance combined with graceful antiques and expensive accessories, a perfect showcase for *Architectural Digest*. His bedroom, however, was its antithesis.

Just like Alan, sweet and juicy on the outside but rotten to the core inside, she thought, giggling at the analogy. The walls and even the ceiling were lined with black smoked mirrors while the floor was covered in gray nubby berber—that is, what little carpet could be seen through the litter of dirty laundry, old newspapers, and magazines. Recessed ceiling lights washed the room in a soft glow, but even the lights couldn't disguise the filth. Rancid scraps of food on dirty plates and filthy napkins were strewn everywhere. She glanced around quickly as a sudden movement caught her eye. A fat brown cock-roach scuttled from inside a half-eaten tuna sandwich and dashed over a pair of dirty jockey shorts directly toward her. At the last moment it swerved and dove beneath a grimy sweat sock. She shuddered in revulsion and clamped her mouth shut before she could involuntarily squeal.

Though she'd never been in his bedroom before, his reputation as a no-holds-barred connoisseur of sex with both men and women was legendary, as was his fetish for videotaping his many escapades. Rumor had it that he kept a camera secreted behind the framed Mapplethorpe print that hung opposite the foot of his bed. She went immediately to the print and lifted it off the wall. Sure enough, there was a Beta Camcorder all set up and ready for action.

"Bingo," she whispered, smiling to herself. She pulled a brilliant multicolored silk scarf from her purse and stretched it across the camera lens, securing it with a rubber band, then carefully replaced the picture.

She walked over to the rumpled, unmade bed, the white sheets dingy. She surmised that they hadn't seen the inside of a washing machine in some time. Cracker crumbs and grape stems lay scattered across the bottom sheet.

She set her glass down on the nightstand next to a half-used tube of hemorrhoid salve and a large wad of tissues. She glanced at them and giggled, realizing that Alan probably had nose problems. The salve was commonly used to shrink swollen nasal membranes from doing too much coke.

There was a McIntosh tube amplifier and receiver on the opposite nightstand and she leaned across the bed and switched on the power. The soft strains of a Jefferson Airplane classic waffled through the Infinity speakers and she sat down on the edge of the bed, mesmerized by the hypnotic voice of Grace Slick. She hummed along with the music and gently stroked the tiny, silver amulet that hung from a braided gold cord around her neck. She dreamily removed the neckpiece, unscrewed the stemmed

top, and reconnected the top to the base, to form a minia-
ture silver pipe. Then she pulled a small bottle, a pair of
long-handled forceps, and other paraphernalia from her
purse and laid everything in a neat row on the nightstand.
Reaching back into her purse, she took out a 500-mg. Red
Flyer and washed it down with a big gulp of rum.

The pill took hold, breaking down in her stomach,
rushing through her bloodstream, and exploding in her
brain. The words and music of Slick's song grew in
intensity and echoed over and over, until she wasn't sure
whether they were coming from inside her head or from
the speakers behind her. She stood up and began swaying
to the music, her shoulder-length platinum dynell wig
ebbing and flowing to the throbbing beat. The pervasive
rhythm drove out all thoughts of yesterday or tomorrow,
leaving only the reality of the next few minutes. A hot
flush rolled over her and she felt a trickle of perspiration
slowly caress its way down between her breasts, the length
of her flat stomach, and into the dark tangle of hair below.
She stripped off her Schiaparelli pink satin jacket to reveal
a lacy black bustier, a tiny black crepe miniskirt, and long
strands of jet-black beads that she had twisted around
her throat. The mirrored reflection of her lovely body
undulating to the music made her moan with pleasure.

Gradually through the early-morning silence and drug-
induced fog, Alan became aware of music coming from
his bedroom. He had been positive that everyone had
left the party, but apparently he was wrong. The sudden
realization that he wasn't alone filled him with trepidation
and raised the hairs on the back of his neck.

He crept cautiously down the long hallway to his bedroom doors, then paused to listen. Music throbbed from
behind the doors and he guardedly pushed them open a
crack and peeked inside. To his amazement and delight, a
delicious young woman sensuously moved to the rhythm
of the music.

Yes, yes, he exclaimed silently to himself, lifting his
hands toward the ceiling in mock prayer. *There is a God*

after all! And, Alan, baby, you're him!

He pulled the doors open. She was oblivious to him as he stood there for a few moments, gazing at her graceful movements and striking beauty. He had never expected to find *her* in his bedroom. He had been wanting to fuck her ever since she had walked through his front door earlier that evening. A large measure of his sexual success, with both men and women, was that he found out what they wanted and he gave it to them; however, he had not been able to get close enough to this one during the party to find out what it was she wanted. But he would find out now and give it to her in spades. His pole was already saluting in anticipation.

"Baby, baby," he crooned as he moved across the room toward her. "Why didn't you tell me you were back here? I would have never kept *you* waiting."

He came up behind her and ran his hands up and down her tall, lithe body. She was a full head taller than he was, but he loved the tall ones. It was such a feeling of conquest to fuck the tall ones. He couldn't believe his good fortune; tonight was truly his lucky night. Her skin was as soft as flower petals and she smelled twice as sweet. He could hardly contain his excitement and he knew she felt the same way; he could tell by the way she trembled at his touch. They all did. None of them could resist his boyish good looks, his thick-lashed brown eyes, and his practiced gregarious smile.

"I can't tell you how much I want to fuck you," he whispered huskily as he turned her around to face him.

"Try," she commanded softly.

Her eyes were deep violet, too intense in color to be natural, he was sure, and she gave him a look of such naked hunger that his cock rose higher.

"Tell me," she repeated, catching her full lower lip provocatively between her teeth, then parting them and sliding her tongue along the upper edge of her lip.

"Oh, God," Alan moaned. He flicked his long layered black hair over his shoulders and ran his lips down the side of her shapely neck, kissing the hollow of her throat. He inhaled deeply and blew his hot breath against her skin. It was a trick he always used and it drove his lovers crazy.

I've got all the moves, he thought confidently to himself.

"Not so fast, darlin'," she said sweetly, extracting herself from his embrace. "We have the whole night. Why rush a good thing, huh?"

"Of course not," he replied a little sheepishly.

Rush? he thought to himself. *By the time I'm finished, I'll have this cunt begging me for more. She's never had a cock that can compare to mine.*

Even so, he mentally stepped back and slowed his mounting excitement. Using one of his most successful ploys, he gazed deep into her eyes with scorching intensity. Suddenly he had the niggling suspicion that beneath the platinum wig and false eyelashes was someone he had seen before tonight, but the thought escaped him before he could fully grasp it.

"Come into my parlor, darlin'—" she murmured in his ear, pressing her warm body against him.

"I'll come wherever you want," he interrupted, turning his full attention back to the luscious creature before him. "But preferably all over you."

She smiled and ran her tongue around the outer edge of his ear and nibbled on the lobe. Then taking his hand, she led him over to the bed and gently pushed him back, her hands pausing to stroke the rock-hard bulge in his pants.

He had to get this action on tape, Alan thought excitedly and flipped a switch on the wall next to the bed.

She reached over to the row of paraphernalia on the nightstand and picked up the silver pipe and bottle. After opening the bottle and sprinkling several crystals of crack in the pipe's bowl, she took a wad of cotton with the forceps, dipped the cotton in the rum, and lit it. She touched the flaming cotton to the rocks and took a deep drag to ignite them.

Alan watched her and wondered again where they might have met, but the answer still flitted away from him in the passion of the moment. Then she passed the pipe to him.

"Here, sweet meat," she whispered, and began to undress him.

Alan eagerly took the pipe and inhaled. "Wow, this is good shit!" The coke hit his brain in a shower of sparks and his body felt electrified, too, as she slowly undressed him, stroking and caressing every inch of him, making him itch with desire. At that moment he would have given her anything: his Mercedes, his condo, his business, anything to slake his thirst for her body. He grabbed for her, but she eluded his grasp and started slowly to unwind the strands of black beads from around her neck.

"Come into my parlor, darlin'," she repeated in a throaty whisper, kneeling before him and encircling him in a long strand.

He impatiently cupped her head with one hand and pressed his lips down on hers. He slipped his tongue against her lips and she parted them with a moan of lust. He probed the hot inside of her mouth with his tongue and flattened himself against her body. He wanted her to feel his turgid, throbbing cock. He wanted her to beg him to put it to her. His other hand slid down the front of her bustier. He grabbed the strands of her necklace and with a quick jerk ripped them from her body, macho style. Beads scattered everywhere.

"Never mind, love," she murmured, taking his hand and sensually sucking his fingers one by one.

Fuck, this was turning into a marathon. If she'd just let him plug her once, then they could go back to the romance part later.

"Here," she said, moving away from him and sliding her hand up under her skirt. She slipped off her G-string and dangled it before his eyes. "I have an extra special little snack for you."

Oh, Christ, Alan thought, *not edible underwear.* He'd thought she was more of a swinger. But what the hell, if it would make her spread those long legs, he'd eat the damn G-string and his shorts, too!

"Anything you say, baby. You're the boss," he said, grabbing the G-string and stuffing it into his mouth. It was cherry-flavored.

It figures, he thought, almost gagging on its sickening sweetness as he swallowed the whole thing in one gulp. There was a bitter aftertaste, too, but he ignored it and reached for the woman.

Suddenly there was something wrong. His stomach flip-flopped and cramped with such excruciating pain that it took his breath away. He felt like his stomach was being twisted and ripped from his body. All sexual desire left him as he struggled to catch his breath. His face changed from red to deep purple to blue, and he grabbed for the woman next to him. His coordination was sluggish and all he managed to catch was empty air. She twisted gracefully away from him and danced to her feet, where she stood watching him intently.

"Help me," he gurgled, through the saliva and mucus that bubbled freely from his lips. "P-please!" His facial muscles spasmed into gross distortions and the convulsions quickly spread to the rest of his body. He thrashed and twitched uncontrollably.

"I already have, Alan, darlin'," she replied, smiling indifferently. "Like I said before, darlin'. Come into my parlor," she repeated, pulling off the platinum wig, "said the frog to the fly."

Alan's eyes bulged as the realization of who she was suddenly impacted on his screaming consciousness, but he knew it was too late. She was one person who would never help him. Pink froth flowed from his mouth and nose, and with a final, massive convulsion, he fell back on the bed, dead before his head hit the pillow.

She watched in morbid fascination.

"Bye, fly," she chirped cheerfully.

CHAPTER
1

Joi Lin Ambernites hit the remote switch on her VCR to rewind the Super Model aerobic tape and, out of breath, dropped into the nearest chair. The tape promised that if she worked out daily, within two weeks she'd see a "new you." She caught a glimpse of herself in the mirror on the other side of the room and made a face.

"I could exercise till the end of time and it would still be the same old me," she said out loud, critically peering at herself in the mirror and turning one way and then another.

It wasn't a bad face, she thought, sucking in her cheeks and trying to look seductive. It just wasn't a model's face. She pushed her shiny black hair behind her ears for a closer examination. There were no smooth planes and sharp angles to her cheekbones, only soft mounds and gentle slopes.

She inspected her pale hazel eyes. Nope, they didn't even vaguely resemble a model's wide-set eyes. Her Korean mother was responsible for Joi Lin's slightly sloe, though not exotic, eyes.

She did have beautiful white teeth, even though she had a tiny overbite. But then so did a lot of actresses.

For example, Lassie. That made her smile to herself. No, she'd never make the cover of *Cosmopolitan*, but what the heck, she liked her face.

What Joi Lin didn't mentally check off her list was her sweet disposition, a dimpled smile that lit up a room and would put a young Shirley Temple to shame, a contagious sparkle in her pale eyes, and a laugh that caused others to join in.

She continued her critical analysis of the rest of her body with a frown. It was something she was determined to change. She tried pulling the gray sweat suit fabric tight against her figure. The top half of her body was fine, with firm upper arms, full breasts, and a narrow waist. It was the lower half that needed help. Her hips and thighs were Rubenesque and, in the back of her mind, she suspected that no amount of exercise was going to change them, although it wouldn't stop her from trying.

Her stomach rumbled, reminding her it was time for her liquid diet lunch. As she stood up to follow the well-worn path to her refrigerator, the doorbell rang and she reversed her direction to the front door, wondering who it could be on a Tuesday afternoon. It was probably her brother, Alan. She hadn't heard from him in several days, since she told him she couldn't come to his party, to be exact. He'd been furious and had tried his usual methods of persuasion: cajoling, guilt, and finally anger. In the past it would have worked; he'd always been able to talk her into whatever he wanted. But she'd stood fast to her decision in an effort to become more assertive.

She really did have other plans that night, and besides, his Hollywood parties weren't all that much fun. For the most part, there were plenty of drugs and a bunch of superficial people trying to outdo each other or to use anyone for their own benefit. Although Alan always went out of his way to introduce her to all the other guests, because she wasn't in a position to help any of them, she usually spent the evening sitting in a corner alone. No, she had told herself, she'd fulfilled her sisterly obligation in the past. Alan fed on the glamour and fast lane, but she'd been to enough Hollywood parties to last a lifetime.

She opened the front door, expecting to see her brother, ready with his standard line when he wanted to make up: "Joi Lin, I'm going to give you one last chance to apologize," even when it wasn't her fault. He always tried to manipulate the situation around to his advantage, but she understood that his ego wouldn't allow him to take any responsibility or blame. He was always right; it had been that way since childhood.

But it wasn't Alan; instead, it was a hulk of a man. He had to be at least six feet four, well over a foot taller than she, and his bulk filled the doorway so completely that she could barely see the sunlight behind him. His face had the look of an ex-fighter, big flattened features, squared jawline, the face of a man who didn't know the meaning of backing down. Only his soulful puppy-dog eyes kept him from being thoroughly intimidating.

"Don't you believe in asking who it is before you open the door?" he boomed in a deep rumbling voice before she could say anything. "Los Angeles is not a place to take chances."

"I—I thought you were my brother," she stammered, taking a step back, intimidated.

"Were you expecting him today?" he asked, watching her closely.

"Well, no—" Joi Lin started to respond obediently, then remembered that this was her home and she should be the one asking the questions.

"Hey, wait a minute, who are you anyway?" she demanded, adopting a stance of authority.

"I'm Lieutenant Frank Hollis, LAPD," he answered, flipping out his badge for identification. "Are you Joi Lin Ambernites?"

"Yes, I am," she told him.

"Alan Ainsley Anderson is your brother?"

"Yes. That's his professional name. It's easier to remember than Ambernites," Joi Lin volunteered nervously. "But how did you know?" Her stomach churned with sudden queasiness as she sensed that something was terribly wrong.

"I saw a signed picture of you in his apartment and then I found your name and address in his address book," Hollis explained.

"May I come in," he continued somberly. He said it as a statement rather than a question and slipped past Joi Lin with surprising catlike grace before she could answer. "I'd like to talk to you for a few minutes."

His tone of voice had softened and that scared Joi Lin more than what he was saying. She knew without asking that something was wrong with Alan, but the words rushed out anyway.

"What is it? Has something happened to my brother? Has he been in a car accident?" she cried before she even closed the door behind Lieutenant Hollis. A feeling of dread overcame her, and in her mind she conjured up a vision of his car twisted and mangled.

"I told him not to drive so fast," she said with a quiver in her voice.

"I'm afraid, Ms. Ambernites, that it's more serious than that." His words hung in the air and suddenly Joi Lin wished that she could suspend time forever. She didn't want to hear his next sentence; she didn't want to hear what her heart already suspected.

"Your brother is dead," he told her quietly.

"Oh, please God, no!" Joi Lin cried. Such pressure mounted inside her chest that for a moment she felt it would burst, then she crumpled into tears. "He can't be! I just talked to him a week ago and he was fine!"

Hollis looked at the sobbing young woman standing before him, such a tiny slip of a thing. This was a part of his job that he never got used to. After twenty years of police work, ten as a homicide detective, he had become callous enough to handle the most brutal of murders and the most heinous of criminals. Yet a woman's anguished tears were the hardest for him to face. He awkwardly patted her shoulder, as he would a small child.

"Alan was all I had. He was my whole family," she muttered through her tears. "How did it happen? What kind of accident was it?"

Hollis looked at her upturned, tear-stained face. Christ, sometimes he hated his job. Why couldn't he just concentrate on catching the criminals and let someone else be the bearer of bad news? Why did he have to be the one to tell her that her brother was found in his bedroom stark naked and stone-cold dead by his maid, who then ran hysterically through the building, shrieking at the top of her lungs? By the time the police arrived, seven eighths of the building's occupants had traipsed through her brother's apartment to have a morbid look at him and had managed to trample any evidence the police might have discovered. The coroner estimated that Anderson had been dead for several days. The bedroom air-conditioning, running full blast, had turned the room into a giant refrigerator and kept Anderson perfectly preserved. "Crisp as a cucumber," Hollis remembered the coroner had quipped with a perverse grin. A police canvass of the building confirmed that the last time anyone had seen or heard Anderson was the night of his big bash three days earlier. Everyone, including the next-door neighbors, heard him that night.

Yes, Hollis thought, why did it have to be him? But he already knew the answer. He was a lieutenant and it came with the territory. All the same, his puppy-dog eyes became even more soulful.

"It wasn't an accident, Ms. Ambernites," he told her softly. "We believe he was murdered."

Derian Delorian loved mornings like this. The pristine sun glittered brightly, quickly evaporating the light moisture that had settled on the pavements overnight. Glancing into the distance, she noticed that the light mist created by the sun and the dew gave the boulevard a vague, dreamlike quality, making her think that Sunset Boulevard was indeed a street of dreams.

Every day, hundreds of people traversed the famous boulevard, people with dreams as different as the imposing white arches of Bel Air were from the gaudy shops on the strip.

Derian, owner of Los Angeles's most prestigious modeling agency, DDL, confidently maneuvered her sleek Jaguar XJS convertible through the bumper-to-bumper morning traffic. There had been a major fender-bender and traffic was backed up in both directions on the boulevard.

Just before the East Gate entrance to Bel Air, there was a break in the line of cars, as some of the cars in the right lane peeled off to continue on to the valley, and Derian saw her opportunity. With the smooth skill of a seasoned California driver, she downshifted into second gear, hit the gas, and swerved around a gray Mercedes. Behind her, the driver, realizing she meant to pull ahead of him, leaned on his horn as he tried to speed up and cut her off. It was one of the unspoken laws of the road in California: Never give the other driver an even break, or any break if you could help it. Derian ignored him and squeezed into the opening.

Sorry, buddy, she thought to herself with a triumphant smile. *You're just not quick enough.* Sharp and manipulative, Derian relished any kind of challenge, and winning was her game. She knew how to go to the mat to get what she wanted but she didn't believe in being ruthless, unless she had to be.

Yes, she could handle any situation. Her thoughts drifted to her beloved brother, Rusty. At twenty-four years old, he was fifteen years younger than she, almost young enough to be her son, and she was fiercely protective of him. After their parents' deaths when he was fourteen, the burden of raising him had fallen on her young shoulders and she had immediately set her priorities—Rusty, her work, and then the rest of the world, in that order.

Thank God her modeling career had been hot and had afforded her the luxury of spending more time with him than a normal nine-to-five job would have. It had also provided them with a life-style free of money problems.

But, still, she was saddened by his being deprived of their parents and over the years she had done the best she could to make it up to him. She had even taken him with her on bookings, which had fascinated him, and he quickly began to learn as much as he could about her work until he knew almost as much about modeling as she did.

At one point, he had seriously considered a career as a male model. A younger male version of Derian, except for his gray-blue eyes, he would have been perfect but his build was just too narrow, so he gave up on modeling. Since then, he had attempted several careers and with undying motherly support, Derian had encouraged each new venture. The agency was her lifeblood, but Rusty was her life.

With a flip of her finger, she pressed a button on the dashboard and the Jag's convertible black top folded back, exposing Derian to the warm southern California sun and the gentle Santa Ana breezes. The sunlight reflected glints of rich copper off Derian's burnished hair, and the wind caught the thick, wavy strands, fanning them out behind her. More than one motorist turned his head to stare at her as she sped by.

She checked her gold Buccellati watch and uttered a sigh of exasperation. "Damn that Alan!" she swore cynically. "Even dead, the jerk's still causing me problems."

The day before, a Lieutenant Frank Hollis from the Los Angeles Police Department had visited her at her agency, bringing the inspiring news that Alan Ainsley Anderson was dead.

"Lieutenant Hollis, you've brightened my day. No, make that my entire week," Derian told the detective with a dazzling smile. "Don't look so shocked," she continued. "You might as well know up front. There was no love lost between Alan and me. Alan was a snake. I taught him everything he knew about the modeling agency business, and he rewarded me by starting his own agency with my account list! It couldn't have happened to a better guy!"

Replaying the conversation in her mind, she laughed out loud at her snappy repartee. Hollis hadn't even cracked a

smile. But then what did she expect of a flatfoot who
wore a ten-year-old suit. Narrow lapels went out with
the Dark Ages, for crying out loud, and didn't he know
pant cuffs were in? Oh, well, it wasn't like she would
be representing him for modeling jobs. The image of the
solemn Lieutenant Hollis as one of her models made her
laugh harder.

After Lieutenant Hollis left, she immediately put in a
call to Mrs. Ritter, the fashion coordinator of Spheres, her
biggest account. If she moved quickly, she was positive
that she could swing Alan's share of the Spheres business to her agency. It could easily mean an extra fifty
to seventy-five thousand dollars a year for her models
and a fat thirty percent commission for her—fifteen from
the models and fifteen from the client. Not too bad a
return from one telephone call and follow-up meeting.
She stayed up half the night preparing her strategy for
this morning's breakfast meeting, and as a result slept
through her alarm. Twenty minutes behind in her busy
schedule, she rushed to finish important errands before
her appointment.

Picking up her mobile phone, she pressed the direct
dial to the dining room at the Hotel Bel Air. Angelo, the
maître d', picked up on the first ring.

"Angelo," Derian said crisply, "this is Derian Delorian.
Is Mrs. Ritter there yet?"

"No, Ms. Delorian," Angelo answered. "Not yet."

"Thank goodness," Derian replied in relief. Although
DDL was the biggest agency in L.A., Alan had been snapping at her heels. His untimely demise held the potential
for her agency to realize a ten percent increase in income
from the Spheres account alone, and she couldn't afford
to offend Lucille Ritter. "If she gets there before I do, see
that she's well taken care of."

"Absolutely, Ms. Delorian," he responded.

She hung up and turned all her attention back to her
smooth weaving in and out of the traffic and finally entered
the exclusive Bel Air community.

The morning traffic on Stone Canyon Road was almost nonexistent as the residents never worried about punching a time clock. They were the owners of the time clocks. On the sides of the road, tall walls and manicured hedges hid lavish mansions from prying eyes, and a profusion of lush trees hung like a canopy, shading the road from direct sunlight and muffling the sounds of traffic from Sunset Boulevard. It was like entering a different world, outside the hectic realm of Los Angeles.

Derian didn't waste time on the scenery. Even in opulent Bel Air there was a social pecking order, and being at the top of the A-list in Beverly Hills, where she was a frequent guest at the most glamorous parties, she knew the most important estates inside and out. With her limited schedule, Derian made it a point to attend only the crème de la crème of parties or ones that would benefit her professionally.

Location-wise, the most exclusive area was the lower east side of Bel Air. But Derian lived closer to the West Gate, high up in the canyon with a spectacular view of the reservoir. She liked separating herself from L.A.'s frenetic pace. In the hills, she felt the same tranquillity she had known in the Pacific Northwest where she grew up.

Derian rounded the final curve and pulled into the hotel parking lot, coming to a dead stop with screeching tires. The waiting valets scurried for cover to avoid the spray of loose gravel kicked up by the Jag's tires.

She checked her watch again. Fifteen minutes late. Without waiting for the valet to open her door, she slid gracefully from the car, her leopard print silk dress catching on the door and revealing the curve of a long, smooth thigh. She flicked the silk skirt down with an impatient brush of her hand and started swiftly across the wooden bridge that linked the parking lot with the hotel grounds.

"Lady, lady," one of the attendants called, hurrying after her. "You forgot your ticket!"

Without breaking her stride, she flashed a warm, amused smile at him over her shoulder.

"Forget it, Shawn," the other attendant said, coming up behind him. "That's Derian Delorian. She doesn't need a ticket. Everyone knows her!"

"The modeling agency owner?" Shawn asked in surprise. "What a knockout! She should be a model herself."

"You moron," Mike said with the exasperated tone of someone who was dealing with a half-wit; sometimes he suspected Shawn was. "She used to be one of the top models in the world."

"Wow," Shawn breathed in awe as he stared at the disappearing figure. "What a looker!"

Smiling, Derian caught snippets of the valets' conversation. She was used to the effect her presence had on people. She knew she was a strikingly beautiful woman and admiring stares were a way of life for her.

The sun's golden rays caught in her russet hair, framing her face in a halo of color. She had the milky white skin of a natural redhead and behind her dark glasses her eyes were large and round, their color varying from jade to chartreuse, depending on her mood. Her nose was narrow and perfectly photogenic, thanks to the skill of a plastic surgeon when she was eighteen. Her best feature, though, was her magnificent height. Just under six feet, almost too tall to model at the beginning of her fashion career, she had quickly learned to market the novelty of her height with her stunning beauty and had parlayed herself into being one of the top models in the world. Throughout the late sixties, seventies, and into the early eighties no one— not Cheryl Teigs, Jerry Hall, not even Christie Brinkley— had come close to her popularity. Shrewd enough to stop modeling while still at her peak in the early eighties, she had used her savings to finance her own agency. And now the thirty-nine-year-old ex-model owed nothing to anyone, and that was how she liked it.

She took a shortcut along a stone path that skirted the gigantic banana palms and birds of paradise, which concealed the hotel walls on her left. To the right, stately swans softly chittered from a small tropical pond.

Rounding a corner, she entered the restaurant through the terra-cotta patio.

"Ms. Delorian," Angelo exclaimed, hurrying to kiss her hand. "You're looking as spectacular as always. Those girls at your agency should be thankful they aren't competing with you for bookings anymore. They'd all starve—"

"Thank you, Angelo," Derian interrupted. She'd always felt Angelo missed his true calling. He would have been a great mayor or at the very least a popular councilman.

"Is Mrs. Ritter here yet?" she asked, looking around the restaurant. "Oh, I see her," she said in the same breath, answering her own question.

Lucille Ritter was a tiny sparrow of a woman, dressed in a monochromatic beige suit that blended with her skin tone; the only colors were her black shoe-button eyes and her trademark Chanel red lips. She sat slump-shouldered as if the weight of the world were resting on her thin back, her little eyes darting nervously about the room. She spotted Derian and weakly fluttered her hand.

Without waiting for Angelo to lead the way, Derian extracted her hand from his lips and hurried over to the table.

"Lucille," Derian said warmly, sliding in opposite the woman and grasping her limp hand in both of hers. "How are you? I'm so sorry I'm late."

"I've been better, dear." Lucille sighed. "And you?"

Without waiting for Derian to reply, she launched into her usual rhetoric.

Derian took a deep breath and steeled herself to be bored for the next hour. She knew the whole monologue by memory and didn't take Lucille's complaints seriously. Listening was just part of doing business with Lucille Ritter, and besides it was well worth the time if it meant getting one hundred percent of Spheres's business.

"I have so many responsibilities that I don't know whether I'm coming or going. The pressure from the store is unbearable," she exclaimed, her pale hands flapping in the air for emphasis. "Why, just yesterday, Mr. Paul, the manager of the couture salon, was complaining because we don't furnish a complimentary buffet lunch for our salon patrons. Can you imagine? Who does he think we are? Let them go to the restaurant on the second floor!

"And Mrs. Roque is only interested in whether the Beverly Hills moneyed set is impressed with her store." She paused for a breath and looked to Derian for sympathy.

Derian took the opportunity to break into the conversation. "You poor thing," she clucked, shaking her head. "Shall we order, dear?" she continued, signaling their waitress before Lucille had a chance to recharge her mouth.

They rattled off their selections to the waitress, and Derian seized the brief lull to change the conversation.

"Did you hear about Alan Ainsley Anderson?" she asked.

"No, what?" Lucille responded distractedly, going down her mental list of complaints. How could Alan Ainsley Anderson possibly be more interesting than her own problems?

"He's dead," Derian announced dramatically, pausing a moment for her announcement to sink in. "He was murdered."

"What!" Lucille exclaimed, simultaneously forgetting about her other problems and realizing that Alan's unfortunate demise presented yet another.

"That's terrible," she cried, the nervous tic in her left eyelid starting up. How could he let that happen? Her biggest show of the year was next month! Half the models were from his agency! "How did it happen?"

"Well, the police haven't a clue," Derian answered. "They said he'd been dead for several days before he was found."

"Oh, Lord!" Lucille wailed, her eye twitching furiously. She thought about Mr. Paul, who'd like nothing better than to see her fall on her face. That fat fag had been eyeing her job as fashion coordinator for years, and if the upcoming show was a fiasco, he'd hammer one more nail in her coffin with Ellysa Roque, Spheres's owner. This was shaping up to be an awful day.

"Lucille," Derian said in alarm, noticing for the first time how distraught she seemed. She'd had no idea that Lucille was so close to Alan. He must have really turned on his phony charm. Thank God he was out of the way.

The waitress arrived with their breakfast.

"I had no idea you and Alan were so close," Derian continued, taking a sip of her coffee.

"We weren't—I mean, that is, I'm so shocked about his death," Lucille stammered, belatedly coming to her senses and trying to preserve her genteel image. It never occurred to her not to bother, because everyone saw through her facade. "How horrible! But what about his agency?" She nervously shredded her toast into tiny pieces, discarding it without eating any. She just couldn't get the vision of her impending doom out of her mind. "What will happen to it? And to his clients? His bookings? And my big show next month! What will happen to *me* if the show falls apart?" she wailed.

"Lucille, Lucille, don't worry," Derian soothed, putting her fork down and patting the older woman's hand. It was the moment she'd been waiting for. "I'll help you. Everything will be all right. Trust me. I have the best models in Los Angeles."

"I don't know," Lucille said dubiously. "I try to make it a point to book models from several agencies, to make sure I have only the best. Mrs. Roque is very particular—"

"I have the perfect solution," Derian announced to Lucille, pushing the plate away, confident that her brilliant plan would appeal to the overanxious woman. "I wasn't going to tell you this yet, but I can see that you're so upset and I want to set your mind at ease. I've engineered a major coup." She paused a beat and took a deep breath. "Here in Los Angeles, I represent *the* top model in Paris, Holly Woodward, and *she* will be arriving in time for your show! It will be the talk of the season!"

"Do you really think so?" Lucille asked, brightening.

She would love to put Mr. Paul in his place, and maybe Mrs. Roque would finally realize just how indispensable she was.

Derian nodded encouragingly. "I guarantee it," she told Lucille positively. Even if she had to wear the clothes herself, she thought.

Lucille gave Derian a small, tight smile. Maybe the day hadn't turned out to be so bad after all.

Back at her desk, Derian immediately placed a call to Paris. While she waited for the connection, she thought back to a year ago, when Holly Woodward started modeling. Derian had sent her to Paris to gain experience, and although Derian would make no money from Holly, she had used her connections to set Holly up with Vogue/Caliber, a new agency and a real comer in Paris. Holly's move had paid off. She had blossomed and done exceptionally well in a short period of time.

Derian realized that Holly didn't owe her anything, but Derian had gambled on her knowledge of human nature when she told Lucille that Holly had already agreed to return to L.A. And she was right, for when Holly answered the phone and heard Derian's proposition, she immediately offered to come for the Spheres show the following month. Pleased with her coup, Derian spent the next hour poring over the headshot book, trying to decide which of her best models to use in the show.

She had just finished making a tentative list when a sophisticated, but noticeably older than the norm, blond model stuck her head around the door. She was tall and lean with the taut body of a woman twenty years younger, but her face betrayed her age. Skillful application of makeup gave her the illusion of youth, but the bright daylight revealed a network of crow's-feet around her eyes and the onset of saggy cheeks.

"Derian," she asked, "may I talk to you?"

"Sure, Charis," Derian answered, motioning for her to come in and sit down. "What's up?"

"Things have been so slow, I don't understand it,"

Charis answered with a puzzled look on her face. "I've hardly had any bookings lately."

Derian fidgeted uncomfortably in her chair. Things weren't slow; this was the busiest season. Her other girls were working like crazy. But she hadn't the heart to tell Charis why she wasn't working.

Charis had been with Derian from the day DDL had opened, and before that, she and Derian had modeled together for years and had become good friends. In fact, during the mid-seventies they were the hottest models in the fashion world. Clients vied to use them and they were flown all over the world at the drop of a hat. At their peak, Derian had retired and opened DDL, while Charis, who was a few years older than Derian, had continued to model. Gazing sympathetically at Charis, Derian knew modeling was Charis's life, the only career she knew, and though she had continued to work through the eighties, in the last year her bookings had markedly declined. Even though it was a fact of life that modeling was not a long-term career, Charis had been doing it for twenty-plus years, and she couldn't accept the fact that the end was fast approaching. Derian was in a quandary as to how to get Charis to accept the inevitable. After all, Derian had made a new life for herself when she could no longer model. She thought about offering Charis a job as a booker at the agency; that way DDL would benefit from Charis's vast experience. But any decision would have to wait until after the Spheres account was under control. DDL's future was Derian's first priority.

"Maybe I should change my makeup," Charis continued, desperately grasping at straws. "What do you think?"

Before Derian could answer another model barged into the office and swiveled over to Derian's desk with a walk that would have turned Jayne Mansfield green with envy.

"Derian, I just heard that the Spheres show was booked and I'm not in it," she exclaimed arrogantly. "I don't understand why."

"Tiffany," Derian said with irritation, "I'm having a meeting with Charis. You'll have to wait until we're finished."

"Sorry," Tiffany said to Charis with a toss of her blond mane, then turned back to Derian, totally ignoring Derian's last sentence.

"But I fit the clothes perfectly," she continued peevishly.

Derian sighed in resignation and gave Charis an exasperated look. It was easier to answer Tiffany's question and get rid of her than to make a scene.

"Tiffany," Derian explained by rote, "I told you before, your hair is too sun-bleached and your skin is too tan. It's fine for sportswear, but not for couture. You have to stop baking yourself in the sun if you want to do couture."

"But this is southern California," Tiffany protested. "I love the sun!" It was impossible to think of herself without a tan. Men loved a sensual, tanned body—specifically *her* sensual, tanned body. She had a quick vision of herself walking down the street with pasty white skin and being ignored by every man she passed. She stole a glimpse of herself in the mirror opposite Derian's desk and couldn't resist fluffing her hair and arranging her full lips into a sexy pout.

"Yes, but it doesn't love you," Derian impatiently told Tiffany, giving the preening young woman a long appraising look. Derian had repeated the same message over and over before, but it never did any good. Tiffany just couldn't get beyond the image of herself as a beach babe. "Another year or so of sun and your skin is going to look like leather."

Tiffany didn't agree with Derian, but she was bright enough not to contradict her; after all, it was Derian's signature on her checks. But she couldn't help making a face when she thought Derian wasn't looking.

Derian, however, caught her expression, and it pushed her over the edge. "Listen to me, Tiffany. I'm tired of your sniveling about your lack of bookings and of hearing the clients complain about your dark tan," she told her bluntly. "If you want to model, you have to be dedicated. Modeling isn't a hobby, for chrissakes. It's a business—big business.

"I want to see you the first of next week and that tan had better be faded or you can start looking for a new agent!"

Instead of replying, Tiffany gave a toss of her head and flounced out of the room. Derian watched her go.

"Well, that was a waste of time," she told Charis sarcastically. "She's striking and she could work a lot more than she does, but you know that went in one ear and out the other. Oh, well." She sighed in resignation. "She knows I won't drop her from the agency. She brings in too much money from her sportswear modeling."

Charis was quiet for a moment in deep thought. "I didn't know Spheres was having a big show," she said slowly, and Derian could hear the hurt in her voice.

"Well, I haven't completely booked it yet," Derian answered, hedging. Although she knew Lucille was looking for younger models, she just couldn't bring herself to tell Charis.

"Maybe I should lighten my hair, to give my skin a lift and then go see Mrs. Ritter," Charis said thoughtfully. "What do you think?"

"I like your hair the way it is," Derian answered truthfully. "Look, Charis, let me handle things with Mrs. Ritter. I'm pretty sure I can get you on the show."

She saw the look of hope on Charis's face as she rose to leave and Derian made a silent promise to herself that one way or another Charis would get the booking.

Derian watched Charis leave her office and her heart went out to her. Sometimes life was so unfair. In any other field, the more years of experience you had, the better it was for your career. In modeling, the more years you had the less you had left. She dismissed her idea of offering Charis a booking job with the agency; Charis would never be able to handle it. Some models could accept reality and make the transition into a fashion-related field, but Charis wasn't one of them. She could never cope with sitting behind a desk and booking other models on jobs she wished she had.

Derian knew she would have to talk to Charis about her future eventually, friendship or no friendship, but she just didn't want to face it today.

CHAPTER
2

Joi Lin opened the refrigerator and perused its interior, finally deciding on a half-eaten Sarah Lee banana creme pie and a can of whipped cream. She had just returned from burying Alan and she needed food to soothe her strung-out emotions. It had been a heavy-hearted occasion that had been made more so by the absence of any other relatives or friends. Although Alan had no other family except her, Joi Lin had been shocked when not even one friend had appeared at his gravesite. She couldn't understand it. Why didn't Alan have any friends?

Joi Lin pulled the pie and whipped cream out and slammed the door closed with her foot. Three days had gone by since she'd had to identify Alan's body, and she had been voraciously eating ever since.

She set the pie on the counter and shook the can of pressurized cream, then absentmindedly sprayed it over the top of the pie. It wasn't that she was hungry, she told herself as she spooned a mound of whipped cream into her mouth, it was just that eating filled an empty void and for a moment or two she was able to forget Alan's death.

Maybe if she had gone to his party he would still be

alive, but instead she'd been pigheaded. Why had she
selfishly decided to pick his party to demonstrate her
newly acquired assertiveness? He had insisted repeatedly
that she come to his "victory party" as he had termed it,
and she should have. Now she might never know what
his victory was. She'd asked him repeatedly what he was
celebrating, but he refused to tell her. Come to the party
and find out, he answered mysteriously.

But she resented his totally orchestrating her life, even
to the point of choosing a career for her. He had told her
with a tone of finality that she would be a CPA because
she had a good head for figures and CPAs were always
in demand. He never asked her what *she* wanted; he just
insisted she do exactly what he told her and finally at
twenty-six, she rebelled. She was old enough to make her
own choices, right or wrong.

Stop it, you stupid fool, she cried silently, swallowing
another mouthful of pie in an attempt to blot out her
mutinous thoughts. She had been so wrong and now Alan
was dead. Why hadn't she listened to Alan and gone to
his party?

"Oh, Alan, I'm so sorry," she sobbed out loud.

He had always been right, and he had always watched
out for her when no one else did. Their mother had died
giving birth to Joi Lin, and Joi Lin suspected their father
blamed her for their mother's death. Sometimes he would
go for days without taking any notice of Joi Lin, but with
Alan he was different; Alan was his golden boy. Slender
and handsome, like their father, he was a total physical
contrast to Joi Lin. There was no one like Alan as far
as their father was concerned and Joi Lin had always
concurred; he was her golden big brother. Her father's
lack of acceptance created her need for Alan's acceptance
and Alan played to her. All through their childhood, he
was the star, he held center stage, and she was his adoring
audience. Her father withheld his love, but Alan loved her
and watched over her as only a big brother could. After
her father's death when she was sixteen, Alan became her

father figure, guiding her, protecting her. And now at only thirty-one years old, he was gone forever.

Tears of sorrow and guilt clouded her vision, overflowing down her cheeks, and she smothered her sobs with a mouthful of the sickeningly rich dessert. She swallowed it without even tasting it and took another bite. She would try anything to dull the jagged edge of her sorrow. It didn't work, but she kept eating.

"Alan, Alan, how can I make it up to you?" she sobbed. "What can I do now?"

Frank Hollis leaned back in his chair, trying to shut out the squad-room din around him and concentrate on the autopsy report on his desk. Alan Ainsley Anderson's preliminary autopsy disclosed some startling and confusing information, and Hollis wanted to review it before contacting Anderson's sister. He needed to decide which tact to take with her, and in light of the autopsy findings just how much of the lurid details he should tell her. The coroner had found cocaine in her brother's system, but he didn't die of an overdose. He also ruled out natural causes and strongly suspected Anderson was poisoned, although initial blood and tissue tests didn't disclose a poison's presence. The coroner was of the opinion that it was a toxin, that is a specific type of poison from an organic source. That would explain why it hadn't shown up in the initial testing. A toxin was able to meld into the thousands of organic compounds that exist in the human body. More specific testing would be required. They did, however, have the way it was administered.

Hollis reread that paragraph of the findings and shook his head in disbelief. He thought he'd heard of every possible method of murder in his twenty years as a cop, but this one beat them all. On the one hand, the sister had a right to know everything, and if the case came to trial, she would hear it all in court anyway. But maybe he should wait until they caught the murderer—if they ever did.

The trail was growing colder by the minute and so far they hadn't come up with any primary suspects. He was in the process of interviewing everyone on Anderson's guest list, which he had found in Anderson's desk, and had started with Derian Delorian, Anderson's former employer and then his major competitor. She had the kind of looks fantasies were made of and she knew it. She was sharp and had been around the block a couple of times. He had the feeling that during the interview she had been mentally grading him on his appearance and hipness, and he didn't think he stacked up too well. But what the hell, he was a cop, not some damn Beverly Hills playboy. All the same, he would have liked the satisfaction of having taken her down a peg or two, but she had an alibi for the time of the murder, though she made no secret of the fact that there was no love lost between them.

Some of the other guests he reached also had alibis and couldn't shed any light on what may have happened that night. He made a mental note of how many more there were left to contact, and checked off Ellysa and Sid Roque as the next ones on his list to see.

Anderson's bedroom had been a filthy pit. Hollis's men had diligently waded through the mounds of dirty underwear and trash, but all their efforts failed to produce any definite clues. And with the exception of Anderson's, there were no clear fingerprints in the bedroom. There were a number of loose jet beads scattered on the floor, but considering the state of the bedroom, there was no way of telling how long the beads had been there. All the same, Hollis followed prescribed procedure and dusted them. They revealed partials of two separate fingerprints, but the lab guys weren't able to identify enough points to use them for a positive ID.

They also found a library of porno films, and behind a picture they discovered Anderson's Beta camcorder with a silk scarf stretched across the lens. The film was given to the lab on the slim chance that something could be seen through the fabric, but all they were able to detect, even with enhancement techniques, was a pair of shadows playing across the film, a vague impression of height and build, and from the way light reflected off one of the shadows, they thought one figure had long blond hair. They weren't even able to identify Anderson as one of the figures on the film.

The lab was also printing up stills from Anderson's porno films and all the players would have to be identified and interviewed. Luckily Anderson kept both a datebook and an address book. With a little luck, all the players would be matched up with the names in the address book.

He reached over and pulled the scarf out of its evidence bag and spread it out on his desk. He caught the fading whiff of a cloyingly sweet fragrance. Bad taste in perfume, he thought, making a face, but good taste in scarves. It was beautiful, imprinted with the hull of a sailing ship on a background of black, red, and gold, and even his inexperienced fashion eye could tell it was expensive. The bottom portion of the square had been ripped away and he suspected it had contained a manufacturer's label. Clever but not clever enough. So far she had covered all her bases, except for this piece of silk, and that would lead him to her. His next step was to track down where the scarf had been purchased, when, and by whom.

Behind him, the cacophony of hoots and catcalls coming from the lineup room became so loud he could no longer ignore it. With a sigh, he got up and ambled out to see what was going on.

Joey Tartella, the precinct's resident entrepreneur, was monitoring the door. "Cost you a buck to get in, Lieutenant," he said as Frank walked up.

"What are you talking about, Joey?" Frank asked as he stood aside to allow a rookie to leave the room. "What's going on in there?"

"I'd give a month's pay to get some of that action," the rookie remarked, rolling his eyes as he passed them. "Hey, Joey, I don't have to pay again if I come back after my shift, do I? You need a stamp or something so the guys who've paid can get back in."

"All right, Tartella," Frank said, looking over Joey's head into the room. "Just what kind of a scam are you running this time?"

"Aw, Frank, it's no scam. It's for a good cause," Joey piously told him. "I'm just trying to get together enough money to throw a really first-rate Christmas party for the homeless kids this year."

Frank moved to enter the room, but Joey stopped him, with an outstretched palm. "For the little ones, Frank," he said solemnly.

"The little ones?" Frank snorted cynically. Giving Joey a withering look, he brushed past him. Frank had worked with Joey long enough to know that Joey's idea of charity was the old adage, charity begins at home.

The room was dark, but Frank could make out the extra rows of chairs that had been set up, almost all of them filled with police officers. Someone had placed a big-screen television with a VCR at the front of the room and a tape was in progress.

Playing across the screen were three people, two women and a man, entangled and writhing on a bedroom floor in the throes of heavy sex. Something about the bedroom looked familiar to Frank, but he couldn't quite place it. The man's back was to the camera, but as he shifted positions, the audience got a clear view of the two girls. Even Frank, whose routine reading material didn't include fashion magazines, immediately recognized one of the girls as a top model. As he watched, the man reached for something off camera and brought back a tiny spoon filled with white powder. He held it under the other girl's nose and she inhaled deeply, then went down on the man. As he turned slightly and winked slyly at the camera, Frank suddenly recognized him with a jolt. Alan Ainsley Anderson. They were running one of the tapes from Anderson's porno library—"evidence"—taken from the murder scene!

"Look at the body on that babe." Someone sighed. "She's got legs that stretch from here to Newport Beach!"

"Some guys have all the luck!" another voice commented.

"Some luck, you bozos, the guy's dead," Frank said, switching on the lights. "Show's over. And since you all seem to have so much free time, I need volunteers to go through and update the mugshot books."

Groans resounded around the room.

"That's what I thought," Frank said, surveying the cops. "Everybody, back to work." Sometimes he felt like he was dealing with a bunch of pubescent boys instead of L.A.'s finest.

After rewinding the tape, he put it back in the container. Outside the door, Joey had conveniently disappeared, so he headed for the property room and checked the tape in. He returned to his desk and absentmindedly fingered the scarf.

"I might as well get this out of the way," he muttered, tossing it back down on the desk and dialing Joi Lin Ambernites's number.

The telephone rang repeatedly and he was about to hang up when she answered, her voice soft and stuffy. He could tell she'd been crying and a wave of sympathy overcame him. He knew what it was like to lose a loved one. A drunk driver had ended his wife Gina's life over three years ago, but sometimes he ached like it had been yesterday.

"Ms. Ambernites, this is Lieutenant Hollis. You asked me to call you when I got the preliminary autopsy report," he explained gently.

"Yes, Lieutenant," she answered. He heard her voice tremble. "What did you find out? How was my brother murdered?"

"Well, it seemed that he ingested poison, but we haven't been able to determine the kind yet. The coroner's report said he'd never come across anything like it," he said, stalling.

He picked up a pencil and doodled boxes within boxes, a habit he lapsed into when something bothered him. He knew her next question was inevitable, but he still hadn't decided how he would phrase his answer. He considered himself a good judge of people, and after his initial meeting with Joi Lin Ambernites and his subsequent interviews

with some of the guests at her brother's party, he was
sure she and her brother were cut from two different bolts
of cloth.

"How was it given to him?" she asked, her voice cracking. "Was it in some food he ate?"

"You might say that," Hollis agreed, deciding in that
instant that she had a right to know all the details regardless of how painful. "We believe it was on rice paper."

"Rice paper?" Joi Lin asked, confused. "Why would
Alan eat paper? I don't understand."

He paused for a long moment and then explained as
tactfully as he could. "His death was almost instantaneous
and the poison was on an edible G-string found in his
stomach."

There was dead silence at the other end of the telephone.

Joi Lin dropped the receiver back into its cradle and
walked barefoot into her kitchen for a diet soda and a
large bag of Cheetos before returning to the living room
to think.

She seemed able to think more easily if she was nib-
bling on something or maybe she thought less if she had
something else to occupy her mind and her mouth. She
wasn't sure which it was. It really didn't matter, she
thought, ripping open the bag.

She thought about the shocking, but unproductive, conversation she had just finished with Lieutenant Hollis,
understanding and sympathetic Lieutenant Hollis, who
was absolutely no help. Talking to him was like talking
to a wall. She was sure that to him, Alan's murder was
just another case. He didn't understand that Alan was
her only family. He had said he now knew how Alan
was killed, but as far as she could tell, he had no new
leads. He was quick enough to tell her the unbelievable
way Alan had died. Didn't she have the right to know
what leads he had? She had questioned him repeatedly,
but the lieutenant's only response had been "I'm not at

liberty to discuss our leads with you at this time." Typical police double-talk for no leads at all.

She dug furiously through the bag after a particularly elusive twist, popped it into her mouth, and washed it down with a gulp of soda. She'd read enough police novels to know that the more time elapsed, the less chance there was of the police catching the perpetrator. Almost a week and a half had gone by since they'd found Alan's body! She just couldn't allow Alan's murderer to go free. Her thoughts raced on. There had to be some logical explanation about how Alan was poisoned, too. She couldn't believe the autopsy report. This was her brother, for God's sake—her brother! She slumped down on the couch with the bag of Cheetos in her hand, wracking her brain, trying to think of how she could find out who murdered Alan.

Rummaging through the bag after more cheese twists, she tried to think things through. She hadn't even been able to convince Hollis to give her a list of the people who had attended Alan's party that night, although she could guess who some of them were. His biggest accounts, all the models from his agency, and, of course, Derian Delorian. He had hinted to Joi Lin that his victory party had something to do with Derian. Though Joi Lin had never met her, she knew that Alan had worked for Derian before opening his own agency. Perhaps a call to her would shed some light on Alan's last night.

She reached into the bag for one last Cheeto, but it was empty, so instead she picked up the telephone. The time for tears was over; now it was time to make up for not being there when Alan needed her.

"C'mon, Ice Angel, give me the look! Yeah, that's it! Cool, aloof," Emil encouraged from his perch at the top of the ladder. "No, don't look at the camera, babe, look away!"

Holly Woodward cautiously readjusted her precarious pose on top of the stone wall that ran along the edge of the Seine's left bank. The predawn mist had coated the wall in a thin skin of moisture and one careless slip would plunge her into the chilly water.

"One more roll!" Emil shouted to her as he reached down to grab another load of film from his assistant. "Quickly, Serge, the sun will be up soon!"

During the brief lull, the makeup artist and hairstylist ran over to poof and powder Holly. They had all been waiting hours for just the right light for this shot and the timing was critical. Five more minutes and there would be too much natural light.

"Move that light to the left," Emil commanded.

Serge hurried in and moved one of the huge tungsten lights. Holly, lying down on the narrow ridge, arched her body, threw her head back, and closed her eyes. The diaphanous white chiffon of her evening gown floated like a cloud behind her in the breeze.

"Perfect!" Emil screamed, his little mustache bristling with excitement. He almost lost his balance on the top rung of the ladder, and for a minute he tottered perilously, then miraculously regained his footing.

"You want me to play some to the camera," Holly called.

"No, my angel, ignore me," he answered.

Holly shifted positions almost imperceptibly and Emil continued to snap away, both oblivious to the entourage behind them. Assistants, stylists, art director, and client stood in rapt attention, ready to correct any flaws that would mar the shooting.

"I got it," Emil called, handing his camera to Serge and climbing down the ladder. "Thank you, everyone."

He hurried over to Holly. "That last roll is going to be magnificent! I could feel it," he squealed in ecstasy, giving her his hand for support as she climbed down from the wall. "I love shooting black and white!"

"I felt really good about it, too," Holly agreed. "But then with your talent, you could make a cow look good!"

"Don't be ridiculous," Emil beamed. "I needed you—the Ice Angel—and that's what I got!"

"The Ice Angel," that was what the French press dubbed Holly and it was an apt description of her pearlescent skin, silver-blond hair, flawless features, and full, pouty mouth—the face of an angel. But it wasn't just her God-given beauty that was arresting; it was the cool strength and arrogance that had gradually metamorphosed during the past year modeling throughout Europe.

"When do you leave for Los Angeles?" Emil asked, taking off his coat and wrapping it around her bare shoulders. Although it was early September, the Paris mornings were already quite cool.

"Tomorrow," Holly answered. "And it should be very interesting."

"Why, *chérie*?" Emil asked, pausing to switch off the tungsten lights.

"When I left Los Angeles, I was just beginning my career. The other models wouldn't give me the time of day. My agent, Derian, was the only one who believed in me," Holly explained. " 'Go to Paris,' she said, so I did and now . . ."

"You're a star," Emil finished for her.

Holly shrugged in acquiescence. It was hard for her to be modest when it was true. "I owe Derian a lot for the help she gave me, and now she's calling in her marker. She needs my help to reel in an important account. The Los Angeles fashion industry is so taken with any successful European model that my presence will practically guarantee Derian the account. I'll only be in Los Angeles a month or two and then I'll be back."

"No longer," Emil advised, shaking his finger at her. "Even two months is a long time in this business. You have to take advantage while you're hot. Another year and I predict you'll be the toast of all Europe."

"From your lips to God's ears," Holly answered.

By the time she changed into her own clothes, the sun was rising. Even though the feathery night mist was slowly dissipating, there was still a chill in the air, and Holly pulled her leather jacket closer to her body. She loved this time of the morning, and after the strenuous shoot, a quiet walk home to unwind was the perfect ending to the night.

Turning off from the river, she headed for the Saint Germain district. Up ahead, the rue Dauphine was wet from its morning hosing and shopkeepers were setting up their market stalls, the lights from their shops bathing the street in a warm golden glow.

Holly could almost close her eyes and guide herself by smell alone, past the fresh produce markets with the tangy aroma of moist loam still clinging to the displays of fresh vegetables, and the stalls with the heady sweet perfume of thousands of fresh-cut flowers. Farther on were the charcuteries where meats were displayed with artistic flair. Ground meats were molded into little quaint animals, each representing the type of meat sold—a little pig with olive eyes, a cow with green pepper slices for horns.

When she reached the row of pâtisseries, the warm fragrance of fresh baking bread was more than she could resist and she sat down at a corner café. A wizened little man with a grizzled face and a tam cocked over one eye scampered over to take her order.

"*Ça va, jolie fille?*" he asked, giving her a flirtatious smile.

"*Merci, bien,*" Holly answered with a smile, assuring him she was well, and then she ordered an espresso and a fresh roll.

Scurrying inside the shop, he returned with the espresso and a still-warm *pain de ménage.*

He presented it to her with a grand flourish.

"How much?" Holly asked, opening her change purse.

He shook his head. "Your beautiful presence in my café is payment enough," he said gallantly.

Above them, a little old woman with a bright-colored scarf tied about her head leaned out of the window.

"Henri," she called in French, "are you flirting with the women again?"

Before he could answer, another window flew open and a second little old woman poked her head out. "Giselle," she shouted to her friend. "That old rooster flirts with all the women. It doesn't matter—pretty ones, ugly ones, young, old."

The old man shrugged his shoulders in resignation. "What can I do?" he complained good-naturedly to Holly. "They watch me like the owl watches the field mouse."

Holly laughed and sipped the warm, thick coffee. She loved Paris; it had such charisma, such richness and flavor, like no other city in the world. Living here was like peeling an onion, one layer more revealing than the last. She'd been here a year and she hadn't yet completely explored the core, the heart of the city. She knew the clubs— *Baindouche, Club Sept, Privé*—the trendy restaurants, the in-crowds, but the people of the streets were the heartbeat of Paris.

Los Angeles had a charisma, too, but it marched to a different beat. L.A. was rap music, Paris a waltz, each one valid, but incomparable.

Yes, she thought to herself, it was going to be a very interesting couple of months in L.A. She was never sure if the other models had snubbed her because she had been their competition or because she had been so green. But whatever the reason, now she was returning a star and she was in control. She knew the fashion world's mentality. They all loved a new face, especially one from Europe, and she would use her European mystique to call all the shots. If she was successful in pulling it off, there would be plenty of Los Angeles models eating crow for the next two months.

She drained her cup and continued her walk. All around her Paris was waking up; the streets had dried and people were beginning to fill them on their way to work.

She paused in front of the Shakespeare & Company Book Store. It would be several more hours before it opened, although its red-framed bulletin board was always hanging next to the door. She glanced in idle curiosity down the blackboard listings.

Just yesterday, she had added her apartment to the listings, and only an hour later an English writer had contacted her. After seeing her apartment, he agreed to sublet it until she returned in a month or two at the most. Amazed at how quickly she had managed her affairs, she had made arrangements for her trip.

Now, with everything taken care of, she already missed Paris and she hadn't even left yet.

She leaned forward and pressed her face up against the window, watching the first purple fingers of night spread across the twilight sky, and the last flickering wisps of daylight drop below the horizon.

It reminded her of Alan. One moment life's light had flickered in his eyes—her face had been reflected in his dilated pupils—and the next moment the darkness of death had descended, leaving her image frozen in his mind for all eternity. There was a poetic justice in that, she gloated. Had he lived, he would have destroyed her and everything she had created. Instead, he would carry her with him forever.

As she watched, the last remnants of twilight faded. It had always been her favorite time of day, a time for peace and contentment, a time for reflecting on the events of the past and planning for the future. A poem by Henry Wadsworth Longfellow came to her and she silently recited it:

> Between the dark and the daylight
> when the night is beginning to lower
> Comes a pause in the day's occupations
> that is known as the children's hour.

Yes, she mused, this was *her* children's hour, a time she set aside each day to devote to her pretty babies. Finally she stood and felt her way through the dark apartment to the back bedroom.

As she noiselessly opened the door, a blast of warm, moist air hit her. She slipped inside, closing the door behind her, and immediately blisters of perspiration rose along her hairline and dribbled down her temples. She wiped them away with the back of her hand and slowly turned up the dimmer switch. A black light bathed the room in its pale glow. She moved slowly so as not to frighten her babies, splaying her spread fingers on the plate-glass wall in front of her and tapping lightly.

"Wake up, my beauties," she cooed softly. "Mama's here."

In the farthest corner of the room, the dark shadows rippled with movement and she sniggered with delight.

CHAPTER
3

Ellysa Roque was in high spirits. Her upcoming fashion extravaganza at Spheres was predicted to be a raging success. All that week after the invitations had been mailed, the phones had rung constantly with friends and clients calling to reserve a seat for the event. *Lifestyles of the Rich and Famous, This Evening, Entertainment Tonight*, and all the local press were already scheduled to attend.

Her purpose for the show was not just to further the boutique's reputation, but more important to show Ellysa's growing significance in Beverly Hills society. It was the culmination of ten years of Ellysa's singlemindedly climbing, politicking, scheming, and buying her way to the top. And from the look of the R.S.V.P. list, the event would be more rewarding than she had dared dream. Every big name in the Beverly Hills social world was planning to attend.

There was a brief moment last week when the whole event threatened to crumble around her. A pedantic lieutenant from the LAPD had paid her and Sid a visit, bringing them the news that Alan Ainsley Anderson had inconveniently gotten himself murdered. Her whole show

teetered on the brink of disaster and all the officer did
was interrogate them on their whereabouts after Alan's
boring little soiree. Boring for her anyway. Nothing but
empty-headed bimbos with plastic faces—just Sid's type.
He had practically drooled through the entire evening.
The officer was a pushy sort. Even after Sid told him
they knew nothing about the unfortunate affair, he kept
chipping away at them. So common, too, no *savoir vivre*.
He obviously didn't know whom he was dealing with.

Surprisingly, though, the mousy Mrs. Ritter saved the
show. She had booked a top Parisian model, and now
Ellysa knew the event would be more successful than
even she had dared dream.

She leaned back in her chair with a self-satisfied look on
her face. "Like they always say: 'Money talks and bullshit
walks,' " she said out loud to the walls of her office.

At that moment there was a light tap at the office door,
and her secretary poked her head around its corner.

"I'm sorry, Mrs. Roque, but I can't seem to locate Mr.
Roque," she reported, nervously switching from one foot
to the other. Mrs. Roque's temper was legendary among
the employees of the boutique, and Susan didn't like being
in a position of being on the receiving end of it.

Ellysa tensed, but managed a cool smile. "That's okay,
Susan," she said with a cavalier wave of her hand. "Just
keep trying."

As soon as Susan retreated, Ellysa's smile faded. She
wondered who Sid's fuck-of-the-week was this time.

His family had made their big bucks in real estate
years ago, so Sid had never really had to work, but he
did dabble and thought of his occasional sale as terribly
backbreaking labor. The truth was he worked at playing.
He had been a player before meeting Ellysa and she was
positive that their marriage hadn't slowed him down at
all. Initially she had ignored his dalliances, but as she
gained acceptance with the moneyed set in Beverly Hills
and her self-confidence grew, she found it harder and
harder to ignore his romantic forays and she wouldn't

tolerate them anymore. With her growing status in the community, she wasn't going to become the center of speculation for wagging tongues. No way! She'd worked much too hard for that.

Ellysa swiveled around in her chair and looked at her reflection in the tinted window. Why wasn't he satisfied with her? She looked pretty good for forty-two. Her sun-streaked hair was cut in the latest style, her nose bobbed, her cheeks implanted, her boobs lifted, her tummy tucked, and her thighs liposuctioned. Besides, she worked out every day without fail. What more could he ask for?

She stood up and strolled into the main boutique. Although Spheres was her vehicle to become a social force to be reckoned with, it was also her pride and joy, the result of her long-time vision to take the pampered environment of a European spa and combine it with the slick chicness of a California fashion boutique, offering only one-of-a-kind garments. Because of her genius— and Sid's family money—she had created the ultimate trend-setting shopping center, first of its kind anywhere, dedicated to making her clients feel and look special, and they traveled from everywhere to patronize it.

She kept two sleek black-windowed limos parked out front, ready at a moment's notice to whisk clients to and from the boutique. A Latino doorman greeted and protected her patrons' anonymity from the ever-present paparazzi gathered outside the boutique with their cameras.

The three-story building was stuccoed Mediterranean apricot inside and out. The various ground-floor areas displayed the latest and trendiest sportswear designer clothes, ranging from swim wear like Touch Me Tahiti to *avant-garde* Issey Miyake. They were divided by glass block walls and Moorish archways with carved terra-cotta pillars.

At the rear of the store was an enclosed pool area surrounded by chaise longues. Patrons were encouraged to spend the day shopping and lounging around the pool;

the store even furnished disposable bathing suits for their convenience. When they got hot, they could retreat to the shade of the lush tropical gardens that encircled the pool and sip icy drinks from the mineral water bar. A revolutionary sheer screen tented the entire area, filtering out the dangerous wrinkle-producing ultraviolet rays while still allowing the sun's warmth and brightness to shine through.

The second floor was devoted to complete pampering and beauty treatments: facials, massages, hair, nails, and private exercise and aerobic rooms with the newest equipment and muscled young instructors to provide the bored Beverly Hills matrons with individual "instruction." No men, other than the instructors, were allowed in this area of the shop. Ensconced on the second-floor balcony and overlooking the pool area was a small café serving tasty low-calorie California cuisine.

The third level housed a couture salon with garments ranging from California chic to black-tie sophistication. There were no racks of clothes; instead, the floor was arranged with comfortable couches and oversize chairs in casual groupings. Clients were encouraged to relax on the couches while waiters served them cocktails and hors d'oeuvres. Salespeople brought clothes to the potential buyer and there was even a staff model to fit the clothes if a client didn't feel up to making the effort. If she did decide to try on the clothes, she was guided to a tastefully appointed changing room with floor-to-ceiling mirrors that were discreetly distorted to make her look thinner than she really was.

Spheres was truly a striking innovation in a city where the creative and the unusual were the norm. Even the jaded Beverly Hills set had seen nothing like it and had selected it as the in-place.

As Ellysa made her way toward the pool area, she stopped occasionally to greet clients and to play the gracious proprietress. Halfway back to her office, she noticed Baroness Von Wittsburg selecting sportswear, undoubtedly for her upcoming Mediterranean cruise.

The baroness, or Chi Chi as she was known to her friends, was an unforgettable presence. Sid had once sarcastically described her as a Rubens trying to pass herself off as a Patrick Nagel and he was right. Although she hid her ample figure beneath voluptuous silk tunics, her face was her pride. She had had so many face lifts and peels that her face was stretched into a perpetual smile—or grimace. The difference between the two expressions was so minor that it could only be distinguished by the tone of her voice. Any softness beneath the flesh on her once-round face had long been liposuctioned away and replaced with silicone cheek and chin implants to add angles and planes.

Ellysa was in no mood for small talk, so her initial reaction was to slip quietly by before Chi Chi saw her. But on second thought Ellysa decided to chat with her for a few moments. The baroness was at the top of the Beverly Hills social roster and it was to Ellysa's advantage to cultivate her friendship.

"Ellysa, my sweet," the baroness gushed in heavily accented English, even though Ellysa knew she'd lived in the United States for the past thirty years. "Have you heard the latest on the literary scene?"

Baroness Von Wittsburg was the reigning queen of gossip and keeper of social smut in Beverly Hills. The oldest joke around was telegraph, telephone, or tell the baroness. She was better than Geraldo Rivera and the *National Enquirer* combined.

"It's about a certain famous women's romance writer, here in Beverly Hills," Chi Chi continued, without waiting for Ellysa's reply.

"You mean the story about all of Colleen Cantrell's novels being ghostwritten," Ellysa replied airily. "That's old news, Baroness." She spotted a speck of dust on the polished floor, snapped her fingers at a passing salesclerk, and pointed to it.

"Oh," Chi Chi said, crestfallen that she had been scooped. Then she brightened as she thought of another, even more delicious tidbit. "I also heard that a certain gentleman who travels in our social circle and hosts a very popular late-night talk show is quite the showman off the air, too."

"Really, tell me," Ellysa demanded, her curiosity piqued.

"Well," the baroness explained, lowering her voice and looking around, wishing she had a bigger audience, "it seems, and I have it from a very reliable source, that Jimmy Novacks asked a certain starlet to his home for dinner and when she arrived, he greeted her at the door stark naked! I guess he planned on being the entree."

"What did the starlet do?" Ellysa exclaimed in shock.

"My pet, she stayed, of course," the older woman finished wickedly. "He told her it was all right. He was kosher!"

"Oh, my God!" Ellysa squealed, and she burst out laughing. "You've got to be kidding."

"It's the truth, I swear on the baron's grave," Chi Chi insisted, solemnly holding up her right hand.

"But your husband's not dead," Ellysa insisted, wiping tears of laughter from her eyes.

"Really," the baroness said with a straight face. "You couldn't prove it by me."

"Baroness," Ellysa said with mock seriousness, "you are so naughty."

"You know . . ." the other woman continued in an innocent tone, then paused while checking the labels on a rack of blouses. She watched Ellysa's expression out of the corner of her eye with the concentration of a predator stalking its prey.

She had another rumor to spread, but she wanted it verified, if not verbally, at least by expression. Sure, Ellysa was nice enough, but life was so boring that the baroness needed diversions. Besides, her gossip never really hurt anyone.

"I heard there were problems in your household, too," she nonchalantly tossed out with a gleam in her eye. "No?"

Ellysa blanched, but managed to look amazed. "I can't imagine where you could have gotten such a ridiculous idea," she lied with wide-eyed surprise. "My marriage has never been better. In fact," Ellysa continued with as much panache as she could muster, "we will soon have an exciting announcement to make."

"Announcement?" Chi Chi queried eagerly.

"Sweetie, I can't say just yet," Ellysa replied with a mysterious smile. "But you'll be the first to know."

"Promise, my pet," the baroness pressed. The tantalizing promise of a new scoop made her feel euphoric, powerful.

"Of course! Gotta go, love," Ellysa said. "Kiss, kiss." She gave the old woman a hug, bussed the air to the left and right of her face, leaving the baroness to digest this latest preview of imminent news.

Chi Chi's words left Ellysa shaken. "Damn him," Ellysa muttered furiously under her breath. The truth was, she did have an announcement to make, one that would change their lives forever, but *she* wanted to pick the time and the place to make it. She had no intention of being forced into making it prematurely as a result of Sid's indiscretions.

If he screwed up all her plans or if she ever caught him with another woman, she swore vehemently to herself, she'd cut his balls off!

"Stay away from me!" the naked, blindfolded woman cried, tossing her thick, black hair from side to side. Her long, lean body squirmed and wriggled, but the silken ropes that bound her to the four corners of the bed kept her from completely eluding Sid's touch.

"Stop struggling, I won't hurt you," he panted, licking his lips in anticipation.

Sid Roque was fifty-three years old, old enough to be this woman's father. The sight of her firm, young body, however, made him feel young again. Gone were his middle-aged paunch, the receding hairline, and the tufts of hair sprouting from his ears that heralded the onset of aging. In his imagination, he was thirty and gorgeous, and his cock grew hard and eager at the sight of her struggles.

"Get away, I told you," she panted, tossing her head from side to side. "What are you going to do?"

Sid picked up an ice cube and knelt down on the bed. Starting at her throat, he ran the ice lightly down the length of her tanned body, taking time to fondle and caress each full breast with the ice. She shivered, gasping in shock at his cold touch, and her struggles enhanced his hard-on. He slid the ice along her inner thighs, pushing it deep inside, stroking her with gentle but probing intensity. Finally he grabbed her by the hair and jerked her head back, forcing his cock into her mouth.

"Suck," he ordered huskily, eagerly watching as she complied.

When he could stand it no longer, he forced her thighs as far apart as they would go, and ruthlessly shoved his cock deep into her. She moaned with pleasure as he repeatedly thrust inside her. Then abruptly her moans turned to wild cries of ecstasy as she matched his strokes and began to come.

"God damn it, Vicki," Sid gasped in exasperation as he rolled off her and lay panting next to her on the bed. "Everything was going great until you had to spoil it! You're supposed to be terrified!"

"Sid, baby," she answered, slipping her hands out of the bindings that held her to the bedposts and pulling off the blindfold. "What do you want from me? I get turned on. I come. It's as simple as that."

She nuzzled his ear. "If you don't want me to come," she whispered in a sultry voice, "then don't turn me on."

"Jesus Christ," he said with forced good humor, "you're as bad as Ellysa. You women are all alike. You're supposed to be terrified and instead you enjoy it. Some fantasy life I have!"

"Well, you certainly took care of my enjoyment by mentioning your wife." Vicki pouted, sliding off the bed and slipping on a celadon-green silk dressing gown. Sometimes Sid had about as much tact as an Uzi.

"It's enough that I have to work for her eight hours a day, without you going out of your way to mention her during my off hours, too."

Sid shrugged and walked into the bathroom to take a leak. Women were all alike. You gave them some cock and they thought they owned you. "Yeah, and if I stop coming over during your off hours to rock you, then you won't have to hear me mention her," he said, putting her in her place. "How does that sound for a plan?"

"Sid, honey," Vicki quickly whined as she slipped on the gold-link bracelet that he had surprised her with earlier and admired how it glistened on her wrist. "I was only kidding. I didn't mean anything by it. I couldn't care less about Ellysa. I only care about being with you!"

"Yeah, well, then act like it," he said, returning to the bedroom and pulling on his pants. "Next time try to put a little more effort into my fantasy for a change, okay?"

"Okay, Sidney," Vicki said in her sweetest voice. She walked slowly to the bathroom, letting Sid enjoy the view, then ripped the shower curtains apart and turned on the shower with a vengeance.

That bitch Ellysa had kept her at the boutique a whole hour longer than usual last night and after work Sid was supposed to take her to dinner, but he never showed. He was probably home giving that hag the old one two. When he had shown up this morning with the bracelet, she was sure of it.

What the hell, she thought, her temper cooling. It wasn't as if Sid was the great love of her life. She'd take what she could get for now. And if it wasn't her getting it, then it would be someone else, and besides, she liked the idea of fucking him right under the princess's nose.

"Hey, babe," Sid called from the bedroom. "I gotta go."

Vicki hurried out to say good-bye and to walk him to the door.

"I have to be at the boutique by two P.M. tomorrow. You're going to stop by, aren't you?" she asked, trying to pin him down. "There's an outfit I'd really, really like, Sid, honey."

"I don't know yet," he answered.

God damn it, he thought, Vicki was beginning to sound like his bitching wife, always wanting something from him. "I have a lot of business tomorrow," he lied smoothly, although they both knew his real estate business was just a hobby. "And it's not a good idea to always show up there when you're working, Ellysa might get suspicious."

"You're probably right," Vicki agreed grudgingly. Maybe Sid wasn't *numero uno* in her life, but she resented taking a back seat to any woman, even one who had been there first. "I'll hear from you soon, though, won't I?"

"Of course," Sid replied, giving her a quick pat on her backside on his way out the door.

Women, Jesus Christ, Sid groused to himself as he drove through the early-afternoon traffic toward his office in Beverly Hills. Vicki and Ellysa reminded him of the old adage: "Give 'em an inch, and they'll take a mile."

When he married Ellysa, she was little Ellen Wheeler from Redding, California, and she was full of wonderment and in awe of the big city and its sophistication, which Sid found delightful and refreshing. She was the total opposite of the moneyed circles he moved in. She was completely devoted to his every whim and accepting of his every action; his "outside interests" were of no consequence to her and if he were to be totally honest, in those days he'd had none.

Gradually, however, she changed. She called herself Ellysa, and became more self-centered. Impressing the people around her became almost an obsession, her demands a way of life. He had hoped that Spheres would keep her occupied and out of his hair, but even that wasn't working.

Now Vicki was starting the same demanding song and dance. Maybe it was time to start looking for a new diversion. He was beginning to wish he had never seen Vicki at Spheres, he thought, and turned his attention back to his driving.

● ● ●

Shifting around in her chair, Derian tucked one leg up under her, and prepared herself for a lengthy conversation. "Look," she reiterated emphatically to the client on the other end of the speaker phone, "I explained the rates to you before I took your booking. I even sent you a rate card."

Some clients were so infuriating. Before the booking, they were ready to promise the moon to get the star model they wanted. But after the booking, they suddenly remembered they had a limited budget or they "forgot" what the rates were.

"There is a fee if you videotape the show and yes, if the press photographs a model in one of your gowns, independent of the show but with your consent," she continued by rote, "that falls in the editorial category and you will be billed accordingly."

Derian looked up as her brother quietly slipped into the office and lowered himself into a chair, leaning forward to catch every word of the conversation. She rolled her eyes and held her palm over the mouthpiece. "Karen 'Her Holiness' Boyle," she mouthed.

"I understand that, Karen, but that's why you called DDL," she explained patiently. "We have the best models in Los Angeles. If you didn't want the best, then you should have called another agency."

Listening politely to the response, she gave Rusty a look of exasperation. "That's right," she agreed, absent-mindedly clicking her lucky sterling silver Dunhill pen on and off with her thumb. "Then we can expect your check by return mail? Thank you. It was a pleasure doing business with you." With that, she disconnected the caller with an angry punch of a button.

"That woman has the nastiest disposition in L.A. What an attitude!" Derian exploded.

"That's why she's known as Karen 'Her Holiness,' " Rusty commented dryly.

Derian gave an exaggerated sigh of impatience and began to sort through the pile of vouchers on her desk.

"She's always quick enough to book the models she wants and even quicker to forget the rates. Let's see how quick she is about paying the bill. Until I hire a new bookkeeper, I'm having to handle everything."

"That's what you get for introducing Bertha to her future husband," Rusty told her unsympathetically. He picked up Derian's pen and began to play with it.

"Who was to know she'd fall in love with the Krystal Klear water man, for crying out loud? I just wanted a discount on his water delivery," Derian lamented good-naturedly. "I tried to tell her she'd be happier single."

"You should have never let them talk to each other in the beginning," Rusty told her earnestly, ignoring Derian's jocular comments. "This agency is much too important to be without a bookkeeper for even a few days."

Rusty stood up and paced across the room, clicking the pen.

Derian observed that he had the same nervous habit as she did and started to make a joke about it, but then she realized how serious he was about the loss of the agency bookkeeper.

"Take a relax pill, kiddo," she said flippantly instead.

Rusty was deep in thought and didn't answer.

"Rusty," she repeated laughingly. "Earth to Rusty, come in."

"Oh, sorry," he answered, breaking his mood. "I guess I was just thinking of something else. What were you saying?"

"Bertha got married on Saturday," Derian said.

"Ah, the trials and tribulations of being number one in the business," he quipped, giving her a broad smile. When he felt like it, he could charm a fish out of water. He sat back down and tucked one leg up under him. "Any leads on a new bookkeeper?"

"As a matter of fact, smartass, I have an appointment with a prospective bookkeeper later this afternoon," Derian told him, paging through a stack of booking sheets. "If she can add two plus two, she's got the job!"

"If that's all you need, why don't you hire one of your models? They can even count to twenty if they take off their shoes." Rusty grinned wickedly.

"Feeling a little catty today, dear?" Derian shot back at him.

Rusty shrugged good-naturedly.

"Anyway, who knows what would have happened if ole Alan Ainsley Anderson had succeeded in consolidating his agency with Jolt before his unfortunate demise?" Derian continued in a more serious tone.

"Yes, who knows," Rusty agreed with studied sympathy. "Tragic, huh?"

"Isn't it?" Derian added, brightening. "He might have given DDL a real run for its money."

"Oh, no," Rusty disagreed loyally. "Not a chance."

"That party he gave two weeks ago when he tried to ram his consolidation plans down my throat was the last time anyone saw him alive. He watched me like a hawk all that night, trying to see my reaction."

"Well, he's not watching you now, and you're at the top," Rusty declared. He restlessly picked up the stack of booking sheets on her desk, then read through them. "How come only five DDL models were booked for the Wings show?"

"Because it was a mini-show and they only needed five models," she answered, taking the booking sheets out of his hand and restacking them on the desk.

"How's your photography going?" she asked.

"It's going." He shrugged noncommittally.

"I almost forgot to tell you," Derian enthused. "Mrs. Ritter wanted the telephone number of Michael Tippton, so she could book him to photograph the Spheres show."

"So?" Rusty replied disinterestedly.

"So, I told her to forget him," she finished, her eyes sparkling with her news. "You're much better!"

"Well, I am, but you don't need to speak for me. Why didn't you just have her call me—" Rusty protested.

"Listen to me, Rusty," Derian interrupted. "I know what's best."

"But I want to find my own jobs—"

"Just do what I say," Derian said, steamrolling his objections. "You know I'm right."

Rusty chewed on his lower lip and Derian caught the unhappy look on his face. "Trust me, I'm the best at pitching," she told him with finality, giving his hand a maternal pat.

Rusty was silent for a moment, then abruptly his attitude changed. "I know you are," he agreed brightly and stood up. "Well, gotta go."

He leaned across the desk, kissed her cheek lightly, and quickly closed the door behind him.

Although he hadn't worked much, Derian knew that he felt with the unshakable certainty that only the young possess—for six months at a time, that is—that fashion photography was his true calling. And with a mother's faith, Derian believed him one thousand percent. He just needed the opportunities she told herself, and she was in a position to give them to him. Never mind that a year ago he capriciously dabbled in costume designing and two years before that screenwriting. She paid for his studio apartment, gave him an allowance to cover all his expenses, and recommended him to as many clients as possible. She knew what was best for him.

Joi Lin sat in the reception area at DDL and fidgeted. Her almost compulsive eating the past week had caught up with her as the waistband on her suit testified. Sitting up straighter and taking a deep breath, she sucked in her stomach as hard as she could. That was better, but it gave her a kink in her lower back, so she exhaled and tried to ignore the tight waistband. She looked at the room. It felt strange imagining Alan working here.

It was even stranger that *she* was here. Earlier in the week, after reflecting on her conversation with Lieutenant Hollis, she decided to do some investigating of her own. She had called Derian Delorian asking to meet with her, hoping that maybe Derian could tell if she had noticed anything unusual at Alan's party.

"Are you calling about the opening for a bookkeeper?" the receptionist had asked before Joi Lin could state the purpose of her call.

It had been on the tip of her tongue to say no, when instead she suddenly found herself telling the receptionist yes. She didn't know whatever possessed her to lie. Well, it wasn't lying really, she told herself, she was an excellent bookkeeper and she was looking for a job. But even so, when she met Ms. Delorian, she would tell her that the receptionist had misunderstood her, that she was Alan's sister, and that she was really there to talk about Alan. All the same, she was dressed in her best suit, a Helga navy blue and white one, and was in between job-hunting appointments.

"Derian will see you now," the receptionist told her, pointing toward a pair of closed double doors at the end of the room.

Joi Lin took a deep breath and entered Derian's office, an elegantly appointed room with walls sponge-painted in a pale seafoam green and thick Chinese carpets covering the pickled pine floor. Derian's desk was lacquered ivory goatskin and behind it an antique Coromondal screen stretched across the width of the room. As Joi Lin walked toward Derian, she stood up with a smile and held out her hand.

"Hello, Joi Lin," she said briskly. "I'm Derian Delorian. Please have a seat."

Though her demeanor was brusque and businesslike, the tone of her voice was warm, and her presence was magnetic.

"Thank you. I'm pleased to meet you," Joi Lin replied, looking up at the statuesque redhead, who stood a head taller than Joi Lin and seemed to radiate personality. More than ever, Joi Lin felt painfully aware of her stubby legs, her round face, and her wide hips. It was like comparing a Shetland pony with a Thoroughbred, she thought.

"Did you bring a résumé?" Derian asked, getting right to the point.

"Y-yes, Ms. Delorian," Joi Lin answered, taking the papers from her bag and handing them to Derian. Her resolution to reveal her identity dissolved in her awe of the agency's owner.

Get serious, she told herself. *I'd look like an idiot if I told her the reason for my visit now.*

"Please call me Derian. Everybody does." She slipped on a pair of reading glasses and studied Joi Lin's résumé.

"You have excellent credentials. Your bachelor's degree, four years experience," Derian read from the page. It was beginning to look like this Joi Lin Ambernites was exactly what DDL needed.

"Thank you," Joi Lin answered, folding and unfolding her hands in her lap. She was beginning to regain her poise. Maybe, she thought, a new plan forming in her head, she might learn more by working for Derian Delorian than by asking her direct questions—and she did need a job.

"Why did you leave your last job?"

"I was going to begin a new job, but it fell through. The owner died," Joi Lin said cautiously.

"Oh." Derian raised her eyebrows.

"Yes," Joi Lin continued, struggling to maintain a casual tone and watching Derian closely for a reaction. "It was another modeling agency. The owner, Alan Ainsley Anderson, was killed and the agency closed."

Derian looked up sharply at Joi Lin. "I knew Alan. As a matter of fact, he used to work for my agency. Did you know him well?"

Joi Lin hesitated a beat, deciding the best way to answer. "No, I only met him once," she lied. *Alan forgive me*, she prayed silently to herself. "But he hired me on the spot. I was supposed to start a week ago. Then I read about his murder in the paper." A lump rose in her throat at the word "murder," but she swallowed it and forced herself to remain calm.

"It was a shock" was Derian's only response as she mulled over Joi Lin's information. She stood and walked over to an Immogene Cunningham photograph hanging slightly askew on one wall and straightened it. If nothing else, Alan was a shrewd businessman. If this woman was good enough for him, then she was good enough for Derian, and furthermore, Derian was tired of being owner, booker, P.R. person, and bookkeeper, too.

She looked speculatively at Joi Lin for a moment before she spoke. "If you want the job, you're hired," she finally told her, making a snap decision.

Joi Lin was taken aback, never having anticipated that she would be offered a job on the spot. Still, it would be an access to Alan's world. Surely Derian and Alan knew many of the same people. She could find out about them firsthand without raising anyone's suspicions. And Joi Lin had not missed the look on Derian's face when Alan's name was mentioned. She was positive Derian knew more about Alan's death than she was letting on.

Joi Lin, she told herself, bolstering her self-confidence, *you may not have the looks and the presence that Derian Delorian has, but you're bright and you're no slouch and you're going to find out who killed your brother.*

"I'll take it," she announced to Derian, making just as quick a decision.

CHAPTER
4

From the moment her plane landed in Los Angeles a week and a half ago, Holly had been working nonstop. Word of her arrival spread like brushfire in the fashion industry and everyone clamored to book her. She knew that several times Derian had canceled other models to make room for her and she suspected that Derian was pushing her in the hope that Holly would remain permanently in L.A. It was hard on the other models, but it had happened to her, too. This was a tough business and there was no room for fragile egos and thin skins. She had paid her dues and she felt she deserved to reap the rewards.

Today Derian had scheduled an all-agency interview at DDL for a series of shows for the Golden Corridor, a new grouping of chi-chi boutiques on Camden Drive in Beverly Hills. Holly knew it was a given that she would be booked solid once they found out she was in from Paris, but she decided to show up for the interview anyway.

She had been visualizing this day from the moment she had left L.A. a year ago as a novice with her tail between her legs. Now she was a star, she was hot, real hot, and she was going to play it for all it was worth.

• • •

Holly gave her black over-the-knee suede boots a final pull, threw her shoulders back, and copped an attitude before she opened the door to DDL. Striking a casual pose in the doorway, she languidly surveyed the room, giving the other models a chance to look her over. She wanted them to see what success looked like and she was rewarded with a drop in the din of conversation as the other models, one by one, turned to stare at her. Then the noise level resumed as they began buzzing about her among themselves.

Fascinated, she noted the different flair between Los Angeles and European models. In Europe the models came to interviews clean-faced and dressed in the antithesis of their fashion career: torn jeans, T-shirts, cowboy boots. Here, the models dressed to the nines. Holly had only to glance briefly around the room to recognize clothes by designers like Azzedine Alaïa, Donna Karan, and Umberto Ginocchietti.

For a second, the old insecurities returned, the anxiety of not being good enough, of being a brown wren among a flock of peacocks. Afraid her Paris-chic boots and casual black mini looked out of place, she panicked but it was only for a brief moment. Then she reminded herself that *she* was the star; she was the one *they* wanted to emulate.

"Holly, Holly Woodward." She heard a bombastic voice call her name and she looked in the direction of the sound.

A tall, well-built, black male model with a strong, square jawline and crystal-blue eyes elbowed his way through the sea of models.

Holly saw him coming and gave a squeal of recognition. "Toney!"

Toney Wayne was one of Holly's few model friends from her early days in L.A. He was at the agency the first day Holly walked in to meet Derian. When the other models snubbed her, he took her under his wing and taught her the ropes: how to put her portfolio together, how to interview, which photographers were on the level and which ones were just on the make. Toney made it a point to know everyone in the business and everyone's business. He grew up in New Jersey and had hit L.A. after a mega-career in Europe. He was not only street smart, but he also knew how to walk the political fence deftly.

Toney swept her off her feet with a big bear hug. "It's so great to see you, little sister," he boomed, setting her back down on the floor.

"You, too," she said, returning his hug.

"So what's shaking?"

"Same old, same old," Holly said modestly.

"That's not the way I hear it," he shot back at her with a grin. "I heard you've been strutting your stuff all over Paris. French *Vogue, Je Suis, Elle*."

Holly shrugged, beaming with pride. "Just trying to keep out of trouble, that's all."

"You back here slumming"—he winked—"or you gonna teach the home girls how to move?"

"A little of both." Holly laughed shamelessly.

"There's been an awful lot of long faces since you hit town," he continued. "The word out on the runway is that bookings for other blondes are drying up. I can think of two in particular who have been canceled from several bookings in the last week."

"It beats last year when no one would give me the time of day," Holly countered. "And I've got some scores to settle. The women around here treated me like Typhoid Mary and if some of them are losing bookings, then that's their problem. Let them go to Paris like I did."

"Revenge never did anyone any good, little sister," Toney warned with a worried look on his face. "It's like I told you a year ago, ignore the petty jive and just do your thing. Listen to me, I've got a lot of years invested in this business."

"I always listen to you, Toney. I just want to rattle

a few cages, starting with this one." She nodded in the direction of an approaching woman who was making her way through the crowd of models toward them. "Holly, hi," Charis exclaimed, a brilliant fake smile plastered on her face.

Charis, too, had been in the business enough years to know that if you can't lick them, join them, and the way her career was going, she needed every bit of help she could get. Having been canceled twice already this week by her regular accounts so that they could use Holly, she was scared and angry. She knew the reason for her progressively diminished bookings in the past year, but she couldn't bring herself to admit or believe she was too old to model. She had nothing else. She had to do something to increase her bookings, and she knew from experience that often all it took was the recommendation from an in-demand model for another model to be hired. Her only hope was that if she played her cards right and established a friendship with Holly, maybe Holly would mention her name to prospective accounts. After all, in her prime, she had done it for other models many times.

"Why, uh, Charis, isn't it?" Holly feigned a lapse of memory, although Holly remembered perfectly well how Charis had tried to put her through her paces when she was starting out. "My God, are you still modeling! I thought you would have retired ages ago!"

Charis winced and her face fell, but she retained her composure. "Me, good heavens, no. I've been much too busy. In fact, this season reminds me of one of my biggest years—1969—when everyone paired me with Verushka. You know, I remember one time—"

"I'm glad to hear that," Holly interrupted before Charis related her tale. "By the way, are you doing the Neiman Marcus show tomorrow?"

Holly knew Charis wouldn't be doing it because she was replacing her. But turnabout was fair play, she thought to herself, remembering how she had been canceled from a print job because Charis had complained to the client about working with a beginner.

It still hurt her to think about it. Holly hadn't been in competition with Charis; she had been a greenhorn just trying to get a break. She showed up at the photographer's studio only to be told to go home. While having her makeup applied, Charis went out of her way to make snide remarks that Holly and everyone else in the studio couldn't help but overhear. Holly was devastated. Soon after that, Holly took Derian's wise advice and left for Europe, working for the Paris agency Derian set her up with.

"Well, no," Charis stammered, struggling for a plausible excuse. She knew that Holly knew the answer before she asked the question, but Charis had to try to save face. "I had another booking," she lied lamely. "I have to go now. I see someone I have to talk to," she finished, beating a quick retreat before Holly could ask any more embarrassing questions.

"Now what did you accomplish by doing that?" Toney asked. "All you did was humiliate her and make an enemy."

"Business, *mon cher*," Holly answered, nonplussed. "Just taking care of unfinished business."

"You had better watch out that it doesn't take care of you," Toney warned her prophetically. "The bigger they are, the harder they fall."

"Yeah, they sure do," Holly agreed, thinking of Charis's fast departure. "How long do we have to hang around here, anyway?" Holly grumbled impatiently.

"Did you sign in?" Toney asked, referring to the standard model's sign-in sheet.

"Nope," she answered. "If you think I'm waiting until after all these bimbos go in, you're crazy."

"Yeah, you crowd in and these girls will slit your throat with their nail files."

"We'll see," Holly said confidently. "Watch this."

As a model came through the door from interviewing with the clients, Holly made her way to the door and started to go in.

"Just a minute, honey," she heard a sultry voice say. "I'm next."

A buxom, tanned blonde positioned herself between Holly and the door.

"Gee, I don't think so," Holly said innocently, and started to squeeze past her.

"No, I've been here much longer than you." Tiffany firmly blocked her path. Tiffany had also been replaced by Holly earlier in the week, and she had no intention of giving Holly her interview slot, too.

"Oh," Holly said sweetly, "I could have sworn I was next. Why don't you go check the list to see for sure?" As soon as Tiffany's back was turned, she intended to head for the interview room. A year in Paris had taught her plenty of tricks.

"Why don't you?" Tiffany countered in an equally sugary voice and before Holly could continue the conversation, Tiffany tossed her long platinum hair and swished through the door, almost colliding with Derian as she came out of the room.

Openmouthed, Holly watched Tiffany disappear behind the door. She had been beaten at her own game.

"Hi, Holly," Derian exclaimed when she spotted the lithe blonde. "How are you today?"

"Who was that girl?" Holly demanded angrily, ignoring Derian's greeting. She hated anyone getting the best of her.

"Tiffany, why?"

"Oh, nothing. We were just chatting," Holly said, calming herself. Then as an innocent afterthought, she added, "You know, Derian, there's something very strange-looking about that girl, don't you think? She's too tan, or muscular or something." It was another old Paris trick, sow the seeds of doubt.

"I never thought of Tiffany as muscular," Derian reflected slowly. "She does do a lot of active wear."

"Oh, that's probably it," Holly agreed, then she laughed. "She has more muscles than some of my ex-boyfriends!"

Derian looked at Holly thoughtfully for a moment, then changed the subject. "Stop by my office before you leave so I can give you the details on the Spheres booking," she said on her way back to her office.

"Told you," Toney said, coming up behind her. "You're lucky it was Tiffany. Some of these other girls would step over your dying body to get to a booking. Tiffany would only scratch your eyes out."

Giving him a sour look that made him laugh harder, she belligerently sauntered over to the sign-in sheet and wrote her name in at the bottom of the list.

Forty-five minutes passed before it was Holly's turn. During that time, some of the models she knew drifted over to say hello: Leslie, Sylvia, Misha, Gayanne, Linda. Their names came back to her as if it were yesterday. All of these women were top models, she thought to herself. Any of them could work in Europe if they wanted, but she was the only one who had actually done it, and as a result, she was at the top of the heap.

Finally, Holly entered the interview room where two women and a man were seated at a table, looking tired and bored.

"Hi, I'm Holly." She walked to the table and extended her hand, expecting them to recognize her, but they barely looked up.

"May we see your book?" the man asked in a monotone, ignoring her outstretched hand.

Typical interview, Holly thought to herself. No "hello" or "how are you?" As usual, these people didn't even bother treating models like they were human, just slices of fashion meat.

"We'd like to see you walk," one of the women explained to her, adjusting a portable tape recorder. "Listen to the music and follow my direction. First, hit the beat, then walk against the beat, then I want a couture walk, and finally a sporty walk. Do you think you can do that?" she asked with a condescending note in her voice, never making eye contact with Holly.

Holly felt like flipping her a sarcastic response, but instead she just answered, "Sure."

Oh, brother, she thought to herself. All of Europe was

into a casual saunter and these dolts wanted a Las Vegas review.

The woman played the tape and Holly moved back to the far wall facing them, but before she could start, the second woman, who had been thumbing through Holly's portfolio, stopped her.

"You've worked in Europe?" she asked, raising her eyes to look at Holly for the first time.

"Yes, I just arrived here a week ago," Holly answered. Deciding to impress them, she added, "I've worked for Sonya Rykiel, St. Laurent, Chanel, all the top designers."

"Really?" All three looked up at Holly, so clearly impressed that she had to keep herself from smiling.

She nodded seriously.

The man cleared his throat. "It won't be necessary to walk for us," he said, looking at the two women. "Will it?"

They both nodded in agreement.

"Thank you for coming in, Holly," he continued with respect in his voice and holding out his hand to her. "Derian will give you the details of the shows. We'll see you there."

"Thank you." Holly picked up her portfolio and shook his hand.

Europe had worked like a charm, just as she had known it would, she thought to herself as she walked through the reception area to Derian's office.

As she pranced by, Charis and Tiffany looked up and glared at her.

"Modelette," Charis scoffed contemptuously.

"What's a modelette?" Tiffany asked, watching Holly disappear into Derian's office.

"It's a woman who's caught up in playing model instead of just being real. She'll get hers. They all do."

Joi Lin was sitting in her little glass cubicle that faced the reception area, watching the models. She had been at DDL for a week and although Alan's death was the main topic of conversation, she had learned nothing that would help her discover his killer. She did learn that he had not been well liked in the industry. Betsy, the receptionist, was a loyal employee of Derian's and she had been more than willing to divulge the details of his departure from DDL and the subsequent opening of his own agency.

"Jerk!" Betsy spat out bluntly when Joi Lin brought up Alan's name. Betsy was not known for mincing her words.

"He was always ordering me around, telling me what to do," she told Joi Lin. "It was always get me this or get me that. You woulda thought he was the king of England or something."

Betsy quickly warmed to her subject. She bounced over to Joi Lin's cubicle and plopped herself down on the corner of Joi Lin's desk.

"There was a scene like you wouldn't believe before he left," Betsy continued, looking around and lowering her voice to a conspiratorial whisper. "Rusty caught him going through our client list, so of course he told Derian. She went ballistic! Read him up one side and down the other, kicked him out of the agency on the spot! Boy, what a weasel! He got what he deserved."

At first Joi Lin was shocked and angry, and it was all she could do to keep from defending her brother. It couldn't be true, she told herself, but after careful reflection on Alan's personality, she realized the stories held some merit.

Several models confirmed Betsy's story that he had used on everyone the same self-centered, self-aggrandizing tactics that he had used on her. And although she hated to admit it, the revelations served to enforce her newly formed assertiveness. However, even the revelations about Alan's personality did nothing to soothe the heavy burden of guilt she felt. Blood was still thicker than water, and Joi Lin knew she would never have any real peace until Alan's murderer was brought to justice.

As for Derian, Joi Lin found her to be a complex woman. She was tough with clients, but fair; calculating and manipulative, yet understanding and sympathetic toward her models. However, she certainly had plenty of reasons to hate Alan. He not only stole her client list to start his own agency, he tried to woo her top models into coming with him. When that didn't work, he started negotiations to merge with another agency. The merger would have made his the biggest and most powerful agency in L.A., and Derian would have been out of business. That was the reason for Alan's victory party. All these reasons made Joi Lin wonder if Derian had something to do with Alan's death.

One afternoon Joi Lin made a point of asking Betsy to take a coffee break at the restaurant across the street from DDL. Circuitously, she asked Betsy if she knew Derian's whereabouts after the party.

"I heard Lieutenant Hollis ask Derian the same question," Betsy volunteered. She diluted her coffee with cream and spooned enough sugar into it to change its consistency to syrup.

Amazed, Joi Lin watched her vigorously stir the thick concoction, take a sip, and then add still more sugar.

"You know, there was something very sexy about that cop in a rugged sort of way—"

"What did Derian tell him?" Joi Lin prompted impatiently. The last thing on her mind was Betsy's impression of Lieutenant Hollis.

"Oh, Derian told him she had a midnight supper with a group of people from the party," Betsy told Joi Lin, gulping the thick coffee down in one swallow. "Say, I'd like to have a midnight supper with the lieutenant. Wonder if he's married. He's never been back, too bad.

"Time to go," she told Joi Lin, bounding to her feet.

No wonder Betsy always had so much energy, Joi Lin thought to herself as she followed Betsy's bouncing figure back to the agency. She was always on a sugar high.

It was lucky for her, too, that Lieutenant Hollis hadn't come back to DDL. She suspected that Hollis would be less than enthusiastic if he found her working there.

Joi Lin had also met Rusty, Derian's brother, and wondered why Hollis hadn't even mentioned him. He was as handsome as Derian was beautiful and though he was almost the same age as Joi Lin, he seemed much more self-confident than she was. From models' conversations she had overheard, she surmised he was a classic pretty boy/playboy. He had only been at the agency once since she started, but the bond between brother and sister was evident to her. Derian almost glowed with maternal pride in his presence, while Rusty watched Derian's every move and hung on each word. Betsy told her that Derian's dedication to her business was second only to her great devotion to her brother.

Since Derian had an alibi the night of Alan's murder, Joi Lin had to cross her off her list of potential suspects. As she looked for other suspects, she studied the models carefully and found they were a unique group of people. Joi Lin expected them to be aloof and conceited; after all, they were some of the most gorgeous creatures she had ever laid eyes on. Instead, she found that the majority were friendly and down to earth. They all came by to introduce themselves to her and to chat, and she commented about it to Betsy.

"Natch," Betsy told her, "models are just regular people with hopes and dreams, goals and aspirations. Like everyone else, they get pimples on their chins, have arguments with their boyfriends, and cry on each other's shoulders.

"But the thing is, they're like salespeople selling the most difficult product of all—themselves." Betsy continued, "They're on perpetual job interviews day in and out. Three hundred and sixty-five days a year, they put their egos on the line. Clients knock them down and they pick themselves up and try again.

" 'Don't take it personally' is their motto, but you know," Betsy finished, shaking her head, "I don't know how they handle someone always tearing them apart."

Joi Lin didn't know either, but she was developing a whole new perspective on modeling.

Earlier that morning, Joi Lin overheard the clients who were now interviewing complaining to Derian about models who were too skinny.

"That's nothing," Betsy said dryly when Joi Lin mentioned their cutting remarks. "Some clients whine about the models' ankles, their lips, their personal style—anything and everything. One client even complained about the chest hair on one of the male models!

"Give me an office job any day," Betsy told her vehemently as she rolled a sheet of paper into her typewriter. "You couldn't pay me enough to be a model."

After what she had seen and heard, Joi Lin was beginning to agree.

At lunchtime, Joi Lin was just starting to eat an apple as she worked on the accounts when Holly Woodward walked through the agency door. Derian had been talking about Holly's return to Los Angeles all week and when Holly showed up for the interview, Joi Lin had no doubt about who she was. Holly exuded an aura of sophistication, sensual grace, and self-confidence. The other models saw it, too, for the room quieted briefly as they all turned to stare.

Curious about Holly, Joi Lin stood in the doorway of her office to get a better view of the reception area. She was close enough to hear the encounter between Holly and Tiffany, and the remarks Holly made to Derian.

She thought about Holly's observations for a moment, and yes, she decided, taking another bite of her apple, Holly was right. Tiffany was too tan, too muscular. She threw the apple core in the wastebasket and headed for the kitchen to get a cup of coffee.

Derian was already there, and as Joi Lin entered, Derian slammed the pot down on the coffee maker. Joi Lin deliberated for a brief moment, uncertain as to whether she should stay or quietly tiptoe away. Her curiosity won out.

"Is anything wrong, Derian?" she asked, concerned.

Derian whirled, startled. "Oh, I didn't hear you come in." She quickly changed her pursed mouth into a smile. "No, nothing's wrong. The pot just slipped, that's all."

She picked up her cup and left before Joi Lin could continue the conversation.

Joi Lin watched Derian, a pensive look on her face. Holly was obviously important to Derian, and Joi Lin had a feeling that Derian would be having a little chat with Tiffany, warning her to back off and not upset Holly.

Guiding his Rolls into the far right lane on La Brea Boulevard, Sid allowed a police car with its siren shrieking to pass him. When he regained his position in the left lane, he gazed after the disappearing patrol car, recalling the visit he and Ellysa had received almost two weeks ago from one of L.A.'s finest, a Lieutenant Hollis. He had come to talk with them about Alan Ainsley Anderson's murder. Of course they had already heard about it. News traveled fast in their set.

Sid stopped for a red light and ogled a sweet young thing in a miniskirt and cowboy boots as she crossed the street in front of the Rolls. She gave him a long sideways glance over the top of her sunglasses and Sid smiled back encouragingly.

It was a real shame about Anderson. His agency had some of the best-looking babes in town. In fact, the night of the party, Anderson pulled him aside and told him that anytime he wanted to meet any of them to just let him know. Sid knew what Anderson wanted in return— an exclusive on the Spheres account.

Of course, he didn't tell Lieutenant Hollis that. Some things were best left unsaid, and even though Hollis looked a little rough around the edges, Sid could read people and he knew a sharp operator when he saw one. Ellysa tried to give Hollis her usual rich-bitch attitude, but it didn't faze the cop in the least. Sid finally got so irritated with her attitude that he took over the conversation and that put her nose even more out of joint. All the schmo wanted to know was where they were after Anderson's party and instead he got a barometer reading on their marriage—chilly. And the bottom line was, they were home. Period. Women always made things so damn difficult.

Sid pulled up and parked in front of the coffee shop

and through the window saw Vicki waiting. "Shit," he grumbled as a look of annoyance played across her face.

Having given his affair with Vicki considerable thought this past week, he'd come to the conclusion that boffing her wasn't worth the aggravation. Her youth and impatience, the very traits that had attracted him in the beginning, were now irritating. Every day, she pressured him for more gifts, more time, and more of him. And at home, Ellysa made a whole set of other demands. There was no peace anywhere as the women clutched at him, making him feel boxed in.

He took a deep breath and steeled himself. Hoping to avoid a scene, he had purposely chosen a public place to meet. Though not *too* public. He couldn't afford to run into familiar faces.

"You're late," Vicki said petulantly as he sat down in the booth opposite her. "You know your darling wife only gives me an hour for lunch." She sipped a strawberry milk shake, then set the glass down with a loud bang to emphasize her anger.

He noticed for the first time the grating tone of her voice and how the corners of her mouth turned down.

"I had a long-distance phone call as I was leaving the office," he explained, signaling for the waitress. "Coffee, dear," he told her when she came to take his order.

"That's how it's been lately," Vicki retorted accusingly. "If it's not Ellysa, then it's business. I always take the back seat and I'm getting tired of it."

The waitress set a cup of coffee in front of Sid. "Anything else, sir?"

"Vicki, would you like something else?"

"No," Vicki barely replied, sulking.

"That will be all, then," he told the waitress.

"That's what I wanted to talk to you about, Vicki," he said, picking up where she had left off. "Business has increased tremendously and I'm not going to have as much free time as before."

"That's okay," Vicki said, only half listening. She had seen a new couch that she wanted for her living room and she was planning how she was going to hit Sid up for the dough to buy it.

"No, it's not okay," he continued emphatically as he poured cream into his coffee and stirred it. "It's not fair to you."

"Sure it is," Vicki said generously. "When things calm down, then you'll come over more." She wouldn't mind seeing the old goat a little less. "You know, Sidney, honey, I saw this rad couch that would look so gorgeous in my apartment."

"No, you don't understand. You should be dating guys your own age. Get involved in a relationship that can grow, not a dead-end one like ours." Sid had never realized before how slow on the uptake Vicki was.

Finally Vicki started listening to him. "Wait a minute!" She frowned. "You're not giving me the brush-off, are you?"

"Not a brush-off exactly. I just think we would both be happier if we both went our own way."

Shit, Vicki thought to herself, *the old fart is dumping me—Victoria del Rio*. She couldn't believe her ears and after all she'd done for him!

As she furiously stirred her milk shake with the straw, she thought of something else. This would be the end of her little perks, her baubles like the gold-link bracelet, the designer clothes, the new couch she wanted, and, most important, her swanky apartment. The thought of losing the apartment alone brought tears to her eyes and she uttered a little sob.

"Don't cry, Vicki." Sid patted her arm comfortingly, misinterpreting the reason for her tears. "I'm not such a great bargain. You'll eventually meet someone else and be just as happy."

Damn, he hated it when women cried. He never knew what to do or how to act. Maybe he had misjudged Vicki; perhaps she wasn't as tough or as demanding as he thought. *Look at her*, he thought, his resolve starting to weaken. *She's so young and vulnerable*. What a louse he was to do this to her. If she would only understand that she would meet someone else.

"You'll fall in love again," he promised earnestly, taking her hand in his. "Believe me."

If he goes through that voice-of-experience routine one more time, Vicki thought to herself, *I'll gag.*

"Oh, shut up, you fool!" She angrily jerked her hand away.

Her words and nasty tone of voice were like a slap in his face and Sid's resolve returned. She didn't sound so broken-hearted after all. He'd better make it clear to her that they should keep their relationship, or lack thereof, confidential, he thought shrewdly.

"Let's just part friends," he continued, trying to keep his anger in check. "There's no need to let anyone know about us." *Especially Ellysa,* he thought in a fit of temper.

"Of course, we'll always be friends and if you ever need a favor—"

That was all Vicki could stand of his patronizing attitude. The old fart was really doing it, she thought furiously. In one swift movement, she stood and threw her milk shake in his face, then stormed out of the door.

"I gotta get back to your wife's salt mine," she snapped over her shoulder.

Ellysa wandered through Spheres, supervising the progress her employees were making on preparations for the fashion extravaganza the following night. Everything seemed to be progressing on schedule. Alan's death could have really thrown her plans into disarray had Derian Delorian's agency not been able to step in and replace the models. It was too bad about Alan, though, she had liked him. She admired his handling of her account. He was aggressive, determined, and ambitious—like her. She hoped they'd catch his killer.

She reflected on Lieutenant Hollis's visit. What a horse's ass Sid made of himself. He was always trying to take command of every situation. She wondered why he lied, because she knew he left the house a half hour after she went to bed. He was probably sneaking off to meet one of his bimbos. It made her laugh to think how he tried to hide it, lying to the police. Pompous fool!

As she continued through the store, answering questions and marking her checklist, her mind kept returning to the wonderful secret she had kept for the past six-plus months. She wanted to savor the knowledge alone for a while, to hold it deep in her heart. It was an event that would change her life with Sid forever and she knew she had to choose the right time to tell him.

Lately, though, he seemed to be making himself scarce. He was working hard, or so he said, but she wondered if he was telling the truth. There had been indiscretions in the past and only God knew about the present. But all of that would be put behind them once she confided in him. There was no other way.

Reluctantly dismissing all thoughts of her secret, she forced herself to concentrate on the last-minute details in preparation for tomorrow night. She had a thousand things to do: reconfirm the menu, interview the waiters, check on the valet parkers, and a multitude of other details, all of which left her nervous and uptight. This show was of utmost importance to her and to everyone connected with the boutique—if they valued their jobs. She was determined that there would be no slipups or else.

She had just returned to her office and finished talking with the rental company, extracting a promise that they would be there by noon tomorrow to set up chairs, when she caught sight of Vicki del Rio returning from lunch. Glancing at her watch, she noted that the young woman was a half hour late, her third time this week. With all of her other aggravation, this was the proverbial straw that broke the camel's back.

"Well, well, well, if it isn't Miss del Rio?" she sniped sarcastically from behind her desk. "How nice of you to grace us with your presence and only half an hour late, too."

During the drive back to Spheres, Vicki's anger had tripled and she was in no mood for any of Ellysa's sarcasm.

"Sorry," she mumbled, and started to walk past Ellysa's office.

" 'Sorry,' " Ellysa mimicked her, making slight effort to contain her temper. "This is the third time this week that you've been late from lunch and all you can say is 'sorry.' Gee, Miss del Rio, I hope we didn't inconvenience you by expecting you back from lunch after an hour."

Vicki slowly turned to face Ellysa. She'd had just about all the abuse she could stand from the Roques. "Well, if Sid hadn't been half an hour late as usual in meeting me, then I wouldn't have been late," she hissed in a deadly tone of voice. "Why don't you impress upon your husband the importance of being punctual for lunches and not just when he's going to get fucked?"

Ellysa's mouth dropped open and for a rare moment she was at a loss for words. Her stomach lurched and she made a concentrated effort to keep from retching. Finally she found her voice. "Have you been having an affair with my husband?" she spat out, trying to maintain her composure.

"Let's just put it this way," Vicki continued, too furious even to consider the consequences of her words. "He likes his balls tapped when he's getting head."

"You're fired!" Ellysa screamed, her face turning a bright shade of purple. Shoving the chair back from her desk, she stomped around it to her office doorway.

Throughout the boutique, people turned and stared. Two exercise instructors walked by and one elbowed the other. "Cat fight," he mouthed with a smirk and the other one grinned. Lucille Ritter ducked behind a rack of clothes she had been pulling for the show, her bad eye spasming with nervousness, and Baroness Von Wittsburg, who was shopping for yet another cruise, scented blood in the air and moved in for a better view.

"Get out!" Ellysa shrieked.

"Oh, go to hell, you fat cow, and take that horny old fart of a husband with you!" Vicki retorted loudly.

Taking a step toward Vicki, Ellysa dug her nails into her clenched palms. Then realizing the entire first floor was watching them, Ellysa turned and stormed back into her office, slamming the door hard enough to rattle the lockers in the spa on the second floor.

Vicki stomped out of the boutique, muttering loudly about being screwed every which way but loose by the ungrateful Roques.

And Baroness Von Wittsburg headed for the nearest telephone, a look of rapture on her face.

CHAPTER
5

Standing under the shower head, the hot water beat down on Derian's neck and shoulders. When she felt thoroughly relaxed, the stress of the day finally having dissipated, she twisted the knob 180 degrees to the right, and shivered as numbing cold water hit her. She had learned this method of revitalization years ago on a photo shoot in Sweden and it always worked.

A small school of black angel fish swam by disinterestedly, but a small seahorse hung suspended at her eye level. He seemed mesmerized by her every action, peering at her first with one eye and then with the other. But when she tapped lightly on the glass, he darted away.

She stepped from the glass shower, letting the etched door swing silently closed behind her, and grabbed a thick bath sheet from the heated towel rack. As she rubbed herself dry, she idly glanced around.

This room had always been her favorite, probably because it was the one room in the house that she completely designed on her own. It was an elegant combination of Imperial granite and glass with her unique shower as the focal point of the room. Large and circular, with granite floors and four-foot-high sides, its curved glass wall above the granite was a huge, double-walled, saltwater aquarium, stocked with schools of brightly colored tropical fish. Although the architect had insisted an aquarium of that magnitude was impossible, Derian had been determined to make it work and eventually she found a way.

Slipping on a silk dressing gown, she walked into her dressing room, which was the size of a normal bedroom. Like most people in the fashion world, she loved beautiful clothes and she extravagantly indulged herself.

Her clothes were divided on racks by the four seasons, and then separated again by garments: blouses, skirts, day dresses, cocktail dresses. Lastly each group of similar garments was lined up according to color, beginning with white, then cream, then yellow, and ending with black. Derian sorted through the row of cocktail dresses, looking for just the right attention-getting dress for the Spheres fashion show that night. She was confident that the event would be a huge success and she wanted to be certain that no one would miss her when it came time for accolades.

Her final choice would have to be between a black silk morocaine suit and a pewter-gray Nolan Miller dress. She held them up side by side, trying to decide which one to wear. Black was the classic color for all formal affairs in Beverly Hills, so Derian purposely chose the gray one. She wanted to stand out and be easily noticed by the other guests. After making her decision, she sat down at her vanity and began to put on her makeup.

Applying her makeup was so much a matter of habit that Derian could do it with her eyes closed. After she applied undercoatings of moisturizer, eye cream, and lipstick fixative, she then used concealer, foundation, shader, a light coating of loose powder to set and blend the three together, and finally blusher.

Her eye makeup varied depending on what the latest trends were and where she was going. She arched her brows with dark brown powder and pencil, and set them with a brow gel. Then she reached for her custom-blended shadows and eyeliner, but she was unable to find them. She searched the top of her vanity table and finally gave up, making a mental note to check with the maid. Luckily, she kept spares and pulled them out. Working quickly, she brushed on a light layer of powder to soak up any oils on her lids, applied the shadows, liner, brushed on more powder to blend the colors into each other, and added mascara.

She outlined her lips with a natural shade of lip pencil and filled them in with a rich red lipstick. Then she gave her face a final light dusting of powder and scrutinized the results from all angles in the brightly lit mirror. She looked flawless.

Unfastening the banana clip that had held her hair in place while she was showering, she shook her hair loose. She brushed it back from her face, twisted it into a sophisticated chignon at her nape, and secured it with hairpins.

Derian pattered back into her wardrobe and peeled the gray dress from its hanger. Stepping into it and shimmying it up over her hips, she fastened it at the neck, then glanced in the full-length mirror. She looked spectacular. The narrow, long-sleeved columned dress was elegant and conservative from the front with its high funnel neck. It was also drop-dead backless, revealing an expanse of creamy skin. A chunky, black pearl and diamond necklace with matching jeweled ear clips and a chinchilla throw would complete her ensemble.

She pivoted in front of the three-paneled mirror next to the bedroom door. "I don't think anyone will overlook me tonight," she confidently told her reflection, then sailed out of the bedroom.

"Who were you talking to?" Rusty demanded. He was standing directly in her path as she opened her bedroom door.

Startled, Derian gasped and involuntarily took a step back.

"What's the matter with you?" Rusty asked innocently. He peered past her into the room. "You got someone in there with you, Derian?"

"Damn it, Rusty," Derian exclaimed, giving him a shove. "You scared the shit out of me! I didn't even know you were here. When did you get here anyway?"

"I just got here. I heard you talking to someone and thought I'd better investigate. Just who've you got in there? The pool boy?" He strained to look around her into the bedroom.

"Very funny. You aged me twenty years by scaring me like that," Derian retorted.

"Well, you don't look half bad for sixty," he teased with a grin, taking her elbow.

Derian jerked her arm away from him and gave him a withering look. "Ha, ha, ha," she said dryly.

"Have you got your camera?" she asked, changing the subject. "And plenty of film?"

Rusty made a grimace and nodded. "You know, in the future, I'd rather handle my own business affairs, if you don't mind. I'm perfectly capable of finding my own jobs."

"Now, baby, don't get your nose out of joint. You know I'm the best there is when it comes to sales," Derian answered, dismissing his protestations with a pat on the arm. "Hey, salesmanship is my business."

Rusty started to make a retort, but then changed his mind.

"Did you say something, Rusty?" Derian asked, draping her chinchilla around her shoulders.

"I said, let's go, Grandma." Rusty grinned.

Derian made a face at him and led the way to the door.

This was a big night for Joi Lin, although she had mixed feelings about it. Even though Alan had owned a modeling agency, Joi Lin never had any interest in the fashion industry, so consequently she had never been to a real fashion show. Since her employment at DDL, however, her interests had changed. She had gotten to know many of the models personally, and she was eager to see them perform on the runway. The show also afforded her an opportunity to meet and observe some of the same people who had attended Alan's party.

It promised to be an exciting evening, but it was going to take all her courage to walk into Spheres alone; and once she was there, she wondered if anyone would talk to her. The thought of standing in a corner alone all night was enough to make her break out into a cold sweat. Each time she thought about the upcoming evening she would begin to hyperventilate. She wanted to go. She knew she had to go—but she was afraid.

She thought how Alan would have handled the evening. He would have been smooth, charming, full of interesting conversation and witty jokes; he would have introduced himself to strangers, confident that they would be interested in meeting him. Perhaps, she told herself, if she adopted his methods, she could at least get through the evening. Feeling slightly more secure, Joi Lin went into her bedroom to dress for the party.

It only took her a few minutes to get ready. She didn't wear much makeup and she just pulled her hair back with a velvet hairband. Since she only had one dinner dress, a little four-ply black silk one, she didn't have to decide what to wear. Her only suitable jewelry was a pair of pearl button earrings that had belonged to her mother. Joi Lin noticed as she passed the mirror that her dress seemed slightly looser and she wondered if she had lost weight, or perhaps the dry cleaner had just stretched it.

She practiced her social banter as she drove toward Spheres, and by the time she reached Melrose Avenue she felt a surge of confidence that made her more determined than ever to find Alan's killer.

Melrose Avenue had always been a kaleidoscope of life-styles, Joi Lin thought, as the shops and restaurants flashed past her. A forgotten street in the seventies, it rose like the phoenix from the ashes with the arrival of the punk rockers in the early eighties, followed by the

yuppies in the mid-eighties, and recently by the Beverly
Hills chic set.

Spheres was twice removed from the so-called fashionable area of Melrose. In fact, it was beyond the outer
limits of the hip-hop shops, beyond even Paramount Stu-
dios. But it didn't matter, because it was beginning to be
known as *the* trendsetter, a legend among legends, and
it was far and above anything as pedestrian as prime
location.

Joi Lin had shopped on the avenue many times and
she knew Spheres by sight and reputation, but nothing
had prepared her for the carnival atmosphere that night.
The police had cordoned off a two-block area around the
store, stopping all traffic except those attending the show.
When she gave her name to the guard who stopped her,
she couldn't help but feel a sense of importance as he
checked it off his list without question.

The police were able to control the motor traffic, but
they were unable to limit the foot traffic. Within a block
of Spheres, the sidewalk was overflowing with crowds and
the entire area looked like the premiere of a major motion
picture as paparazzi and stargazers elbowed for front-row
positions.

As she pulled up in front of the boutique, all eyes
focused in her direction and several red-jacketed valets
snapped to attention. It was all too much for Joi Lin, even
with her newly primed self-confidence, and she stepped
on the gas and sped off. She circled the block and parked
on a quiet side street, hoping she could slip through the
entrance without being noticed.

Hundreds of tiny white Italian lights hung from the front
of Spheres and a wide red carpet stretched from the
entrance to the street. On either side, spotlights lit up
the starless sky.

As she scurried self-consciously across the carpet, her
resolution again began to falter when a liveried guard met
her halfway. He politely asked for her name, and Joi Lin
held her breath until he found it and checked it off his

list. She started through the entrance when a murmur
went up from the crowds. Turning in the direction of
the street, she saw Derian's pearl-white Jag pull up and
Rusty slide out of the driver's side. Then, Derian stepped
out of the passenger's side. The crowd swarmed around
them and the paparazzi called Derian's name, vying for
her attention. Derian gave them a dazzling smile, and in
response, a dozen flashbulbs exploded. Rusty stood out of
camera range, but Joi Lin could tell that Derian adored
being the center of attention. Then taking Rusty's arm she
slowly walked up the red carpet, milking the moment for
all it was worth. She looked so regal and intimidating that
Joi Lin, who was still standing in the entrance, glanced
around for a corner to squeeze into.

"Good evening, Joi Lin," Derian exclaimed, spotting
her before she had a chance to melt into the background,
and linking her arm in Joi Lin's, Derian swept her through
the entrance with them. "Perfect timing!"

Tuxedoed waiters stood at the entrance with silver trays
of caviar and chilled flutes of Roderer Crystalle champagne. Derian handed Joi Lin and Rusty each a flute,
and then with both in tow, she got down to business—
working the room.

She was a master at it, smooth, gracious, and she made
sure Joi Lin and Rusty met everyone she spoke to. Joi Lin
met movers and shakers, not just from L.A., but from all
over the country: people like Vinny Lundstrom, one of
the largest commercial real estate developers on the East
Coast; the glamorous film star Sabina Dawson, who was
holding court to a group of adoring men; and her famous
sister, novelist Starla Dawson. Television news commen-
tator Meredith Williams and her husband, TV mogul Mo
Ahlberg, were deep in conversation with industrialist Hap
Davis and the timeless Ina Fairchild, but when they saw
Derian, they hurried to greet her. Derian introduced Joi
Lin to them all, and with Derian acting as her guardian,
they were all cordial to her. Joi Lin marveled at the
difference it made to have someone take an interest in
her; it was so unlike Alan's parties where she had always

been left to her own devices after he quickly introduced her around.

A sudden hush came over the room and all eyes turned toward the door as former President Jerry Hartford and his first lady, Beatrice, entered the room with the dime-store heiress, Sissy McCormick. A small entourage of Secret Service men followed close behind. Joi Lin saw a lacquered-looking young matron and a paunchy middle-aged man move quickly to greet the group.

"That's our host and hostess," Derian explained to Joi Lin. "The Roques."

Joi Lin stood on her tiptoes to get a good look at the couple. "I've got to meet them," she said tightly, more to herself than to anyone else.

"Oh, I'll make sure you meet them before the evening's over," Derian responded breezily, missing the intensity in Joi Lin's voice. "If all my plans go right, we'll be seeing a lot more of the Roques."

Rusty, however, picked up on Joi Lin's tone and he looked at her curiously.

"Get a load of that," Tiffany hissed to Charis. The two women were on the top floor of the store in the models' dressing area, leaning over the balcony and watching as Holly made her way through the audience below. "We were told to use the back entrance, but here comes her royal highness up the escalator. God, I can't stand that bitch!" Tiffany whirled and stalked over to one of the mirrors.

Charis watched Holly's ascent thoughtfully. She suspected that what upset Tiffany the most was that *she* hadn't thought of walking through the crowd. Since their last meeting at the agency interview, Charis had given Holly a wide berth, but then, so had most of the other models. Holly hadn't hesitated to lord her privileged status over the other models and more than one model's bookings had bit the dust because of her. She constantly bragged about her Paris successes and some of the other models who had also worked Paris tried to compete with her patter. But she quickly silenced them by mentioning recent shows and current in-photographers of whom they had no knowledge.

Charis, however, still believed in the old adage that one could attract more flies with honey than with vinegar, so she waited to greet Holly and to once again try to ingratiate herself with the young woman.

"Hi, Holly," she said enthusiastically as Holly reached the top of the escalator.

"Oh, hi," Holly responded as she started to brush by Charis. She took a step or two, then turned back and gave Charis a sharp, appraising stare. "I didn't expect to see you here. I guess they needed someone the old buzzards in the audience could identify with." And she walked off, leaving Charis speechless.

She felt like she had been slapped. Her face burned with embarrassment and she fought back tears. She quickly looked around the room to see if anyone else had overheard Holly's remark, but no one had.

All around her, models were putting on makeup, checking shoes, matching up jewelry. A current of excitement crackled through the room as the models geared up for the show. Charis walked to a mirror and peered at her face. Sure, there were small lines around her mouth and crow's-feet at the corners of her eyes, but she still looked good for forty-two. But that was the problem. She looked good for forty-two, but all the other models were no more than thirty-two. How could she compete? Tears threatened to spill over and wash down her cheeks, and she took a deep breath, struggling to control her emotions. All she ever wanted to be was a model and she was a good one, too, but what was she going to do when no one wanted her? A tiny sob found its way from deep inside her chest and escaped before she could stifle it.

Linda, who was standing next to her applying false eyelashes, turned to look at her. "Are you all right, Charis?" she asked, concerned.

Charis, afraid to trust her voice, nodded and attempted a smile.

Linda stopped her ministrations and put an arm around Charis. "You know, I meant to tell you how pretty you look tonight."

"Really?" Charis mumbled, her voice cracked, but she was desperate to believe her. "You know, Linda, I look in the mirror and all I see are wrinkles. Holly said the only reason I was hired for the show was so the old buzzards in the audience would have someone to identify with!"

"Silly girl." Giving her a hug, Linda lied, "You look gorgeous and you don't have any wrinkles. You just put on your false lashes, and you go out there and strut your stuff. You'll be the envy of everyone in that audience!"

Behind them, Holly dominated the conversation. In a loud voice she lectured any model who would listen on the benefits of using Bleu-Blanc, special eyedrops she brought from Paris that made the whites of her eyes whiter and brighter.

"What a fool," Linda said disgustedly, picking up on Holly's conversation. "I worked Paris, too. Everyone knows Bleu-Blanc contains liquid cocaine. If she keeps using those drops, she'll be out of modeling before she really gets started."

"Ten minutes," Mrs. Ritter called from the top of the escalator.

"Come on, sweetie," Linda told Charis gently. "It's showtime."

The overhead lights dimmed as Ellysa stepped away from the podium and squeezed through the tables toward her seat. Along the way guests plucked at her clothes and grabbed her hands, congratulating her on her introduction and the forthcoming entertainment. She barely made it to her seat before the first tinkle of bells and haunting strains of mandolins filled the air.

Three spotlights set up in different positions parted the darkness and focused on the first three models posed dramatically at the top of the moving escalator. As the audience gasped at the stunning tableau, Ellysa swelled with pride. She knew without a doubt that no one could top this show and that she would be the center of the fashion scene in Los Angeles for the rest of the year. Charity groups would vie for her attention and she would have her choice of social events.

Every eye in the room focused on the three Asian models at the top of the escalator, dressed in beautifully embroidered Japanese wedding robes in striking combinations of black, white, and gold. Each model's long, glossy black hair was twisted up and held with a single gold chopstick. As the escalator carried them down to the runway, the music swelled, and the sound man dropped in an overlay track of throbbing futuristic music. On cue, the three stepped gracefully from the moving escalator onto the ramp, keeping their robes wrapped tightly around them. When they reached the T of the runway, they simultaneously dropped the robes to reveal the skimpiest thong swimsuits that Ellysa had been able to find. They pulled out the chopsticks and their long hair shimmered down their backs. Behind them, a second group of models robed in brilliant reds and oranges began their descent down the escalator. More models in beachwear followed them, twirling colorful Japanese paper umbrellas until both the escalator and the runway were ablaze with movement and color.

The first group chevroned stage right, followed by the second group who dropped their robes and chevroned stage left. Tuxedoed male models picked up the robes as the women worked dual runways that snaked throughout the room and ended at the ascending escalator and the waiting male models. Then the women gracefully slipped on their robes and posed on the returning escalator as it carried them upstairs to their next change of clothing.

For a few moments, the audience was speechless, and Ellysa, who had been anticipating applause, twisted nervously in her chair trying to see the expressions on the faces around her. Finally as the sequence ended, the audience came to life, clapping and cheering enthusiastically.

Ellysa swelled with pride. She couldn't believe the magnitude of the response; she had managed to mesmerize the jaded assemblage.

Sid, who was sitting next to her, slipped an arm around her and gave her a squeeze. "Congratulations, baby," he whispered in her ear. "You've done it!"

As the applause died down, Ellysa leaned back in her chair and took a deep breath. This *was* her night. She had her husband by her side, a wildly successful boutique, and the crème de la crème of Beverly Hills society at her feet. For the first time in weeks, she felt her tension beginning to ease. Her hard work and long hours had finally paid off. At the next table, Ina Fairchild and Princess Guyroche of Yugoslavia whispered animatedly to each other, and at the table beyond, Chi Chi Von Wittsburg caught her eye with a nod.

Sid possessively draped his arm across the back of her chair, and for a few moments Ellysa's mind drifted back to memories of a happier time in their lives, to the beginning days of their marriage—before Spheres, before Sid's extramarital affairs—when they were enchanted with each other. In those days, Sid used to insist that Ellysa come to his office to keep him company, and she could still remember how his face would light up at the sight of her. They would lunch together in cozy little bistros and afterward, they'd slip away for an hour or two of lovemaking. In those days, love filled his eyes and it was only for her.

Tender memories, warmer than a summer day, filled her, and she temporarily forgot the incident with Vicki del Rio as she leaned over to stroke his face affectionately. She longed to see the special little smile that he had always reserved only for her.

But Sid was enthralled with a blond model strutting down the runway in front of him.

"Wow," he breathed under his breath. "She's hot stuff!"

Ellysa clenched her hand into a fist and let it drop into her lap as she struggled with an almost uncontrollable urge to slap him. She felt her face burn with fury and she closed her eyes for a moment until she could regain her composure. When she opened them again, she glanced over and saw Baroness Von Wittsburg staring at her, so she forced herself to smile.

There was a sensual excitement in the air as the models preened and pranced down the runway. The audience had never seen such staging, such fashions, or such an array of beautiful models. Applause was like an aphrodisiac to the models and each round of applause drove their showmanship up a notch. Each woman played to the audience trying to top the model before her.

The runway was like an elixir to Charis, clearing her head of her problems, giving her strength, and enabling her to think clearly. On the surface she moved with her usual grace and poise, but on the inside, her mind was turning her situation over and over, examining it from every angle. There had to be some way for her to increase her bookings, and whatever it took, she decided she would do it.

As she came down the escalator in her third change, she saw at the apex of the T her salvation—Sid Roque. Everyone had heard the rumors about him, that he was a player from the get-go. If she played her cards right, or at least played him right, Spheres could be her biggest account. Although she had always thought of him as pudgy and over-the-hill, now she saw him in a new light. He was powerful, rich, and the answer to her future might very well lie in his control. She added an extra swing to her hips as she slinked down the runway and when she pivoted in front of him, she gave him her best sultry look, of course making sure Ellysa Roque didn't notice. But Sid did and he gave Charis a broad smile.

Joi Lin was having a wonderful time and with all her heart, she wished Alan were here with her. He would have loved the flash and glamour. The models were magnificent and the show was even more exciting because she knew the girls. Rusty had left her and Derian earlier so he could photograph the models from various angles as they came down the runway, but she was sitting next to Derian and as each girl came down the escalator, Derian would critique her performance.

"Look at Linda," Derian whispered to Joi Lin. "That girl walks like butter! And Syl, can that girl strut or what . . ."

One by one the models peeled off and worked the runway, in their own distinctive style. Theresa came down the runway with her I-don't-give-a-damn attitude; then Jacquie followed close behind with her classic walk. Linda and Suzanne came next, both gliding to the ends of the runway and back, in shoulder-to-shoulder elegance.

From meeting the models at DDL, Joi Lin had been unsuccessful in picking up any clues as to whether any of them had dated Alan. Though she thought none of their names had appeared on his guest list, she wondered if one of them had shown up uninvited to his party. Joi Lin had discovered each girl was a distinct individual with assets and liabilities, strengths and insecurities. But she was amazed that once they were out on the runway, they all acted with poise and confidence and had the ability to hold the audience. They were the best of the Los Angeles modeling world, graceful and beautiful to look at, experts at showing a designer's clothes. They knew how to project just the right mood for each garment, how to flip a skirt, eye the audience from beneath the brim of a hat, or drag a sable with luxurious decadence. But not one of them had given her any indication that they had known Alan intimately.

"Here comes Tiffany. Damn, she's still too tan!" Derian continued. Even though she no longer modeled, Derian felt a buzz of excitement and energy. "Look at Holly! Look, she's upstaging Tiffany and can she ever move. Paris did wonders for her!"

"Tiffany looks pretty good to me," Rusty whispered lecherously. He had moved up behind them to get a wide angle shot. "How come I've never met her?"

"Sh-h-h," Derian ordered. "Just keep snapping pictures. What do you think, Joi Lin?"

"They're fabulous," Joi Lin breathed. She was having a wonderful time, though she hadn't forgotten her real purpose for being there. She looked around the room and spotted the Roques. Derian had promised to introduce her to them, and Joi Lin intended to make sure she met them before the end of the evening.

As the show reached its finale, the ascending escalator was reversed so that both escalators ran downward to the runway. The entire room went black, and suddenly the top of each escalator exploded simultaneously in arches of sparklers. Holly led the procession from one escalator and Linda from the other as the models slipped through the flaming arches and struck poses, gliding down to the runway. They were dressed in jewel-studded gowns that reflected the light from the burning fireworks. Gasps of awe and disbelief went up from the audience at the sight.

"Oh, no! This is too dangerous," Derian whispered fearfully. "I would have never let my models do that if I had known."

She held her breath, hoping that no one would catch fire. Once all her models were through the blazing arch, she exhaled in relief. She had to admit it was a spectacular ending and the audience was crazed with applause.

But it wasn't over yet. As instructed, the models stepped down off the runway and into the audience. The women randomly selected men in the audience and led them to the dance floor for the first dance to keep the momentum of the evening going.

As Tiffany passed near Rusty, he laid his camera down on a nearby table and grabbed her hand. Never one to pass up an opportunity, Tiffany, without missing a beat, swiveled back to the dance floor with Rusty in tow.

Charis saw an opportunity, too. She headed toward Sid Roque, holding out her hand with an inviting smile.

"Dance?" she asked.

Behind her, Holly watched Charis and Sid walk to the dance floor and from the look on Charis's face, she deduced that Charis was making a play for Sid.

Pretty sharp, Charis, Holly thought to herself. *But not sharp enough.*

She grabbed the nearest man in the audience and followed Charis and Sid to the floor. Barely noticing her dancing partner, she maneuvered him next to them, and when Charis was gazing at Sid with adoration and speaking in soft husky tones, Holly tapped her on the shoulder.

"Time to switch partners," she told Charis gaily.

"I don't think so," Charis retorted sharply, keeping a firm grip on Sid. She wasn't about to let Holly get the upper hand this time.

For a moment it was a standoff, both models glaring at each other, neither willing to budge. Sid was in seventh heaven. Two beautiful women were fighting over him and his ego went into the stratosphere as he looked from one to the other, trying to calculate which one was the best deal. Finally, he decided that Holly was the youngest, the prettiest, and the biggest boost to his ego. God, he hoped the other men noticed these two beauties arguing over him!

"Ladies, please, let's not argue. There's enough of me to go around," he told them magnanimously. "Didn't your mothers teach you to share?"

With that, he dropped Charis's hand, grabbed Holly around the waist, and twirled her away. Charis, beside herself with anger and humiliation, turned and stomped off, leaving Holly's partner standing alone in the middle of the floor.

"What am I," he exclaimed to her quickly disappearing back, "chopped liver?"

Derian had sent Joi Lin down to find Rusty, and now she impatiently watched them make their way through the crowd. She motioned for them to hurry.

"I'm trying to get you some new business, and all you're doing is fooling around," she told Rusty crossly. "I've been telling Ellysa Roque about you and she wants to meet you!"

"I'd rather get—" Rusty started to protest.

"Sh-h-h," Derian interrupted. "Come on!"

She linked her arm through his and pulled him through the crowded room, Joi Lin trailing behind.

"Ellysa," she called, breaking through the group congratulating the Spheres's owner. "I want you to meet my brother, Rusty."

"How do you do, Rusty." Ellysa smiled, holding out her hand. "I understand you got some great shots tonight."

"Yes, he's a fabulous photographer," Derian bragged before Rusty could answer. "Rusty, say hello to Ellysa."

"It's nice to meet you, Ellysa," he answered, shooting Derian a warning look. "Wonderful show."

"Thank you," Ellysa said thoughtfully. "I've been thinking of mounting a full-scale advertising program, starting with a full-color monthly catalogue. Would you be interested in shooting it?"

"He'd love to do it," Derian enthused before Rusty could answer. "Wouldn't you, Rusty?" Derian added, nudging him.

"Yes, I would," he agreed, giving Derian an exasperated look.

"Then it's settled," Derian finished. "I've got some great ideas for the catalogue, too. Perhaps we should all get together in the next few days to discuss them. What do you say?"

"That's just fine," Ellysa said, unaware of any dissension between the two.

At that moment Sid Roque joined the group, and although Ellysa graciously introduced him to the three of them, there was a definite iciness to her tone. As they turned to walk away, Joi Lin heard Ellysa hiss something about hitting on anything in a skirt.

Once they were out of earshot, Rusty angrily turned on Derian. "Why do you always do that!" he exclaimed, his face flushed with anger.

"Do what?" Derian asked innocently.

"Talk for me!" he exploded. "You never think I'm capable of doing anything."

"Excuse me," Joi Lin broke in, feeling uncomfortable in the middle of a family discussion as personal as this one threatened to become. "I'm going to talk to some of the models." She made a quick exit, but neither Derian nor Rusty noticed.

"That's not true, Rusty," Derian protested. "I'm just trying to help you. I've had more experience in these things, and I was just trying to help you promote yourself."

Rusty chewed on his lower lip without answering. Derian affectionately brushed back a stray strand of hair from his forehead. *Maybe I am too pushy,* she thought to herself. *Maybe I should just let him handle things his own way. He'll learn eventually. But, I love him so. I'd hate to see anyone take advantage of him. The fashion business is a tough field and he's such a good kid I don't want to see him hurt.*

"Look, Rusty," she told him, ruffling his hair. "It's no big deal. The important thing is that you get the business, right? Lighten up."

"I guess you're right," he said, his bad mood dissipating. "I'm going to catch up with Tiffany."

Derian watched him cross the dance floor and approach Tiffany. *He's a good kid, but he's so young. Will he ever be able to take control of his life?*

Joi Lin watched Sid Roque head for the open bar in the corner of the room and she wove through the crowd to his side. She wasn't sure what she was going to say to him; she just knew she had to at least make an attempt to gain any information that might be pertinent to Alan's murder.

"Wonderful show, Mr. Roque," she began, accepting a glass of chardonnay offered by the bartender.

"Thanks. The boutique is my wife's baby," he answered, sipping on a gin and tonic. "But the models were the ones who made the show."

"Yes, I know. All the models came from DDL. Originally, though, weren't some of the models supposed to be booked from Alan Ainsley Anderson's agency?"

"I'm sorry, I wouldn't know anything about where the models came from. But unfortunately for Alan Anderson, the point is moot. He's dead," Sid answered casually. He canvassed the room, hoping to see Holly before she left.

"Yes, I know," Joi Lin answered, trying to figure out what questions she could ask without making Sid suspicious. She couldn't very well ask him if he murdered Alan. This was more difficult than she had imagined. "I heard he gave a big party the night he was murdered."

"Yeah, I was there. It seems he was on the verge of acquiring a second modeling agency and that would have made his the largest agency in L.A.," Sid explained with a shake of his head. "A real shame about Alan. He threw one hell of a party."

"You and he were friends?" Joi Lin asked quickly. She had heard so many negative comments about Alan, her heart leapt at the thought that she might finally hear something positive. Maybe he wasn't perfect, but he was her brother.

"Well, we weren't exactly friends," Sid countered vaguely, spotting some of the models leaving. Perhaps he'd just mosey over and casually run into Holly as she left; that babe was quite a number. "But he always had the prettiest girls in L.A. at his parties. Look, it's been nice talking to you, but I see someone I have to speak to," he explained quickly. "Enjoy yourself, and thanks for coming. Bye."

Joi Lin watched his disappearing back with frustration. It was obvious that he had given her the brush-off and she had hardly learned anything. Damn it! She wasn't a detective. She was a bookkeeper, for heaven's sake.

No one seemed to have liked Alan and that saddened her. Sure he was a jerk sometimes, but so far, no one had told her anything he had done that would have pushed someone to kill him.

Hollis double-checked the address on the side of the apartment building with the one on the slip of paper he held before killing the car's engine and with it the air-conditioning. No use giving himself heat stroke. In the summer, the valley was always at least ten degrees hotter than the rest of L.A. The temperature had shifted as soon as he crested the hill and began to descend, the hot smoggy air hitting him like a drunk's bad breath, sapping his energy. If his air-conditioning had been on the fritz, he would look like he'd walked through a sauna with his suit on.

Thank God it was working this morning, because KNIK radio had announced one hundred five degrees and still climbing. He sorted through the file on the seat next to him, procrastinating in the cool car before having to face the inevitable blast of sweltering heat.

He had completed his interviews with those who attended Alan Ainsley Anderson's party and had turned up nothing. Now, he was starting with the first of the eight women who had starred in Anderson's private home videos. Naturally, he had plenty of panting volunteers standing in line to help him with these interviews, but instead he perversely assigned the eager beavers to computer duty and background files, checking to see if any other murders could be linked up with the same M.O. It was worth a dozen trips to the valley without air-conditioning just to see the look on Joey Tartella's face when he was assigned to the computer. Hollis smiled at the memory. *Ah, the sweet taste of payback.*

He scrutinized the building and surrounding tree-lined block. It was a pretty ritzy neighborhood for a woman who said she was a salesclerk. The building was one of those new Mediterranean affairs in pink and turquoise stucco, a style that seemed to be popping up all over southern California. He speculated on whether she had a roommate with whom she was splitting the rent. Well, he'd soon find out.

Slamming the car door, he plodded up the apartment steps. The air was so thick and hot that he felt as if he were parting it with his body. Not so much as a leaf stirred and the greedy heat seemed to suck the cool breath from his lungs.

He ran his finger down the list of occupants next to the security phone until he came to the one he wanted,

Victoria del Rio, and punched in her code number. She was waiting for his arrival and immediately buzzed him in, giving him directions to her apartment.

Victoria del Rio looked the same as she did in the video, Hollis thought—except she was wearing brightly printed leggings and a sweatshirt, instead of her birthday suit. She was a pretty, sexy, young Latino woman, probably in her early twenties, he estimated, attractive enough to be a model except for her annoying pout and her whiny voice.

"Nice apartment you have, Ms. del Rio," Hollis noted, surveying the room.

"Thanks, I saw that Anderson guy you asked about earlier a couple of times at Spheres—the place I used to work," she told Hollis, getting right to the point. She didn't like the way Hollis was looking around her apartment and she wanted to get rid of him as soon as possible. Cops were always sneaking around trying to stick it to people. Even if they hadn't done anything.

"Course I don't work there anymore," she volunteered, tossing her long dark hair arrogantly. "I quit. I couldn't stand that bitch Ellysa Roque, who owned the place. She was always picking on every little thing I did. I think she was jealous of me, 'cause I was younger and better-looking."

"What about Anderson?" Hollis asked, drawing her back to the subject before she went off on a tangent. "Did you ever see him other than at Spheres?"

"No, he came by the store trying to get the bitch to book his models. Of course, I never talked to him. Personally, though, I don't think he had much of an agency. I've heard DDL is the best agency in L.A."

"You're sure, then," Hollis persisted. "The only times you ever saw him were at Spheres and you never talked to him?"

"That's right, Captain Hollis," Vicki reaffirmed. She reached out and lined up a stack of fitness magazines on her coffee table.

There was something about this cop that was making her nervous. She felt like he knew something about her that she didn't. And how did he come up with her name in connection with that slime bucket Alan Ainsley Anderson anyway?

Hollis noticed a slight tremor in her hands and knew it was time to shake a few branches to see what dropped out. "It's Lieutenant Hollis, and you might want to think over your answer for a few minutes," he said, fixing her with an unwavering stare.

"What do you mean?" Vicki asked nervously, the corners of her mouth drooping even more.

"I mean we've got a video of you, Anderson, and another woman that would never make it through the censors at *America's Funniest Videos,*" he told her dryly. Her voice was beginning to grate on his nerves.

"I don't know what you're talking about," Vicki insisted, but her voice wavered and her hands were shaking so hard that she had to clasp them together and hold them in her lap.

"I'm not playing games here, Ms. del Rio," Hollis said in a weary tone of voice. Why did people always think they could bluff their way out of a situation? "We've got you in living color, in the buff, snorting enough blow to put you away for a long time. Now do *you* want to tell me about it here, or do you want to tell me down at the station?"

"No, no, I'll tell you," she said quickly, her bravado collapsing.

"I met Alan at Spheres. I wanted to become a model and so we partied a few times. But I never knew he was videotaping us! I guess I shouldn't be surprised, though," she continued bitterly. "One time the sonofabitch even had another woman join us—a big-time model. But then he had the best shit around and it was free, so I thought, what the hell. No big deal, right?"

"Then what happened?" Hollis asked, jotting down a few notes in his little notebook.

"I finally got around to asking him to sign me with his agency and you know what the little shithead said?" Vicki spat out. "He said I was too short!

" 'Sorry, sweetie, I only take on girls over five-nine,' "
she repeated, mimicking Anderson's voice. " 'You should
have asked me that in the beginning.'

"I'm glad he's dead!" Vicki spat out vehemently. "He
got what he deserved!"

"And you made sure of it," Hollis stated flatly. "You
went to his place after the party and told him you wanted
one last hump, for old times' sake, so to speak, and then
you gave him a little late-night snack—poison."

"No, I didn't! I hadn't even seen him in a couple of
months." Vicki was badly shaken, her hands refused to
stay folded in her lap, and she wrapped them around her
body to keep them still.

"If you weren't with Anderson, then what were you
doing that night?" Hollis hammered at her.

"I was here alone, watching television," Vicki sniveled.
She thought about turning on the tears, but she sensed that
it wouldn't faze a man like Lieutenant Hollis.

"Right. Somehow it's hard for me to picture you as the
little homebody type. Maybe you were knitting, too, huh?"
Years of observation told Hollis that there was more to
her story: the way her eyes kept darting around the room,
avoiding his; the folded arms around her body; and the
spots of perspiration that appeared along the armholes of
her sweatshirt.

"We're dealing with a murder here, Ms. del Rio. You
have the right to remain silent. You—" he bluffed.

"Wait, wait, I forgot. I wasn't alone," Vicki interrupted
in panic. "Sid Roque was here! Just ask him."

"You were with Sid Roque?" He was trained to keep
the surprise out of his voice, but Vicki's admission caught
him completely off guard. So Roque had lied to him. He
had gone out after the party. No wonder he detected a
chill between the Roques. Sid was playing house with one
of Ellysa's salesgirls. The pieces fit. Now he understood
how Vicki could afford such a swank apartment. And
that was why Vicki was no longer working at Spheres!
Ellysa Roque found out and fired her. "How long has this
arrangement been going on?"

"It's not. That is, not anymore," Vicki admitted nastily. "We broke up. I couldn't stand making it with the old fart any longer or working for his wife either.

"At least Alan was young," she added.

"So much for falling in love," Hollis commented, scribbling furiously in his notebook.

"Get serious," Vicki said bitterly.

Hollis's next stop was DDL. From his interviews, he'd discovered that the whole purpose of Anderson's party was to announce his intention to buy out another agency, giving Derian Delorian a run for her money in the fashion agency business. Hollis wanted to question Ms. Delorian further about Anderson's impending purchase.

The reception area was deserted when Hollis walked in. The same little receptionist who had greeted him before bounced up to the counter. He wondered where she got all her energy.

"Hi, Lieutenant Hollis!" she bubbled, giving him a big smile. "It's really terrific to see you again."

"It's nice to see you, too," Hollis responded, surprised at her warm reception. "I wondered if Ms. Delorian was in. I'd like to speak to her."

As he spoke, he glanced around the room and caught sight of a familiar face in one of the back cubicles. Startled, he craned his neck to get a better look. There was no doubt about it. Alan Ainsley Anderson's sister, Joi Lin Ambernites, was sitting at a desk! Hollis looked again. What the hell was she doing there? He felt a smoldering anger slowly rise within him. This investigation was difficult enough without a meddling civilian compromising it.

"Lieutenant? Did you hear me?" Betsy was saying. "Earth to Lieutenant Hollis, come in please—"

"I'm sorry," Hollis apologized, forcing his attention back to Betsy. "I guess I had my mind on something else. What did you say?"

"I said that Derian is out for the rest of the afternoon," Betsy repeated slowly, emphasizing each word as if he were deaf. "Do you want me to have her call you?"

"No," Hollis answered, focusing on Joi Lin. She hadn't looked up, and he was pretty sure she hadn't seen him. "Don't bother even mentioning I stopped by. I'll catch her another time."

"Okay. Whatever you say. You know, you look like you could use a cup of coffee, whaddaya say?" Betsy said, giving him a big smile and leaning over the counter.

"Thanks, but I just had one," Hollis answered distractedly. What was Joi Lin up to? "Thanks for your time Ms.—"

"Betsy. Nice seeing you, too. Stop back again soon, okay?"

Hollis walked back to his car and got in, but made no attempt to leave. What was Anderson's sister doing there, and why hadn't she told him she worked at DDL? He decided to sit tight and wait for her to leave and then have a little chat with her.

Joi Lin pushed open the front door of the agency and a gust of warm air enveloped her. After sitting for eight hours in a stale air-conditioned office, the summer breeze was rejuvenating. The temperature had dropped and the late-afternoon sun cast long shadows along the street. She paused for a moment, recalling the endless summer days of her childhood when she and Alan used to play tag with their shadows and the responsibility of adulthood was only a child's dream. Gradually, the vociferous traffic intruded upon her thoughts, rudely snapping her back to the present, and with a sheepish grin, she continued toward her car.

One of the benefits of being the bookkeeper was that she got off at five, instead of six like everyone else. It left her with several hours of daylight in which to run errands or to just relax. Lately, she had taken to driving to Santa Monica and walking the length of the little park that ran along the cliff above the ocean. It felt good to stretch her legs after spending the day behind a desk.

As she reached her car, deep in thought, she sensed someone standing near her. Startled, she looked around and up into Lieutenant Hollis's unsmiling face.

"Just what are you doing at DDL?" he exploded, not bothering even to say hello.

He towered above her and though his anger intimidated her, she stood her ground.

"Working. I work there," she said defiantly.

"Get in the car," he ordered, opening her car door. "I want to have a talk with you."

Joi Lin got in and waited for him to come around to the other side. *I have a right to work wherever I want*, she told herself firmly.

"Look," she began when he eased into the seat and shut the car door. "It's a free country. I can work wherever I want. I am not doing anything wrong."

"It may be a free country, but you're right in the middle of my murder investigation and I don't like it," he told her. "If you want me to catch your brother's killer, then butt out and let me do my job!"

"You don't seem to be doing it very fast. Weeks have gone by and Alan's killer is still on the loose," Joi Lin retorted. Two bright spots of color appeared on her cheeks as her temper flared. "It seems to me you could use a little help."

"Just where do you get off critiquing *my* job perfor- mance and how are *you* helping me by working at DDL?"

Joi Lin saw an opening and went for it. "I can keep my ears open! Just by being there on a day-to-day basis, I may hear things that might help you. Already, I found out the reason for Alan's party," she rushed on. "It was to announce that he was buying a second agency, one that would rival DDL. I also know that the Roques were at the party and that Sid Roque has a roving eye and that Ellysa Roque is aware of it!" She paused for a breath.

"I already know all of that," he told her curtly.

"But did you know that Rusty caught Alan stealing DDL's account lists?" she pressed.

He had to admit that he didn't. Maybe there was a benefit to having someone on the inside of the agency. If nothing else, it would keep Joi Lin from meddling in other areas of his investigation.

"Look, I'm not quitting and that's final," she said, interpreting his silence as an objection. "Besides, I'm an excellent bookkeeper so even if you told Derian who I really am, I doubt that she'd let me go."

Hollis looked at the stubborn, defiant expression on Joi Lin's face and suppressed a smile. He admired her spunk and determination, but he wasn't about to tell her that.

"Okay," he told her grudgingly. "You can stay at DDL for now. But you're there to do bookkeeping—nothing else. And you're to stay out of my investigation. Deal?"

"Deal," she agreed. "But if I hear anything, I'll call you right away. I'm going to be a big help to your investigation, you'll see."

Yeah, right, Hollis thought to himself.

CHAPTER

6

Everything was working out perfectly for Sid. It was all a matter of timing, he had always maintained, and as usual, he was right. Ellysa's secretary had telephoned to say his wife would be working late at the store, something about vandals and price tags or some such thing, and then he had gotten the second phone call.

Never in his wildest fantasies had he imagined that he'd have the opportunity to fuck a chick as young and beautiful as Holly Woodward. Sure, she came on to him at the fashion show, but hell, that didn't mean anything. He figured she was just stroking him because he was the owner of Spheres.

But then she called him, asking if he'd like to meet her for a drink. Would he ever! He immediately made plans to meet her at Le Dome on Sunset Boulevard. It had just the right ambience, yet it was not a place he would run into anyone he knew. Now, sitting across the table from her after a couple of glasses of champagne, Holly invited him back to her apartment!

Sid, you dog, he thought to himself. *Looks like you'll be putting the wood to her tonight*. He glanced into the mirrored wall of the restaurant and smirked. *Yeah, baby, it's all me, every gorgeous inch.*

He looked around and noticed the couple at the next table staring curiously at him, and he quickly pretended he was straightening his tie.

"Let's get out of here," he said in a seductive whisper when Holly returned from the ladies' room.

"Follow me," Holly replied, leading the way out of Le Dome. As she did, Sid noticed all the male eyes also following her.

"Easy, baby," Sid murmured in a husky whisper as Holly peeled his suit off in a frenzy. Sid didn't do drugs but Holly did and minutes before, after pouring them chilled glasses of chardonnay, she popped an XTC pill that she told him she'd brought from Paris. The pill worked its magic as she acted like a cat, rubbing her naked body against him, stroking his aroused cock through his clothes, and playing his sex slave. He just hoped she didn't shred his new Armani suit in her wild efforts to separate it from his prostrate body.

Starting at her throat, he ran his hands down the length of her undulating body, his tongue following, discovering every part of her. Her breasts were full and perfectly formed, the hard nipples a delicate shade of pink and her skin as soft as a baby's cheek. Her stomach was flat, the muscles taut, and her body shuddered as his hot tongue traced a downward path. When he reached the hot wet crevice between her long legs, he made a discovery that made him gasp in ecstasy. Holly was completely shaved and her skin was like warm satin.

"See something you like, Tiger?" she breathed, pushing hard against him. She already knew the answer. Every man she'd been with liked it. Why should Sid be the exception?

She swallowed another XTC with a sip of wine and grasped his face, pulling him upward, exploring his mouth with her tongue. The drug gave her the sexual appetite of an animal. But it wasn't just the XTC. It was Sid. She had only decided to seduce him on a whim, but he was a more exciting sex partner than she ever thought he would be.

The drug made her dizzy and she felt herself spiraling toward an orgasm. "Now, do it now," she cried in a delirium of passion. She reached out, trying to guide his cock inside her.

Sid wasn't about to take any chances. He adroitly slipped on a Trojan and lowered himself onto the thrashing young woman. Matching her pace, he felt himself building. At the last possible moment, Holly abruptly flipped Sid over, pinning his arms above his head. Simultaneously, she began to come, and her moans became a loud wail.

"Sh-h-h!" Sid gasped, unnerved. He pulled one hand from her grasp and clamped it over her mouth, trying to muffle her cries. He felt his hard-on shrivel and his balls drop like lead. Just his luck, a screamer! God, how he hated screamers, they turned him off like nothing else. He wondered what her neighbors were thinking.

Holly collapsed on Sid's chest panting, completely unaware that Sid's efforts hadn't reached fruition. "Oh, Sid, you're the best," she wheezed, trying to catch her breath.

She ran her fingers along his chest and twirled the hair—something else Sid detested. "You had a good time, too, I could tell," she continued coyly. "You like my little shaved pussy, huh?"

"Yeah, baby," Sid answered distractedly. His balls hurt and he wondered how soon he could leave without being rude. But to his horror, he felt her hand slip down to his wilted member.

"Sid," Holly whispered confidently, massaging him with a vengeance. "I know you still want me. Men can never get enough of me."

"Of course I d-do," he stuttered, rolling out of her reach and grabbing for his clothes. "It's just that I have a very early breakfast meeting tomorrow, so I've gotta go *now*."

He threw on his clothes and made a beeline for the door, her voice ringing in his ears.

"Let's do this again soon," Holly called from the bedroom. "I'll be waiting for your call, Tiger."

Betsy leaned around the doorway. "Derian, Neiman Marcus is still waiting on line two. The Germans are calling about a print contract on line three, and Misha is calling you from her car phone on four. She can't find the address you gave her for her interview," Betsy announced.

Derian threw her arms up in a gesture of surrender and signaled Betsy to tell them all to hold.

Since the Spheres show, DDL's business had quadrupled. Everyone wanted to book the agency's models, and it wasn't only local clients. Press shots from the show went out across AP news wires and now she was getting international calls as well. Several German cigarette companies were traveling to L.A. to book and shoot whole advertising campaigns for Europe; a leading Japanese auto manufacturer wanted to shoot a series of television commercials; and several Italian and French magazines wanted to shoot editorial segments on the DDL look. In addition local and East Coast clients were clamoring for first priority, and Holly was at the top of everyone's list.

"Yes, I understand completely," Derian assuaged her telephone caller. "Yes, Holly is fabulous, but she's booked solid all week. I have several other models who are just as remarkable and are available."

Although she impatiently played with her pen as she listened to the response, her impatience never translated to her voice. "You'll love Tamara. She's one of our best," she pitched. "Tamara has the face of a Mona Lisa and she's so easy to work with. I know you'll love her. Call me back right after the booking.

"Misha, where are you?" Derian asked brusquely as she took the next phone call. At the same time, she began thumbing through the model's "bible," *The Thomas Guide to Streets in Los Angeles County.* "Okay, I gotcha. Go south on Grand Street, and turn right on Central. It's a little dead-end street that runs alongside Union Station. Got it? Good luck, call me after the interview."

Without a break in her pace, Derian switched to line two. "Clarice, how are you, sweetie? I'm glad you called. Holly's booked, but Suzanne would be perfect. Wonderful. Then I'll book her for both days."

Derian was using standard operating procedure for modeling agencies. When a requested model wasn't available, she would substitute another model, thereby giving the other model an opportunity for a booking and maybe acquiring a new account.

Derian handled line three in the same smooth manner, substituting another model for Holly as well. She realized the importance of pushing Holly and DDL now, while they were on everyone's lips.

She took a gulp of stale coffee and gradually noticed that her office was silent. No telephones ringing, no models barging in with a disaster for her to handle—it was heaven. Her thoughts returned to Holly and the phenomenal number of bookings she was pulling into the agency. Derian had anticipated a big response but not this big. Thanks to Holly's popularity, DDL was now the hottest agency in town. But to stay that way presented its own problems and she was facing two of them now. Number one, Holly planned on remaining in L.A. only six more weeks, but the agency needed at least six months to hit its stride. By that time, Derian would have other models who would be peaking and who could easily pick up the slack of Holly's departure. She would have to convince Holly to lengthen her stay. She was positive that would be easy. Derian could always talk anyone into anything.

The second obstacle was more difficult—it was Holly's attitude. Derian had heard through the rumor mills that Holly seemed to be on a mission dedicated to making the L.A. models squirm. Derian was well aware of the difficulties Holly had had when she first began modeling over a year ago, but they were par for the course. Every model had a hard time being accepted initially. New models were generally considered a threat to the established ones. But that was the nature of a business that preyed on insecurities. If left alone, the situations gradually worked themselves out. Models were slow to change, but eventually they did and friendships developed naturally. Holly on the other hand seemed determined to pay back any perceived slight she had encountered during her earlier modeling days and Derian would somehow have to discourage Holly's get-even attitude while encouraging her to stay in L.A. Not an easy task and one that would require every manipulation of which Derian was capable.

Holly woke early from a sound night's sleep and walked barefoot into the kitchen to make herself a cup of instant coffee. Even made extra strong, it couldn't compare with the rich espresso served in the little café she frequented around the corner from her apartment in Paris. Coffee cup in hand, she crossed the narrow room and perched on the windowsill. Gazing northeast across the skyline from the studio apartment Derian had found for her, Holly studied the sprawling concrete and steel jungle of downtown L.A., backlit by the orange and gold ribbons of early dawn. Across the street, a grizzled old wino huddled in an empty doorway, sucking on a grubby bottle. To her left, she heard the sound of voices and she craned her neck to look farther down the street. The deserted lunch wagon that had been parked along the curb overnight was no longer deserted. Now two Mexican men were busily loading it with supplies in preparation for their route throughout the downtown area. It was a different city, different people and languages, but their actions invoked memories of Paris and she longed for home.

The growing cold silences at bookings had little effect on Holly. She was there to pay back some old debts and make as much money as she could before returning to Paris. A few models still talked to her and attempted to buddy up to her, but she knew it was only because they were hoping to get more bookings by associating with her and she had no intention of accommodating them. She enjoyed flaunting her star status, but her longing for Paris was stronger and she made the decision at that moment to leave three weeks earlier than she had planned.

Her booking today was a catalogue shoot with Rusty at his studio. She took a quick shower, threw on a pair of jeans and a man's white tuxedo shirt, and departed. A makeup artist and hairstylist would take care of the details at the studio.

Holly thought Rusty's studio was impressive in its size by any standard, American or European. It was a huge whitewashed loft. The front entrance opened into a small reception area with the studio itself behind. To the left of the studio was a makeup/dressing room/bathroom area and next to that a small Pullman kitchen. On the right side of the studio were Rusty's living quarters and darkroom. The walls and floor of the studio were painted a typical flat white with rolls of colored backdrops, spare photography umbrellas, reflectors, light boxes, and miscellaneous equipment filling all available corners.

Rusty walked with Holly to the makeup room and introduced her to Leatrice, the other DDL model she would be working with for the day, and to Skeeter, the makeup girl. Holly sized up Leatrice. She was a dark brunette about Holly's age, with an English peaches-and-cream complexion and big brown doe eyes. She was very pretty in a midwestern, wholesome way that was perfect for catalogue work, but her looks were no competition for Holly. Holly's reputation had obviously preceded her because Leatrice merely acknowledged her with a cool nod; while Skeeter on the other hand gave her a friendly wave with a blusher brush.

Skeeter was a very pretty pipsqueak of a girl, about nineteen years old with shiny chestnut, China-bobbed hair, big round Kewpie doll eyes, and a freckled turned-up nose. She was dressed completely in black: turtleneck, suspendered slacks, and thick-soled men's shoes.

"What's shakin', girlfriend?" she greeted Holly, in between chews on a big wad of pink bubble gum. "Relax, I'll be with you after I finish with Leatrice."

Holly sauntered over and slouched down in a chair to wait her turn.

"All finished, Leatrice," Skeeter said after a few minutes.

"Thanks, Skeeter," Leatrice answered. Without a word to Holly, she walked over to change into her first outfit.

"Yo, dudette," Skeeter summoned Holly. "You're up."

Holly took a seat in the makeup chair and Skeeter began working, while asking nonstop questions.

"You're not from here," she guessed. "East of the Atlantic, right?"

Holly nodded, stifling a yawn.

"Don't clue me—Milan. No, Munich. No, too loose for Munich." She punctuated each city with the pop of bubble gum.

"I know! Paris!" she exclaimed. "I could tell. You have that look!"

"I do?" Holly asked, becoming more interested in the conversation because it revolved around her.

"Yeah, you know, that confident, I-don't-give-a-damn look," Skeeter told her. "How long you been hangin' here?"

She saw the blank look on Holly's face and rephrased her question without the colorful colloquialism. "How long have you been here?"

"Oh," Holly replied. "Just a few weeks."

"Hey, gnarly! We should do a little hip-hop at the Steam Club!"

Holly had no concept of jive talk, however, she could decipher it enough to grasp that Skeeter was suggesting the two of them go out to some club together. But she had no intention of spending an evening with a nobody makeup person. Any of her available evenings were going to be spent with Sid Roque. There was something exciting about screwing a middle-aged man with millions.

"Thanks, but I won't be here that long." She sniffed, quelling any further conversation. "Hadn't you better get my makeup finished? I think they're waiting for me."

Skeeter hurriedly completed Holly's makeup and Holly had to admit that Skeeter really knew her stuff. It was as good a job as any she'd had in Paris. As a final touch, Holly leaned her head back and squeezed a couple of drops of Bleu-Blanc in each eye.

"Hey, dudette, I wouldn't be squirting that stuff in your eyes, if I were you," Skeeter warned. "I've seen that shit before. You could end up with no eyes if you aren't careful."

"Please," Holly said disdainfully. "I *always* use them and I've never had a problem."

"Hey, Skeeter, do you have Holly almost ready?" Rusty asked from the doorway.

"I'm ready," Holly answered, dropping the bottle in the top of her makeup bag. She walked over to the rack. "What do you want to shoot first?"

"The navy one, gorgeous," he answered, pointing to a blue suit hanging on the rack. "Come on out when you're ready."

"And you, sweetpea—" he grinned, turning to Skeeter and towering over her—"why don't you hang around for a while in case we need some touch-ups."

"What a hunk," Skeeter breathed, collapsing into the makeup chair after Rusty had left and fanning her face. "He has this way of looking at a girl that makes me weak in the knees. Don'tcha think?"

"He's okay," Holly answered noncommittally. Pretty faces never really interested her; power and a fat bankroll did. She zipped up her skirt and buttoned her jacket. Then as an afterthought, she defiantly added one more drop of Bleu-Blanc to each eye and with a toss of her head she walked out the door.

Shooting with other models had never been Holly's idea of an ego-satisfying booking, but she worked the situation to her advantage. She knew all the methods of subtly drawing the attention to herself. Like positioning herself slightly in front of the other model, throwing the woman's concentration off with a minute movement just before the photographer clicked the shutter, or using the model as a prop instead of a partner—and she used them all today.

She had raised one hand and brushed a lock of hair from the side of her face, effectively blocking Leatrice's face for the third time when Leatrice leaned over and whispered so that only Holly could hear her.

"If you block me one more time, I will rip that arm from its socket and stuff it down between those phony silicone breasts of yours. Do you understand?"

"I don't know what you're talking about," Holly lied with a shocked look on her face.

"I have worked the catwalks in London, dodged horny photographers in Barcelona, and endured the sweatshops in Tokyo, and I am not about to let some snot-nosed bitch get the better of me in my own territory," Leatrice continued in the same calm undertone. "Once more and you will be the only one-armed model in the Western Hemisphere. Do you understand me?"

"I—" Holly started, turning to face her.

"Do you or don't you?" Leatrice interrupted, not giving Holly an inch.

"I understand," Holly agreed in a subdued voice.

"Hey, beauties," Rusty called from behind his camera, "is there a problem?"

"Of course not," Leatrice answered sweetly, striking a pose.

Skeeter and Rusty looked at each other. Despite what Leatrice said, the vibes in the studio were so strong Skeeter swore they could power the whole building. There was a grim set to Holly's mouth and a brittle hardness in Leatrice's eyes, and the two seemed out of sync in their movements. Rusty's lighthearted demeanor changed, and Skeeter noticed his jaw working. She knew he was also feeling the tension.

Finally, Rusty called an end to the shoot and dismissed Holly and Leatrice for the day. Skeeter stayed behind ostensibly to straighten things up, but deep down, she hoped to get to know Rusty better.

"Well, that was a guaranteed reshoot," Rusty muttered angrily after the models departed. "I couldn't seem to get my sense of rhythm."

"Maybe not," Skeeter replied encouragingly. "Anyhow, it wasn't your fault. Those models were ready for rattail combs at ten paces."

"That may be, but it's still my fault," he answered, refusing to be appeased. "I should have smoothed the situation over. Derian would have had no problem." He turned his back on Skeeter and started dismantling the light box.

Skeeter didn't know what else to say, so she quietly made her way back to the models' dressing room and began cleaning up.

"Hey, sweetpea," Rusty said later, leaning against the door frame of the dressing room. He was smiling and his dark mood had lifted. "Don't work so hard."

"I'm not," Skeeter answered, throwing tissues and used cotton swabs in the trash. She glanced up at him. "I'm just putting things in order before I go. It'll be less work for you later."

"Let it go," Rusty told her easily with a smile that turned her knees to butter and took away her train of thought. "Let's go get a bite to eat, I'm starved."

"Okay," Skeeter exclaimed. She didn't need a second invitation. She couldn't believe her good fortune; Rusty was the cutest dude she'd met in ages.

Joi Lin turned the final page of *Seventh Heaven*, and closed the book with a sense of satisfaction and a pang of regret that the story had come to an end. Alice Hoffman gave her characters such empathy and simple dignity that reading about them transmitted strength and determination into Joi Lin's own life. She turned off the lamp by her bed and snuggled down, pulling the comforter up beneath her chin. She had always loved books, she mused, her thoughts drifting toward sleep. Their characters were like

trusted old friends to whom she could return again and
again, and on whom she could always depend. It wasn't
that she didn't have friends, it was just that she had been
so shy growing up that books many times were easier to
relate to than people.

But of course she had always had Alan who had always
insisted on including her in his fun. She remembered the
time that he and his buddies decided they would learn to
smoke. They had no cigarettes, but they knew where to
get them—Joi Lin's father, who was sprawled out on the
couch asleep. Joi Lin wanted to tell Alan that she was
afraid their father would wake up and catch them, but
then he made her his captain of reconnaissance, so she
swallowed her fear and listened to his plan. Her mission
was to crawl quietly across the living room and take the
cigarettes out of their father's shirt pocket, then crawl back
to where Alan and his buddies were waiting. The first part
was easy; the tricky part, however, was to retrieve the
cigarettes without waking her father and take them back
to the boys, who were waiting in the hallway.

Joi Lin eased the pack out of his pocket and across his
arm when the loose cigarettes fell out, landing on his arm.
His eyes popped open and instantly focused on her leaning
over him with the forbidden cigarette pack in her hand.

"What are you doing!" he roared, grabbing her by
the shoulders. Joi Lin looked back for help from her
commander, but the hallway was empty—the boys had
fled.

Her father jumped to his feet, and lifting her by the
back of her collar, he shook her like a dog with a rab-
bit.

"Why can't you be more like your brother!" he shouted,
his voice echoing in her ears. "You're always so much
trouble!"

She was so scared that she peed her pants and she hung
like a limp rag in his grasp, feeling the warm water dribble
down her pants leg. But she didn't cry.

"Dummy," Alan said to her later. "Why'd you drop the
cigarettes and embarrass me in front of my friends? You

know, you're lucky I even let you hang out with me."

At the time, Joi Lin solemnly nodded in agreement. He was right, most brothers wouldn't be bothered with a little sister.

She restlessly rolled over in bed and flipped her pillow over to the cool side. However, as she thought back, perhaps that wasn't the way to treat a little sister. Was there an edge of cruelty in Alan that she hadn't noticed before? Her thoughts drifted then to Derian and Rusty. From what she had observed they, too, had a close relationship. Derian, who was almost obsessively driven when it came to agency business, softened when Rusty entered the agency. A maternal pride colored her attitude and many times Joi Lin had seen Derian put aside DDL business in order to give Rusty her full attention. Derian was a perfectionist and it extended to her attitude toward Rusty, and although Joi Lin knew it was steeped in love, perhaps Derian was trying to control Rusty's life the way Alan had done to her.

Rusty was handsome, boyish, and charming. And while he was an incorrigible flirt who enjoyed exercising his charms on any woman crossing his path, Joi Lin had observed that around Derian he was immature. Their relationship seemed to be almost parent-child in nature, with Derian calling all the shots.

Just that day, Skeeter, a cute, petite makeup artist, stopped by the agency. Betsy was at lunch, so Joi Lin was acting as receptionist, too.

"Yo, dudette, my handle's Skeeter," she told Joi Lin, blowing a big pink bubble from the wad of gum in her mouth. "I just stopped by to leave some of my cards for any models who want to do testing."

"Great," Joi Lin answered. She had learned that the models were always testing, trying to improve their portfolio.

"I've worked a lot," Skeeter continued. "In fact, I recently did a shoot with two of your models, Holly and Leatrice, at Rusty Delorian's studio. He's Derian Delorian's brother, you know."

"Yes, I know Rusty," Joi Lin answered. She got the impression that Skeeter was maneuvering the conversation toward a particular point, so she waited for her to continue.

"Cute guy, huh," Skeeter said after a moment.

"Yes," Joi Lin agreed.

"We grabbed a bite after the shoot," Skeeter continued, fidgeting with her portfolio. "I thought we had a good time, but I haven't heard from him since. Do you, ah, know if he's involved with someone?"

So that's where it's heading, Joi Lin thought to herself. "No, not that I know of," she answered truthfully, feeling sorry for the girl. Skeeter wasn't the first woman Joi Lin had seen smitten by Rusty in the two weeks she had been at the agency. Several of the models had also fallen for his playboy charms.

"I left a couple of messages on his service, but he never called back. I thought maybe he was out of town," she finished hopefully.

"No, he's in town," Joi Lin said kindly. "Look, Skeeter, if I were you, I wouldn't get too caught up with Rusty. I don't think he's looking for a steady relationship right now."

Skeeter's face fell. "Oh," she said quietly, then brightened. "Hey, you win some and you lose some. At least maybe I'll pick up some more work, if you'll pass out my card."

"Sure," Joi Lin agreed. "I'd be happy to."

She watched Skeeter walk out the door. She suspected Rusty's cavalier attitude where women were concerned was a result of Derian's indulging him and erecting a protective barrier of love around him. He seemed to have the cocky confidence of youth and the simplistic logic a teenager had before the complexities of life complicated his thoughts. But his affection for Derian was evident to Joi Lin in the way he hung on Derian's every word and the practiced way he tried to imitate her mannerisms.

At times, Joi Lin thought sleepily, she caught glimpses in Rusty of the same single-minded determination she saw in Derian. But his was cloaked in charm while Derian's was part of her everyday disposition.

As sleep overtook her, her thoughts returned to Alan. Joi Lin still believed there was a link between DDL and his murder. She had spent the past few weeks learning her job at DDL and talking with Betsy and the other models. She hadn't found any potential girlfriends among the women. So where was the link? Now she had to concentrate on finding it elsewhere. Perhaps by going through the agency's files, she would find a clue to Alan's murder, and she promised herself to start looking the next day.

Joi Lin awoke to the hollow pinging of rain as it struck the metal drainpipe by her bedroom window and gushed out the bottom into ever-widening rivulets, crisscrossing the tiny courtyard behind her apartment. She looked out the window and saw that the gutter at the far side of the courtyard was clogged with debris accumulated from months without rain, and a lake of water was rapidly developing. The giant birds of paradise that lined the courtyard were bent backward, their broad leaves beginning to shred under the storm's assault.

She dressed, poured black coffee into her travel mug, and hurried to her car, trying to keep as dry as possible. The streets were like parking lots. Rain in southern California was so unusual that it paralyzed the city, and many times it dampened the streets only enough to liquefy the oil and exhaust left by months of traffic, making the streets as treacherous as black ice. Other times, like today, it came down in sheets so heavy that it was almost impossible for automobile windshield wipers to sweep it away. The up-side was that the torrents usually lasted for only a short time, washing away the smog and leaving the city sparkling clean and smelling of salt air and orange blossoms.

When Joi Lin finally reached DDL, Betsy told her that Derian would be coming in late, because the rain had gotten into the engine of her car and it was stalled on Sunset Boulevard.

"She called AAA, she said," Betsy relayed, absently shuffling and reshuffling a stack of composites on the desk. She was on her fourth cup of coffee and between the caffeine and sugar she was already buzzed. "But you know how slow they are. In the meantime, I've got a dental appointment that I can't miss. Do you think you can hold the fort down? Derian should be in in a couple of hours at the latest."

"Sure," Joi Lin answered. What luck! This would be the first time she'd been alone in the agency. This could be the opportunity she had been hoping for. "Don't give it another thought, Betsy."

For this time of morning, the agency was unusually quiet. The rain had undoubtedly dampened business all over the city for the phones were eerily silent. But Joi Lin waited a good fifteen minutes after Betsy left before she began her search. She wasn't sure what she was looking for, but she knew the best place to start was in Derian's office.

As she opened the door to the office, Joi Lin guiltily glanced back over her shoulder to survey the empty reception room. Even her dedication to her cause could not completely erase the feeling that she was doing something she shouldn't. Outside, the rain continued to beat down, while inside the weak light that accompanied the storm filtered through the skylight in Derian's office and caused long gray patterns on the pale green walls.

Joi Lin slipped through the door and went to the filing cabinet by Derian's desk, where she methodically started with the top drawer and worked her way down. The top drawer contained current correspondence, mostly having to do with agency business, and some personal business, and the second drawer was filled with correspondence from past years. Joi Lin sorted through both drawers, but she didn't find anything connecting Derian with Alan's death. The third drawer was filled with résumés, filed current year first and going back to the opening of the agency. Joi Lin found her own résumé and then Alan's. She paused for a moment to read his and to her shock and embarrassment she discovered that he had lied. He had listed agency experience that Joi Lin knew he didn't have, and it angered her. Incident after incident showing his deception and ruthlessness was beginning to add up, and she wondered if she had ever really known her brother. What else didn't she know about him? She jammed the résumé back in the file and slammed the drawer shut.

"Darn him," she muttered out loud.

The bottom drawer was locked and Joi Lin's hopes leapt. She searched Derian's desk for a key, being careful not to disturb anything, and just as she concluded that Derian must have it with her, she spied a key sitting in an ashtray. Grabbing it, she stuck it in the cabinet lock and it turned stiffly, as if it hadn't been opened in a long time. Joi Lin tugged at the heavy drawer, praying that there would be something inside that would help her find Alan's killer.

It was filled with clippings and tear sheets. Joi Lin sat down cross-legged on the floor and started to thumb through them, wondering what they were. The answer readily became apparent as image after image of Derian wearing different expressions and every costume imaginable stared back at Joi Lin. The chronicle of pictures of Derian as a model showed her in the bell-bottoms and Twiggy eyes of the sixties; the Farrah Fawcett hair and Halston gowns of the seventies; and on and on. There were hundreds, if not thousands, of photographs and tear sheets; ads and editorial layouts from *Glamour*, *Vogue*, *Harpers Bazaar*, and a score of other magazines. It was a fascinating fashion display of the past three decades.

Joi Lin was so engrossed in the tears that she didn't hear the sound of footsteps behind her.

"Some collection, huh," a voice said above her.

Joi Lin started and twisted around, looking up into Rusty's face. "I was just looking for some invoice books," she explained innocently, but her voice sounded hollow and unconvincing. She gathered up the materials and put them back in the drawer.

Rusty sat down in Derian's chair and picked up her pen, clicking it off and on. "We keep the invoice books in the storage cabinet in the reception room," he said, looking her directly in the eye.

Joi Lin could almost see the wheels turning in his head and she had the uncomfortable feeling that he was looking into her mind and that he could see she was lying.

"Betsy should have explained where everything is kept," he continued. For a long moment the only sound in the room was the clicking pen.

"Oh, that's right," Joi Lin exclaimed, closing the drawer and relocking it. "Betsy did show me. I guess I forgot. Sometimes it takes a while to remember where everything is when you're new." She nervously dropped the key back in the ashtray and started for the door.

"Oh, by the way, Joi Lin," Rusty called as she reached the door.

Joi Lin turned around apprehensively.

He had replaced the stern look on his face with a broad grin. "You look very beautiful this morning," he joked, his humor returning. "I've been thinking, they always say 'Still waters run deep.' Maybe we should explore those waters together."

Joi Lin felt the tension drain out of the room and she laughed shakily. "Do you make that stuff up or does it come out of a book?" she shot back at him.

"Joi Lin, you cut me to the quick," he chided, giving her an exaggerated puppy-dog look.

Joi Lin walked back to her desk, dropped into the chair, and took a couple of deep breaths to calm her pounding heart. Betsy walked in at that moment.

"Look, Ma, no cavities," she joked, but then she saw the strained look on Joi Lin's face. "Hey, what's up? Why is your face bright red?"

"No reason," Joi Lin answered, burying her head in her accounting figures.

The rest of the day, Joi Lin performed her job by rote. Her surprise meeting with Rusty had left her shaken, but more than that she was frustrated that she hadn't discovered anything tangible to link DDL with Alan's murder. She also hadn't heard from Lieutenant Hollis since the day he found out she was working at the agency almost two weeks ago, and she decided that it was time for them to meet again. She wasn't about to let him brush her off. She was positive that he must have learned something new about her brother's death by now. She waited until she was sure no one could overhear her and then she called him.

"Lieutenant Hollis," she said firmly when he answered. She had made up her mind that he wouldn't put her off with excuses.

"This is Hollis, who is this?" he asked, but he had already recognized her voice.

"This is Joi Lin Ambernites," she told him. "I want to find out what's happening with my brother's case. What have you found out?"

Hollis paused for a moment, weighing his response. Finally he decided to take a chance and fill her in on the basics. Maybe some of his findings would tie in with DDL. Perhaps it would jog something in her memory that she had observed without realizing its importance.

"We have made some progress," he began, then he realized it would take some time to explain it all to her. "How about meeting me after you get off work and I'll tell you what we've found out. Let's say the Beverly Hills Grill at five-fifteen?"

"I'll be there," she answered without hesitation.

The restaurant was quiet. It was too late for lunch, yet too early for dinner, and Joi Lin had no problem spotting Hollis at a table at the back of the restaurant. He stood up when she approached, and again she was struck by the incongruity between his intimidating bulk and his gentle brown eyes.

"What have you found out?" Joi Lin asked eagerly after the waitress had placed a cappuccino in front of her and a double espresso in front of Hollis and retreated.

Hollis took a sip of his espresso. It was his tenth cup of coffee that day and he winced as he felt it working on the lining of his stomach.

"First of all," he reminded her, "I want you to understand that I'm under no obligation to fill you in on the details of my investigation; I'm trusting you. Everything we discuss is confidential; I could get into a lot of trouble confiding in a civilian. *Capisce*?"

"Of course. I promise I won't say anything to anyone," Joi Lin answered impatiently. "Now what have you found out?"

"The lab has been backed up, so it took them almost a week to analyze the dyes in the silk scarf we found in your brother's bedroom. But we got lucky," he explained, pouring cream into his coffee. Maybe the cream would neutralize the burning acid in his stomach. "The silk in the scarf isn't new. The lab estimates that it's eighteen to twenty years old."

"Oh," Joi Lin said, disappointed. A twenty-year-old trail didn't sound particularly lucky to her.

"But here's the lucky part," Hollis continued. "The scarf had been colored with special dyes used only by the Hermès Company in Paris. I faxed their main shop in Paris and found out that although the company has designed hundreds of patterns over the years, each pattern is registered by year and records are kept as to where the scarves are sent. I figured that if the scarf was purchased at one of the Hermès shops, there would be a record of the purchaser. But if it had been purchased at any one of hundreds of other locations we would be out of luck. So, I sent close-up photographs of the scarf to Paris, crossed my fingers, and hoped for a miracle. And guess what?"

"What?" Joi Lin asked, sipping her cappuccino. She was thoroughly intrigued by the whole investigative process.

"Five days later, I got my response. Hermès recognized the print as a very limited edition produced twenty years ago for a special promotion. I've sent them a fax requesting all information they might have regarding who purchased the scarves."

"That's wonderful," Joi Lin enthused. "It's amazing how you were able to glean so much information from a piece of silk."

Hollis looked at Joi Lin, intending to continue with the rest of what he'd found out about her brother's murder, but instead he found himself noticing what a pretty smile she had. He'd never realized she had dimples, and she had a cute way of hanging her head when she smiled as if she were embarrassed about something.

"What's the matter?" Joi Lin asked, self-consciously fidgeting with her mug. She noticed that Hollis was staring at her with an odd look on his face and she wondered if she had done something wrong.

"Nothing," Hollis answered curtly. Embarrassed by his thoughts, he picked up the thread of his story. "I also have some information on what killed your brother."

"You mean you know the kind of poison?" Joi Lin asked.

"Well, technically, it's a toxin. But it's organic and blends in with the thousands of other organic compounds that are normally present in the body, so unfortunately the lab hasn't been able to identify it," Hollis explained. "They've been working on isolating and identifying it with a gas chromatograph, but so far they haven't had any success. It just takes time."

"Haven't they been able to find out anything else about it?" Joi Lin asked. It seemed like everything was taking so much time.

"They do know how it works," Hollis told her. "It causes irreversible damage to nerve synapses and muscle cells, so the lab techs are working under the premise that it is—"

"A neurotoxin," Joi Lin finished, remembering her college biology.

"Very good, I'm impressed," Hollis praised. And he was with her mental agility in picking up concepts, taking them one step further, and drawing conclusions.

"How long before they know?" Joi Lin asked.

"I wish I could tell you, but it's a matter of one test after another. The Hermès scarf, though, is another story. I should be receiving information on it in the next few days."

"You know, there is something about that name that seems familiar to me," Joi Lin said slowly, searching her memory. "But I just can't seem to grasp it. It just keeps slipping away from me."

"Is it something to do with DDL?" Hollis prodded.

"I'm sorry, Lieutenant, I just can't put my finger on it," Joi Lin apologized, shaking her head.

"Frank," Hollis said.

"What?" Joi Lin questioned.

"Since we're working together, so to speak," he said with a grin, "you might as well call me Frank, partner."

"Frank," Joi Lin repeated with a smile. "You got it, partner." He had an easy way about him. She liked his forthright nature and the fact that he trusted her by confiding the aspects of the case.

Later, he walked her to her car and held the door open for her. "Let me know if you can remember anything about the scarf or if you find out anything of interest at the agency," he said, closing her car door.

He didn't really expect she would, but she was useful to him because he liked bouncing his ideas about the case off her. He watched her drive off and idly wondered how soon before he would see her again. Then guiltily he caught himself. It was the first time he had thought about another woman since Gina had died, and he felt a pang of guilt about betraying her memory. But that was stupid because Gina would have told him to get on with his life. She had been that kind of a woman. And maybe it was time he did.

She stormed into the bedroom, slamming the door behind her. "Damn that Holly and her nasty behavior! I'm fucking tired of hearing about her condescending attitude and Queen Bitch behavior at the shoots!" she screamed out loud, kicking her bedroom door again and again with each curse.

But it didn't make her feel any better. If anything, it fueled her fury even higher. She stomped across the bedroom and swept everything from the top of the vanity to the floor. Makeup went flying; lipsticks rolled under the bed; eye shadows shattered; and her wigs fell off their stands, landing in heaps like little dead animals. Her anger was still not quenched and she turned to her closet, and in a frenzy began ripping clothes off their hangers. Finally she sank to the floor, panting, with her knees drawn up under her chin.

"Calm down, calm down," she mumbled, her body twitching as if an electric current were surging through it. "I feel at peace. I feel peaceful."

An emerald sequined gown lay crushed under her feet and she stared at it, mesmerized by the sparkle of sequins. Still twitching uncontrollably, she picked it up and draped it on the bed. Then she stripped her clothes off and stepped into the green dress, wriggling it up over her hips and shoulders.

She was still mumbling to herself in a singsong voice as she picked up a raven wig from the floor and adjusted it on her head. She managed to crawl around on the floor, picking up the scattered bits of makeup. But when she sat down and began to make up her face, she had to stop several times to try to stabilize her jerky movements. It took both hands to steady her lipstick, and when she tried to put it on, she smeared it all over her mouth. She let out a shriek of frustration.

"It's not my fault!" she screamed in a fresh blaze of temper. In a fury, she bit off the lipstick and chewed it up. Then she grabbed a tube of cream eye shadow, slit it open with nail scissors, and ate that, too.

Raging from room to room in the apartment, she slammed doors and swept knickknacks, books, anything she could find off tables and counters. Her wig was askew; there was a crazed light in her eyes; and her teeth were stained bloodred from the lipstick.

"Fucking ingrate! Holly, Holly, Holly," she chanted over and over in a singsong voice, kicking at the wall, but it still wasn't enough.

Out of control, she reached the door at the end of the hall and wrenched it open. Hot, tropical air swirled around her as she entered the room, ramming the door up against the wall. The loud noise set up a chain reaction and behind the protective glass there was a startled flight of movement in all directions.

Realizing what she'd done snapped her back into control. "My babies, my babies," she crooned, dropping down to the floor in front of them. "I'm so sorry. I didn't mean it! I didn't mean it!" She stroked the glass and tapped on it softly with the pads of her fingers.

"That bitch Holly made me do it," she whispered in a flat, cold voice. "But she'll pay. She'll pay, my babies."

CHAPTER
7

A month had passed since the Spheres fashion extravaganza and although Charis had hoped that the show would stimulate more bookings for her, it hadn't. Instead her bookings were dropping and her self-confidence was plummeting with them.

Just the day before, when she had learned about an upcoming go-see from another model, she had initially been confused and angry that Derian had not given her the interview. But when she had shown up at the appointment, she had found out the reason. All the other models had been fresh-faced with flawless skin and glossy hair, and vibrant with the brash confidence of youth and the grace of young colts. She took one quick glance around the room and as unobtrusively as possible slid back out the door.

Deep down, she realized she had to make some changes in her career, but she couldn't bear to face the facts. Instead, she kept assuring herself that things would get better. But it was hard to keep her spirits up when just last week she was replaced yet again by Holly on a show, and worst of all, Holly flaunted it. It was as if Holly had a personal vendetta to destroy Charis. God, she hated that girl!

Today she was booked for an informal at the Joseph Goodman Department Store in Century City. In the past she would have turned down such a mundane booking, but more and more frequently, informals were becoming her bread-and-butter accounts. She tried to convince herself that stores and designers must be doing fewer and fewer shows. But she knew that a glance through the *Los Angeles Chronicle*'s society section would undoubtedly prove her theory wrong.

She would just have to try harder, she told herself. That was the answer. From now on, she'd be so perfect and so professional that everyone would want her. It would be a repeat of her unqualified success in the sixties and seventies, when everyone had clamored to book her. She could do it; she knew she could; she *had* to do it.

She made sure she arrived early at the store and was touching up her makeup when Julie and Cragan, the other two models, arrived. Her buoyed spirits, which she had so carefully cultivated, dropped when she saw them. Why hadn't Derian booked two brunettes instead of two more blondes? She was sure the fashion coordinator would be comparing the three of them.

She peered nervously in the mirror and then furtively at the other two girls. She minutely inspected both of them, looking for any flaws that might help to bolster her failing self-esteem. But they were such natural beauties that Charis felt like a painted hussy compared to them. Why had she put on so much eye shadow? It would be too difficult to remove some of it at this point, so she thought perhaps she could convince the other two women to add more makeup, so that they would look more like her. It was a teenage mentality—security in peer sameness.

"You probably should do more eyes," Charis suggested authoritatively to Julie. "These clothes are pretty dramatic."

"I don't know," Julie answered doubtfully. "I hate putting my makeup on too heavy."

"Well, do whatever you want." Charis shrugged. "Did I ever mention that you look just like a model I worked with in Paris in '75 and '76? She had a great look. She was the hottest model around—next to me, of course."

"Really?" Julie asked, flattered.

"Yes," Charis continued, studiously selecting panty hose from her lingerie bag. "But then all of a sudden, her face fell. It was the strangest thing. One day she was gorgeous and the next day she looked like somebody's grandmother. Her eyes had suitcases under them!"

She looked closely at Julie's eyes. "I guess she was about your age."

"Oh," Julie said, turning a little pale and inspecting her own eyes in the mirror.

"My eyes are my best asset," Charis bragged, holding the panty hose up to the light and checking them for runs. "And everyone tells me that my skin is incredible. Anyway, do whatever you think is best as far as your makeup is concerned."

"Oh," Julie said. "Well, maybe you're right. I'll put more on."

"I will, too," Cragan quickly added, brushing on more shadow and hoping Charis wouldn't tell her she reminded her of someone else who had shriveled up and blown away.

Charis figured that they would change their makeup. No matter how beautiful and poised models were, they all had the same trace of insecurity. It bolstered Charis's lagging self-esteem and gave her a slight sense of control over her own situation to throw Julie and Cragan off balance. She envied the years of modeling they had ahead of them.

"Here are your outfits," the fashion coordinator announced, wheeling a clothing rack into the room. "Pick out what you want to wear."

Charis immediately stood up and casually strolled over to the rack. She wanted first choice, so that she could be sure she got the best clothes. She selected an outfit that she thought would make her look young and then she selected two of what she considered the ugliest outfits for Julie and Cragan.

"Here," she told them, holding up the three ivory-colored outfits. "These three all seem to coordinate. We'll wear these first."

The other two women, who could wear potato sacks and look terrific, nodded in agreement. All three changed and went out onto the floor where the fashion coordinator was waiting for them. Charis noted how chic Julie and Cragan looked in their clothes and nervously squirmed.

"Cragan, you walk around the store and, Julie, you and I will stay in the department to talk to patrons," Charis decided. "Then we'll rotate and change outfits every twenty or so minutes."

The two models were surprised at Charis's bossiness. As a model, her place was to follow the fashion coordinator's instructions, not to give them, and they looked at each other and then the fashion coordinator, wondering what had gotten into Charis.

But the coordinator nodded in agreement. "That's fine," she told them. It was the same thing she had planned on telling them anyway.

Cragan left the department to walk around the store, talking to people and hopefully sparking some interest in the clothes they were modeling, while Charis and Julie took a position on a small pedestal within the department. For a few minutes everything was fine.

Then Charis began watching Julie out of the corner of her eye. A strikingly beautiful woman, her makeup looked wonderful, and the clothes were perfect on her. Beside her, Charis felt shopworn and second-rate. She imagined that everyone was comparing her to Julie, thinking how withered she looked.

Nervously, she sneaked a finger up and patted her crow's-feet, while looking quickly around the department to see if people were actually staring at her. Thankfully, she didn't notice anyone looking, but perhaps, she thought, if she went back into the dressing room and double-checked her appearance or changed into a different outfit, she would look better.

"I'll be right back," she told Julie, stepping off the pedestal.

She hurried into the dressing room and checked her face in the mirror. She had been right. Her forehead was slightly shiny. She quickly blotted it with a powder brush and added more lipstick. Then she thumbed through the rack trying to find an outfit that might look better on her. She decided on a pink dress, quickly changed into it, and hurried out of the dressing room. Once on the floor, Charis looked up at Julie on the pedestal and again observed how perfect she looked.

"One second," she called, and raced back to the dressing room.

She added more mascara to her lashes and blusher to her cheeks. Glancing at the rack, she spied a bright red dress that she felt would look much nicer on her than the pink one she had on, and quickly changed into it. But that required a change in her lipstick from pink to red. Once again she did a final check in the mirror, and headed back out on the floor.

Cragan had returned and to Charis she looked wonderful. She had a perfect figure. Charis looked down at her own figure. Her dress would look much better, she decided, if she was wearing a strapless bra. So once again, she went back into the dressing room.

"What's Charis doing?" Cragan asked in confusion.

"You got me," Julie answered dryly. "I'm just paid to wear the clothes, not to think. But she hasn't been out here for more than a minute yet."

Finally, as Charis took her place next to the other two women, the coordinator appeared.

"Time to change, ladies," she said, unaware of Charis's strange behavior.

The three of them returned to the dressing room, and again Charis took charge of assigning them outfits. Long after the other two models had changed and gone back out on the floor, Charis stood in front of the three-paneled mirror looking at herself.

"When is she coming out?" Cragan asked, looking at her watch. "She's been in there ten minutes already."

"She's been acting weird during this whole booking," Julie answered. "She hasn't even been out to model. All she's done is change her clothes. She just comes out, looks at us, and then goes back in to change. She's acting like a nut case."

"You know," Cragan said thoughtfully, "I think I know what the problem is. I noticed her watching us when she thought I wasn't looking. I'll go in to get her."

Cragan found Charis primping in front of the mirror. When she caught the look of sadness in Charis's eyes, she immediately forgave all of Charis's earlier digs and desperate manipulations.

"Hey, what's up? Are you coming out?"

"I think I look best in this lighting," Charis quipped, attempting a light demeanor. "So, I think I'll stay in here and model."

Cragan smiled at Charis's self-deprecating humor. "I meant to tell you earlier, Charis," she said sincerely, "you look very pretty today."

"Do I? I just felt like my makeup wouldn't go on right," she confided, her face lighting up. "Do you think I look fat? I really feel fat in these clothes."

"You've got to be kidding. You don't have an ounce of fat on your entire body and your skin looks great," Cragan assured her. "But maybe we'd better get out on the floor before they wonder where we are."

"Uh, right," Charis agreed. "You're sure this dress looks good on me?"

"Positive, come on, sweetie," Cragan said, putting her arm around Charis's shoulders.

The rest of the time, Cragan and Julie were able to keep Charis out on the floor with them by constant encouragement and praise, but both knew they would have to have a talk with Derian. Something had to be done soon; Charis was starting to unravel.

• • •

"It's like I told you before," Derian lectured Rusty as they sat in Derian's office drinking coffee. Derian had one leg tucked up under her, and Rusty was sprawled out in his chair across the desk facing her. "You've got to push harder if you want to build your clientele. That's how I got started and now look at DDL. It's number one in L.A., and there's not another agency that comes close."

She gestured with her favorite pen for emphasis.

"DDL is number one, now," Rusty agreed. "But who knows where it would be if Alan Ainsley Anderson were still alive? I hate to say it, Derian, but his death was a real boon for DDL."

"He didn't have a chance," Derian disagreed, angrily flicking her pen on and off. Even the mention of that weasel's name made her blood boil. He got what he deserved!

"Let's be honest here," Rusty persisted. "You made a poor business move hiring him. If he had merged with that other agency, you would have had a battle on your hands."

"I don't think you're in a position to judge what's best for DDL. It's my agency. Besides," she told him curtly, "we're discussing how to improve your photography business, and I have some fail-safe ideas. If you listen to me and do what I say, you'll succeed."

Rusty looked down at the floor and was silent.

The silence made Derian realize that perhaps she was being too hard on him. He was only a kid after all and a good kid, too, but she was only trying to help him. She knew how tough it was to get a business off the ground. She was just trying to protect him from making stupid mistakes, and if he would take her lead, he'd be fine. Kids today. On the other hand, maybe she was being overprotective. Maybe she should let him make his own decisions.

She was just about to tell Rusty that when Holly stuck her head in the door.

"Derian," Holly said, stepping into the room, "may I talk to you?"

"Sure," Derian said. "Come on in. Do you want to talk privately?"

"No, Rusty can stay. I'll only take a minute of your time," Holly answered. She took a seat next to Rusty opposite Derian.

"I'm leaving Los Angeles soon," Holly announced.

"What do you mean?" Derian asked, leaning forward in her chair. She had been hoping to convince Holly to stay indefinitely.

"I mean, I'm going back to Paris," Holly explained. She felt that she'd repaid her debt to Derian and there was no challenge left here. She was tired of playing a big fish in a small pond.

"Well, when?" Derian asked, at a loss for words. Holly's presence at DDL had greatly increased the agency's popularity. Since the Spheres show, the agency's telephones had been ringing off the hook with new business. When those in the L.A. fashion world had learned that DDL had a European model in its stable, they had all wanted to book Derian's models and as a result revenue had increased dramatically. The last thing Derian wanted to hear was that Holly was planning on leaving earlier than Derian had expected.

"In about two weeks, I think," Holly said.

Rusty sat up straight and chewed on his lower lip, listening intently.

"But why?" Derian asked. "I'm sure I can get you more work. We're just now hitting our stride with you. You can become a superstar here."

"I am a superstar in Paris," Holly retorted haughtily. "And let's face it, I'd rather be a superstar in Paris than in Los Angeles."

"But what about—" Rusty started to say.

"I'll handle this, Rusty, if you don't mind," Derian interrupted him brusquely. "What about the jobs I've already booked you on for the next few months?" Derian protested.

"Who told you to do that? I told you I was only going to be here two months. Cancel them." Holly shrugged with nonchalance. What did she care about a few book-ings? She was bored with L.A. and its provincial models. They weren't even a challenge anymore. She'd gotten the revenge she wanted. Screw everyone else. Replacing her was Derian's problem.

"Holly, I want you to think about this," Derian began. She had to convince Holly to stay. "I've been in this busi-ness a lot longer than you have and I know what's best—"

"*I* know what's best for me and it's not Los Angeles," Holly broke in firmly. She knew how convincing Derian could be and she was not about to let her get on a roll. "My mind is made up. I'll finish up my bookings through next week and then I'm history.

"Later, guys," she finished airily before Derian could continue the conversation, and she walked out the door.

Rusty looked at Derian. She was so pale that for a moment he thought she was going to be sick.

"What am I going to do?" she whispered.

It was the first time he had ever seen his confident sister at a loss for words.

"All my new business is dependent on her," Derian moaned. "She can't do this to me. DDL needs that busi-ness to maintain its number-one position."

Rusty picked up her pen and began clicking it off and on. Derian noticed his copycat mannerism, but she was much too distracted with the bombshell Holly had dropped on her to give it much thought.

"I've got to figure a way out of this. I've just got to," she murmured. She stood up and began pacing. There had to be an answer—a way to either make Holly stay or to at least turn the situation around to her advantage.

"Maybe—" Rusty started to say.

"Look, honey, do you mind leaving me alone for a while?" Derian dismissed him. "I've got to think this through."

"Sure," Rusty answered.

Joi Lin was walking back to her office with her comput-er printouts when Holly walked out of Derian's office.

"Hi, Holly," she called out sociably. "How are things going?"

"Hi, Joi Lin," Holly answered, walking over to Joi Lin and leaning on the door frame. Joi Lin was only the bookkeeper, and Holly had nothing to gain by being arrogant with her. "Things are going great."

Joi Lin believed her. Holly was gorgeous, thin, her career was going like gangbusters, and she probably had half the men in the city chasing her. How bad could things be? Of course Joi Lin had heard the rumors about Holly's not-so-great attitude, but Holly had always been nice to her.

"I need to give you my address in Paris, so you can forward my check."

"Paris?" Joi Lin repeated in surprise. "Are you leaving L.A.?"

"Yes," Holly continued. "I was never staying here permanently. I'm just going sooner than I had planned."

"How come?" Joi Lin asked. She set her stack of computer papers down and casually sat down on the edge of her desk to continue the conversation.

"Eh, I'm tired of this town." Holly shrugged. "I'm tired of the smog, the cheap bookings, and the boring models. I miss Paris."

"Well, there's nothing we can do at DDL about the smog," Joi Lin joked, "but I'm sure Derian could raise your rates. You're in such demand that I'm sure the clients would pay more to use you."

"It's not just the money," Holly confided. "I miss the sophistication of Paris, and besides, I've had it with the small-minded models around here. They don't even know a superstar when they see one. Instead of treating me with the respect due me, they treat me like the plague."

Joi Lin had heard about Holly's superior attitude from several of the other models, but she refrained from making any comments.

"And they're thieves!" Holly declared emphatically.

"What?" Joi Lin exclaimed. She couldn't believe her ears.

"That's right," Holly continued, lowering her voice and speaking in a confidential tone. "Just a few days ago, someone stole my bottle of Bleu-Blanc!"

She saw the blank look on Joi Lin's face. "My eyedrops," she explained. "I use them to make the whites of my eyes brighter. They're all the rage in Europe. I know some jealous model took them. A model is the only one who would have had the opportunity."

"Are you sure?" Joi Lin asked. "Maybe you just misplaced it. I can't believe one of our models would steal. They all seem so nice."

"Well, believe it. Those bitches would do anything to eliminate the competition. Of course you wouldn't know anything about that. You're hardly competition to anyone!" Holly told her.

"Oh," Joi Lin sputtered, flabbergasted. It was all she could think to say. Granted she wasn't model material, but she certainly wasn't the bride of Frankenstein, either. No wonder the other models didn't like Holly.

Holly noticed the look on Joi Lin's face and for once she realized that perhaps she had said something rude.

"Did I say something I shouldn't have?" she asked innocently. "I only meant from a modeling standpoint." But she could tell by Joi Lin's expression that the bookkeeper wasn't convinced. She thought she'd better try harder to smooth things over.

"Really, you look good," she went on. "You look like you've lost some weight and your face has lost some of that bloated, pasty look."

Joi Lin just stared at her. She didn't know whether to say thank you or to tell Holly to get out of her office. The truth was that without trying Joi Lin had lost weight. Finally, she decided that the easier route would be just to thank her. "Thanks, Holly, I have lost about fifteen pounds."

"Hey, that's great! Now if you started using a little makeup and got a new hairstyle, you'd look . . . good," Holly advised. "Anyway, before I leave, I want to make sure you have my Paris address." She rattled it off as Joi Lin wrote it down.

Holly turned and almost bumped into Rusty, who had come up in the course of the conversation and had been listening.

"I wouldn't count on her leaving," he said to Joi Lin thoughtfully, watching Holly saunter out of the agency.

"Why, what do you mean?" Joi Lin asked, confused. "She seemed pretty determined to leave."

"I just mean that Derian is pretty determined that Holly won't," Rusty explained. "And you know how Derian is. She usually gets what she wants."

"Hi, guys!" Joi Lin and Rusty heard from the front door. "What's shakin'?" Skeeter bounced into the agency and made a beeline for them.

"How are you, Rusty?" She beamed. "I left a couple of messages on your answering machine, but I never heard from you."

"I've been really busy, but I'll give you a call when I need a makeup artist. You do good work, kid," he replied, smoothly dodging the real meaning of her words.

"Thanks, Rusty, but I meant—" Skeeter started to explain.

"Oh, God, look at the time. I have to go," he exclaimed, eyeing his watch and heading toward the front door. "Bye!" he called.

"Call me!" Skeeter shouted after his disappearing figure.

"Shoot," Skeeter complained. "I was hoping Rusty and I would get together again. When we went out that night, he seemed really interested, but he's never returned any of my calls. Oh, well, the reason I came by was to drop off some more of my cards."

It was obvious to Joi Lin that a chance meeting with Rusty was the real reason Skeeter stopped by, but she was too tactful to say so.

"I'll take them," she said, holding out her hand. "Let me ask you something, Skeeter," she said thoughtfully.

"Do you think I'd look better if I wore some makeup? Holly told me I would."

"Holly!" Skeeter sputtered. "That woman is such a witch!" Then she stopped and thought for a moment. "But you know what? She's right. With just a little makeup and maybe a different hairstyle, you would look darling! Hey, I could show you. My makeup kit is in the car. I'll go get it."

"No, that's all right," Joi Lin protested. She didn't know if she was really ready to change her image; she'd always liked the way she looked.

"No problemo. I'll be right back," Skeeter called, already out the door.

She was back in a flash. "I brought my scissors, too. I give a great haircut," she told Joi Lin. "This will really be fun!"

Before Joi Lin could protest further, Skeeter sat her down and started going through her makeup palette, selecting the right colors for Joi Lin's complexion.

Forty-five minutes later, Skeeter handed Joi Lin a mirror. "Voilà," she said, smiling at her results. "You look gnarly."

Joi Lin looked into the mirror and was surprised with the results. She did look good, even pretty. Skeeter had evened out her complexion with a light coating of foundation and blusher and she had emphasized the exotic tilt of Joi Lin's eyes with neutral shades of shadow. Then she used mascara to bring out thick eyelashes Joi Lin didn't even know she had. Finally Skeeter had recut and shaped Joi Lin's hair into a style that brought out the best in her bone structure.

"It doesn't even look like me," Joi Lin said, studying her face from every angle in the mirror.

"Of course it does," Skeeter assured her. "It's you with a little projection. It's like the difference between writing with a pencil and a pen."

"I think I like it," Joi Lin said slowly. She'd hardly ever worn makeup before because her self-image always dictated that she stay quietly in the background. But with her new independence and assertiveness, she felt the makeup suited her. It was another example of her taking charge of her life. "Do you think I would be able to do this myself?"

"Of course," Skeeter reassured her, writing down what makeup she used. "All it takes is practice. Here's a list of everything you'll need, and if you want, I'll come by and give you another lesson anytime you want."

"Thanks," Joi Lin said. The makeup felt strange on her face, but she felt good about it—and herself.

"It's nothing," Skeeter dismissed with a wave of her hand. "Gotta fly!"

For several minutes afterward Joi Lin sat and looked at her face. Yes, she definitely liked her new image.

Later that day, Joi Lin received a telephone call from Hollis asking her for a quick dinner meeting at La Scala Presto in Brentwood. Rush-hour traffic was exceptionally heavy that afternoon, and she was twenty minutes late as she pulled into the parking lot, narrowly missing two rollerbladers who careened down the sidewalk and darted in front of her car.

Hollis was again already waiting when Joi Lin entered the restaurant. It was early and the place hadn't started to fill up yet. He stood up when she approached the table.

"Sorry I'm late," Joi Lin told him, sliding into the booth. "I had some work I had to get out today."

"I just got here myself," he admitted, sitting down next to her.

A waiter came to take their drink order.

"I'm off duty, so I think I'll have a glass of Chianti. What about you?" he asked.

"I'll have a white wine spritzer," Joi Lin replied.

After taking their order, the waiter was back within minutes with their drinks.

"I'm sorry, I don't have much to report," Hollis said, taking a sip of his wine. "But I wanted to touch base with you and see if anything was happening at DDL."

"I haven't found out anything new either. Just run-of-the-mill stuff."

"Like what?" Hollis asked, interested. Sometimes the most seemingly unimportant things turned out to be vital when combined with other facts.

"Oh, just things like Derian's top model from Europe is leaving to return to Paris and Derian's trying to find a way to keep her here," Joi Lin reported casually. "And then the fact that Derian is always orchestrating Rusty's life—sort of the way Alan used to run mine. I guess Rusty doesn't mind, though, because he never protests. He's quite the playboy. He's got girls coming out of the woodwork. Nothing more important than that."

Hollis found himself staring at Joi Lin. There was something different about her. A gradual transformation had taken place in the grief-stricken young woman whom he first met. Her growing self-confidence was evident, but it was more than that. She looked different, too—prettier, more vibrant.

He became aware of the waiter standing at his elbow.

"Frank, I think the waiter wants to know if we're ready to order dinner," Joi Lin said, putting a hand on his arm.

"Oh, yes," Hollis said. The light pressure of her fingers sent a warmth surging through him and he felt like a teenager on a first date.

"What would you like, Joi Lin?"

"I'd like the Leon chopped salad, no dressing," she explained, ordering one of the specials of the house. "And that's it."

"I'll have mozzarella marinara, the house salad with oil and vinegar, veal scallopini with a side order of gnocchi, a chocolate soufflé, and two more wines," Hollis said, indicating their half-empty glasses.

"You're not eating much," he observed after the waiter left. "Are you on a diet?"

"Not really, the chopped salad is a meal in itself. Speaking of which, it's evident that you're certainly not on a diet. You ordered everything on the menu but the kitchen sink," Joi Lin needled him with a smile. "The restaurant will be lucky if there's any food left for the rest of the diners."

Hollis liked the way Joi Lin's eyes sparkled when she teased him. She had a sweet, easy-to-be-with disposition, and to his surprise, he found that he was having a great time. He liked being with her and he wanted to know her better. Then a sudden realization hit him. Their meeting was more like a date than a business meeting.

"Why are you looking at me like that?" Joi Lin smiled. The spritzer was giving her a light, warm buzz.

"I'm trying to decide whether I should arrest you for harassing an officer," he said with an easy grin, his eyes catching and holding hers.

Joi Lin was quiet for a moment. Either the wine or his gaze was causing her stomach to flutter. She liked this relaxed side of Frank: his warm sense of humor, his kind-hearted way, his dedication to his profession. She found that she wanted, really wanted, to develop a more personal relationship with him. But she had seen the ring on his fourth finger of his left hand and knew he was married. Besides, she was sure that his only interest in her was in solving her brother's case.

After the waiter brought their dinners and wine, Frank gave Joi Lin a rundown of his investigation over the past few days. He still had not received a response from Hermès in Paris and the lab was still eliminating compounds in an effort to track down the toxin.

The conversation digressed into casual conversation.

"It's so hard sometimes," Joi Lin confided over coffee and half of the chocolate soufflé. "I'll think I'm handling Alan's death, but then all of a sudden a stranger walking down the street, a song, even a smell, will remind me of him, and then the realization that he's gone will hit me all over again. It's so hard to explain how it feels."

Her eyes welled with tears and she quickly looked down at her plate so that Frank wouldn't see. They were having such a good time, she didn't want to spoil it. But he'd already noticed.

He put his hand over hers and gave it a pat. "You don't have to explain," he told her gently. "I already know. Gina, my wife, was killed by a drunk driver three years ago, and I still get twinges. But it's okay. It's part of life. Certain things, situations, will probably always bring back memories, but that's normal. Alan was a big part of your life—Gina was of mine—and you'll always carry him with you. But after a while the memories will be sweet, not painful, then you'll know things will be okay. Trust me."

"But you still wear your wedding ring," Joi Lin observed as she looked at his left hand. "Are your memories still painful?"

"Actually, it's my father's ring. He was a cop, and it was the ring he got when he graduated from the police academy. Now I wear it more in his memory than in Gina's," Frank explained. "And, no, my memories aren't painful anymore."

"And maybe someday mine won't be either," Joi Lin said.

Frank squeezed her hand gently.

Frank's admission that he was a widower made her imagine again seeing him on a more personal level, but she dismissed the thought. She knew he was just being kind; he would never be interested in her.

Almost a month had passed since Holly's last facial so she booked a late-afternoon appointment at Gigi Fontaine's Salon of Beauty for a seaweed facial. Like most models, she regarded regular facials as a necessity rather than a luxury. Even with proper cleansing, her skin needed periodic deep cleansing to offset the rigorous abuse it took from makeup.

The lavish salon with its brushed copper and etched glass facade and its interior of plush carpets and muted colors was considered the keystone of skin care in Beverly Hills. So she was looking forward to her treatment as she entered the chic establishment.

"Your facialist is Miss Yasmine and she will be with you momentarily," the receptionist told Holly as she stood at the front desk.

"Miss Yasmine, Miss Yasmine," she announced with a nasal twang over the intercom, "your client is waiting."

A slender young woman of Middle Eastern extraction approached Holly. "I am Yasmine. You will come with me." She led Holly through a mirrored makeup area with rows of cosmetic chairs, up a narrow spiral staircase, and down a hall to a small dimly lit facial room.

"Please take off your clothes and put on this robe," Yasmine instructed Holly, giving her a pink dressing gown. "I will be right back."

Holly complied and sat back in the contoured chair that dominated the room. A few moments later Yasmine returned and after wrapping Holly in pale pink sheets, she adjusted the chair horizontally.

Holly loved facials, as all the tensions of the day seemed to melt away during the relaxing treatment. Yasmine expertly removed her makeup and then after placing cool cotton pads over Holly eyes, she wrapped Holly's face in warm wet towels to open the pores. Then she massaged Holly's hands with moisturizing lotion and put them in heated mitts so the lotion would soak deep into the skin.

"I'm going to leave you for a few minutes. You relax," she told Holly, dimming the lights and closing the door behind her with a gentle click.

The muted sounds from beyond the door faded as Holly's mind drifted and she dozed off. Images of France floated behind her eyelids, and suddenly she was on a shoot with Emil in the little country village of Betschdorf in the region of Alsace. Half-timbered little shops dating back to medieval times crowded the narrow worn streets, many of them selling the town's distinctive blue and gray stoneware.

Against this historical backdrop, Emil was shooting her wearing incongruous contemporary sportswear and she was the center of attention. Villagers stopped in their tracks to stare at the glamorous superstar from Paris. An old woman in a black overcoat and babushka bicycled slowly up the street toward them, her bicycle squeaking sharply as she approached.

The sound ground into Holly's subconscious like nails on a chalkboard, gradually awakening her to the present. Above her, she heard the sounds of someone stealthily moving about the room and she surmised that Yasmine had returned. She waited for the facialist to speak to her, but there was only a hush that filled Holly with growing unease.

"Yasmine?" Holly asked, her voice muffled beneath the warm towels.

Tightly wrapped in sheets, her hands inside the electric mittens, and her face covered in hot towels, she felt vulnerable and slightly disoriented from sleep. Again she heard the squeaking noise followed by Yasmine's surprised voice. "What are you doing in here?"

"Oh, I guess I'm in the wrong room," Holly heard the other woman's soft reply.

Before Yasmine could continue the conversation, Holly again heard the sound of the door opening and closing.

"What happened?" Holly asked in a voice made almost unintelligible by the towels.

"It was nothing," Yasmine explained, dismissing the incident. "Just some client who walked into the wrong room. It happens all the time."

The thought of someone in the room with her while she was in such a helpless position gave Holly a creepy feeling. But Yasmine didn't seem concerned, so Holly tried to do likewise, although her uneasiness persisted for the remainder of her appointment.

By the time she was finished, the sun had set and the final vestiges of twilight had faded into darkness. Because it was after closing time, the doorman escorted her to the back alley employee's entrance, closing and locking the door firmly behind her.

The sounds of traffic from Camden Drive echoed in Holly's ears as she started toward her car, which was parked in the lot at the far end. The moon's illumination lent an eerie, surrealistic glow to the alley, backlighting and distorting everything it touched. Trash cans became huddled figures; stacked boxes, hiding places; loose garbage took on the shapes of creatures of the night. She hesitated and looked back at the salon, but even as she turned, its lights blinked out. She told herself she was being silly. The safety of Camden Drive was only seconds away so she determinedly continued walking the alley, her shoes tapping out a rhythm that steadily increased as her apprehension grew.

Halfway down the alley she heard—or did she only imagine?—the sound of footsteps. She paused to listen, but all she heard was the soft rustle of trash being whisked about by a playful Santa Ana wind. She crossed to the center of the alley, as far away as possible from the dark shadows, and kept walking. The pounding of her heart roared in her ears, and again she was positive she heard footsteps tracking her. She whirled to face her pursuer, but all she could see were inky-black shadows filling the corners of the alley.

A sliver of cloud passed in front of the moon, and the black shadows in the alley seemed to reach out toward her. With a cry, Holly broke into a run. She pounded down the alley and, not waiting to shut off her car alarm, jumped into the driver's seat and hit the automatic lock. The screaming alarm further unnerved her, and it took several long moments before she could stop shaking long enough to disarm it. Then she leaned back in the seat gasping, her heart racing, trying to gain control of herself.

Suddenly there was a knocking at her window. She jumped and turned to the window with a scream. Only inches away, a dirt-streaked homeless woman stared back at Holly, her eyes flat and her hair hanging in greasy dreadlocks. The woman jabbered something Holly couldn't understand, and Holly didn't wait long enough for her to repeat it. She turned the key in the ignition, shifted into gear, and floored the gas pedal. Her car shot out of the lot, leaving two black lines on the pavement and the smell of burned rubber hanging in the air.

From her cover beside a Dumpster, she watched the exchange between Holly and the homeless woman before Holly peeled rubber in her haste to leave. She had been on the verge of making her move on Holly when she spotted the old woman sprawled in a dark doorway, and she had melded into the shadows before the old hag saw her. It was the second time in one day that her plans had been thwarted, and she could feel frustration building inside her. First that damn facialist and now the old homeless woman. As she stepped out of the shadows into the alley, the old woman turned and spied her. Dragging one foot, the old woman stumbled toward her, waving her arms. As she approached, the moon reappeared from behind the clouds, bathing the alley in cold light and illuminating the face of the younger woman.

The old homeless woman stopped in her tracks, suddenly warned by a sixth sense that the young woman standing before her was dangerous. Nervously the old woman reversed her path and hobbled off down the alley, looking over her shoulder every few feet to make sure the young woman wasn't following her.

As she watched the rapidly retreating figure, her fingers closed around the shaft of the small tube she held in her pocket, and she suppressed an urge to follow. Her anticipation of the kill was almost palpable, and she struggled to control the urge to vent her pent-up needs. Finally when she could no longer contain her frustration, it burst forth in a scream that echoed off the alley walls.

Still unnerved, Holly raced into her apartment, slammed the deadbolt across the front door, and threw herself into the nearest chair facing the door. She'd checked her rearview mirror constantly on her way home and was fairly sure no one followed her, but that didn't rule out the possibility of someone's knowing where she lived.

She drew her knees up under her chin and huddled in a corner of the big armchair, racking her brain for someone to call, if for no other reason than for the sound of a sympathetic voice. She thought of Derian but quickly discarded the thought when she thought of their last conversation. She thought of Toney. When she first returned to L.A. she hadn't wanted to waste her time on someone who couldn't benefit her. Now how could she call him after she had dodged his repeated calls? Suddenly she felt terribly alone.

She picked up the telephone and dialed Sid's number. Although she hadn't seen him since their afternoon fling, they had spoken on the phone several times. Apparently he was extremely busy, because each time she suggested they get together, he said his schedule wouldn't allow it. The phone rang ten times before Holly hung up.

It took her two more hours before she was calm enough to go to bed, and even then, she spent most of the night awake, listening for footsteps outside her door.

Joi Lin was reviewing call sheets when Holly burst into the agency. Her face was pale and her eyes sunken with dark circles.

"Where's Derian?" she demanded, stomping toward Derian's private office.

"I'm sorry, she's not here," Joi Lin told her. "She had an early-morning meeting. Are you all right?"

"No, I'm not all right," Holly exclaimed. "Some nut case is after me!"

"What are you talking about?" Joi Lin asked, putting down her call sheets and giving Holly her full attention. "What nut case?"

"Some crazy woman is after me! She's been stalking me all over town," Holly explained, telling Joi Lin exactly what had occurred.

"It's just like what happened to Jodie Foster, Theresa Saldano, and Rebecca Schaffer. An out-of-control loony-tune fixated on them and next thing they knew, they were being chased around town with a butcher knife!" Holly concluded, pacing around the agency and flailing her arms for emphasis.

"Calm down. Take a deep breath," Joi Lin said, trying to placate the agitated young woman. Joi Lin felt Holly's reaction was extreme, by putting herself in the same category as Jodie Foster or Theresa Saldano. She had hardly experienced what they had. "Remember, Holly, you're not in the public eye like they are."

"Oh, yes, I am. I'm a celebrity of the nineties. The whole world knows my face—or they will! People envy me! They want to be just like me. That's why some schmuck model stole my eyedrops!" Holly insisted in exasperation. "And now I'm positive some creep is after me!"

Joi Lin couldn't imagine anyone wanting to be like Holly. Her arrogance and condescending attitude negated any beauty Joi Lin may have initially thought Holly had, and she believed this was yet another excuse for Holly to leave DDL sooner than planned. Regardless, she felt it was her responsibility to try to calm the woman down.

"Sit down," she said soothingly, giving Holly's arm a pat. "Let me get you a cup of tea or a soda."

"I don't know why I'm even bothering to tell you all of this," Holly snipped nastily, shrugging off Joi Lin's attempts at placation. "After all, you're only a bookkeeper. How would you understand what it's like to be a superstar model? Listen, just tell Derian to call me the minute she gets in!" With that, she sailed out of the agency.

Joi Lin watched her leave. Holly's words stung, but instead of depressing her as they would have in the past, they angered her. With her new sense of self-esteem and confidence, she saw Holly for the shallow, self-absorbed young woman she really was. Maybe she even made up the whole story of someone stalking her. Nevertheless, she made a mental note not only to tell Derian, but to tell Frank about Holly's accusations too.

CHAPTER
8

The polo ponies thundered down the grassy field at Will Rogers Park, the sod torn up by their hooves, flying in their wake. As the clock ticked off the final seconds of the third chucker, the star of the home team, in a last-ditch effort to score, urged his pony onward, bumping his nearest competitor out of the way. He leaned against his lathered horse and swung his mallet backhand, connecting with the ball and driving it across the goal line. The spectators on the grassy sidelines cheered their approval.

Watching polo practice at Will Rogers Park on Sunday mornings was a popular Angelino event. It was one of Derian's favorite pastimes, too. She never tired of the fervor of the players, the gracefulness and beauty of the horses, and the relaxing atmosphere of the park. Today, however, though her friends rallied around the efforts of the home team, she couldn't seem to keep her mind on the game. As hard as she tried, her thoughts kept returning to DDL.

Over the weekend, she and Holly had repeatedly discussed the incident in the alley, but she wasn't able to persuade Holly that no one was after her, and that it had only been a one-time occurrence. But Holly was convinced that she was being followed, and although she hadn't noticed anyone suspicious since that night, she was determined to leave Los Angeles. Derian had tried every argument she could think of to convince Holly to stay.

"This is the film capital of the world," she told Holly. "You should stay here and eventually pursue acting."

"I'm not interested," Holly said flatly.

"But, Holly, with acting, the sky's the limit. It's a natural segue from modeling," Derian argued hopefully.

"There's plenty of time to go into acting if I decide that's what I want to do," Holly declared. "Right now, I'm hot as a model and I want to go with that. In another year, when I'm even more well-known, Hollywood will be chasing me!"

Derian had to admit Holly's thinking had some validity, but that didn't help DDL any. Just when the agency was starting to hit its peak, Holly's departure would pull the rug out from beneath it. The agency would suffer not only a big loss in revenue, but also in prestige. Next to Rusty, DDL was Derian's lifeblood, and she wasn't about to let Holly jeopardize its future so easily. She vowed to talk to Holly again; after all, she was Derian Delorian and she always got what she wanted, one way or another.

In the meantime, it wouldn't hurt the agency to have a new supply of up-and-comers. Then in a year, or six months even, she wouldn't need Holly Woodward because her new girls would be at their peak. She reviewed various ways of attracting fresh new faces. One way was sifting through the eager young girls at modeling schools, though she'd done that before with little success. The schools were more interested in making money than in discovering and teaching girls with real potential. Another way was to promote an exchange program with agencies in Europe and the Orient. That had possibilities, but it would take a fair amount of time to implement and she needed more immediate results. Perhaps holding a contest would do the trick. She could offer a modeling contract as first prize. Girls all over the West Coast could enter. Every high school, college, and local newspaper would receive a press kit. She had a built-in photographer, and Rusty could use the winner and runners-up on some of his jobs. That way both he and the agency would benefit.

With all those fresh faces, however, it would mean she would have to cut some of her models who were no longer financially productive. In the extremely demanding and fickle fashion world superstars and new faces brought an agency publicity and new clients. Even though the steady money-making models were the backbone of the agency, after a few seasons of seeing the same model, many times a client didn't want to book her again. Not because she wasn't a good model, but because she seemed "old," her face was too recognizable. Many models drifted into other occupations and some developed enough of a loyal clientele that they continued to model steadily for years. Eventually, however, it all came to an end. Modeling just was not a "forever" career.

Derian started mentally to weed out the models who were not big revenue producers and she almost immediately thought of Charis. Her bookings had steadily decreased over the past year with a dramatic drop this season. She hated the thought of cutting Charis loose from the agency— they had been friends for so many years—but DDL's welfare came first.

Several times during the past few months, Derian had hinted to Charis that perhaps she should consider finding another career, but Charis had refused to listen. Now she would have no choice. She had to release Charis from the agency. DDL was number one in the city and Derian was determined that it would remain in that position, even at the expense of losing her friendship with Charis. Painful as that thought was, she vowed to talk to both Holly and Charis tomorrow. The future of her agency was at stake and nothing would stand in its way. Certainly not two models.

Finally, resigned to her decisions, she leaned back on the grass and reached for her mimosa, enjoying the feel of the California sun on her body. On the field, the home team scored another goal and Derian cheered them. God, she loved winning.

Derian's good mood continued on into the next morning and she was humming as she came into the agency. She had been in such a bad mood on Friday after her conversation with Holly that Joi Lin and Betsy had deliberately stayed out of her way.

"Hi," she practically chirped to them.

The two women looked at each other in relief. Although Derian was rarely in a bad mood, when she was, no one was immune from her wrath.

"Betsy," Derian said, grabbing a cup of coffee from the kitchen, "would you call Holly and Charis and tell them I'd like to see them today, if possible?

"Then you and Joi Lin decide where you'd like to send out for lunch. I'm treating," she called gaily as she walked into her office.

Derian sat at her desk and for the next two hours, after returning phone calls and fielding bookings, she mapped out her plan of action. She'd whittle the agency down to only the money-makers, instigate plans for her model contest, and convince Holly to stay for at least a few more months until she had the first influx of new girls in the agency.

"Derian," Betsy said, leaning around the doorway. "Charis is on her way over and I left a message on Holly's service. According to the call sheets, Holly's at a booking."

"Thanks, Betsy," Derian said, returning to her plans.

She continued working on her plans for another hour and was about to break for lunch when Rusty showed up.

"Hi, Sis," he said, leaning over the desk to kiss her on the cheek and at the same time filching her coffee.

"Hi, I thought you had a shoot this morning."

"I did." He sipped her coffee, leaning back in his chair, sitting on one leg. "A headshot for a composite, but she canceled. She called and said she had an allergic reaction to something she ate yesterday. Tomorrow, though, I have a real busy day.

"How were the polo matches?"

"Great," Derian said. "Actually, they were very productive. I've figured out how to keep DDL on top in L.A."

Betsy stuck her head in the door. "Derian, Charis is here."

"Thanks, Betsy," Derian answered, then turned to her brother. "Sweetie, I need to talk to Charis privately for a few minutes. But don't go away. We'll have lunch."

But as Rusty stood up to leave, Derian had a brilliant inspiration. "Hold it," she said excitedly, motioning Rusty toward the chair. "I just had a great idea! Stay after all."

"Why?" Rusty asked, sitting back down.

Before she could answer, Charis walked in. She was beautifully dressed in a pale aqua sweater and matching slacks, but her face was openly lined with stress. She had no idea why Derian had called her into the agency, but she felt that anytime an agency owner requested her presence, it was not a good sign. However, she attempted to cover her unease by being overly upbeat.

"Hi, Derian!" she exclaimed. "Rusty, how have you been? Just as darling as ever, I see. When are the two of us going dancing?"

"Hi, Charis," Rusty responded with an easy grin. "Anytime. I keep my dancing shoes in my car for short notice."

"All right! I've been so busy," Charis chattered on brightly as she sat down across from Derian. In her lap, however, her fingers compulsively worked the strap on her purse. "I'm in the midst of redoing my composite and as soon as it's finished and Derian does a mailing, I probably won't have any spare time. Hey, I should shoot with you. Do you have time to do any testing? I—"

Derian had been quietly watching Charis. She could read the tension in her face and the stiff way she held her body, and she felt her resolve to cut Charis from the agency weakening. She wondered again whether Charis could handle not modeling. If only the wonderful idea she just had would work. But of course it would! She could talk anyone into anything. And she was sure Rusty would love it!

"Charis," she began, "there was an important reason I asked you to stop by."

"Yes," Charis said. Her stomach quivered and she gripped her purse strap tighter.

"Rusty's photography has taken off and gotten extremely busy," Derian said.

Rusty looked at Derian in surprise. They hadn't talked about his photography being *that* busy.

"He needs help," Derian continued, carefully threading her way between the two egos. "He's very talented, but he needs someone who can take care of details and free him so he can concentrate on being creative."

Both Charis and Rusty leaned forward in their chairs, trying to decipher the point of Derian's thoughts.

"It would be a big responsibility for someone. This person would have to know the modeling end of things. She'd have to guide the models, and style the shoot. It would have to be someone who had years of experience behind her."

Charis finally understood what Derian was getting at. Rusty needed a stylist and Derian wanted *Charis* to take the job! She blanched at the thought. She didn't want to be a lowly stylist. She wanted to model and that's all she wanted to do! She thought about the embarrassment and the comments she would have to endure from the other models. They would all surmise that she had started styling because she couldn't get work as a model.

"Gee, I don't think I'm the right person for Rusty," she began nervously. She knew she would have to be very tactful with Derian. Her future bookings lay in Derian's hands. "He needs someone who can stay with him, grow with the business. I wouldn't be reliable. He'd be depending on me and I'd get a booking and have to cancel on him. It wouldn't be fair."

"I think Charis is right," Rusty agreed. He didn't need a stylist, but if he did, he'd want to choose his own.

"Yes," Charis chimed in. Rusty didn't think it was a good idea either, and it gave her more courage to disagree with Derian.

"Nonsense," Derian said, ignoring the two unhappy faces in front of her. This was a terrific idea and if she could get Charis interested in styling, she wouldn't have to tell her that she was being dropped from the agency.

Charis's years of experience would be a big help to Rusty, too. With Charis's help, he would develop an eye for detail and composition, and his sense of fashion style would increase. Even if she had to subsidize Charis's salary, she would. Yes, she knew she was right and she wasn't about to listen to any further protests from either one of them.

"It's a great idea. I'd really like you two to give it a try."

"But—" Rusty started to say.

"Come on, one time for me," Derian interrupted, shooting him a warning look. "Charis, I'm asking you as a favor to me."

Charis looked from Derian to Rusty. When Derian put it on a personal level, she knew she couldn't refuse. But she also feared that if she didn't acquiesce, Derian might cut her bookings in retaliation.

"Okay, I'll do it," Charis agreed.

"Good." Derian stood, indicating their meeting was over. "You and Rusty can connect and figure out the details."

She walked around her desk and put her arm around Charis, guiding her out of her office.

"I think you and Rusty are going to work out fine," she said cheerfully, opening the door of the agency for Charis. She was pleased with how things were working out and she was convinced this union would be the best for everyone, including DDL.

"I'll talk with you soon, Charis," she said, closing the door.

"Why didn't you tell me you were going to offer Charis a job in my studio?" Rusty exploded, having followed Derian out of her office. "It's my studio!"

His voice carried throughout the agency, and Joi Lin and Betsy looked up in surprise at his tone. But before he could continue the conversation, Holly walked in.

"Hi, I got a message on my service that you wanted to see me," she said to Derian. "But I was on my way over anyway. I've made arrangements to fly back to Paris at the end of the week and I wanted to see if you will advance me the rest of the money I've made on my bookings."

"Yes, I can do that," Derian said slowly, her mind racing. So Holly was making good on her threat. Panicking, she thought about the billings. Joi Lin had sent out a lot of them for Holly in the last few weeks, but most of them hadn't been paid. Many of them were new clients and DDL normally didn't advance money from clients until they had established a track record with the agency. If the agency had to pay out everything it owed to Holly by the end of the week, it would mean operating short for the next month or so. Additionally, Derian desperately needed Holly to remain in L.A. until she could put her new plans into action.

"Look, Holly, it's just not a good idea to leave L.A. right now," she tried reasoning with Holly yet again. "As I told you, big things are just starting to happen. Spheres is mounting a big ad campaign and I know Mrs. Ritter will want to feature you. And I've gotten a call from *L.A. Life*. They want you for the cover *and* the editorial inside. Plus, you've been booked by a couple of dozen other big accounts. It would be a big mistake for your career to leave now, trust me."

"Cancel them. My mind is made up," Holly said firmly. "I was never planning on staying any length of time, I told you that from the beginning. And now with some crazy person stalking me, I can hardly wait to leave."

"But you said you hadn't noticed anyone following you since that night," Derian said persuasively. "I'm sure it was all just a misunderstanding."

"I don't care what it was, I'm going," Holly declared, starting to get impatient with Derian.

"Listen, Holly," Derian said frankly. "I'm asking you again as a favor to me. Stay—at least for another month or two. I need you here until then. The agency is on an upswing and in two months—or even one month—I'll have a better handle on it. I'll have some fresh faces and I'll be able to continue the momentum. If you leave now, you'll destroy it all. You may even ruin me. I'll lose my credibility.

"What do you say, Holly?" Derian wheedled. "I was there for you last year. You would have never made it to Paris without my help and now I need yours. You owe me a favor."

"I told you before, not a chance," Holly said without hesitation. She was tired of listening to Derian's sob story. Why didn't *Derian* understand what *she* wanted? So Derian made a little phone call introduction a year ago. Did Holly have to repay that favor for the rest of her life?

"Derian, we've already gone over this. I've repaid your favor. You called and asked me to do the Spheres show and I did. That debt is paid. Now if you'll just make arrangements to have a check ready for me on Friday, I'll stop by then."

Without waiting for a response from Derian, she tossed her head arrogantly and walked out.

For a moment no one spoke. Rusty waited for a response from Derian, while Joi Lin and Betsy quietly busied themselves with their files.

Derian turned and without a word stormed back into her office, slamming the door and leaving Rusty standing alone in the middle of the agency with a look of amazement on his face. No one ever said no to Derian. After a moment, he, too, went into her office.

"Look, I don't want an argument from you, too," she snapped as he closed the door behind him. "You'll use Charis as your stylist and that's the end of it."

"Okay, okay, I'll use her," he answered, raising his hands in a posture of submission. "But what are you going to do about Holly?"

"I really don't know! I'd hoped I could stall her, but obviously it didn't work!" Derian said angrily, furiously snapping her pen off and on. "DDL, everything I've worked for, could go down the tubes. I'll lose my credibility if I have to cancel her bookings!"

"Why didn't you lock her into a contract from the very beginning? You could have avoided this—" Rusty started to say.

"Not now," Derian cut him off. "Just go away and let me think about this. There must be a way to turn this situation around to my advantage. No snotty little bitch of a model is going to get away with destroying everything I've worked for." She walked over to the window and stared out.

For a long while, Rusty sat waiting for her to continue, but when she didn't, he stood up and started to leave.

"Bye," he said as he closed the office door, but Derian didn't hear him.

"She won't get away with it," she mumbled numbly, over and over to herself.

"Here's that list you asked for, Lieutenant." Officer Kathy O'Conner dropped a stack of pages on Hollis's desk.

"All ready? Thanks, Kathy," he said, picking it up and perusing it.

Kathy was the right person to assign to a task if he wanted it done fast and correctly. She was a tall, big-boned woman with a quiet demeanor, a mind like a steel trap, and a razor-sharp sense of humor. Several times, he'd seen some loudmouth in the department single her out to make her the butt of a joke only to find himself cut down to size with the twist of a phrase or a single word. She didn't know the meaning of doing the minimum. She not only completed a task, but if possible she would extrapolate the pertinent information and take it to the next level.

When he asked for volunteers to help him contact all the exotic novelty shops in L.A., the arms of several detectives went up like the SS saluting Hitler. *It figures*, he thought dryly to himself. *Ask for someone to canvass sex shops and everyone wants a piece of the action. Ask for anything else and the whole department becomes deaf and dumb.*

"Officer O'Conner, I'm assigning this to you," he said.

"What're you assigning it to her for? She didn't even volunteer," Joey Tartella complained. "She probably doesn't even know what an exotic novelty shop is."

"She didn't volunteer, that's why I assigned her. The rest of you are too eager."

"Maybe the lieutenant was afraid he'd get his reports with tongue tracks and drool on them," Kathy piped up with only the faintest hint of a smile.

" 'Tongue Tartella.' It does have a sort of ring to it," one of the rookies in the back of the squad room mused. "Doesn't it?"

The room broke up with peals of laughter and from that moment on, Joey had been labeled "The Tongue." Knowing Joey, Hollis was sure he relished the nickname. Cops loved nicknames, and one like "The Tongue" would make Joey a legend.

Kathy was terrific. She not only listed all the addresses and telephone numbers of exotic novelty shops within Los Angeles proper, but she also underlined the ones that carried edible G-strings. Of those, she requested copies of their general mailing lists, incomplete or otherwise. Of course some of the shops never did mailers and other shops only had names and addresses of people who made credit card purchases. But it was better than nothing. She cross-referenced the mailing lists with the department's lists of known female offenders who had an M.O. of using any kind of sex apparatus in connection with a crime. She also did a computer run on exotic catalogues throughout the country and printed the ones she located with their names and addresses for him. If nothing panned out from a canvass of the local shops, they could start on the catalogues.

He had just started going over the lists when one of the departmental clerks brought him the fax from Hermès, which he had been waiting for for days. He skimmed the information, his excitement growing with every line of copy.

The silk scarf had been a part of a very special and select promotion entitled "The Hermès Women of 1972." In fact, he read, only a score were manufactured. A score! This could be his big break in the case. What followed was general information explaining the promotion, what it entailed, and so forth. At the bottom of the page was a list of everyone who received a scarf and their addresses at that time. One scarf was kept by the company for its archives; various high-level executives of the company received a number of them; ten of them went to their most important clients (most of whom had European titles). At the bottom of the list, four were given to the models who were booked for the company's advertising campaign. Hollis gave Kathy the list.

"Kath, track these names down, will you? I want current addresses and phone numbers for all of them."

Hollis sensed that he was finally on the right trail, but he decided to wait until he had something more concrete before confiding in Joi Lin. He didn't want to see her hopes dashed, although he had observed that disappointments only seemed to make her more determined.

He just hoped it wouldn't take too long, because he was already looking forward to seeing her again. He really didn't completely understand why himself, but she was like an unsuspecting magnet, drawing him to her.

Holly had called Sid several times trying to set up an encore to their last sexual encounter, and the more he made excuses, the more intrigued she became. The thought never entered her mind that he might not want to see her. After all, who wouldn't be interested in her?

She was walking down Camden Drive when she recognized Sid's familiar figure ahead of her. She hurried to catch up with him and pinched him on the backside. Startled, he jumped and whirled around.

"Holly, hi," he said, surprised. "How are you? You look beautiful." She did, too. He had almost forgotten how really breathtakingly beautiful she was. For a moment he felt that familiar hardening, but then he recalled their one-night stand and everything wilted. Once in the sack with her was enough. She was an animal. Besides, he had discovered she was a mental lightweight and outside her favorite subject—herself—she had nothing to contribute to a conversation.

"Sid, honey," she purred, "where have you been? I was hoping we could get together before I went back to Paris." She stood several inches taller than he and she draped her arms around him possessively.

Sid nervously stole a look around him, hoping no one he knew saw him with this young woman hanging on him. Even as he looked over her shoulder, she leaned down and nibbled on his ear.

"Don't," he protested. "Someone might see us."

"They'd only be envious of you, Sidney," Holly answered, continuing to nibble. She'd had a great time with him and she was determined to bed him one more time before leaving L.A. "Hey, let's go back to my place."

"I can't. That is, I don't have time," he stammered. She was making him very nervous. What if Ellysa should drive by and see them in front of God and the whole world? He had to get off the street.

"I'm not leaving you until you say yes." Holly pouted, twisting a strand of his hair.

He quickly brushed her hand away.

God, he thought to himself, this was becoming a nightmare. Maybe he could at least get her off the street and into a restaurant, where fewer people would see them.

"Let's get a cappuccino," he suggested. They were standing in front of Prego's and he steered her toward the entrance of the restaurant.

"Table for two," he told the hostess, scanning the restaurant for any familiar faces.

The hostess led them to a table only one row from the window, but it was far enough back so that Sid didn't think anyone passing would notice them.

Instead of sitting across from him, Holly slid in next to him, running her hand up his thigh. He grabbed her hand and held it to keep it from exploring higher, and stole a quick look at the hostess to see if she noticed Holly's movements.

She had.

"Lovebirds, that's so sweet," she trilled, misinterpreting their actions.

Sid flushed and wished he had never left his office. There was something so unappealing and threatening about being chased. *He* liked to be the hunter, not the hunted.

"Two cappuccinos," he said gruffly.

Holly rubbed up against him and stuck her tongue in his ear. He jumped and tried to scoot away from her, but she followed him, pinning him against the edge of the banquette.

"Sidney," Holly cooed, "you're so jumpy. You need a little relaxation and I'm just the one to relax you."

"Behave, someone will see us," he said, trying to push her away. "I am a married man."

Ellysa, who had a sudden sweet tooth, was walking down the street on her way to Teuscher Chocolates and happened to glance into Prego's window just as Holly leaned over and chewed on Sid's ear. All thoughts of candy left her and it took all her willpower to keep from marching into Prego's and creating a scene that Sid and Holly would never forget. Only the thought of being seen by one of her Beverly Hills society friends held her back.

All the way home she fumed. She had immediately recognized Holly from her Spheres show and as the model she had booked for her upcoming print campaign. It incited her even more to think that she was supporting

Holly with bookings while Holly, in turn, was having an affair with her husband.

When she entered the house, her first impulse was to dial her attorney and start divorce proceedings, but she forced herself to sit down and to think the situation through rationally before acting. Eventually, she decided to confront Sid and demand his version. Although she was positive that he would lie through his teeth, for once in her life, she knew she had more important considerations than her temper tantrums and his sordid little affairs. She had her social status and monetary future to think about.

It was past dinnertime when Sid arrived home. He had managed to extract himself from Holly only after two cappuccinos and a promise to call her. A promise he had no intention of keeping, but it was the only way he could get rid of her.

The house was completely dark and he surmised Ellysa must have given the housekeeper the night off and gone to dinner with one of the "girls," as she called her clique of Beverly Hills matrons. Personally, he couldn't stand any of them. All they talked about was who was doing what to whom, where, and who could go through the most money. Ellysa was probably at the front of the line in that department, he thought grimly. He remembered how good their marriage had been in the beginning, when their lives revolved around each other instead of social climbing. Boy, had times changed, he thought with a sigh.

He pressed in his code to deactivate the alarm next to the front door and heard the lock click. Switching on the light in the foyer, he continued into the living room to draw the drapes across the front window, when he discovered Ellysa sitting alone in the dark.

"Jeez, you startled me," he exclaimed, taking a step back. "What the hell are you doing, sitting here in the dark?"

Ellysa stared straight ahead out the window without answering him. All afternoon she had rehearsed what she was going to say one hundred and one different ways and now that the moment was here, all her plans flew out the window.

"I drove into Beverly Hills to pick up some champagne truffles at Teuscher Chocolates today," she said dully without looking at him.

"So," he replied in confusion, thinking it was a very strange statement for her to make.

"Teuscher is next door to Prego's," she reminded him pointedly.

Sid knew immediately what she was talking about, but he decided to use the traditional spousal cop-out—playing dumb. "Hey, *I* was at Prego's this afternoon."

"I know you were," Ellysa said nastily. She tore her eyes away from the window and stared at him. "I saw you and your little blond bimbo-of-the-week."

"What are you talking about? It was a business meeting. You should have come in and joined us," he said, adopting a tone of righteous indignation.

"Right, Sid," Ellysa retorted cuttingly. "Her tongue was so far in your ear that it was coming out the other side, and she was pressed so tightly against you that the label on her dress is probably permanently imprinted on your chest!

"You slime bucket! How could you?" Her voice rose with each word as she struggled to maintain her composure. "I pay that bimbo's bills! And, furthermore, she's young enough to be your daughter!"

Without pausing she stood up and paced the room, her rage growing with each step. "What is it with you? First that bitch Vicki, now this bimbo, and God knows how many others. Am I constantly going to have to worry that you'll be having affairs with our daughter's friends? I can't take any more."

"What are you talking about?" Sid asked, baffled. "We don't have a daughter."

"I mean it, Sid," Ellysa continued. "Let's call it quits right now. I'd rather be a single parent than married to a cheater and bring up a child in a hostile environment. My child's happiness is more important to me!"

In two steps, Sid was across the room. He grabbed Ellysa by the shoulders and spun her around to face him. "We're going to have a baby? I'm going to be a father?"

"How blind can you be, Sid? Don't you ever notice anything except a pair of big boobs and a pretty face?" she asked incredulously. She pulled up her oversize top to expose her obviously pregnant stomach. "What do you think this is, you fool? Water retention?"

Sid picked her up with a whoop and swung her around in a circle.

"Put me down," Ellysa said sternly, but his excitement was contagious. She had had no idea he would be excited about the prospect of being a father. She always thought he didn't like children.

"You're right. I'm sorry, I'm sorry." He put her down and led her to the sofa. "Can I get you a drink . . . No, you can't have that. Milk. Can I get you some milk?"

He was so flustered and had such a look of tender concern on his face, it was hard for Ellysa to stay angry. He kept bombarding her with questions. Why didn't she tell him? When was she going to have it? Was it really a girl? He was so boyish and enthusiastic, reminding her of how he was when they were first married, and against her will, she felt her resolve melting.

"I know it's a girl, because I had an ultrasound and the doctor told me it was," she patiently explained.

"I can't believe I didn't notice. Why didn't you tell me?"

"I didn't tell you because I didn't think you'd be interested," she told him pointedly. His words reminded her of Holly and Vicki. "You always seem to have plenty of other things to occupy yourself with. This baby is the focus of my life, and *I* don't want her to grow up in a part-time family with an absentee father. I want her to have a happy, wholesome childhood, with two devoted parents."

"Wait a minute!" Sid protested loudly. "It isn't just me! You're at fault, too! You've always been more interested in your social status and my money than you have been in our marriage!"

"That's not true," Ellysa denied, her temper rising again. "I was just trying to increase our standing in the community."

"And what about Spheres?" Sid continued, walking over to the wet bar and pouring himself a healthy shot of Wild Turkey. "You spend more time at that damned boutique than you do with me."

"Don't you tell me about spending time on our marriage," Ellysa retorted nastily. "*You* seem to have plenty of diversions to occupy your time! And I don't mean real estate deals either!"

"I already told you," Sid insisted, belting down his drink and setting the glass down on the bar with a loud bang. "I don't know what you're talking about." But he found it impossible to look Ellysa in the eye.

"Look, Ellysa, arguments and accusations aren't getting us anywhere," Sid continued, making an effort to bridge the chasm between them. "We've both made mistakes. But now we have a reason to wipe the slate clean and start over. What do you say?"

"You have more to wipe clean than I do," Ellysa groused. Deep down she really wanted to give their marriage another try, but she kept seeing Holly with her lips against Sid's ear. "What will your little bimbette say?"

"I'm telling you again, there was nothing to what you saw," Sid insisted earnestly. He sat down next to her and looked into her eyes. "Ellysa, I don't know if our marriage can survive, but I'm willing to give it a try. We'll take it one step at a time. What do you say?"

Ellysa tried to keep from crying. Here were all the words that she had ached to hear, but never in her heart of hearts did she believe their conversation would end with this. Sure she loved the prestige of being Mrs. Roque, but she truly did love Sid. If only she could forgive him. Until this moment, she had thought their life together was too far gone and divorce the only way out.

"What is it? Why are you crying?" Sid exclaimed, panicking. He grabbed a magazine and began fanning her face. "You aren't going into labor are you? Shall I call the doctor?"

Ellysa started giggling through her tears. Sid stopped pumping the magazine up and down, and gazed at her. It had been a long time since he'd heard her giggle like that.

"God, you're beautiful," he said.

She leaned into the mirror and carefully applied a false eyelash and then sat back to inspect the effect. She looked marvelous. It was amazing what a pair of false lashes did for a girl. Next, she slithered into a tight, black cylinder of a dress that accentuated her pencil-thin figure. She cupped her hands over her breasts and then slid them sensuously down her body, striking various sexy poses in the mirror. Then, perching on the edge of the stool, she combed her long russet tresses, making sure every lock was in place, and as a final touch, she picked up Holly's bottle of Bleu-Blanc and administered a drop in each eye.

She admired the results. Her eyes sparkled with blue-whiteness, her lips were deep scarlet and moist, and her body was long and lean. She tossed her mane of hair and seductively eyed her reflection in the mirror, pretending the face looking back at her was one of her "chosen," as she liked to call them.

"Come into my parlor," she said to the face in the mirror, wetting her full lips with her tongue.

Alan was only the first; others would soon follow. Now that she'd discovered her true path, no one would stand in her way. She reached for a bottle on the vanity and shook out a 500-mg. Red Flyer and swallowed it dry.

In another room, a timer went off and she checked her watch. Her babies were waiting. It was feeding time.

She donned surgical gloves from a drawer in the vanity and hurried down the hall to the last door. Tonight, she had a special treat for them: ants. She stuck her gloved hand into a large jar and the ants swarmed over her hand. Then she stuck her insect-covered glove through a special trapdoor she had devised in the glass wall.

Her babies knew the trapdoor meant mealtime and they trampled on each other in their haste to reach her.

"Patience, my sweethearts," she cooed to them. "Mama has enough yummies for everyone."

Behind the glass, her babies milled in a profusion of color as brilliant as a polar dawn, but uncomparably more deadly.

It was a hot, sweltering night. During the day the temperature climbed past ninety and hovered there, even though it was after 10 P.M. The heat seemed to bring out the people, and La Brea Avenue was still crawling with cars, their exhaust perfuming the air and filtering the street lamps with a beige haze.

She peeled back the roof of her car, hoping for a cool breeze, but the hot night engulfed her like a vacuum. Her hair stuck to the sides of her face and forehead in damp ringlets, and she could almost feel her foundation sliding down her cheeks. Even so, she knew she looked good, and she wanted to be seen and envied for her beauty.

Up ahead, a long queue of people were waiting to get into one of the underground clubs that dotted the area. Black leather was the dress code of choice for both sexes, but many of the young women had shed their uniform leather jackets in the heat to reveal black bras or bustiers. Most of them were in their late teens or early twenties, and they had a freshness about them that even their heavy makeup couldn't conceal.

As she pulled alongside two pallid-faced young girls, their eyes ringed in black, she had a brilliant inspiration. She motioned them over to her car.

"Have you two girls ever thought about becoming models?" she asked when they leaned on the passenger door.

The two of them giggled and elbowed each other.

"You're putting us on," one finally said dryly. "Don'tcha think we're a little short to be models?"

"That's the old way of thinking," she told the two girls. "I represent the top modeling agency in Los Angeles, and I'm going to be starting a whole new division: shorter, more realistic models. Women want models they can identify with."

"Wow, gnarly," the other girl said.

"Here's my card." She took a business card from her purse and handed it to them.

"Call me, if you're interested," she said as she sped away.

She continued on aimlessly, stopping from time to time to repeat her spiel to other girls and to give them her business cards, until she realized she was in front of Holly's apartment building. She pulled around the corner into the alley and concealed her car in the shadows.

She knew Holly's apartment was on the second floor, its bedroom opening onto a narrow landing and fire escape. Removing her heels, she cautiously crept up the escape and onto the landing. The bedroom was dark except for the phosphorescent glow of the television set. From her vantage point, she could see Holly was in bed alone, watching television.

She didn't know how long she stood there peering in the window, five, maybe ten minutes, when Holly abruptly turned her head and caught sight of her white face through the window. Screaming, Holly leapt from the bed and ran into the next room.

Holly's actions made her laugh and she wanted to track her movements through the apartment, but she would almost bet that Holly was dialing 911. So instead she quietly stole back down the fire escape to her car, and as she started her engine, she heard the whine of a police siren in the distance. But she was long gone before they arrived.

Backstage was a mass of confusion. Workmen, putting final touches on the stage, pushed their way through the models, dressers tried to organize the clothes racks for the show, and photographers hung about snapping candid behind-the-scenes shots.

Even Joi Lin was there. Derian had suggested to the coordinator that Joi Lin work as a caller so she could see firsthand what things were like backstage at a fashion show.

Holly, still shaken from her encounter with the prowler, arrived early. She had spent the night in a hotel, but she was not able to sleep. There were dark circles under her eyes, and after she cleared a space in front of one of the makeup mirrors, she attempted to cover them. At one point she saw Rusty, but she didn't feel like wasting her breath on useless conversation.

One by one, the other models began to arrive, although by now none of them bothered to acknowledge her. Charis and Tiffany came in together, and although Charis glared in her direction, she didn't say anything.

"A prowler tried to break into my apartment last night," she said in a loud voice, but no one picked up the thread of conversation.

"I had to call the police." Still no one said anything, and embarrassed by the silence, she gave up. In another couple of days, she thought to herself, she would blow this town, and she had no intention of ever returning.

Earlier this morning, she picked up a message on her service from Derian, again wasting her time in an attempt to talk Holly into staying. She wondered if Derian ever gave up on anything.

A workman walked by with a two-by-four and knocked her makeup bag to the floor with a crash, scattering the contents.

"Can't you clods be more careful!" she yelled after him as she bent over to pick up her belongings.

To her surprise, she spotted her bottle of Bleu-Blanc, the one she thought one of the other models had stolen.

"Well, at least one thing is going right today," she muttered out loud, placing the bottle on the table for later use.

She donned her ensemble and was getting ready to line up when she remembered her eyedrops. She wondered if they were still there or if some model had filched them again. She hurried to the table and to her relief, the bottle was where she left it. She unscrewed the lid, put a drop in each eye, and started to screw the lid back on when she dropped it.

The pain was instantaneous, so excruciating that it felt as if someone had driven white-hot pokers into her eyes. Her pupils immediately constricted, and she fell to the floor, screaming in agony and tearing at her eyes. Her only thought was ridding herself of the terrible pain. Everyone in the room turned and saw Holly's facial muscles contort her trademark angelic face into a hideous mask. The torturous burning was so great that she ripped at her eyes with her nails, managing to completely pop one eyeball from its socket before her body began thrashing in violent convulsions. She drew her legs up to her chest, trying to ease the horrible cramps, but nothing helped.

Frozen in shock, no one moved as blood streamed down Holly's face. One of the dressers screamed in terror and that snapped Joi Lin into action. She knelt on the floor, shoved the handle of a makeup brush between Holly's teeth to keep her from swallowing her tongue, and laid Holly's head on her lap. Holly was beginning to foam at the mouth, and saliva bubbled over the handle of the brush mixing with the blood from her injured eyes.

"Hold her hands down, so she won't hurt herself any more!" Joi Lin shouted, taking charge of the situation. Two of the models quickly assisted her. "Call the paramedics!"

Holly's suffering was so great that she was unaware of the people around her. Firm hands held her down, but she couldn't feel them. Waves of fiery torment washed over her and she threw her head back, uttering a long keening cry that was to haunt those present for the rest of their lives. She was blind.

"Please, God, help me," she moaned as green mucus drooled from her mouth.

"Where are those paramedics? She's getting worse!" Joi Lin shouted, holding Holly's thrashing body in her arms.

"They're on their way," somebody yelled.

"Hold on, Holly, hold on," Joi Lin whispered urgently, holding Holly close to her body. "Help's coming!"

Through the red mist, Holly prayed for God to ease her pain. She promised never to say anything spiteful again; to help anyone who needed help; even to give up the only dream she'd ever had—her modeling. She promised Him her life and He finally listened.

With one tremendous convulsion, her back arched and she fell limp against Joi Lin. Her convulsions stopped and the pain stopped.

Holly was dead.

CHAPTER
9

Four other homicides had occurred and were solved; but during that time Hollis had to push the Anderson case to the back burner. No new evidence had emerged from the interviews with the women on Anderson's sex tapes, and if Hollis hadn't gotten a break in the case, he would have had to drop it completely, despite Joi Lin.

But Holly Woodward's death pushed the Anderson case to the forefront again, and Hollis could now redirect his energies to solving Anderson's murder. In fact, some progress had been made. Kathy gave him her completed list with the names and addresses of the recipients of the special promo Hermès scarf, and to his surprise, one of the models, named Charis, was living right here in L.A. and was represented by DDL. But before he could contact her, the call came in about the death of a model at a fashion show. Upon his arrival at the scene, he discovered not only Joi Lin, but also Charis, the very model he was planning on questioning.

It had taken him two days since Holly Woodward's death to wade through all the reports and evidence. From what he gathered through the initial coroner's observations and brief interviews of the witnesses, the eyedrops that the victim had used may have caused her death. He had given the bottle to forensics for analysis and just this afternoon they gave him a startling report. There was a link between Anderson's and Holly's deaths. Both were killed by the same toxin. Now that Holly's death had been ruled a homicide, he could hardly wait to discuss the findings with Joi Lin.

He had been impressed with her calm, controlled behavior in the room of hysterical women when he questioned her about Holly's death at the fashion show. She told him the way she handled the situation, succinctly apprising him of the circumstances, while keeping a firm grip on her own emotions. Her actions and observations made his job easier, and his first piece of business was to schedule in-depth interviews with everyone who was at the fashion show. As a matter of fact, this afternoon he was meeting with the models, including Charis, whom he was very eager to talk to.

One of the first models to show up was Tiffany. She paused in the doorway of the squad room, then spotting Hollis, she walked toward his desk, hips swiveling like they were double-jointed. Hollis, who was reviewing some reports, looked up when the entire room went silent. Every male eye was focused on Tiffany. When she got to Hollis's desk, she paused in front of it.

"I'm Tiffany," she said breathlessly. "You wanted to talk to me?"

Before he could answer, Tongue Tartella rushed over with a chair. "Here's a chair for you. Can I get you some coffee?" he asked, straightening his tie. "By the way, I'm Joseph Tartella."

"Oh," Tiffany said, her china-blue eyes never leaving his. "I'm Tiffany. And yes, I'd love a little coffee, if it isn't any trouble."

"I'll take one, too, Joseph," Hollis quipped sweetly as Tartella turned to hurry to the coffee machine. Tartella turned and gave Hollis a dirty look when he heard the syrupy inflection in Hollis's voice.

Hollis's businesslike demeanor returned when he began his interview with Tiffany. From some of his brief interviews at the show he learned that Holly had not been well liked and he asked Tiffany if she agreed.

"I'll say," Tiffany sniffed.

"And why was that?" Hollis prodded.

"She blew into town with an ego as big as the state of California. She was always bragging about Paris! For crying out loud, half the models at DDL have worked Europe," Tiffany explained.

"I understand there was no love lost between you and Holly?" He asked the question, but he already knew the answer. He'd heard rumors that the two had words on several occasions, but he wanted to hear it firsthand from Tiffany.

"You got that right. She was a real operator. She didn't care how she got a booking or who she had to step on to get what she wanted," Tiffany said. "That bitch cost me a lot of money, and I, for one, was counting the days until she left."

"She was leaving L.A.?" Hollis asked. He was surprised, this was the first he'd heard about Holly's leaving.

"Yes, that was the rumor. She just came into town, picked up the choicest bookings, and then she was planning on leaving again."

Tartella brought over two cups of coffee and set them down on the desk.

"Thanks, Joseph," Tiffany said, giving him a coquettish smile. Joseph was pretty cute; she wondered how he was in bed.

"No problem," the Tongue said, sitting down on the edge of Hollis's desk. "Let me know if I can get you anything else." He emphasized "anything." Then he gave Tiffany his best Don Johnson look and swaggered off, macho style.

"When was she planning on leaving?" Hollis continued, picking up his pencil.

"Well, I think she was originally leaving in a couple of weeks," Tiffany explained, pulling her eyes away from

Tartella's tight buns. "But she may have decided to leave sooner."

"Sooner? Why was that?"

"I don't know for sure, but I know from some of the other models that she thought she was being followed. And that day at the show, she looked awful, like she hadn't slept. She was yakking about a prowler and having to call the police or something."

"She called the police?" If Holly did, there would be a record of it and he made a note to check the police logs.

"That's what she said," Tiffany answered.

Hollis asked her to contact him if she thought of anything else that might be helpful and she agreed. As Tiffany stood up and weaved her way toward the door, Hollis noted that Tongue Tartella was waiting to hold the door open for her.

He shook his head. *Young love*, he thought to himself dryly. *Or at least young lust.*

Charis was one of the last models to come in to see Hollis that day and he was eagerly anticipating questioning her. So far, Charis was one of his strongest links to both murders. He had learned that she and Holly had disagreements on several occasions and the Hermès scarf found in Anderson's bedroom had a good chance of belonging to Charis.

As she sat down at his desk, Hollis observed that she was a beautiful woman, though she lacked the fresh confidence of youth and her eyes had the glaze of too much experience. Her eyes never quite met his, and she surveyed the squad room apprehensively, twisting the handle on her shoulder bag. When she spoke, she had a way of beginning a thought with confidence but ending it by hanging her head apologetically.

"What was your relationship with Holly Woodward?" Hollis asked.

"She and I worked together. That is, we were with the same agency."

"Were you friends?" He'd heard of the disagreements between the two, but he wanted to hear Charis's explanation.

Charis hesitated before she answered and Hollis noted that her eyes seemed to dart around the squad room, as if looking for an escape route. "No," she answered, measuring her words.

"But you must have known each other. Didn't your paths cross on bookings?" Hollis probed.

Charis started to shake her head. Then she changed her mind and the words seemed to tumble out. "I'll say our paths crossed. She was stealing my bookings left and right. She got what she deserved, but I didn't have anything to do with it."

"Stealing your bookings? What do you mean?"

"Lieutenant, as soon as she waltzed into town, I started getting replaced by her on all my regular bookings," she explained bitterly. "And she loved it. She went out of her way to rub it in.

"I tried to be friendly, so did some of the other models, but she wasn't interested. She was greedy and she had a real attitude. You know, I remember in '69, when I just started hitting my stride, there was this other model," Charis mused, a vacant look coming over her face. "Her name was . . ." Charis searched her memory for the name. " . . . Colleen. Anyway, this model was a real snake, always after everyone's bookings and she'd rip you to shreds in the process. One time . . ."

She was drifting and Hollis cut her off before she could continue. "I understand the two of you had an argument at the fashion show at Spheres," he said, leading her back. "A serious blowup. It sounds to me like she pushed you over the edge and you retaliated by killing her."

"No!" Charis exclaimed vehemently, tears filling her eyes. "Look, modeling is my life. You can't imagine what it's like to see younger, prettier versions of yourself come onto the modeling scene; to look in the mirror each day and count the new lines; or to feel eighteen in your heart and look forty in the mirror. I know that my clients are watching me age before their eyes and the other models are whispering behind my back, but I have no place to go. My only experience is modeling." Her voice broke and she struggled to regain her composure.

Hollis pitied her, but he also knew he had to press while she was vulnerable. "Why were you following her?"

"I wasn't! The first I heard about it was at the fashion show, and I just thought she was making it up for the attention," Charis said, dabbing at her eyes.

"Did you see anyone tampering with her makeup before the show?"

"No one. Everyone was too busy getting ready themselves. Besides, she was like the plague. No one wanted anything to do with her."

"You did a modeling job for Hermès about twenty years ago, right?" Hollis asked, changing the subject.

Charis frowned for a moment trying to recall, then she remembered that frowning caused more wrinkles, and she quickly arranged her features into a neutral expression. "Yes, that's right. It was a print job, a promotional in Paris," she said slowly. "I remember because they changed their schedule to accommodate mine. Everyone wanted to book me then."

"I understand they gave all the models a commemorative scarf," Hollis said conversationally, while watching her reactions closely. "You still have yours?"

"Of course," Charis replied without hesitation. "It's a collector's item. They only made a few."

"You do?" Hollis asked, surprised. He had been so sure the scarf from Anderson's apartment belonged to Charis.

Charis nodded. "Why do you ask?"

"It has to do with an ongoing investigation," Hollis answered vaguely. "Do you remember the three other models who were booked with you?"

"No, it was twenty years ago. I haven't the faintest idea who else did the booking with me," Charis said. "Sorry."

"That's all right. I've no more questions for you right now, but if you don't mind, I'd like to borrow your scarf.

I'll have one of my men follow you home and pick it up."

"Sure," Charis said with a shrug.

"Thanks for stopping by," Hollis said, indicating the interview was over.

Another day passed before Hollis had an opportunity to question Derian. When he entered DDL, he caught sight of Joi Lin sitting at her desk and their eyes met. He nodded to her with feigned casualness as Betsy hurried to greet him and to usher him into Derian's office.

Derian Delorian was every bit as striking as he remembered. Her black outfit looked as if it cost a month's salary, and a faintly familiar fragrance floated in the air. Any of the men in his division would have given their paid holidays for an opportunity to be in the same room as the illustrious Ms. Delorian, but Hollis's thoughts were on Joi Lin. The sparkle in her eyes when she saw him and the dimples in her smile were mesmerizing. Reluctantly, he pulled himself away from his thoughts of Joi Lin to address Derian.

"Ms. Delorian," he said bluntly, "you're our number-one suspect. You have the strongest motive to have murdered both Alan Ainsley Anderson and Holly Woodward. Anderson stole your account lists, opened a competing agency, and was on the verge of merging with another modeling agency. The merger would have made his agency the biggest in L.A.

"Holly Woodward had been making big money for DDL and with her departure, your revenues would have taken a nosedive. It's common knowledge that you repeatedly tried to convince her to stay and when she refused, you murdered her."

Derian's face blanched. "That's not true," she protested vehemently, rising to her feet, then sitting back down. "I had nothing to do with Alan's death, and what good would it do to murder Holly? Either way, I still lost her revenue."

"In my book, revenge is a strong reason. Their deaths weren't pretty," he said, hammering at her. He was positive that she was hiding something. "The pain must have been indescribable. The murderer put a substance in Holly's eyedrops so excruciatingly potent that she almost ripped her eyes out to get rid of the pain."

Derian's face remained impassive and she swallowed hard, but she was silent.

"And Anderson," he continued relentlessly, "his body was so twisted by the convulsions that the coroner had to hack his limbs off to fit him in his coffin."

Derian shuddered and her eyes pooled with tears. For a moment Hollis thought she was going to break down, but then she summoned an inner strength and met his gaze head on.

"I had nothing to do with those murders," she said coldly, "and unless you're arresting me, we have nothing more to discuss."

"I'm not arresting you yet," he told her, emphasizing the word "yet." "But I'm going to be on you like white on rice, and if you're hiding anything, I'm going to find it."

Hollis could see over the top of her desk into her lap, where she clenched and unclenched her fists.

"That's all for now," Hollis finished. He stood and made his way to the door. "Have a nice day, Ms. Delorian."

Hollis assigned Kathy to follow up on Holly's murder, while he set to work tracking down the other three models booked for the Hermès shoot. Charis had given her scarf to one of his men and now he was able to compare it with the piece of silk taken from Anderson's apartment. The patterns were identical. Now he just had to find the owners of those three remaining scarves. Twenty years was a long span of time and his first attempt was to contact the agencies representing the women.

Of the three women, two were represented by an agency in Paris and the third by a different agency, in Munich, that was no longer in business. He started with the Paris agency. It took several attempts to contact it because of the time difference. They put him in touch with the now

semiretired owner of the agency. With the help of his
old files, he recalled the two models. One, he said, had
married a rich American businessman and had moved to
the United States. He remembered her married name, he
said, because it was the same as the greatest of all actors,
Maurice Chevalier. But he couldn't remember the exact
name of the city, although he knew it was the same as
the title of an old Clark Gable movie. Hollis hadn't the
faintest idea what city the old agency owner was thinking
of, but he gave it his best shot: Dallas, Chicago, New
York, he even threw in Atlanta. Between the agency
owner's typical French attitude and his failing memory,
Hollis felt like he was auditioning for a television game
show instead of conducting a murder investigation. None
of his answers was right.

The second model was easier for the owner to recollect.
She died of a drug overdose eighteen years before, he told
Hollis. On a chance Hollis asked him if he'd heard of
the third model, who hadn't been registered with the old
man's agency but the old man hadn't.

Hollis hung up the telephone. The field of suspects
was narrowing. He called the American Academy of
Motion Picture Arts and Sciences' Research Department
and requested a list of Clark Gable's films. At that
moment, Kathy stopped by with an updated report on
the toxin.

"Have a look at this, Lieutenant," she said excitedly,
waving the report.

Hollis grabbed the paper and skimmed it, his amazement growing as he read.

"My God," he said over and over. "This is the strangest
murder case I've ever had."

"There is a definite connection between your brother's
murder and Holly Woodward's murder," Hollis explained
to Joi Lin.

It was three days after Holly's murder and they were
sitting in Angel City on Melrose. Hollis was eating a goat
cheese designer pizza and Joi Lin was sipping coffee.

If he were being totally honest with himself, he knew this meeting wasn't really necessary, because he could have accomplished the same results with a telephone call. The truth was, he wanted to see Joi Lin. Though it was uncomfortable, he found it exciting to think about another woman, the first since Gina's death. The more he tried to convince himself she was only a case contact, the more he wanted to see her. Once when their fingers accidentally brushed, he felt as if an electric current was jolting his body.

"We've been able to isolate the toxin that killed your brother, and it's the same one we found in Holly's body," he continued, taking a mouthful of pizza and washing it down with coffee.

"Oh my God," Joi Lin breathed, resting her forehead on her open palm.

"It was very difficult to isolate. Our lab uses an instrument called a gas chromatograph and it's been a long process of elimination. They've had to run thousands of tests, and cross-reference Alan's and Holly's symptoms with those of various toxins.

"They think it's a batrachotoxin. It doesn't just block the pathway to a nerve, it destroys it by depolarizing the nerve pathways at the synapse."

"Wait a minute. You're losing me," Joi Lin said. "Explain in terms I can understand, what is it?"

"This is the kicker. It's one of the most lethal toxins known to man!" Hollis said excitedly. "It's the same thing the Indians of South America use on their poisonous darts! An ounce of this stuff is enough to kill two point five million people!"

"Oh, please." Joi Lin took another gulp of coffee. "You're not saying some crazy Indian from South America is running around murdering people?"

"Of course not. It could be a bacteria of some kind, or even a type of venom, but this certainly narrows the field. We're checking pharmacies, labs, our black market sources. Any place where the toxin could be obtained here in the States."

"How was the toxin administered to Holly, anyway?" Joi Lin asked. "And please don't tell me it was on edible underwear again."

That brought a small smile to Hollis's lips. "No. This time it was in some eyedrops she used."

"What!" Joi Lin exclaimed, stunned by the news. "I can't believe it! Holly told me she suspected that one of the other models stole her eyedrops! If that *is* the case, it would mean the murderer was one of the models who was at the fashion show!

"But that's impossible. I know those women, none of them could possibly be the murderer," she concluded emphatically, dismissing the whole idea as preposterous.

"Look, Joi Lin, Holly wasn't exactly winning popularity contests," Hollis reminded her. "From what I've learned, Holly was lucky the other models didn't band together and take out a contract on her."

"You know," she said, shaking her head, "if the murderer had waited just a while longer, Holly would have been gone. She told me she was leaving soon to return to Paris. She was even more determined to go when she believed she was being followed. If the murderer had known that, perhaps Holly wouldn't have been killed."

Hollis sat back and looked at Joi Lin. He could almost see the wheels of her mind turning as she excitedly connected one point to another. She reminded him of a rookie cop in her enthusiasm.

"That's presuming Holly was killed because she was taking another model's bookings. We don't know that for sure," Hollis reminded her. "There could have been another motive that we don't as yet know."

"Well, there's the jealous wife theory," Joi Lin said thoughtfully. "The rumor around DDL was that Holly was having an affair with Sid Roque."

"What!" Hollis exclaimed. "Why didn't you tell me that before?"

"Because I just remembered. Besides, from what I've seen of Sid Roque's behavior at the Spheres fashion show, he's on the make for anything in a skirt. His wife would have had to kill off half the women in L.A."

"Is that so," Hollis said thoughtfully. This was a new angle to the case. Maybe Joi Lin's employment at DDL was paying off. It would certainly bear looking into and he made a mental note to pay Sid and Ellysa Roque another visit.

"I'll let you know immediately if I learn anything else helpful. Maybe I can find out more about Holly and Sid Roque from some of the other models."

"You just let me handle the investigations, and you do your job," he told her sternly. He didn't want her asking the wrong person the wrong question and jeopardizing her safety or his investigation.

"What do you mean? I thought I was your partner!" Joi Lin protested.

"That was before Holly Woodward's murder," he said. "My instincts are telling me that DDL is involved in these murders. And though Derian Delorian has an alibi for Alan's murder, she still might be tied into the two murders in some way."

"But, Frank—"

"I'm not asking, I'm telling you," Hollis said firmly, signaling the waitress for the check.

"But if DDL is involved and Derian is a suspect, you could use someone on the inside," Joi Lin insisted.

"Look, don't forget, one of the victims was your brother," he reminded her.

Joi Lin thought about what he had said and she knew he was right, but she couldn't let it go. One victim was her brother. She said nothing, but in her mind she vowed to continue her investigation.

The waitress brought their check and both of them made a grab for it. As they did, their fingers touched again and this time both of them felt the jolt of electricity. Joi Lin quickly pulled her hand away and clasped it tightly in her lap.

Hollis's mouth went dry. When he tried to swallow, it was as if he had a mouthful of cotton, but he made up his mind that it was time.

"You know, I make what is perhaps the best pasta primavera in all of Los Angeles," he said, trying to sound casual. Instead, he thought he sounded like a hick. "I thought maybe you'd like to have dinner with me tomorrow night."

Joi Lin looked up in surprise. "Is it business or pleasure?" she asked cautiously and held her breath, hoping he'd say the latter.

Hollis reddened, but he answered without hesitation. "It's not business, Joi Lin." He looked her directly in the eyes. "It would be my pleasure."

Hollis went over the conversation he had with Joi Lin yesterday as he drove to the Roques' home in Bel Air. The rumor about Sid Roque's alleged affair with Holly Woodward put a whole new slant on his investigation. Perhaps Roque tried to break things off with Holly and she threatened to tell the wife; or maybe Ellysa Roque found out about the affair and killed Holly. Whatever the reason, he formulated questions in his mind that would cover every angle.

Hollis stopped his car in front of the high wrought-iron gates that guarded the entrance to the Roque estate. Earlier that day he had notified Sid Roque that he would be coming by, so when he pressed the intercom, Sid himself answered and a moment later the huge gates slowly swung outward, admitting Hollis. A housekeeper led Hollis to where Sid Roque was waiting in the library.

It was an impressive room with tall book-lined walls on three sides. A fourth wall, the backdrop for Sid's desk, was floor-to-ceiling windows that revealed a panoramic view of the grounds.

"Lieutenant Hollis, how are you?" Sid boomed, using his best good-ole-boy tone.

He stood up from his desk and held his hand out, letting Hollis walk the length of the library to reach him. It was a calculated effort to impress upon Hollis the magnitude of his wealth and at the same time subtly attempt to put Hollis on notice that he, Sid Roque, was very important and not someone who had time to waste. However, that in itself was a wasted effort. Hollis had been around the block too many times to be impressed by a few bucks and an overinflated ego.

"More questions about Anderson's death?" Sid asked before Hollis could disclose the reason for this interview.

"No, Mr. Roque, actually I'm here in connection with another case," Hollis said brusquely. He sat down in an overstuffed wing-backed chair and fixed Sid with a direct appraising gaze. "Holly Woodward's murder."

Sid paled but managed to keep his voice nonchalant. "Isn't she that model who was killed recently?" He felt a warm line of sweat soak through his Sea Island cotton shirt and resisted an impulse to mop his forehead. How had the police connected him with Holly Woodward? He'd been very discreet in his liaison with her.

Hollis, who missed nothing, noted beads of perspiration edging Sid's hairline and the way he involuntarily clenched his jaw. But even without these obvious signs, Hollis knew Sid was lying about knowing Holly. It was a sixth sense that all cops acquired. His instructor at the police academy used to say a good cop could detect a lie in one sentence. Hollis knew at a glance.

"I understand you were friends," he said, emphasizing the word "friends."

"Well, I did meet her once at my wife's fashion show," Sid admitted, squirming uncomfortably under Hollis's piercing gaze and racking his memory in an effort to discover the origin of Hollis's information.

"My sources tell me that you and Holly were having an affair—" Hollis began.

"That's not true!" Sid shouted, jumping to his feet. "I barely met the girl, and I won't stand for these accusations!"

Sid was shaken. Wide bands of sweat ringed his underarms and perspiration trickled down his temples.

"Sit down," Hollis said firmly. "You were having an affair with her, she threatened to tell your wife and to destroy your marriage, so you killed her!"

Sid's bravado crumbled and he slumped in the chair. All he could see was Ellysa's face. Since the day Ellysa told him about her pregnancy, their marriage had undergone gradual changes. There had been a renewal of their commitment to each other and an infusion of romance. But more important, an intimacy was starting to develop between them that had not been in their relationship for years. He was eagerly looking forward to the birth of his daughter, and he was convinced that Ellysa believed him when he told her that there was nothing between him and Holly. But now with just a few words from this detective, he could lose it all.

"Okay, okay, I did make it with her, but only once. It wasn't what you'd call a love affair. I was horny and she wanted to get laid. That's all it was for both of us!" he blurted out. He had to make sure Hollis understood that he had nothing to do with Holly's death. "We were just diversions for each other. My God, she was going back to Paris in a few days!"

"When was the last time you saw her?" Hollis asked, knowing Sid was telling the truth. In actuality, he never believed Sid was the murderer, but he needed to establish Holly's actions during her stay in L.A.

"I ran into her in Beverly Hills a few days ago and we had a drink together, but that's all, I swear!" Sid said earnestly. He knew he was babbling, but he had to be sure Hollis believed him. "Sure she wanted to hop into the sack again, but I said no."

"What about Victoria del Rio?" Hollis asked. He was a little tired of Sid's "innocent" act. "Did you tell her no, too?"

Sid went white and stammered, "I—I— How did you know about her? That was a mistake on my part. She was more demanding than Ellysa. I felt like I had a second wife! I broke that off weeks ago!" He explained, "Look, it's a curse I have. Women can't seem to get enough of me."

Hollis looked at the paunchy, balding, middle-aged man sitting before him and tried to maintain a poker face.

"Listen, Lieutenant Hollis," Sid pleaded, "my wife and I are going to have a baby soon and we're working on our problems. I don't want anything to jeopardize that."

"Congratulations, Mr. Roque," Hollis said dryly. *What a change*, he thought to himself, *a "born-again" husband*. Then another thought occurred to him. "What about Mrs. Roque? Did she know you and Holly had an affair?"

"Yes, I mean no," Sid stammered. He hoped Hollis didn't suspect Ellysa. "She saw Holly and I having a drink together once, but no, she didn't know that we'd slept together. And it wasn't an affair. We were together only once."

At that moment Ellysa entered the room. In the last few weeks, her pregnancy had blossomed so much that even loose clothes could no longer conceal her condition, and she didn't so much walk as list from side to side.

"Yoo-hoo," she called. "Consuela said we had company." When she saw Hollis, she held her hand out coolly. "Hello, Lieutenant Hollis."

"Hello, Mrs. Roque. It's nice to see you again. I had a few questions to ask you and Mr. Roque," Hollis said politely. "I'm finished with Mr. Roque and I'd like to speak with you for a few minutes."

"Of course." Ellysa's reluctance to endure Hollis's presence was evident in her voice. She slowly lowered herself into a chair.

"May I get you some herb tea, dear?" Sid asked solicitously. "What about you, Lieutenant?"

"No, thanks," Hollis answered.

"I'd love some, darling," Ellysa responded sweetly with a smile that faded as Sid left the room and she turned to Hollis.

"Now, what can I do for you?" she asked condescendingly.

Sid absently listened to the drone of their voices as he walked down the hallway to the kitchen. He wondered if Ellysa believed him when he denied having any involvement with Holly. For a brief moment he wondered if Ellysa could have had anything to do with Holly's murder, but he immediately dismissed the idea. Ellysa might have a nasty temper, but she wasn't a murderer. He was sure of that.

"I understand Holly Woodward worked for you on several occasions," Hollis said to Ellysa.

"Yes, she was booked for our fashion extravaganza and she also did some print jobs for us," Ellysa explained.

"Did she ever talk to you about any of her friends?" Hollis asked.

"*I* didn't talk to her at all. She was an employee." Ellysa straightened in the chair with a haughty attitude.

"Did you ever see her with any men? Any men you knew?" Hollis asked casually.

His implication wasn't lost on Ellysa. She knew exactly what he was getting at. "If you mean, did I know my husband was seeing her? Then the answer is yes. I knew and I also know it was a one-night stand, not a love affair," she said, adopting a cavalier attitude. "They all stray once, Lieutenant. You're a man, you should know that."

Inside she was steaming. How dare this common cop delve into the privacy of her life! She wasn't about to let him know he was upsetting her.

Hollis listened to her words and thought of his own marriage. In all of those ten years he had never once looked at another woman, nor had his own father.

He saw her chin quiver, and he pitied her because all her wealth and social airs hadn't brought her fidelity or happiness. But he also had to know the truth.

"So you didn't care that your husband was making love to a beautiful, young model, while you were paying her bills?" he asked, baiting her.

"Of course I cared!" she cried out in anger. "But I didn't kill her! Things are different now!"

She took several deep breaths and fought to control her emotions. "Look, Lieutenant," she said plaintively, dropping all pretenses. "I know Sid slept with her, even though he won't admit it to me. There have been others, too. A wife knows these things—another woman's fragrance, a sock wrong side out, an intimate gesture between two people. But I also knew when it was over."

She took another deep breath and continued, "More than anything in this world, I want my marriage to work. We're giving it another try and this time I know it will.

"Please, you have to believe me. I had nothing to do with Holly Woodward's murder and neither did Sid. He's a good man, and he's only human, but I love him," she implored. "Sid thinks I believe that he and Holly didn't sleep together, and you can't tell him otherwise. Lieutenant, please, I'm begging you, don't rip this marriage apart."

She stopped and waited anxiously for Hollis's reply.

Hollis shrugged his shoulders. He knew the truth when he heard it or maybe he was getting soft in his old age. Ten years ago, he would have gone for her jugular; now all he wanted was the real killer. He felt tired and he just wanted to go and leave them with their secrets.

"Ellysa, dear, I have your tea," Sid called, walking into the room carrying a tray.

Ellysa looked quickly at Hollis and silently formed the word "please" with her lips.

"I have to go now," Hollis said, standing. "I'd like you to make yourselves available in case I have further questions. I'll find my way out. Good-bye."

Ellysa took a leisurely stroll through Spheres to check merchandise and displays. She paused in front of a glass case displaying one-of-a-kind African jewelry made from seed pods and beads. Absentmindedly she ran her finger across the shelves, checking for dust as she thought about Lieutenant Hollis's visit. She felt a wave of relief wash over her that her marriage had withstood another test. It was funny how her priorities were changing. Six months ago, she would have been mortified that her Beverly Hills friends would find out about Sid's fling and Hollis's visit to the house. Now it really didn't matter to her. Sid, her marriage, and their soon-to-be-born daughter had become priorities in her life. The energies she had used on Spheres, she now devoted to her marriage.

As it was, even her interest in her precious Spheres was waning. It had been one o'clock in the afternoon today before she came to the store. She knew she should be at the store every morning when it opened, but she just didn't care. The employees sensed it, too. A month ago, she would have never found a trace of dust anywhere, but now, a casual inspection turned up dust, messy displays, and poor merchandising. She didn't care and neither did they. But she couldn't help herself.

What interested her now was Sid and the upcoming birth of their daughter, not the newest trends from Europe or the latest gossip in Beverly Hills. Still, something had to be done. She couldn't just let Spheres fall apart. Suddenly she had an inspiration and she hurried to her secretary's desk.

"Susan, find Lucille Ritter and tell her I'd like to see her immediately."

Three minutes later she heard a tentative knock on the door.

"Come in," Ellysa said briskly.

"You wanted to see me?" Mrs. Ritter asked, peeking around the door. She couldn't imagine what Mrs. Roque wanted, but being summoned to the owner's office was never a good sign.

"Yes, come in. Sit down, Lucille. I want to talk to you about your future at Spheres."

Good Lord, she's firing me! Mrs. Ritter thought, her bad eye starting to spasm.

"What about my future?" Mrs. Ritter asked timorously.

"I've come to a decision," Ellysa said, getting right to the point. "With the upcoming birth of my child, I'm not going to be able to devote the time needed to run Spheres, so for the time being, I'm going to put you in charge. You've been doing a good job handling the fashion end of things and I think you will do just fine handling the managerial aspects, too."

Mrs. Ritter was speechless. She thought she was going to be fired and instead she was being promoted to boss!

Ellysa waited for a response from Lucille, and when it wasn't forthcoming, she thought that perhaps Lucille didn't feel qualified. Maybe she had overestimated Lucille's talents.

"Look, if you don't feel you can handle the responsibilities, please tell me. I was thinking that Mr. Paul would also be a possibility."

Mr. Paul! Mrs. Ritter almost choked. She hated that fat fag! Firing him would be her first pleasant task as manager.

"Oh, no, Mrs. Roque," she said quickly, a smile creasing her usually dour face. "I was just momentarily overwhelmed by your generous offer. I'm perfect for Spheres—that is until you feel up to returning."

In her mind Mrs. Ritter anticipated the look of shock on Mr. Paul's face when she handed him his walking papers and her smile became even broader.

As Derian returned from lunch, Betsy greeted her with problems concerning Spheres. Mrs. Ritter had just canceled a big print booking the day before it was to shoot. The models had been booked for weeks; some had even been taken off other bookings to accommodate the Spheres account. Derian was furious. Cancellation of the job would cost her models and DDL revenue that would be irreplaceable at such a late date. Under the terms of the contract, Spheres was obligated to pay the agency a cancellation fee and she called Joi Lin and directed her to call the boutique's accounting department immediately and to inform them that they would be required to pay the fee.

Returning to her office, Joi Lin placed the call but to no avail. Getting up from her chair, she crossed the reception area and entered her boss's domain.

"Derian, I spoke to Spheres's head accountant, but he refuses to pay our cancellation fee according to Mrs. Ritter's instructions," Joi Lin reported.

"He did?" Derian said, immediately picking up the telephone and dialing. "We'll see about that.

"Mrs. Ritter please. Derian Delorian calling."

Derian turned on her speaker phone, so that Joi Lin could listen to both sides of the conversation.

"This is Mrs. Ritter."

"Lucille, this is Derian Delorian. How are you?" Derian kept her tone cordial, but businesslike.

"Crazed, dear, crazed. I never realized what was involved, running a business. I haven't had a moment to myself. Everyone wants my attention and there's always a crisis. Why just this morning I got a call that our biggest sportswear line is going Chapter Eleven! Do you know what that means? We're into them for two hundred thousand dollars and we may not get our merchandise . . ." She rambled on, sometimes sounding on the verge of incoherence.

"Lucille, calm down," Derian said soothingly. "I'm sure everything will work out. I'm sure you'll get your merchandise. In the meantime, I want to talk to you about the catalogue."

"Catalogue!" Mrs. Ritter practically shouted. "Derian, I can't even think about the catalogue when I have thousands of dollars slipping through my fingers. What will I tell Mrs. Roque?"

"But, Lucille," Derian patiently explained, "you need the catalogue to stimulate business. That catalogue will draw your customers. It's as basic a marketing principle as supply and demand. You have to stimulate demand to increase business."

"I can't think about this now," Mrs. Ritter said, and Derian could hear the distraction in her voice.

"Lucille, listen to me," she said, trying another tact, "if you cancel the shoot at this short notice, the agency is unable to rebook the models on other jobs. You booked these women weeks ago. At your insistence, I took some of the models off other accounts to accommodate you."

"I can't help that now," Mrs. Ritter insisted.

Derian sighed. "Lucille, I'm sorry, but the agency policy is to charge you a cancellation fee that is half of the booking fee. If you cancel this job, you'll end up paying

half as much as you would for the catalogue and have
nothing to show for it."

In reality Derian knew that if push came to shove, she
probably wouldn't hold Spheres to DDL's policy, based
on the volume of past bookings and in anticipation of
future ones. But she was banking on her ability to convince Lucille that it was in Spheres's best interest to go
ahead with this job.

"I'm sorry, I just can't think. If it's not one thing, then
it's another!" Mrs. Ritter wailed.

Derian could see trying to save the booking was hope-
less; Lucille was much too fragmented. She hung up.

"She sounded like she was on the verge of a nervous
breakdown," Joi Lin said sympathetically. "You did your
best, Derian."

"Yes, but it wasn't good enough." Derian frowned,
thinking about the lost revenue. She had to think of something to build up the agency coffers. She seemed distracted
and didn't notice when Joi Lin left her office.

Joi Lin quietly walked back to her office. Even though
she knew Derian was a potential suspect in Alan's and
Holly's murders, she couldn't help but feel sorry for her.

As she got to her door, she stopped short. Rusty was in
her office, his back to the door, going through her filing
cabinets. For a moment she didn't know what to do. Then
he must have sensed her presence, for he whirled with
a start.

"I didn't hear you," he said.

"Sorry, I didn't mean to startle you," Joi Lin replied,
trying to see what he was looking at. "Was there something I could help you find?"

"Not really," he said, closing the file. "I was just going
through the account lists. I figure that the more I know
about the agency, the better I'll be able to help Derian."

He walked to the doorway where Joi Lin was standing,
took her hand, and began to stroke it. "You know, Joi
Lin," he said, changing the subject with a mock leer,
"you've been looking very delicious lately. What do you
say we go out to dinner tonight?"

Joi Lin started laughing and pulled her hand away. "Get a life, Rusty. Go practice on one of the models!"

Rusty gave her an exaggerated hurt look and walked out of her office.

Joi Lin already had a dinner date that evening—with Frank Hollis. She tried to convince herself he just wanted to be friends, but she couldn't keep the eager anticipation of the evening out of her mind. It took her half an hour to make up her mind about what to wear, but finally she decided upon a red wool blazer over a slimming black catsuit. She had unintentionally been losing weight and to her happy surprise, she'd dropped a whole dress size. On impulse, she'd bought the catsuit, after she'd seen them on many of the models, but she hadn't had the nerve to wear it until tonight.

Using the techniques she'd learned from Skeeter, she carefully applied her makeup and twisted her hair up into a casual knot and surveyed the results in her mirror. She had to admit she'd never looked better as she picked up her car keys and left the house.

Twenty minutes later she arrived at Frank's house on a quiet little tree-lined street in Westwood. When he answered the doorbell, Joi Lin entered the comfortable living room that still had remnants of a woman's touch.

"I haven't gotten around to changing much since the accident," Frank explained as he ushered her into the dining room. "In the beginning it was comforting to leave things the way they were, and in the last year I haven't had the time."

As Joi Lin sat at the table, she was amused by Frank's culinary skills or lack of. He prepared dinner in true bachelor style. He got takeout: pasta primavera and Caesar salads from Angeli in West Los Angeles, and Ben and Jerry's ice cream from the grocery store. He held a wineglass and a bottle of Chianti and Joi Lin noticed the bottle shake a bit as he poured her wine. It was comforting to know she wasn't the only nervous person in the room.

The wine relaxed them, and before long they were joking with each other like old friends while they ate. As the evening progressed, their mutual attraction increased. Frank built a fire in his not-used-in-years fireplace, but forgot to open the flue and the room began to fill with smoke before they could find the lever to open it. They collapsed against each other in front of the fireplace, laughing like teenagers, and suddenly they were kissing. It was such a natural progression of events that it didn't, yet did, come as a surprise to either of them. Their attraction toward each other was born out of mutual respect, honesty, and the rapport that had developed between them in the past weeks since their first meeting. Frank had always admired Joi Lin's quick mind and forthright opinions, and the more he got to know her, the more beautiful she was to him. Joi Lin discovered Frank had a sensitive side and was someone who listened to her opinions and encouraged her strength and individuality without feeling threatened.

As he slowly unzipped her catsuit, she felt he had the gentlest hands and softest lips she could ever imagine. His palms were rough, but his fingers sensuous. And as her own hands explored his body, she discovered that as rough as his palms were, the rest of his body was as smooth as velvet. He was passionate, but he treated her like a delicate flower, nurturing, encouraging her every movement. As their touches evolved from tentative to passionate to urgent, Frank rolled her over on top of him, engulfing her in his arms. Joi Lin drew him deep into her, while they murmured the tender words of passion they had been holding back from each other.

In the distance, the wail of a siren screamed and nearby a dog barked, but the lovers were as oblivious to the sounds as if they were on a deserted island.

In another part of the city, a stray cat, backlit by the dim light of a crescent moon, howled in hunger. Nearby in her darkened bedroom, the killer paced in frustration, the cat's cries grating on her taut nerves.

She tried to block out the sound with her thoughts. *She* had done the agency a service by killing Holly. She knew in reality that there was no way that cunt would have stayed to honor her bookings with DDL. But Holly's death had made the front page of every major newspaper in the country and all the news networks. Regardless of what she said in public, there was no real stigma surrounding the agency as a result of the murder; instead, once again, *she* had been the one to put DDL into the limelight. Let everyone think Holly's murder had upset her. It was a perfect diversion. Now all she needed were some new faces and steady bookings to keep DDL at the top.

But if Spheres continued to pull all its bookings, the agency's future would again be jeopardized, and she wasn't about to let that happen, even if it meant another murder.

She thought about the silk scarf. Perhaps she should have removed it from the Beta camcorder; surely the police had found it. But she dismissed her apprehensions; she was positive that there was no way it could be traced to her.

Outside, the cat's insistent cries turned into wails and she could stand them no longer. Her head was throbbing with pain. Wheeling into the kitchen, she opened a can of tuna. Then taking a small bottle from the corner of the refrigerator, she carefully extracted a drop of liquid with an eyedropper and mixed it into the tuna with a spoon.

Then she hurried outside and called the unfortunate cat to her. Eagerly, it ran to her and gobbled down the fish without hesitation. In seconds the poor animal went rigid with convulsions. By the light of the moon, she could see it frothing at the mouth and panting. Within three minutes it was dead.

She hungrily watched the little creature's final struggles. They left her feeling relaxed and in control again. Killing was an aphrodisiac to her, making her feel powerful, omnipotent, and as satisfied as if she had just had the most thrilling orgasm of her life.

CHAPTER
10

It was predawn, the soft, fuzzy time before the sky became streaked with pink light and promises of a new day. It was an hour in which the morning dew dampened the city with a light mist and the only sounds were the occasional cooing of the doves nesting on the hillside behind the house.

Ellysa, lying in their Kriess bed, stirred restlessly in her sleep. So huge now, she could only lie flat on her back, and when she needed to go to the bathroom in the middle of the night, it was a major production. Gradually from the depths of sleep, she became aware of the ever-increasing waves of pain gripping her lower back from behind and rolling around to her front. Though the baby wasn't due for another month, she immediately knew it was time.

She lay in her bed for a few minutes thinking about how her life was about to change forever. She wanted to cleave to the emotions she was feeling, to imprint these moments on her heart. It was the day her daughter was to be born. She imagined the kind of child she would be and the woman she would eventually become. She looked forward to sharing the girlish laughter and feminine secrets that were part of the mysticism of womanhood. As these thoughts played through her mind, she timed her pains and realized they were coming closer together. It was time to wake Sid.

She listened to his soft breathing and watched the rhythmic rise and fall of his chest. He had a cute little way of wrinkling his forehead when he slept and only another contraction from deep within her ponderous belly kept her from impulsively leaning over and hugging him. Instead, she reached over and gently shook his shoulder.

"Sid," she said softly. "It's time to go."

Sid awoke with a start. He leapt from their bed, threw on his clothes, and was waiting by the door before she was even dressed. He solicitously half walked, half carried her to the car. As she leaned against him for support, she could feel his heart pounding and she knew he felt the same way she did. In a few short hours their lives would never be the same.

All the way to the hospital, Sid kept asking her if she was all right until it started to irritate her, but then she understood he was trying to reassure himself. His knuckles were white against the black steering wheel and he had a look of near-panic in his eyes. *Men are conditioned to always being in control of their lives,* she thought, watching his face, *while women find it easier to trust the hand of fate.*

Sid coasted to a gentle stop in front of the emergency entrance to St. Luke's Hospital. Leaving the Rolls engine running, he guided Ellysa inside, then raced back outside to park it.

Ellysa's baby made her debut later that day, and Sid stayed at Ellysa's side the entire time. She took comfort in his presence. When she panted, he counted for her; when her forehead dripped with perspiration, she felt his tender touch, mopping it away; and when her throat was parched, he fed her ice. When their daughter came into the world, Ellysa saw Sid rocking her in his arms and quieting her tiny cries.

Later, they gazed at their daughter as she lay sleeping in Ellysa's arms.

"I've been thinking, Sid," Ellysa whispered, stroking the baby's tiny pink fingers. "What if we name her Sydny Ellen? It's a combination of both our names . . . and she is a combination of both of us."

"I like that," Sid said. There was a lump in his throat and a tightness in his chest as he gazed down at the child who was a part of him. "It would also reflect our commitment to our marriage."

Ellysa felt tears well in the back of her throat and nodded without speaking.

"You know, Ellysa," he confessed quietly, "I finally realize the real source of my own youth and immortality. For years I've been fighting the passage of time, but now with our daughter's birth, I realize that this is the only way to continue my youth. I don't think I've ever been this content in my whole life."

"Me neither," Ellysa agreed softly, reaching over and gently taking Sid's hand in hers. "And I want our marriage to work more than anything else, not just for us but for Sydny Ellen."

"It will, I promise," Sid whispered, bending to kiss the two most important people in his life.

Hollis struggled to focus his attention on Kathy's progress report on Holly Woodward's murder, but his mind kept wandering back to Joi Lin. It was amazing how his life had changed in the space of one short night. A week ago, he was a workaholic police lieutenant and now he was like a teenager giddy in love.

"Good work, Kathy," he said when she finished. "Now I want you to track the victim's movements in the days preceding her death. I understand she thought someone had followed her from a facial salon. Find out what salon and go there. See if anyone else saw anything suspicious."

Kathy went back to her desk, and he forced himself to concentrate on the list before him. It was the list of Clark

Gable movies that he had requested. There were five titles that incorporated the names of cities: *Manhattan Melodrama, San Francisco, Saratoga, They Met in Bombay,* and *It Started in Naples.* He called the Paris agency owner back and read off the titles to him.

"It's the last one," the owner exclaimed. "*It Started in Naples.* Now I remember because I thought they were moving to Naples, Italy, and she said, no, that it was a Naples in the United States."

Hollis thanked him and hung up. Even though he was going back years and the Chevaliers may have moved several times since, it was the best lead he had. He suspected that the city the owner meant was the one in Florida, although there was also a Naples in southern California that was near the city of Long Beach. A search of the California Naples turned up no Chevaliers living in the Long Beach area, although there were eight listed in the greater southern California area. Three were listed in Naples, Florida, one as G. Chevalier, which coincided with the first letter in the name of the former model he was looking for—Gretchen.

He crossed his fingers and dialed that number first.

A woman answered and said she was indeed the former model, Gretchen Van Wie. He questioned her closely but found out that she had no knowledge of any Alan Ainsley Anderson. She and her husband were cruising the Caribbean in their yacht at the time of Anderson's murder and she hadn't seen her Hermès scarf in the last eighteen or so years.

Hollis was disappointed but not surprised. It would have been too easy if all the pieces had fallen into place. Contrary to motion picture portrayals, cases were solved not with single monumental breakthroughs but by a series of small steps and endless detail work.

Gretchen was, however, able to help him with the whereabouts and telephone number of the fourth model. She was living in Dover, England, where she owned an exclusive bed-and-breakfast. By then, it was too late to call her, but

Hollis made a note to call her at 9 A.M. British time.

Again his thoughts wandered back to Joi Lin and he conjured up a vision of her sweet face and the feel of her smooth skin against his, and he felt himself stirring. Embarrassed, he looked around and then quickly began sorting through the files on his desk. But it was no use; he couldn't keep Joi Lin out of his thoughts. Finally he gave up and dialed her number.

Joi Lin hung up the telephone and picked up a stack of computor printouts, humming softly to herself.

"What are you so happy about?" Betsy asked, watching Joi Lin closely.

"Oh, nothing," Joi Lin answered, smiling.

"For the past several days, you've been positively radiating happiness and goodwill. And right now, you're glowing so much you could probably light up the Forum," Betsy probed. "I know something's up. What is it, a new man?"

Joi Lin didn't answer, but she continued to grin giddily. She thumbed through her printouts and made notes in record time.

"I think I'll leave early today," she announced a little later in a casual tone. "I've got a bunch of errands to run this afternoon."

Betsy looked at her suspiciously. "Sure you do," she answered in a disbelieving tone.

Joi Lin hurried home, showered, changed, and reapplied light makeup. Frank had called her earlier in the afternoon and asked her to dinner at Chinois on Main Street in Venice.

She had seen Frank several times since the dinner at his house, and he had made a point of calling her at least once a day. From the beginning, he was forthright in his intentions and he made it clear to Joi Lin that he intended to be a continuing part of her life. Suddenly in the space of a few days, her life had flip-flopped. She had gone from being a lone individual to becoming a partner in a relationship. It was a strange and new concept for her because although she had dated occasionally, she had never had a serious relationship. Yet it seemed so natural. Their personalities meshed with complete ease on many levels. What started out as a common goal to find Alan's killer had evolved into a friendship and now into a full-blown romance. Thinking of Frank gave Joi Lin a warm glow that nothing could dampen.

She thought about how she as a person had changed, not only by becoming more assertive and confident, but physically as well. Without any effort on her part, the pounds had melted from her body, and she was developing a strong sense of personal style.

She idly wondered whether or not Frank would have been attracted to the "old" Joi Lin, but immediately dismissed the thought. The new Joi Lin was here to stay.

As she pulled up to the restaurant, Frank was just getting out of his car.

"Hi," she called. He turned and waved, waiting for her to catch up with him.

When she reached him, he bent down and gave her a light kiss on the lips. The moment was so natural, it was as if they had known each other for years instead of weeks.

"Hi, you," he said with a grin. Then he pulled her out of the way as two tanned cyclists streaked past them.

"Dangerous neighborhood," he joked as he took her arm and guided her inside Chinois.

The restaurant was both noisy and chic. Its decor, Frank explained, was as eclectic as its nouvelle Japanese/French cuisine. It was the second of super-chef Wolfgang Puck's phenomenally successful restaurants, and patrons called days in advance for reservations. However, Frank had once caught two would-be thieves climbing out a back window of the restaurant, and now he could always get a table at a moment's notice.

They were seated immediately, and Frank ordered a bottle of St. Michelle Chardonnay and an appetizer of rare Ahi tuna in a nest of shoestring potatoes. The wine was superb and the tuna was a house specialty, but Joi Lin and Frank might as well have been eating Dodger Dogs and drinking beer for all they noticed.

"To you," Joi Lin toasted, raising the wineglass that the waiter had just filled.

"No," Frank corrected, giving her a look that made the pit of her stomach quiver with butterflies. "To us."

They sipped their wine, nibbled the tuna, and chatted about their day, but their bodies were speaking a different language altogether. The sexual tension between them was almost tangible.

This was a new experience for Joi Lin. All her adult life, she had prided herself on maintaining self-control. She had always kept her emotions, like her bookkeeping, precise and disciplined. But now, her feelings for Frank made that impossible. She was no longer analyzing every move, she was taking her cues from her heart.

Frank reached over and touched the back of her hand and she turned her hand over. He gently stroked her palm, then each finger, and her body turned to liquid.

"What is it about you?" he murmured, weaving his fingers through hers. "I feel hypnotized by you."

In any other circumstances, Joi Lin's practicality would have made her cringe with embarrassment. She had never thought of herself in a sexual sense. But she felt the same draw toward Frank. She looked down shyly, but then lifted her eyes and gave him such an intense look that she saw him hold his breath for a brief moment.

"I—I know what you mean," she breathed, returning his touch. Part of her wanted her control back, but another, stronger part of her wanted to give in to the emotions of the moment, regardless of what the future might bring. But intuitively she sensed their relationship was not destined for brevity.

"Joi Lin, I've never had this feeling with anyone—not with Gina—no one," Frank told her. "This is all so new and totally unexpected, but it's like—"

"Like we've known each other for years," Joi Lin finished for him. "I know, I feel the same way."

Between them, their food and wine remained unfinished as the entwining of their fingers became more passionate. It was as if they were speaking through their touch.

"I'm not really very hungry," Frank said tentatively. His mouth was dry and the words caught in his throat. He didn't want dinner, he wanted Joi Lin, but he didn't want her to think he was only out for a good time. He waited fervently for her response.

"Actually, I don't think I could eat anything," Joi Lin confessed without hesitation. Her stomach fluttered and her body ached to feel his against hers.

"Then let's get out of here," Frank said, throwing some money down on the table and standing up. "I've got some other ideas on how to spend the evening."

Joi Lin smiled, her eyes glowing, and picked up her purse. Frank took care of the valets, and while they waited for their cars, they decided that Joi Lin would follow Frank back to his house. When they got there, she pulled up behind his car in the driveway.

The front door barely closed behind them before they were in each other's arms—lips searching out lips, arms encircling arms, fingers touching, exploring, caressing. There was a sexual thirst within them that they strove to slake and they pressed themselves against each other as if they were trying to melt into each other.

With one effortless move, Frank swept Joi Lin up into his arms and over to the sofa, and with frenzied movements, they tore each other's clothes off. The first time they had made love, it was with the tentativeness of new lovers, full of discovery and wonderment. This time, their lovemaking was full of passionate anticipation, and the knowledge of each other's bodies and the desire to please one another. Frank stroked Joi Lin's body, his fingers tracing the curve of her back, cupping her buttocks in his hands, and pressing her against him. He ran his tongue down her neck and kissed the soft hollow of her throat. Shivering with pleasure, Joi Lin lowered her head to his chest, kissing his nipples. She heard his sharp intake of breath and felt his urgent, hard cock pushing against her legs.

"Come here, baby," he whispered, starting to pull her on top of him.

"No," she replied, wriggling beneath him. "I want you on top." She marveled at her own candidness, but then everything between them had always seemed so natural, from the onset of their relationship.

"I'm too heavy for you," he protested. "I'll squash you."

"No, you won't." She caressed his cock. "I want to feel you—feel your weight on top of me."

Frank engulfed her in his arms and she guided him inside her. Her body had still not grown used to his size and it struggled to accommodate him. They matched each other stroke for stroke. Dizzy with pleasure, her body seemed to vibrate, every nerve ending alive, stimulated, and with a gasp, she gave herself to the waves of pleasure that exploded inside her.

"I love you," she thought she heard Frank murmur, his lips against her hair, but she assumed she must have misunderstood him.

As they lay exhausted in each other's arms, Frank gently stroked Joi Lin's hair. Then he cupped her face in his hands and lifted it to his.

"I love you, Joi Lin Ambernites," he whispered hesitantly. "Do you love me?"

She nodded, not trusting her voice. There was a lump in her throat and tears of joy sparkled in the corners of her eyes. She had never been so happy in her entire life.

Then they made love again, this time languidly, relishing each movement.

Ellysa sat in a rocking chair in the nursery, cradling Sydny Ellen. Although the new Swedish nanny, Greta, had started work several days ago, she had not yet held the baby. Ellysa did everything. The energy she had thrown into developing Spheres, she now devoted to being the perfect mother. Greta was relegated to answering the telephone and acting as a gofer.

"Mrs. Roque," Greta said, entering the nursery, "telephone for you. It's Mrs. Symington."

"Take a message, please," Ellysa instructed. "I'll have to call her back after Sydny Ellen is asleep."

Greta returned after a few moments. "Mrs. Symington was calling to remind you of the exciting benefit coming up next week. She said she wanted to make sure you and Mr. Roque were going to attend."

Ellysa sighed impatiently. She no longer had any interest in attending such events. Several of their friends had called with tantalizing invitations, but Ellysa turned them all down. With Sydny Ellen's birth, she had become the antithesis of the self-centered social climber she had been only a few months before.

Ellysa looked up at the nanny. "Now I ask you," she said, "what could be more exciting than holding this adorable little girl?"

"I don't know, Mrs. Roque." Greta smiled. "You haven't let me hold her yet."

Ellysa grinned sheepishly, but didn't offer the baby to Greta.

"Oh, yes," Greta said, "Mrs. Ritter called again and asked that you call her as soon as possible."

"Did you notice, Greta," Ellysa said, deliberately ignoring Greta's words, "that Sydny Ellen smiled today?"

"I'm sorry, Mrs. Roque, but babies who are only a few days old don't know how to smile. It was probably just gas."

Ellysa looked at the nanny. "It was a smile," she insisted firmly.

"Come on, Rusty," Derian said, holding the telephone tightly against her ear with her shoulder while thumbing through call sheets. "Let's stop by and see Ellysa Roque and her new baby."

Expecting an argument, Derian was pleasantly surprised when Rusty agreed to go for she wanted him with her. This wasn't strictly a social call and could prove uncomfortable, if not difficult for she had two very important reasons for seeing Ellysa. First, she hadn't had any response from Lucille Ritter regarding upcoming bookings. Her ability to make decisions seemed to be eroding, and Derian was desperately trying to save the account before DDL lost it completely. And secondly, she had developed a plan to ingratiate herself with Ellysa.

Ten minutes later Rusty met Derian at the agency and they left for the Roque residence. The housekeeper met them at the door and showed them into the frilly pink and white nursery, where Ellysa was rocking the baby by the window.

"Ellysa, darling," Derian gushed, giving the new mother a big hug. "You look marvelous. How did you ever get your figure back so soon? It's unbelievable. And look at this child! Isn't she the prettiest baby you've ever seen? Rusty, just look at her!"

She pulled her brother over to look at the baby. Ellysa beamed with pride and held the blanket open for them to see.

"Oh, yes," Rusty agreed dutifully. "What a beautiful baby."

Then he looked around the room. "I never realized how much equipment it took to raise a baby," he said in amazement. The room was filled with a changing table, bassinet, stroller, toys, and all sorts of foreign-looking baby paraphernalia. He picked up a little pink pacifier and dangled it between two fingers.

"What's this thing do? It looks like a big plug."

The two women laughed.

"It doesn't *do* anything. Actually the baby sucks on it between feedings," Ellysa told him. "It keeps the noise level down."

"May I hold her?" Derian asked, reaching out for Sydny Ellen.

"Well," Ellysa hesitated, "I suppose so."

She reluctantly gave the baby to Derian.

"Rusty, do you want to hold her?" Derian asked, turning to him.

Both Rusty and Ellysa said "No," and then they laughed at their identical, though for different reasons, responses.

"I'll take her back," Ellysa said, holding out her arms. She didn't like her baby's being out of her arms for any length of time.

"I just had the most divine inspiration," Derian exclaimed as if she just had a spontaneous idea.

"Why don't you have Rusty take a series of photographs of Sydny Ellen?" she suggested excitedly.

She looked at Rusty. For a moment he looked as if he was going to protest, and she worried once again that perhaps she was controlling his career and his life too much. But, instead, he agreed with her suggestion.

"What a great idea," he said. Then brainstorming, he added, "In fact, maybe you should think about incorporating the baby's pictures with advertising for Spheres!"

What a wonderfully inspired idea, Derian thought to herself. She couldn't have come up with a better one. She was proud of Rusty for thinking of it. It was a perfect way to turn the Spheres account around and stimulate business for DDL.

"Fabulous idea, Rusty," Derian enthused before Ellysa could respond. "We could have pictures of Sydny Ellen being held by various models wearing fashions from Spheres."

Ellysa shuddered at the thought of strange women holding her daughter and breathing their germs on her. She could just imagine her Sydny Ellen contracting some awful disease as a result of some dirty model touching her. Everyone knew models slept around and God only knew what germs they carried.

"I don't think so," Ellysa immediately said, squelching the idea.

"Why not?" Derian asked. It worked for her; she saw it as the perfect solution to the agency's current money problems.

"Because Sydny Ellen is too young to have strangers holding her," Ellysa said.

"Well, what about in a month or so?" Rusty asked.

"No," Ellysa said emphatically. "I'm not interested in exploiting my daughter. I want her to have a normal life outside of the spotlight."

Ellysa even surprised herself with her words. Only a few months ago she would have jumped at the chance to generate all the attention she could. Now it was no longer important. What *was* important was the child in her arms, not Beverly Hills society, not even Spheres.

Derian's high hopes plummeted, but she wasn't about to give up so easily.

"Did you know, Ellysa," she continued, "that Lucille has canceled all of Spheres's planned bookings—the ads, the shows, the mailers, and the monthly catalogues?"

"No, I didn't," Ellysa admitted, making baby faces at Sydny Ellen.

"Well, she did," Derian said, "and quite honestly, I'm afraid that without maintaining a regular advertising schedule, Spheres will lose a vast majority of its business. I know how hard you worked to build Spheres, and I'd hate to see it go down the tubes. Frankly, Ellysa, I don't know if Lucille is really capable of handling the responsibility for a whole store. Perhaps you should go back to work at least part-time to keep things from completely falling apart."

Derian held her breath and waited for Ellysa's reply.

Ellysa hesitated for a moment. While she had no idea that DDL's future lay in her hands, she did know that she was happier now than she'd ever been in her life. She had a newly recommitted marriage, a doting husband, and a beautiful daughter. The thought of returning to manage Spheres was more than she was willing to consider. Spheres was a symbol of her old unhappy life. Sure, she'd put her heart and soul into the business, and she didn't want it to fail. It was just that she didn't want to think about it right now. Mrs. Ritter *had* been calling constantly with questions and problems concerning the store. Perhaps she wasn't as capable as Ellysa had first thought, but Ellysa was unable and unwilling to address the issue at this moment. Surely, she told herself, Lucille could handle the boutique management for a few months.

"No, Derian, I'm sorry," she said, "but I don't even want to consider part-time. I think Lucille can handle the boutique just fine. I trust her judgment. If she thinks we should suspend advertising for a while, then I bow to her decision."

Derian exhaled. Then this was it. Somehow she would have to find another way to boost the agency's revenues without the Spheres account. She didn't know how, but she did know that she'd been down before and had come out on top. She'd do it again.

Derian slumped in her chair and absently peeled the polish off her fingernails. It was a nasty habit she had broken herself of years before, but with her current pressures, it resurfaced. Now that Ellysa had made it clear to her that the Spheres account would not be forthcoming, Derian had to do something fast. She began reformulating the plan of action she had thought of weeks ago at the polo games. She'd hold those model interviews in all the hicksvilles up and down southern California to "discover" new faces. And she would teach them the basics of the modeling world and Rusty would photograph them.

With her agency contacts in Paris and Milan, she would create an exchange program, bringing budding European models to L.A. Americans loved European models and with her sales abilities, she was sure she could convince Neiman Marcus, Saks, and some of the other big chains to build their advertising campaigns around a "face" from DDL.

But from the moment she knew she would lose Holly she also realized that to initiate all of her plans she would have to downsize the agency in order to control it. Derian doggedly returned to the list she'd made of models to cut. She knew that many of the models would be able to sign with smaller agencies, which made her decision easier. But then she came to Charis's name.

She would never be able to sign with another agency. The blunt truth was she was too old. Derian should have dropped Charis long ago, but their friendship had always prevented her from doing so. She had tried to help Charis, but it hadn't worked. She had shown up at Rusty's studio, but she had been useless as a stylist. Now the agency's future was at stake and nothing and no one would stand in its way. Before she could waver in her decision, Derian picked up the telephone and left a message on Charis's service for her to come in for a chat as soon as possible.

It was late afternoon when Charis showed up at the agency. Derian was scanning some color transparencies belonging to a new girl she was thinking of signing when Charis knocked lightly on her door.

Derian motioned her in.

"Take a look at these," she said, handing Charis a strip of tranparency.

Charis picked up an extra loupe off the desk and went over the pictures.

"Pretty girl. Her nose is a little broad, though. A photographer will have to be careful to shoot it at least three-quarters instead of full on. She's a little stiff, too," Charis observed.

"Her nose is no problem," Derian said, selecting another strip and viewing it through the magnified loupe. "I know a good plastic surgeon who can shave the sides, plus he'll give my referrals a break in the price.

"And as for her stiffness, practice makes perfect. They all have to start somewhere."

"You're right," Charis agreed, handing Derian the transparent strip. It made her nervous to look at pictures of other, far younger models. It only served to remind her of her own age.

Putting her loupe down, Derian took a deep breath, taking note of Charis's tight-lipped expression. It was evident to her that Charis anticipated some sort of unpleasant discussion, and she didn't want to keep Charis agonizing any longer than necessary.

"Look, Charis," she said, coming immediately to the point, "DDL is in trouble. We've lost the Spheres account, and unless I make some drastic changes immediately, the agency will find itself at the bottom of the list of agencies in L.A. I have got to generate new revenue!"

"I had no idea about the Spheres account," Charis responded sympathetically, totally missing the direction of the conversation. "What are you going to do?"

"Well," Derian continued, "first of all, I'm going to conduct a search for new faces and also begin an exchange program with some of my agency contacts in Europe."

"What a great idea!" Charis exclaimed. "American accounts are always impressed with European models and vice versa!"

"But I'm also going to have to whittle down the size of the agency," Derian continued. "With all the new models, I'll have to make sure things don't evolve out of my control."

"Oh," Charis said, squirming in her chair. Suddenly she didn't like the direction the conversation was taking.

"Charis, DDL is going to have to let you go," Derian said gently. *There*, she said to herself, *I've said it*.

Charis jumped to her feet. "What are you talking about?" she cried. "You can't let me go!"

"I have to," Derian explained, "for the sake of the agency's future."

"What about *my* future? What am I going to do?"

"Charis, try to understand, I either make my move now, or DDL will never stay the number-one agency in L.A. DDL has a reputation to uphold, to represent only top models. I simply cannot have nonproducers in the agency."

"Derian, I'm just going through a little slow time right now. It won't last, you'll see!" Charis said desperately, tears glistening in her eyes.

"I know. I'll go to that plastic surgeon and have him do a couple of tucks and a little lift! I'll look nineteen again. Derian, please—"

"It won't work, Charis," Derian said firmly. She had made up her mind and nothing Charis could say would dissuade her. "Look, the agency has carried you long enough. Your modeling days are finished. The time has come for you to make a career change. I did my best to try to interest you in other related areas. I made suggestions. I even set you up with Rusty, but you blew it off."

"Be a stylist!" Charis spat out. "Me? I used to be one of the top models in the world! Why I—"

"That's the operative phrase, Charis," Derian interrupted. " 'Used to be.' You aren't anymore and you never will be again. Perhaps if Spheres had continued its advertising campaign, I could have kept you on. But Ellysa Roque doesn't have time for Spheres anymore. Her whole world revolves around her baby."

"Damn it!" Charis swore. "Then you have to convince her. I have no other way to make money!"

"Believe me, Charis, I've tried. It just won't work."

Charis was devastated. Her emotions out of control, she broke down and wept. In the course of a few short moments, her future had been swept away. She knew no other fashion agency would take her on at her age.

"Please don't do this to me," she begged. "Derian, I was there for you when you started DDL. I was on top, and I was the one who took a chance with you. I'm the one who influenced other models to switch to DDL in the beginning! You owe me!"

"I've paid you back many times over, Charis," Derian said, unmoved by Charis's tears. "I gave you a chance to learn from Rusty. You could have had a whole new career, but you weren't interested!"

Charis dropped back into the chair and sobbed uncontrollably for a few moments, then with a supreme effort attempted to pull herself together. Derian's heart went out to her, but she remained firm in her decision.

"Rusty," Charis said disdainfully, with a toss of her head, streaks of black mascara tracking her cheeks. "What was I supposed to have learned from him? How to steal?"

"What are you talking about?" Derian's anger immediately erupted. How dare Charis say anything derogatory about her Rusty! Maybe she had snapped under the stress.

"Your oh-so-perfect brother is a thief! I saw him take something from a model's bag!" Charis screamed at her.

"And on top of that, he's a lousy photographer, but you're too blind to see it!"

With an animalistic wail, Charis swept the loupe and color transparencies from Derian's desk. Suddenly, it was as if all her pent-up hostilities boiled over: the gradual onset of her insecurities, her loss of bookings, the nasty comments and pitying looks from other models. She couldn't hold back any longer. She ground the fragile slivers of film into the carpeting with her heel.

"Are you crazy?" Derian shouted, jumping up. "Get out of here!"

Charis dissolved into another wave of tears and fled.

Joi Lin looked up from her computor sheets as Charis ran through the agency waiting room, tears streaming down her cheeks, a distraught look on her face. Without hesitation, Joi Lin dropped everything and ran after her.

"Charis, Charis, wait," Joi Lin called.

Charis was a half block from the agency, but she hesitated at the sound of her name. As Joi Lin hurried up to her, Charis looked around wildly as if she were looking for a path of escape. But when Joi Lin put her arms around her to comfort her, she leaned her head on Joi Lin's shoulder and sobbed.

"It's all right. Sh-sh-sh," Joi Lin comforted her, patting her on the back. "Sh-sh-sh."

Joi Lin continued talking quietly to her until Charis's tears subsided.

"Come on, sweetie," she said, still patting her on the back as she would a child. "Let's go get a cup of tea. It'll make you feel better."

They walked to the coffee shop. As they crossed the street, they passed in front of Rusty's car. He had been on his way to see Derian when he observed the scene on the sidewalk. Parking his car, he trailed them, hoping to find out what had upset Charis. The two women sat down in a booth at the back of the coffee shop, and Rusty slid into a booth directly behind them. He had no trouble hearing their conversation.

"Derian is dropping me from the agency," Charis stuttered between sobs. The waitress brought them pots of herb tea, and Charis took several sips before continuing. The tea had a calming effect and she managed to stop crying. "And after all I've done for her and DDL!"

Knowing Charis needed a sounding board, Joi Lin waited without comment for her to continue.

"We've known each other for over twenty years," Charis said. "We were the hottest models around. We were always getting booked as a duo. We made the superstars of today look like Girl Scouts.

"Accounts flew us all over the world—the Caribbean, Africa. We even did a shoot at the North Pole. Boy, was that ever something! Avedon shot it and that was a coup in itself. He told us he would have never done it if it had been any other models but us! Joi Lin, I'm telling you. We were the best!"

As she continued to reminisce over her intertwined friendship and career with Derian, Rusty prepared to leave. These were stories he'd heard before and they were a waste of his time. But then something else caught his attention.

Beginning to feel remorseful, as she remembered the good times, Charis said, "I'm sorry now that I told Derian about Rusty."

"What do you mean?" Joi Lin asked.

At the mention of his name, Rusty paled and inched closer, listening intently.

"About Rusty's stealing."

"What about Rusty's stealing?" Joi Lin prodded, her radar going on.

"I caught Rusty going through one of the model's totes," Charis explained. "I was on my way into the models' dressing room at his studio to get something, and I saw him take a pair of pearl earrings from a tote bag. I just backed out without him seeing me.

"I thought about saying something to Derian, but she's practically obsessed with him and I didn't want to upset her, so I let it drop until today. I just blurted it out in a fit of anger. God, Joi Lin, Derian loves him so much, and if she believed me, it must have really hurt her to find out about him."

Joi Lin's mind was clicking and she filed Charis's statements away as another thought occurred to her. "How well did Rusty and Alan Ainsley Anderson get along?" she asked.

"Now there was a real creep," Charis sniffed, but Joi Lin no longer winced at the words. She had come to expect to hear the worst about her brother. "From the beginning, Alan tried to get Derian to drop me from the agency. He and Rusty had it out, too. It seems Rusty caught him going through the account lists. They had a huge blowup and Rusty told Derian, but by then Alan had already made copies of all Derian's accounts. He tried to get all of DDL's models to join his agency, too.

"All except me," Charis finished ruefully. "Derian was livid. I don't know which made her madder—Alan stealing her account lists or his argument with Rusty. Nobody crosses her brother."

Charis hadn't told Joi Lin anything she hadn't already known. Knowing everything she did about her brother, she really couldn't blame Rusty for trying to protect his sister's interests. But that raised another issue.

"I wonder how far Derian would go to protect Rusty," Joi Lin mused rhetorically.

"As far as she needs to," Charis answered promptly.

Behind them, Rusty, a strained expression on his face, quietly slipped out of the booth and tiptoed to the door.

Another typical day, Hollis mused, mopping the sweat off his forehead. The air-conditioning was on the blink in the squad room and the midafternoon sun blazed through the windows, leaching the energy from everyone in the room and frying tempers. In the hallway a gaggle of cops crowded around the Coke machine, and across the room he could hear the monotone drone of Kathy's voice as she took a statement from the department's resident nut case as he confessed to the latest crime taken from the front page of the *Los Angeles Tribune*.

There was a small flurry of movement as Tartella brought in two gang members, high on God only knew what. They were part of a smash-and-dash gang, and they couldn't have been over fifteen. One was sporting a hairnet pulled low on his even lower forehead, and the other had a series of home-drawn tattoos marching up his arms and across his tank-topped shoulders.

Blocking out the commotion, Hollis dialed the number of the fourth Hermès model in Dover, England, by memory. For the past three days he had been trying to reach her without success. This time when someone answered on the first ring, his hopes soared.

"I'm trying to reach Ms. Annabelle Knight," he told the stilted English voice on the other end of the line.

"This is Annabelle Knight. Who is this, please?"

Hollis identified himself. "I'm calling in connection with an ongoing murder investigation. I understand you used to be a model."

"Yes," Annabelle answered. "But that was a lifetime ago. I haven't modeled in fifteen or so years. I'm an innkeeper now. I run a small bed-and-breakfast here on the coast."

"Yes, I know," Hollis said. "But I'm interested in a booking you did approximately twenty years ago."

"Constable Hollis, I'm lucky if I can remember twenty minutes ago," she told him dryly. "But go ahead. I'll do my best."

"It was a job for the Hermès company in Paris, a special event promoting 'The Hermès Woman.' "

"Doesn't sound remotely familiar. How long ago did you say it was?"

"Twenty years ago. It was a two-day print job and they used four models representing the ideal Hermès women: two blondes, a brunette, and a redhead," Hollis prompted. "After the shoot, they gave each of you a special promotional Hermès scarf."

"Nope, sorry, I don't remember," Annabelle said, searching her memory.

"Wait a minute!" she cried after a few moments of silence. "I do vaguely remember something about an Hermès booking! It was a prestigious booking, and I was supposed to do it, but then I booked a job in the Orient, so I canceled Hermès. I remember because of the scarf; I'm a pack rat for that sort of thing, and I later heard they gave the models each a special scarf. I would have liked to have had it to keep as a memento."

Hollis was deflated. Another dead end.

"You don't remember who replaced you, do you?" he asked, without really holding out any hope that she would.

"Sorry, I don't," she said. "Like I said, it was twenty years ago."

Hollis thanked her, then slammed the receiver back onto the cradle in frustration. The scarf had been his strongest lead, and all he had wanted was a little luck; instead he'd hit a wall.

Two desks over, he heard a shout of anger. He looked over just in time to see the tattooed kid throw up all over Tartella's desk.

"God damn it!" Tartella shouted, jumping up and trying to salvage some of the papers on his desk.

In the melee, the other kid made a break for the door.

With a roar of rage, Tartella overtook him, grabbed him by his hairnet, and jerked him back down on the chair.

Yup, it was another typical day.

The next morning as Joi Lin pulled on a white Gap T-shirt and a new linen DKNY jacket and skirt, it occurred to her that working at the agency was developing her fashion sense. By just watching the models, she was learning how to put herself and her wardrobe together.

She hurried into the kitchen and took the makings of a salad out of the refrigerator. Her sense of style wasn't the only change, she thought to herself as she chopped up lettuce, hearts of palm, and artichoke hearts.

With her blossoming self-confidence came a quiet asser-tiveness and she noticed that with growing frequency the models seemed to gravitate toward her, asking her opinion. They seemed to regard her views with respect, she reflected as she quartered tomatoes and tossed in some sunflower seeds and raisins before sealing the mixture into an airtight container.

Life was full of strange twists, she mused, wrapping a few carrot sticks in plastic as an afternoon snack to tide her over until dinner. She was happier than she could ever remember being, yet all these new changes, including her relationship with Frank, had come in the aftermath of Alan's death.

She made a final sweep through her apartment, putting her breakfast dishes in the dishwasher, closing closet doors, and generally straightening up the place, and then she left for DDL.

Derian rummaged through her closet, pulling out first one suit and then another. She was looking for her favorite suit, a fitted Thierry Mugler in purple barathea. She was going to Lester Harrington's fashion show and she wanted to make a strong statement. Until this point, Lester had been booking models from several different agencies, but today Derian intended to convince him to use only DDL models.

While she searched her closet, she visualized how the Harrington shows would be her first step in rebuilding her agency's revenues. She was determined that DDL would continue to be the tops in L.A.; after all, she was Derian Delorian, and she didn't know the meaning of impossible. After searching her closet, garment by garment, she came to the conclusion that the suit had to be at the dry cleaners, and decided upon a monochromatic Armani with matching suede pumps in its place. It was not as dramatic, she thought, but the "lunch-bunch" recognized an Armani like Marvin Davis recognized a good deal.

She checked her watch and realized she was running late. Jumping into her Jaguar, she gunned the engine and wove through the traffic. As she drove, she reflected on Holly's funeral. Holly had no family and Derian had handled all the funeral arrangements. The moneys due Holly from her bookings paid for her funeral, and Derian was sad to see that only Rusty, Joi Lin, Betsy, and she herself attended Holly's gravesite.

She had been so caught up with the funeral arrangements and with her problem with Charis that she hadn't had time to think about her conversation with Hollis. She hadn't even discussed it with Rusty because she didn't want to worry him. But now during her drive to the show, she wondered what Rusty's reaction would be once she told him.

The Beverly Regent Hotel loomed on her right, and she entered through the ornate wrought-iron gates on El Camino Drive. Leaving her car with the valet, she hurried into the Grand Ballroom.

Derian was assigned to table five, directly next to the runway. Tables one through twelve were always considered the most prestigious, and she made sure the right seat had been reserved for her. She was amused by the fashion show and could hardly wait to tell Rusty about it.

At the beginning of the show, the quirky designer selected a woman from the audience and invited her up on the stage, where he critiqued what she was wearing. Naturally, everything she had on was all wrong because it wasn't one of his designs, so Harrington sent her backstage with his assistant/lover who did a make-over on her. At the conclusion of the show she was brought back on stage, her hair restyled, makeup done, and, of course, wearing one of Harrington's creations.

Personally, Derian thought the woman looked better before the assistant had worked on her. Nevertheless, the audience loved it and they applauded loudly when Harrington traded the woman's "old clothes" for one of his exclusive, but in Derian's opinion thoroughly ugly, designs. Derian made a mental note not to leave him any openings for a barter situation, such as modeling for clothes, should he suggest it to her.

Harrington wound up the program with a syrupy song that he had written. Holding back a snicker, Derian looked around expecting to see others laughing at his rendition, but to her amazement many of the women in the audience were sniffing and dabbing at their eyes. As sappy and eccentric as he was, she decided, he certainly had his fingers on the pulse of his audience.

Hollis set his parking brake, slammed the door on his car, and walked into DDL. His appointment with Derian Delorian was for three o'clock, and he had been marking time all day, knowing he would see Joi Lin. As he approached the counter, he scanned the agency for Joi Lin and was rewarded to see her look up from her desk. He loved the sweet smile that crossed her face when she saw him. He wanted to rush back to her desk, sweep her up in an embrace, and feel the softness of her body against his, but he knew their relationship had to remain a secret for the time being. Instead, he gave her a slight nod, and Betsy a smile as she hurried up to the counter.

"Lieutenant Hollis, hi!" Betsy cooed, beaming at him. "It's so nice to see you! How are you?"

"Fine, thank you," he replied uncomfortably. Betsy's attentions were obvious, and he hoped Joi Lin could see he wasn't remotely interested. "I have an appointment with Ms. Delorian."

"Oh, I'll tell her you're here," she said, rounding the counter to announce his arrival to Derian.

"Go right in, Lieutenant," Betsy said, escorting him to the entrance of Derian's office and quietly closing the door behind him.

"Isn't he the cutest," she asked Joi Lin, fluffing her hair, "in a kind of teddy-bear way. It's always the quiet ones who are hot in bed! You know, still waters and all that stuff?"

Joi Lin didn't know what to say. She couldn't very well tell Betsy she was having a love affair with Frank, but it was maddening to listen to another woman speculate on the man she was involved with.

• • •

"Hello, Lieutenant Hollis," Derian said curtly. Her meeting with Harrington had not gone well. She had been unable to convince him to use only her models and now she was in a black mood. "What can I do for you?"

There were too many more important things on her agenda than talking to the lieutenant, and she was determined to get him out of her office as soon as possible.

"Hello, Ms. Delorian," Hollis said easily. He took his time crossing the room and seating himself in front of her desk. He was convinced that Derian knew more about the murders than she had let on previously, and although he had no concrete evidence, he was sure that if he shook her up enough, she'd crack. "I wanted to go over your connection with the Anderson and Woodward murders again."

"What do you mean, my 'connection'?" Derian exclaimed, her voice rising an octave as all thoughts of Harrington and business left her. "I told you before, I don't know anything about their murders!"

"And I told you that you are a suspect since you knew both people," Hollis replied. His attack strategy was working; he could see she was visibly shaken.

"I thought you might be interested to know that Holly was murdered by a rare deadly batrachotoxin that we found in her eyedrops. We've linked her murder with Alan Ainsley Anderson's. The same toxin killed both of them," he explained. "I think it's time you talked."

Derian sprang at his words. "What do you mean, 'talk'? About what?" she exploded. "I didn't have anything to do with their murders! I told you I didn't. Why do you keep insinuating that I do?"

"Because as I told you before, you have the strongest motive for their deaths," Hollis said calmly, unperturbed by her outbreak.

"But I didn't kill Alan or Holly!" Derian insisted. "Nor did I have any reason to. Sure, DDL would lose some revenue because of Holly's leaving the agency, but not enough to affect the business. Models come and go, and they're all the same! In a couple of weeks, I'll have ten women that can replace Holly!"

Her hands pumped the air to emphasize her point and Hollis noticed that her nails were bitten to the quick.

"And as for Alan stealing my account lists," she concluded, "businesses that book models are public knowledge. It's a free world; Alan could contact whomever he wished."

"Including your models?" Hollis asked pointedly and he saw that he had hit home.

"I—I don't know what you're talking about," Derian stuttered. "My models are all loyal to me. None of them would ever leave me." But her voice had lost its convincing tone.

"Seems to me, they would go where the money was. After all, you've said yourself, modeling is a business, not a hobby," Hollis speculated dryly.

"But not with Alan," Derian spat out. "He was a slime bucket and he got what he deserved."

"He may have been a slime bucket, but he didn't deserve to die and neither did Holly Woodward," Hollis said. "As I said, you have the strongest motive for murdering both of them—"

"And I'll tell you again, I didn't," Derian stubbornly insisted.

"I'm going to find out who did and then I'm going to nail him—*or her*," Hollis pointedly concluded. "If you have anything to hide, I suggest you tell me now."

"I don't," Derian said, but her voice faltered.

For a brief moment she looked tormented. Her eyes were wild and her lower lip quivered, but then she seemed to draw from some inner reserve and gathered her strength. For a moment the two faced each other in silence; Derian glowered at Hollis with undisguised fury, and Hollis returned her stare with cold appraisal.

Finally Derian broke the silence. "Was there anything else, Lieutenant?" she asked, glaring at him balefully.

"Only that I'll be watching you, Ms. Delorian."

"Get out!" she hissed.

Hollis stood up and walked to the door. "Have a nice afternoon, Ms. Delorian," he said pleasantly.

As Hollis opened Derian's door, Betsy jumped to her feet. She reached his side as he started to leave the agency and brushed his arm with her fingertips.

"Hey, it's almost time for my coffee break," she said with a flirtatious little smile. "You look like you could use a break, too."

"Only in this case," Hollis told her as he walked out of the agency, completely missing the inference in her words.

Betsy watched him leave, at a loss for words. At her desk, Joi Lin suppressed a smile and thumbed through her billings without looking up.

As Hollis pulled away from the curb, Rusty drove in behind him, taking the parking space he had just vacated. Rusty recognized the cop from a distance and he hurried inside to find out the purpose of his visit.

"Yo, Betsy," he called, letting the door to the agency slam behind him. "Wasn't that John Law just leaving?"

"Hi, yourself," she answered. "It sure was, in the flesh. Lieutenant Hollis had a meeting with Derian.

"I'd like to have a little meeting with him, myself," she added slyly.

"Why, Betsy," Rusty said in feigned shock, "I didn't know you went for a man in uniform! I thought your heart belonged to me. I'm crushed."

"It does. It's just that my hair's turning gray waiting for you to make your big move," she shot back at him.

"Timing, darling." He grinned. "It's all in the timing."

"You're too fresh for me," she answered.

"Is my sister in?" Rusty asked. Without waiting for an answer, he opened the door to Derian's office.

"She's in her office," Betsy said, picking up a ringing telephone. "Good afternoon, DDL."

Rusty walked in on a strange sight. Derian, her face blotched red with anger, was slamming one of her file drawers closed over and over, as hard as she could.

"Is this a private destruction derby, or can anyone participate?" he quipped, walking across the room and sitting down with one leg tucked under him.

"That Lieutenant Hollis makes me so angry that I could chew a portfolio," she spat out. She gave the filing cabinet one final furious slam and sat down at her desk. Picking up a pen, she began clicking it off and on.

"Temper, temper, big sister, don't freak out on me," Rusty said, unperturbed by her tantrum. "What did the lieutenant want?"

"He came by to harass me again. He all but accused me of murdering Holly and Alan." She slammed her pen down on her desk and started shuffling through some papers. "Didn't you know that your illustrious sister is the lieutenant's number-one suspect?"

Rusty picked up the pen and absentmindedly snapped it off and on. "No, I didn't. What did you say?"

"I told him the same thing I told him the first time he said I was a suspect—that he didn't know what he was talking about. God damn it, Rusty," she exclaimed, suddenly focusing her anger on his mimicking her. It was the final straw in an all around awful day. "Would you stop that!"

For the moment Lieutenant Hollis was forgotten as Derian turned her attention to her brother.

"Every time I turn around, you are mimicking me! And I'm tired of it!" she screamed. "Put my fucking pen down!"

Rusty dropped the pen in shock.

"And look at the way you're sitting! Christ, sit up straight, will you! Can't you come up with your own bad habits without always copying mine! And that's another thing! What the hell have you been doing? Charis told me you were stealing from the models! I've got enough problems without having to defend you!"

"That's a lie," Rusty shot back, putting both feet on the floor and leaning forward. "Think about it, Derian, what reason would I have for stealing anything from any of your models?"

She stopped her tirade and listened to him.

"Didn't you tell Charis you were dropping her from the agency?" he asked shrewdly.

Derian nodded.

"Then the answer's obvious," he said. "Charis said that to get back at you. She decided to pay you back for dropping her. She knew it would hurt you. That's why she said it. I mean get serious! What possible reason would I have for stealing from *anyone*—least of all some model.

"Hollis upset you and now you're overreacting by jumping me," he told her, his voice rising. "Derian, put the blame where it belongs, not on me."

Derian was silent, thinking. Rusty's explanation made sense. Hollis had infuriated and frightened her, and having to drop Charis from the agency did upset her, though not as much as it had Charis. She'd never known Charis to be a vindictive person, but then she'd never seen Charis with her back to the wall like she was now.

Rusty was right. He was her flesh and blood. She'd raised him like her own son these past ten years and she knew him backward and forward. Still . . .

"I'm your brother, for God's sake, and I don't deserve this treatment," he said defensively. "If you don't believe me, then we have no relationship!"

He stood up ready to leave.

"I believe you, Rusty. Really I do," Derian said quickly, hurrying around the desk. She threw her arms around him and hugged him desperately. "I'm sorry, I overreacted. I know you would never steal!"

Rusty stood his ground, a hurt look on his face. It pained Derian to see him upset. How could she be so mean? Any rational person knew Rusty couldn't steal; he was, after all, her darling brother.

"Sit down, please, baby," Derian said, stroking his hair.

After a moment's hesitation Rusty sat back down.

"It's been such a terrible, terrible day," Derian said, standing over him, still stroking his head to soothe him.

"First, I tried to get the Harrington account as an exclusive and the old geezer turned me down cold. He said he'd heard a rumor that we had lost several of our top models," she explained. "I tried to set him straight, but he wouldn't listen.

"Then if that wasn't enough, I started going over the accounts and we are down thousands from our projected income. And just when I thought the day couldn't get any worse, that awful Lieutenant Hollis came by to frighten and intimidate me.

"I've got to do something," she continued, pacing the room, speaking more to herself than to Rusty. "But I don't know what to do. I've overextended DDL based on projected income, and now it's come up short. I don't think you realize what a severe blow Holly's death was to the agency. It makes our accounts nervous to deal with an agency whose models get murdered. And wait and see what happens if it gets out that I'm a suspect in Holly's and Alan's murders.

"To make matters worse, Ellysa is so caught up in that kid of hers, she's completely neglecting Spheres. Without that revenue, the agency will barely survive, never mind staying at the top.

"I've got to do something immediately to convince Ellysa that she's got to forget about that kid and tend to business! She has to resume Spheres's advertising program or everything is lost!"

Derian began to ramble and didn't seem aware that Rusty was still in the room. "Lucille Ritter doesn't know what she's doing. Ellysa has no choice but to go back; DDL's future could very well depend on it.

"I've started a campaign to sign new models and find new business, too, but it all takes time. Ellysa has got to go back to managing Spheres now! She's just got to!"

Rusty quietly stood up and walked out of Derian's office; behind him, Derian was still muttering to herself.

Hollis turned onto Santa Monica Boulevard and headed back to the station. For a few moments he knew Derian Delorian had been on the verge of cracking, but then she'd rallied. He had to admit, she was one tough woman.

He reviewed the other aspects of the case in his mind. He had assigned people to track down sources of the toxin, but so far they had come up empty. They hadn't been able to find any legitimate outlets in the United States that imported that particular toxin and the feelers they had put out for black marketeers who may have smuggled it into the country had also come up negative.

He had also instructed Kathy to follow up on other people who were given the Hermès scarf on the off chance one of them had moved to the United States in the past twenty years. The cases were moving at a snail's pace, but he wasn't about to let them slip through his fingers. The toxin used was so rare and unusual, and the murders so close together in time span and social circle, that he hoped against hope he didn't have a serial killer on his hands.

He had promised Joi Lin, but he had also promised himself when he saw Holly's twisted body, that he would find the killer. And he intended to keep that promise.

Ellysa awoke to find the other side of the bed empty. She could hear Sid's voice through the bedroom door and she slipped on her robe and followed the sound. He was in Sydny Ellen's room and Ellysa silently walked to the doorway and looked in.

Sid was sitting in the rocking chair near the window, holding the baby and softly talking to her. He was making plans with the baby, telling her of the adventures they would share as she grew up. It brought a lump to Ellysa's throat as she watched her husband cuddle his tiny child. The baby reached up and grasped one of Sid's fingers with a fist so small and delicate that it seemed more like a doll's than a real person's. At that moment, Ellysa didn't think life could be any sweeter.

Sid sensed her presence and turned to her with a smile. "Sydny Ellen and I were making some serious plans," he said.

"Oh, really," Ellysa said, playing along. "What did she say?"

"She said she wanted her and Mommy to have lunch with Daddy today at the Hotel Bel-Air and afterward I'd show her the swans in the pond."

"That sounds like a lovely idea," Ellysa agreed. "Do you think she will understand what a swan is?"

"Of course," Sid said. "She's a very smart baby. After all, she's my child."

Ellysa smiled with happiness.

After Sid left for the office, Ellysa busied herself giving Sydny Ellen a bath and dressing her for their luncheon date with Daddy. Even though she had hired a full-time nanny, she still hadn't grown tired of caring for the baby herself, except maybe to allow the nanny to change a diaper or two.

Three times during the morning her mothering routine was interrupted by hang-up calls. By the third one, Ellysa began to feel a little uneasy. It was almost as though someone was checking to see if anyone was home. There had been a rash of burglaries in the neighborhood and Ellysa made sure both the housekeeper and the nanny were aware of the calls. She asked them to keep an eye out for anyone suspicious.

By ten-thirty, Ellysa had Sydny Ellen dressed and ready to go. Because they had two hours before meeting Sid, she decided to take the baby shopping in Beverly Hills. She loaded the child into her Rolls and headed into the business district. It was still early by Beverly Hills standards and she had no trouble finding a parking place. She parked on Brighten Way, unloaded the stroller, and put the baby into it.

It was a beautiful sunny morning and strangers kept stopping her to look at Sydny Ellen. There was something about a baby that captured everyone's attention. She walked into Baby Guess? and purchased a pair of denim shorts with a matching shirt and sunbonnet and then walked to Pixie Town.

Suddenly, inexplicably, she had the uncomfortable feeling that someone was watching her. So what, she told herself, people had been watching her all morning and talking to her, too. People always approached people with babies and dogs.

But this was a different feeling. She stopped and looked around quickly but when she didn't see anything out of place, she dismissed the feeling.

Later as they were eating lunch at the hotel, Ellysa thought about mentioning her uneasy feeling and the hang-up calls to Sid, but they were having such a good time, she didn't want to dampen the mood with her overactive imagination.

CHAPTER
11

Restlessly she roamed the rooms, absentmindedly picking up a magazine here, fluffing a pillow there. She finally found herself at the door to her babies' room and she quietly entered, being careful not to startle them. She sat on the floor in the gloom with one leg tucked under her and watched them in silence. Being with them had a calming effect on her. Some of them, conditioned to associate her appearance with food, came up to the glass and eyed her solemnly.

For the past week, she had been biding her time, watching and waiting. She kept hoping right up to the end that Ellysa would realize the critical importance of Spheres to her beloved DDL's future. All it would take, she told herself, was for Ellysa to make an attempt to set things right at Spheres—for her just to go to Spheres—but it didn't happen. Ellysa Roque's world revolved around that damned kid.

"If only that kid had never been born," she said harshly, and the sound of her voice made the creatures behind the partition scatter. "That kid is at the root of all my problems. DDL would never, never be in the position it is now, if that kid wasn't around. Ellysa would still be in charge and DDL would still be riding the crest of success—success thanks to my efforts. Ellysa's rightful place is at Spheres, not with that brat."

Gradually, her babies congregated against the glass again, patiently waiting and watching. Eventually they drew her attention, and she slowly leaned forward and softly tapped the glass with her fingers.

"There, there, my babies," she whispered gently to them. "Are you ready for dinner?" Sometimes, she believed they understood every word she said to them.

Carefully she slipped on thick rubber gloves.

"I have another special surprise for my babies," she told them, taking a tight-lidded container from a paper bag. "Flies! I bought them just for you!"

Sliding the container into the cage with one hand, she carefully unscrewed the top and shook the flies out. The creatures overran her hand and the container, trampling each other in their hungry fervor to reach the food.

"You understand, don't you? You're the only ones who do. I won't allow anyone to destroy my precious DDL. Alan tried.

"That little bitch Holly tried to destroy it, too. If she would have stayed here where she belonged, everything would have been fine. She had DDL to thank for her entire career and what did she do? She tried to leave. But I fixed her good."

She withdrew her hand from the cage and watched her babies with delight. They never ceased to hold her attention; it was like watching a living, breathing kaleidoscope.

"They don't understand. I won't let anything hurt DDL. DDL is my life! Ellysa Roque doesn't understand either, but she will. Once she doesn't have that kid to distract her, DDL will be safe."

Another idea occurred to her and she went to her bedroom. Picking up a paper sack from her vanity, she returned to the glass partition. With reverent care she took a tissue-wrapped package from the sack and unwrapped it. It was a baby's yellow pacifier she had purchased a week earlier. She donned the latex gloves and carefully reached into the glass cage and caught one of her babies. It struggled with fear, but she held it.

"It's all right," she crooned to it. "Mommy's not going to hurt you. Hold still."

Gently she rubbed the nipple end of the pacifier back and forth across the creature's back. It struggled in panic and droplets appeared from a gland on its back. She held it even tighter until she was certain that she had rubbed the entire nipple in the liquid, then she released it.

"See, my beauty, I told you I wouldn't hurt you," she whispered. "I would never hurt one of my babies unless, of course, it was to protect DDL. Nothing is more important than DDL."

Then she withdrew the pacifier from the cage, and when it was completely dry, she carefully rewrapped it in the tissue paper and put it back in the sack.

"It won't be long now, my sweeties."

It was the first night Sid and Ellysa had been out together alone since the birth of their daughter. Even so, it was difficult for them to leave her with Greta. Ellysa made sure that the nanny had not only the telephone numbers of the restaurant, the police, the fire department, and the neighborhood security patrol, but also the pediatrician and the hospital.

"Any more phone numbers and you might as well give her the whole telephone book," Sid teased.

He had made reservations at the romantic Saddle Peak Lodge in Malibu Canyon, and although it was a bit of a drive for them, it was well worth it. A restored turn-of-the-century hunting lodge, it was nestled halfway up a mountain. Magic, the maître d', greeted them as they entered and led them to a special banquette table Sid had reserved in front of the huge fieldstone fireplace.

The ambience was intimate and romantic. Rough-hewn log walls in the main dining area were decorated with wild game heads and rich oil paintings of Rubenesque women. The tables were set with snowy linens, candle-lit hurricane lamps, and flowers.

Sid reached out and took Ellysa's hand, stroking it. He didn't think he had ever seen Ellysa look prettier. He wasn't sure if it was motherhood or their renewed trust and commitment to each other, but he had to admit, he hadn't been this happy in a long time.

Looking across at Sid, Ellysa knew her trust in him was gradually returning. There was a reassuring aura about him. She felt more confident about their relationship than she had ever hoped for.

The waiter came to take their drink order.

"We'll have a bottle of Acacia Carneros Chardonnay," Sid told him.

When he returned with the bottle and poured it, Sid waited to make a toast.

"Here's to more happiness than I've had in ages and to the two women in my life who have made me feel this way," he said, tapping his wine glass against Ellysa's.

His toast reminded Ellysa of Sydny Ellen. "Maybe I'd better check on things at home," she said after sipping her wine. She stood and hurried to the telephone.

Sid smiled to himself as he watched Ellysa move through the dining room. She was a completely different person from the self-absorbed ballbuster of the past few years. And he had changed, too. He no longer had any interest in chasing bimbos in an effort to prolong his youth. With the birth of Sydny Ellen, he finally recognized his own immortality in the form of his daughter.

"What are you smiling about?" Ellysa asked as she returned and sat down on the banquette.

"You," Sid answered. "Everything okay at home?"

"Everything is fine everywhere," she told him.

"You look so pretty tonight," Sid said, stroking the side of her face with the back of his hand, and Ellysa blushed like a teenager.

"Are you ready to order?" their waiter asked before she could answer.

Sid asked for a few minutes more because it was a difficult decision to make. The Saddle Peak was one of the top restaurants in southern California and it specialized in wild game in addition to standard fare. Sid finally decided on country pâté and a Caesar salad to start, and an entree of wild boar chops with corn crepes. Ellysa selected a green salad and the nested game hen stuffed with wild mushroom foie gras. Sid gave the waiter their order and selected a bottle of Ridge Zinfandel to accompany his boar chops.

Their dinners were excellent and the fun they were having with each other even better. They laughed and joked and flirted with each other. For Sid, it was like having back the wife he had thought he had lost. And for Ellysa, she had no doubt in her mind that Sid only had eyes for her. And for both of them, the joy their daughter brought to their lives was without measure.

Too soon the evening was over, but they both understood that it was only a preview of the joy the rest of their lives had in store for them. That night, they made love for the first time since Sydny Ellen had been born, and it was tinged with a tenderness that had never been present before.

In the morning, Ellysa was still beaming from their evening at the Saddle Peak Lodge. She sang Beatles' songs from the sixties to the baby as she fed and dressed her. It was like playing dolls, Ellysa thought, only more fun. Even pricking her finger with a duckie diaper pin made her smile.

Ellysa's response to motherhood was all so unexpected. She never dreamed she could feel such fulfillment as a mother and housewife. Any lingering desire to return to Spheres had completely disappeared. She knew that she should at least stop by the boutique or check on it, but she was unable to force herself to do it. Ellysa had had several calls from the store, from Derian, and from the baroness telling her that Mrs. Ritter was not the best possible choice to manage the boutique, but she just couldn't concentrate on the business long enough to make any changes. Each time she tried, her mind would return to Sydny Ellen. She realized that sooner or later, she would have to make some decisions, but she had convinced herself that they could wait for a few months.

Since her daughter's birth, Ellysa's numerous friends had extended invitations to luncheons and various social functions, but she had refused them all. She was no longer interested in impressing casual friends with her possessions and social status.

She was in the middle of taking snapshots of Sydny Ellen when Chi Chi Von Wittsburg called.

"Darling," the baroness crowed. "I simply must see you and the little one today."

"I don't know, Chi Chi," Ellysa said doubtfully, her mind racing to think of an excuse to refuse.

"Now, I won't take no for an answer! You've put me off long enough," the other woman insisted. "Besides, Sydny Ellen has to meet her aunt Chi Chi."

"Well," Ellysa said thoughtfully. It was a beautiful day. It would be nice to take the baby out for some fresh air.

"It's all settled," Chi Chi said, taking Ellysa's hesitation as a yes. "I've already made reservations at the Polo Lounge. It's Friday. Everyone will be there."

Ellysa didn't care who would be there. But the baroness was not about to take no for an answer, so she finally acquiesced.

"Okay, what time?" she asked, jiggling the baby in her arms. Maybe it would be fun to show Sydny Ellen off.

While Ellysa showered and dressed, Greta entertained the baby.

Ellysa dressed carefully, because she knew Chi Chi would be reporting everything about their luncheon to anyone who would listen. She was pleased that she was able to fit into her prepregnancy clothes so soon after the baby's birth.

When she was ready to leave, she carefully placed Sydny Ellen in the back seat of the car and securely belted her in her carrier. She made sure she had all her baby equipment: extra diapers, powder, disposable washcloths, an extra bottle of milk, even some little toys. She felt like she was carrying a suitcase of supplies every time she left the house. But she didn't care.

On the way, she stopped to drop off laundry. It was a production to leave the car, because Ellysa had to unsnap Sydny Ellen and take her with her. But the clerk oohed and aahed over Sydny Ellen, and Ellysa beamed with pride.

As she came out of the laundry and started to place the baby back in the Rolls, she discovered that in her absence, someone had sideswiped her car, pulling the chrome from a side panel.

"Shoot, Sydny Ellen," she said after inspecting the damage, "Mommy will just put you in the car and try to fix it."

The baby looked up at the sound of Ellysa's voice and gurgled. It made Ellysa smile. How could she possibly be angry when her precious baby was with her. She never wanted her child to experience unhappiness, or pain, or sadness, especially not as a result of Ellysa's actions.

She put Sydny Ellen on the back seat and attempted to bend the chrome back in place. It was too strong for her and all she succeeded in doing was severely slicing her fingers on the sharp metal.

"Ouch! Ouch!" she cried, shaking her hand in pain. Bleeding profusely, she looked around for something to stanch the flow. She spied one of the baby's diapers poking out of the diaper bag and she grabbed it. Quickly wrapping it around the injury, she applied pressure to stop the bleeding. It took a few minutes and a lot of blood, but she finally succeeded in slowing the bleeding, though she decided to keep her fingers wrapped in the diaper.

By the time she drove up to the valets at the Beverly Hills Hotel, her fingers had stopped bleeding and she was able to remove the makeshift bandage. She gently lifted the baby from the car and hurried into the Polo Lounge.

The baroness was already waiting for her, and upon seeing Ellysa, Chi Chi stood and hurried over to greet her.

"Ellysa, darling," she cried loudly, enveloping Ellysa and the baby in an elaborate embrace.

The baroness was in her element. She was cognizant that the eyes of the entire restaurant were upon them and she made the most of the attention.

"Emilio, darling," she called to the maître d'. "Come, come, look at the bambino. Isn't she precious?"

Emilio was a landmark at the Polo Lounge; he'd been with the hotel for decades and he knew everyone who was anyone and all of their stories. Of course he knew Sid and Ellysa Roque, and he had heard of the birth of their baby.

"Mrs. Roque," he exclaimed, coming toward them. "It's so good to see you." Unaware of Ellysa's injured fingers, he grabbed her hand and shook it enthusiastically.

"Ouch," Ellysa squealed, pulling her hand out of his grasp.

"I'm so sorry," Emilio apologized. "What happened? Oh, no, look you're bleeding! Here, let me go get you a tissue!"

"Lupe, Lupe," he called to his assistant. "Get Mrs. Roque a tissue immediately."

"No, no," Ellysa said quickly. She didn't want to make a scene; she just wanted to sit down and enjoy her lunch. "It's all right. Look, it's already stopped bleeding. See!"

Lupe rushed over with a tissue and handed it to Ellysa, who thanked her and dabbed it on the cut.

"Look at the little princess," Emilio continued after he had reassured himself that Mrs. Roque was indeed all right.

Ellysa lifted the blanket so Emilio could see.

"She looks just like you, Mrs. Roque," Emilio said politely.

Emilio escorted Ellysa and Chi Chi to their table and the baroness spent the next few minutes raving over Sydny Ellen. When the waiter came, they ordered their usual MacArthur salads.

Ellysa had to admit she was having a great time. Chi Chi was a delightful conversationalist and she regaled Ellysa with the latest gossip making the rounds in Beverly Hills. Sydny Ellen was adorable, too. She slept through the entire luncheon without a peep.

"I have to tell you, Chi Chi," she said at the conclusion of the meal. "I've had such a good time. You never cease to amaze me with your stories. How in heaven's name do you ever find out this stuff?"

"I don't know, darling," the baroness replied, rolling her heavily mascaraed eyes. "The people just tell me. By the way, my dearest, I heard that Sid has been telling everyone who will listen that he has never been so happy in all of his life."

Ellysa beamed at her. "Neither have I," she told the other woman sincerely. "It's a miracle. Sydny Ellen gave our marriage new life."

"I'm so happy for you, darling," Chi Chi said. "Good marriages are rare in our circle."

Ellysa could tell her friend really meant it. Chi Chi wasn't a bad person, she thought; it was just that her life had no focus.

Ellysa gave her a big hug. "Thank you for inviting me to lunch," she said, and meant it. "Let's do this again real soon."

"Of course, darling," the baroness agreed with a wink. "By next week, I will have news on Ina. I heard she's been seeing her pool man! In fact, I was supposed to call her back this morning, but I forgot. I'll do it now while I have another tea.

"Emilio, the telephone, please!"

Ellysa laughed and picked up Sydny Ellen, who was still asleep. She waved good-bye to Emilio, who was hurrying over to the baroness with a telephone.

A crowd of tourists, identifiable as non-Angelinos by their cameras and Hard Rock Cafe T-shirts, had gathered waiting for their cars, but upon recognizing Ellysa, Chris, the doorman, immediately signaled one of the valets to retrieve her car. As the Rolls pulled up, the crowd eyeballed Ellysa, trying to decide if she was a recognizable celebrity and if they should be snapping pictures of her.

Tourists in Beverly Hills were as common as ants at a picnic, and Ellysa was oblivious to them as she opened the rear door of the Rolls. As she started to put the baby on the seat, she spied an unfamiliar pacifier. She picked it up with her injured hand for a closer inspection. Before she could even place her daughter on the car seat, she was gripped by pains so intense they took her breath away.

She held Sydny Ellen tightly in her arms as her eyes began to contract and tear. Then she started foaming at the mouth. Her muscles twitched uncontrollably, and she dropped to her knees on the pavement, still cradling her baby against her breast to protect her.

All around her, people were still not completely aware of what was happening. Some thought she had fallen, while others thought she was having an epileptic seizure, so they were slow to respond. A small circle gathered around her. No one knew what to do.

Ellysa's vision faded, and the contractions intensified, twisting her muscles into knots. She sensed that she was dying, and tears coursed down her cheeks. Through the waves of pain came the realization that she would never see her daughter's first step, or hear her first word, or comfort her through her first teenage heartbreak. And she cleaved to her child one last time, fighting with all her willpower to live.

Her thoughts focused on Sid and the joy they had shared in the past few weeks. Throughout their turbulent life together, she had never ceased loving him. The words "I love you" came to her mind, but with one massive convulsion, she died before they could pass through her lips.

The crowd was in chaos. Women screamed, and several people retched at the sight of Ellysa, her body twisted by the final throes of death. A rumor raced around the perimeter of the group that she died by inhaling a deadly bacteria from the air.

"Biological warfare!" one man shouted, and three-quarters of the crowd stampeded in panic.

Chris pushed his way through the pressing crowd and upon seeing Ellysa shouted for someone to dial 911. Then he tried to calm the panic-stricken people.

Chi Chi Von Wittsburg finished her telephone calls, and drawn by the noise, she made her way through the pink and green lobby to the hotel's entrance. She saw the Rolls and noted that it looked similar to the one Ellysa drove, but she couldn't imagine that Ellysa would still be there. She used her bulk to forge a path through the crowd to see what was causing the commotion.

As she pushed through the mass of people, the baroness passed a tall, chic redhead who was squeezing through the crowd in the opposite direction. It registered in Chi Chi's mind that there was something familiar about the woman, but in her haste to reach the front of the crowd, she dismissed it. Having made it through the crush, Chi Chi looked down. Seeing Ellysa's body and her baby still held protectively against her breast, she collapsed. For the first time in her life, she was unable to get to a telephone.

Frank had planned a special afternoon with Joi Lin. He was not scheduled to work and Joi Lin was taking the afternoon off. He booked a room overlooking the ocean at the Malibu Sands Hotel in Malibu. A cozy little hotel with peach-colored stucco walls, its rooms had wide balconies opening out over the surf. On his way to pick Joi Lin up, he stopped by a Mexican restaurant and bought a picnic lunch, complete with salsa, chips, and the makings of margaritas.

"Where are we going?" Joi Lin asked when she opened her front door. "I don't know what I should bring."

"It's a surprise," Frank answered with a mysterious grin. "Just bring your bathing suit, your toothbrush, and your clothes for work tomorrow."

It was a day made for the beach. The temperature crawled upward, past ninety-nine, past one hundred. The palm trees seemed to droop under the weight of the summer heat. Even the doves stopped cooing and perched lethargically in the jacaranda trees, holding their wings away from their bodies in a vain attempt to cool off.

The drive along Pacific Coast Highway was beautiful. The sun reflected off the water, and the ocean breezes whipped the surf until it was as frothy as newly fallen snow before continuing on to cool the traffic-parched land.

It brought to Joi Lin's mind childhood memories of running along the beach, wind streaking the hair back from her face, and the hard grainy texture of the sand between her toes. Days of building sand castles, and of dreams written in the sand, only to be washed away with the sweep of a wave.

When she told Frank of her memories, he smiled at the disparities in their childhoods. He remembered sweltering summers in Jersey City; the pungent smell of oil, and humidity so thick, cigarettes would go stale before they could be smoked. There were long summer days of hanging with the guys, of posturing, macho images, and of hiding their not too distant childhood fears in the furthest recesses of their hearts. And he remembered cool nights, drive-in movies, and young girls, their mouths ripe with the sweet flavor of Sen Sens.

As the highway snaked along the coastline, it was punctuated by high, eroding cliffs that crumbled down on the highway during the dry season and dissolved into mud slides in the rain. On the other side of the highway, the scenery alternated between breathtaking views of the ocean and the less than spectacular views of beach homes wedged together like sardines in a tin.

It had been years since Joi Lin had been in Malibu and the new Malibu Sands Hotel stood like a little Mediterranean oasis among the local restaurants and surf shops.

"This is it," Frank exclaimed. "I thought we needed a day together, away from everything—a sort of mini-vacation."

They checked in and went to their room, which was California-styled in soft pastels and bleached wood. The back wall was sliding glass, and the room was drenched in sunlight.

"What do you think?" Frank asked Joi Lin anxiously. He had never been a suave, hearts-and-flowers sort of guy and he was afraid that this time he might have climbed out on a limb without a safety net. What if she laughed at him?

Joi Lin was silent for a moment and then she slowly smiled. "I think this is the most romantic thing that has ever happened to me," she said simply.

Frank looked at her dimpled smile, the soft light in her eyes, and he knew he was lost. In the years since Gina's death, he'd been content, after a fashion, to be alone. His job had been his lover, but now after meeting Joi Lin everything had changed. He didn't know what she felt, but he knew he wanted her by his side forever.

"Well, then," he said, opening his picnic basket, "how about a margarita?"

He had made arrangements earlier with the hotel for ice, a blender, and margarita glasses, and as Joi Lin changed into her bathing suit, he blended thick Cuervo Gold margaritas and opened a bag of nacho chips and a container of fresh salsa.

They sat out on the balcony, lazily sipping their drinks and watching the surfers ride the waves. Overhead, an occasional sea gull floated on the air currents, while keeping an eye out for the flash of a silver fish under the waves. It was the first opportunity they'd had to relax, away from the stress of the murder investigation that had initially brought them together and still colored their lives.

As Frank was blending their second batch, his beeper went off. "Damn," Frank said, switching it off and reaching for the telephone. "I knew I should have left this thing at home."

"But you know you wouldn't have," Joi Lin said. "You're too much of a professional. I'll start packing things up."

Frank made a sad face, but didn't protest.

As he spoke on the telephone, Joi Lin heard the change in his tone and immediately knew something was seriously wrong. When he turned to face her, his face was grim.

"There's been another murder and it looks like the same M.O. as Alan's and Holly Woodward's. It's Ellysa Roque."

"Oh, my God, no," Joi Lin whispered in shock.

"She's at the Beverly Hills Hotel. At this time of day, Highway 10 to the 405, to Sunset Boulevard exit will be the fastest," Frank said, planning his route out loud.

"I want to come along," Joi Lin told him resolutely. "I'll stay out of the way, but I know there has to be a connection between the three murders."

"I think you're right," Frank acknowledged. "We may have a serial killer on our hands."

The ride to the hotel was a subdued one as both were wrapped in their own thoughts about the murder. Joi Lin wondered what the common link was between the murders and thought now how trivial her information about Derian's overprotectiveness of Rusty seemed. While she mulled that over in her mind, Frank worried about stopping the killer before he murdered again.

When they reached the hotel, the driveway was bottle-necked with people who ignored Frank's attempts to drive up the passageway. In frustration, he finally hit his siren and even then they were slow to move.

"What's with people anyway?" he asked rhetorically. "They have such a morbid fascination with death. If they came in contact with it as much as the police do, they wouldn't want any part of it."

Joi Lin shrugged her shoulders in silence. She knew he wasn't really expecting an answer from her.

There was a white Rolls parked in front of the hotel's entrance, and Frank pulled up as close behind it as possible. The uniformed police had already cordoned off the area with a barricade and the growing crowd strained at the perimeter of it for a view.

"You'd better wait in the car," Frank told Joi Lin.

"Not on your life," Joi Lin responded quickly. "You forget, my brother was the first and I had to identify him, and Holly died in my arms."

"Okay," Frank said. "But stay out of the way."

They pushed through the crowd and ducked under the barricade. One of the cops recognized Frank and filled him in on as many of the particulars as they had so far. Ellysa Roque's body was where she had fallen next to the Rolls. Her limbs were still twisted in final agony and her face was a grotesque mask. A department photographer was busy taking pictures from all angles, and off to the side the doorman was holding a tiny baby, its thin wails drowned out by the buzzing crowd.

As Frank knelt down by the body, a shout went up from the back of the gathering. Both Joi Lin and Frank looked toward the sound as a man shoved his way through the crowd and under the barricade. Sid Roque's eyes were wild and his face contorted in anguish as he rushed to the car and looked at his wife. His face crumpled as he bent down and reached out as if to gather up her body in his arms. But Frank grabbed him before he could touch her.

"I'm sorry, Mr. Roque," Frank said as gently as he could. "You can't touch her yet. You have to wait until we're finished."

"Ellysa, Ellysa!" Sid whispered over and over, covering his face with his hands. "Please, dear Lord, not my wife!"

Joi Lin's heart went out to him and it was all she could do to keep from crying. She knew what he was going through and in her heart she cursed the murderer.

Suddenly Sid remembered his daughter. "Sydny Ellen," he cried, looking wildly around. "Where's my daughter?"

Chris came forward with the baby. "Here she is, Mr. Roque. She's as right as rain. I have two of my own." He placed the baby in Sid's arms, and she immediately stopped crying.

Sid held his child tightly and laid his cheek against the blankets, sobbing.

"Mr. Roque," Frank said, "do you have someone to drive you home?"

Sid shook his head, unable to speak.

"Joi Lin"—Frank turned to her—"would you mind driving Mr. Roque home?" He took out his wallet and extracted several bills. "Here's cab fare to get you home afterward."

Joi Lin waved away his money. "Of course I will," she answered, putting an arm around the stricken man. "Come on, Mr. Roque, let's go home." As she started to leave, one of the uniforms came up to Frank.

"Several people reported seeing a tall, redheaded woman—a real looker—pick something up by the car and then disappear into the crowd."

Frank looked at Joi Lin over Sid's head. They both had the same thought—Derian Delorian.

"I'll call you as soon as I can," he mouthed to her, and she nodded, understanding.

"It was a slight miscalculation, my darlings," she mumbled, pacing back and forth in front of the glass partition. She threw herself down in front of the glass and pulled one leg under her. "But they have no clues." She giggled, pointing to the pacifier on a table in the corner. "And I have a new trophy for my collection." She congratulated herself on her quick thinking to have spotted it near the tire and to have had the presence of mind to whisk it away.

She stood up, walked to the table, and pulled on a pair of surgical gloves. Then she picked up the pacifier and cupped it in both hands, studying it intently. There was a smear of Ellysa's blood on it and in her eyes that gave her trophy even more importance. She went over to a shelf and placed it with her other trophies—the label from the silk Hermès scarf she had used to cover Alan's Beta camcorder and some color transparencies of Holly.

"Someday, I'll put up a display at DDL to show the whole world my trophies and my successes! I just have one more teeny-weeny obstacle standing in the way of DDL's future," she told her babies. "Just one last one!"

She turned and left the room. Her heels echoed along the hallway as she went to her bedroom. She sat down at her vanity and carefully retouched her makeup. Then she changed into a fresh business suit with matching pumps, a pearl choker, and pearl button earrings. Finally, she slipped on a pair of fashionable color-coordinated gloves, before making one last stop in her babies' room.

My plan for a new model contest has got to work! Derian thought. She listed possible sources of new women—area high schools and colleges, other agencies in Europe and Japan. The newly independent Eastern European countries would be a terrific source of new women. They had great photogenic bone structures. She would travel to the countries and hold interviews at the agencies. Maybe she would take Rusty with her to do some test shots before signing the women.

Derian was working late and she was determined to formulate concrete plans before leaving for the night. Time was running out and she had to set her plans into action as soon as possible.

Abruptly she heard the squeak of the agency's front door. Someone had come in. She rose to her feet in alarm, but before she could move, her office door swung open.

A tall, chicly dressed redhead stood posed in the doorway. Derian looked at the woman. She was an exact replica of Derian! Without a word, the woman swept into the room and gracefully folded herself into a chair across from her, tucking one leg under her in a perfect mimicry of Derian.

Derian gazed at the woman intently, the blood draining from her face in horror as she realized the woman sitting across from her was *Rusty*. He was dressed in her missing Thierry Mugler suit, a long red wig, pearl earrings, and was made up to look exactly like her. *Exactly!* He was even wearing her favorite scent. The expression on his face was one she knew well—one she herself had used on numerous occasions—a mixture of amusement, slight patronization, and self-confidence. His performance was flawless and it terrified her. A shiver ran up her back. She felt like she was looking through Alice's distorted Looking Glass.

"Just what do you think you're doing, Rusty!" she demanded, summoning all her composure in an effort to control the situation. "Why are you dressed like that? Those are my clothes! My perfume! Just what is this— some sort of idiotic joke?"

For several minutes they faced each other. The room was silent, except for the hum of the water cooler in the reception room; and Derian held her breath, praying for a logical explanation from Rusty. But when he spoke all her hopes disappeared.

"Shut up," Rusty retorted in a high falsetto voice. "My name's not Rusty! You're in my chair," he added calmly.

Horrified at the tone of his voice, Derian was unable to move. How many times had she spoken with exactly the same inflection?

He removed a bottle of pills and a small box from his purse and carefully placed them on the desk. Then he shook out a red pill and popped it into his mouth.

"What kind of a pill is that?" Derian asked. She had never seen him take pills before. "What's it for?"

Instead of answering her, Rusty picked up the small box and rested it gently in the palm of his hand.

Derian strained to get a good look at it.

"Rusty's gone," he continued, and his voice began to take on a trancelike quality. "He was an impotent weakling and I had to get rid of him."

"What are you talking about, Rusty?" Derian asked, bewildered.

"I told you, my name is not Rusty!" he snapped back, glaring at her. "My name is Derian!"

For once, Derian was too shocked to reply. She watched as Rusty lovingly opened the box, revealing a tiny creature no more than an inch in length. At first Derian thought it was an insect. Then she realized it was a *frog*. Its little body was a brilliant shade of golden yellow and its eyes glistened like onyx. It perched in the box like a glittering jewel and surveyed its surroundings. Derian cringed, hoping it wouldn't jump at her, and she wondered if frogs bit people.

"For his entire life, Rusty's parents berated him on a daily basis. 'What's the matter with you? Why can't you be like Derian?' Nothing he ever did was ever as good as what Derian could do," Rusty said, taking a fountain pen from her purse. "When Derian accomplished something it was extraordinary. When Rusty did something, he was ignored or, worse yet, punished because it wasn't exemplary enough."

Derian immediately recognized her fountain pen, which had been missing for several weeks.

"You can't imagine what it was like growing up in his sister's shadow. He never really existed for his parents. Derian was always the center of their life."

Derian was too stunned to move, and she was confused. Why was Rusty speaking about them as if they were two other people?

Rusty held the tiny frog down with one gloved hand, and with the other hand, he calmly rubbed the edges of the fountain pen back and forth down the length of the frog's struggling back, as if he were stropping a straight-edged razor. As Derian watched in disgusted fascination, the terrified frog released a liquid and it collected on the ridges of the fountain pen. All the while Rusty continued his monologue.

"For a long time—years really—Rusty listened as his parents drilled his sister's superiority into him, over and over and over. They were relentless and he tried as hard as he could to be the obedient little boy and follow in her footsteps. After they were gone, his sister continued where they left off, insisting that only she could make the best decisions. He always listened to her, too," he rambled on in the same high-pitched tone. "She was perfect and he was less than nothing!"

"That's not true," Derian protested.

"Shut up!" he screamed, becoming more agitated. "You're right. It's not true! I'm the only one making the right choices! I was the only one willing to do the right thing to protect the agency. You would have let DDL fall apart!"

Derian uttered a low moan. He was the baby she'd never had, more her child than her brother. He had always been so sweet, so obedient. She couldn't believe what she was seeing and hearing.

"You failed! You didn't care enough about DDL, but I did! *I* was the one who saved it from Alan," he hissed, leaning across the desk so that their faces were only inches apart. His eyes were wild and unfocused and spittle clung to the corners of his red lips.

Derian pressed herself as far back in her chair as possible. She wished she could close out the bizarre creature before her who bore no resemblance to her darling brother. But it was impossible to take her eyes from him.

"And I put DDL in the limelight by killing that bitch, Holly!" he shrieked, his voice cracking with emotion. Saliva flew from his mouth, showering Derian's face, but she was too petrified to wipe it off. "You would have just let her walk away! Only I thought the situation through and made the most of it!"

Rusty jumped up and began to pace, gesturing wildly with the fountain pen.

"What kind of a business woman are you anyway," he taunted her, pointing the fountain pen at her. "You failed DDL and you failed me!"

"Oh, God, no, please say you didn't kill those people! I didn't fail you. I loved you," Derian pleaded with him. Tears glistened in her eyes and she tried to hold them back. How could their lives have gotten so twisted, so confused. Even now as she looked at him, all she saw was the sweet, tousle-headed little boy who used to hang on her every word. *Think*, she told herself, *somehow, you have to find a way to reach him.*

"Listen to me, Rusty, you have to hear what I'm saying," she begged him, pushing back the hysterics that threatened to boil up inside her. "We're going to be fine. DDL is going to be fine; I have ideas to increase revenues, and who knows, maybe Spheres will begin its advertising campaign again."

"I told you before, stop calling me Rusty! My name is Derian, and of course Spheres will be fine," Rusty exploded in exasperation. "Thanks to *me*, Ellysa Roque won't be standing in DDL's way any longer!"

"What are you saying?" Derian cried in alarm. "What did you do to Ellysa?"

"I handled the situation. I proved myself! I proved that I'm the only one competent enough to run DDL!" he raved, edging closer toward Derian. "Thanks to me, DDL will be a success! Everyone will know my name, Derian Delorian, the Derian who never fails! And now there's only one last obstacle to handle."

As Rusty strode toward her in his pumps, Derian edged out of her chair and backed away, frantically racking her brain for some way to reason with him. There was no resemblance between the brother she loved and the demented creature before her. His made-up face was garish in the overhead lights. There was a crazed look in his eyes, and his lipstick-slashed mouth was contorted into a grimace. She had always been able to use words as her weapon, but they were having no effect on him.

"You!" he screamed menacingly, swiping at her across the desk with the fountain pen. "You're the failure! You're a black mark on DDL's reputation and I won't stand for it!"

"Rusty, no!" Derian cried, flattening herself against the wall behind her desk.

"I'm Derian, Derian, Derian!" he shrieked and lunged at her, the deadly fountain pen in front of him like a blade.

After parking his car in the driveway, Joi Lin dropped Sid and the baby off. Sid was too distraught to think clearly, and Joi Lin was thankful that the nanny was there to take care of Sydny Ellen. When she was sure Sid had her number in case he needed her, she called a cab.

During the ride home, Joi Lin reflected on the events of the past few weeks. She tried to organize her thoughts around the facts known about the murders, and the facts all pointed to Derian. She had dismissed Derian as a suspect at first because of her alibi the night of Alan's murder. But now Derian seemed to be the key. Even the witnesses at the Beverly Hills Hotel reported seeing a redheaded woman near Ellysa when she died. But still she wasn't convinced. Her gut feelings told her Derian couldn't be the murderer, not the Derian she knew anyway. The Derian she knew hired her and took special care to make her feel a part of DDL. She kept Charis on as long as she could out of friendship and loyalty. She adored her little brother, even though she patronized him, and she had worked hard to build a career from model to businesswoman.

Joi Lin recalled her last conversation with Charis and a thought kept lingering in her subconscious, just out of reach. She strained to bring it back and finally it clicked into place. When she had been looking through Derian's old portfolio and tear sheets, weeks before, she had seen an Hermès tear sheet showing a much younger Derian, Charis, and two other models. She was sure the date on it had been 1972!

When the taxi dropped her off at her apartment, she didn't go in; instead, she raced to her car. She had to go to the agency and get the tear sheet to show Frank!

Joi Lin pulled up in front of the agency and left the car in a no-parking zone, knowing she wouldn't be staying long enough to get towed. She started to unlock the front door to DDL, but to her surprise, it was already open. Cautiously she turned the handle and stepped inside. The reception area was dark, but there was a light on in Derian's office and she could hear voices. Quietly she tiptoed to the door and peeked around the corner.

Derian was trying to edge herself along the wall, a look of terror on her face. A tall, redheaded woman stood in front of her, holding a box in one hand and brandishing what looked like a fountain pen in the other. As Joi Lin moved into the room, the woman screamed incoherently at Derian and with her arm upraised, holding the fountain pen like a dagger, she attacked. Derian threw her arm up to protect herself, but she was trapped, she had nowhere to run.

Simultaneously, without thinking, Joi Lin leapt forward and tackled the woman from behind. All three of them collapsed to the ground in a tangle of arms and legs. Joi Lin landed on the woman's legs, and she desperately clawed her way up the woman's body toward her arm.

Derian was on the bottom of the pile, pinned beneath Rusty. She struggled to fight him off, and with all of her strength, she raked her nails down the side of his face, leaving deep trails of blood in their wake from his temple to his chin. She could feel his flesh curl under the onslaught of her nails, and she winced, knowing the pain she was inflicting on her brother.

Rusty was beyond feeling pain, only rage. With a scream that was more animal than human, he sank the sharp poison-laden point of the pen deep into Derian's neck over and over again. With a gasp, Derian fell back against the floor, clutching at the pen still protruding from her throat. She began to convulse.

Joi Lin was only vaguely aware of what was happening to Derian. Her only thought was to hang on to the strange redheaded woman, but she was no physical match for her. As the woman wriggled from beneath her, Joi Lin made a last effort to stop her. She grabbed the woman by her long red hair, but to her shock, it came off in her hands. The woman screeched in rage and twisted away. Then she turned and knocked Joi Lin out of the way with a blow to her stomach. Joi Lin crumpled against the wall, unable to breathe, and when she looked up, she looked directly into Rusty's face! His eyes were crazed and she wasn't sure if he even recognized her, but she braced herself, positive he would come after her. Instead, he picked up the wig and fled from the room.

Joi Lin started to follow him, but, instead, crawled to Derian's side. Derian gasped for air, but it was too late. There was no time for recriminations, or hate, or even amends. There was only the sadness of failure. Even in her final moments, Derian's thoughts were for her beloved brother. She gripped Joi Lin's arm as Joi Lin cradled her head in her lap. As convulsions racked her body and saliva foamed from her lips, Derian whispered Rusty's name for the last time.

"Forgive him." She sighed, the effort causing her to break into a wet spasm of coughing. "My fault." And then she was gone.

Joi Lin gently laid Derian's head on the carpet. Holding back a sob, she dialed 911, although she knew it was too late for Derian. Then she paged Frank on his beeper. He immediately called back.

"Oh, Frank," Joi Lin cried at the sound of his voice. "Derian's dead!"

"What!" Frank exclaimed in disbelief. "What happened?"

"It was Rusty! Rusty killed her!"

"When?"

"Just now," she explained through her tears. "I tried to stop him but I couldn't!"

"Is he still there?" Frank asked quickly, concerned for Joi Lin.

"No, he ran away. Frank, he was dressed like a woman!"

Relieved that she was safe, her words about Rusty's dress registered with him. Now his biggest concern was where to find Rusty.

"Do you know where he was going?" he asked her.

"Not really. But I have a feeling that he went to the studio."

"I think you're right. I'll take a couple of men and go there right now. In the meantime, I'll send Officer O'Conner to DDL. I want you to lock the door and wait until they arrive. Understand?"

"Yes," Joi Lin said, her voice cracking. "Frank, it was so horrible! I couldn't stop him!"

"I know, baby. I know. You did your best."

She slammed the studio door, deadbolted it, and leaned against it, out of breath. She had to have time to think.

Her head was pounding, the side of her face where that bitch had scratched her throbbed, and everything was a jumble of disjointed thoughts. She'd had everything under control, but then out of nowhere, that stupid bookkeeper had jumped her. Didn't Joi Lin understand she was the only one who could save DDL, save that bookkeeper's job? And what about her baby! Where was her precious golden baby? The box had been in her hand one minute and the next, it was gone. When things calmed down, she'd have to go back for it. It was her responsibility to protect the tiny creature.

Above the pounding in her temples, she became aware of a police siren, the sound increasing as it drew closer. When it abruptly stopped, she knew the police had arrived. In a matter of seconds, someone began beating on the other side of the studio door, and she lurched toward her apartment. On the way, her pump caught on a wire, and she tripped over a power pack. She hit her head on the floor and for a moment she lay there, disoriented. Slowly she staggered to her feet and ran into the apartment, desperately looking for a place to hide. She thought of a perfect place—the terrarium.

She hurried down the hallway into the darkroom and through the door in the back wall. A blast of moist, black air assailed her, and she stepped into the darkness. She shut the door behind her and turned the dimmer up only the slightest bit. She was so familiar with the room, she could almost find her way by touch.

There was a rustling behind the glass partition as the creatures sensed her presence. She had never been behind the glass wall, but she was positive her babies wouldn't hurt her. There was no other place for her to hide; the thick foliage at the back of the cage was her only hope.

She opened the cage door, and the floor of the cage flowed with color as her babies dispersed in all directions away from her. Behind her, she could hear the police coming closer, and she closed the cage door. As she took a step forward, the bodies of several unfortunate babies crunched beneath her feet. Shuddering, she fought off an attack of hysteria and kept moving. More of them snapped beneath her step as she ducked up under the thick foliage and tried to make herself invisible. She knew it would only be seconds before the police came through the door, but she felt she could elude them in her hiding place.

The creatures panicked at the intrusion, scattering in all directions, their defense mechanisms releasing their deadly toxin. Scores of them hopped to the foliage at the rear of the compound, seeking refuge from what their primitive brains deemed a predator.

In her haste to hide under the foliage, she bumped against an overhead branch and knocked a dozen or so of the little creatures out of their hiding places. They fell on top of her head and shoulders; and in terror, they scrambled up the sides of her face trying to escape. Their suctioned feet were unable to find purchase on her bloody skin and their secreting wet bodies rubbed against the open wounds on her face.

Three tries and the studio door collapsed under the weight of Hollis and his officers. As it buckled inward, Hollis caught sight of Rusty disappearing behind a door at the far side of the studio. He pursued him at a run, his men close at his back. Kicking open the second door, they found themselves in Rusty's apartment and they methodically began searching the rooms.

Suddenly Hollis heard muffled screams coming from a door at the end of a long hall. Yanking it open, he found himself in Rusty's darkroom. Loud screams of pain and terror issued forth from the back wall of the darkroom, and Hollis ran his fingers across its expanse, searching for the seams of a door. His nails caught on an almost invisible line and he looked around for something with which to pry the door open. He grabbed an artist's spatula off a table and shoved it into the crack and applied pressure. He was sure the spatula would break, but instead he heard a loud crack as the catch gave and the door swung noiselessly outward.

Immediately a blast of hot, damp air hit him. The screams had stopped, and the room lay in almost total darkness. Hollis, his gun drawn, felt along the wall for a light switch. His fingers found a dimmer switch and he twisted it, filling the room with an eerie black light.

Directly in front of him, the room had been glassed off. Behind the glass was a huge terrarium from which radiated a blaze of brilliant jeweled colors. There were frogs everywhere, hundreds of them, ranging in size from three inches to three quarters of an inch and in every possible hue: sapphire blue and black striped ones, shocking pink and green iridescent ones, black and white zebra-striped ones, pure yellow ones. Disoriented by the noise and light, they were all moving around the terrarium like a field of tropical blossoms rippling in a breeze and in the center of them was Rusty's convulsing body.

CHAPTER
12

After the coroner finished, officers in protective suits removed Rusty's body, and Hollis notified the ASPCA to pick up the frogs. To the right of the darkroom, Hollis had found a small second room Rusty had used as a makeup room and closet with women's clothing and an assortment of women's wigs in various colors. Three of the walls were lined with exquisite color photographs of Rusty's frogs. They were amazing in their composition.

"This guy should have worked for *National Geographic*," one of the officers muttered. "He coulda made a killing."

He may have made several killings, Hollis thought to himself grimly.

The fourth wall was covered with a complicated collage of snapshots, magazine articles, and papers depicting the history of Rusty's frogs and their black market arrival at his studio. There were pages torn from magazines and stacks of books telling of their deadly nature. Hollis briefly skimmed through some of the articles.

He learned that the frogs were native to the jungles of South America and that they were part of two groups or genera of frogs called *Dendrobates* and *Phyllobates*. The most virulent toxin-producing species of the *Phyllobates* genera was the *P. terribilis*. It was a tiny golden yellow frog with a poison gland on its back that secreted one of the most lethal toxins known to man. Even handling the frog without protection would cause severe irritation.

For centuries, he read, the South American Indians used the poison secreted by the various frogs on their arrows and dart guns. In the case of the *P. terribilis* species, Indians only had to hold the frogs down with a stick and rub their arrow tips on the frog's back. In other species, the Indians would skewer the frogs and hold them over a fire, catching the deadly liquid that dripped off them.

The toxin was lethal for up to a year and the magazine reaffirmed what Hollis already knew: that one ounce of it was enough to kill two and a half million people. A mind-boggling concept.

He continued to search through the papers and collected a number of them to read in depth. Just as he was preparing to leave, a small lockbox caught his attention. He jimmied the lock and found a photo album and journals Rusty had kept over the years. He took the lockbox with him, intending to read the journals at home.

Hollis was exhausted, but before going home, he stopped by Joi Lin's apartment.

She saw him drive up and she met him at the door. "Did you get him?" she asked, giving Frank a welcoming kiss.

Frank gave Joi Lin a tired nod and hugged her tight.

"I wanted to make sure you were all right," he explained. "Are you?"

"I am now," Joi Lin said, leading him over to the couch. "I just feel so awful about Derian. I kept praying she wasn't dead, but deep down, after seeing how Holly died, I knew there was no way she would make it. There was nothing I could do to help her. All I could do was hold her head. I tried to make her last moments as comfortable as possible.

"I feel awful, too, that we thought she was the murderer.

She had nothing to do with them. It was all Rusty. He was a dead ringer for Derian in that red wig!" Joi Lin said. "I'm so glad you caught him!"

"I didn't exactly catch him. He's dead," Frank explained.

"What!" Joi Lin exclaimed, shocked. "How, Frank? What happened?"

"Make a pot of coffee and I'll fill you in on the details."

Joi Lin went into the kitchen to make coffee and Frank followed her. Sitting down at the table, he told her of the evening's events.

"Frogs?" Joi Lin said incredulously. She took two cups from the cupboard and poured steaming coffee into them. "Frogs of all things? I've never heard of anything so bizarre. Where did he get them? Where did the poison come from?"

Frank told her about the collage and articles he had found in Rusty's apartment. He showed her Rusty's journals and changing his mind about going home asked Joi Lin to stay up with him all night, if necessary, to read them.

"By the way," Frank said, taking a sip of coffee, "what were you doing at DDL? You were supposed to drop Sid Roque off at his house and go directly home."

"I did," Joi Lin said. "But on the way home, I suddenly remembered Charis telling me about how she and Derian modeled together and seeing an Hermès tear sheet in Derian's filing cabinet and I put two and two together—"

"And came up with Derian as the murderer," Frank finished for her.

"Yup," Joi Lin said. "I wanted to get the tear sheet to show you. But when I got to the agency, the door was open and I heard voices coming from Derian's office. The rest you know."

"You took a big chance, taking on Rusty," Frank admonished gently. "He could have turned on you. You were very lucky."

"I know, but I had no idea it was Rusty until I pulled

his wig off. All I could think of was helping Derian. Poor
Derian. She loved Rusty so much. You know, her final
words to me were to forgive him."

Joi Lin's voice broke, and she struggled to keep her
composure.

Frank reached across the table and took her hand comfortingly. "Hey," he said, changing the subject, "let's start
on those journals."

"Okay," Joi Lin agreed, wiping her eyes and taking a
large sip of coffee to steady her nerves.

Chronicled in Rusty's journals was the whole tragic story of Rusty's life: the murders he committed, his motives,
and his murder weapons. For his entire life, Rusty had
taken second place to Derian. Derian had always been
the favored child. She was considered the prettiest, the
brightest, the one destined for fame and fortune. Rusty was
repeatedly told to be more like his sister. He was admonished and beaten for any small infraction. He learned
that the only way to avoid rebuke was to watch Derian
constantly and to emulate her actions.

Finally over the years, Rusty's state of mind slipped
over the edge until he thought he *was* Derian. Although
he began to second-guess her decisions, he was unable
to confront her directly. Instead, he would keep in the
background, secretly making plans.

Next to Rusty, DDL was Derian's focus in life and it
became Rusty's, also. When Alan threatened the agency's future, Rusty fought back with murder. And when
Holly wanted to return to Paris, Rusty perceived it as an
attack on DDL and acted accordingly. Losing the Spheres
account was the last straw and he blamed the baby for
it. He saw the agency's loss of revenues as a failure on
Derian's part, and his murders as triumphs of his superior
judgment over hers. His end results justified the means in
his mind. He saw himself as DDL's savior, and because
he had so closely imitated Derian, he became Derian while
she became just another obstacle to eliminate.

Tears streamed down Joi Lin's cheeks as she read
Rusty's story. She could identify with him, because

their stories were so similar. She knew the pain of growing up in someone else's shadow, of being the invisible child. But despite her feelings of inferiority, she had been strong enough to rise above the constant comparisons and demands. Rusty's insecurities drove him into madness, until he strove not only to be like Derian, but to become Derian.

The story wrenched at Joi Lin's heart. She finally had her brother's murderer, but not before other lives were destroyed, and she wept, not only for them, but for the twisted and unhappy life Rusty had lived.

"If only I had known what he was feeling," she wept, huddled against Frank's shoulder. "Maybe I could have helped."

Frank was silent, letting her cry. Even if she had known, he suspected that Rusty had been too far gone at that point to be helped. For his part, now the investigation was almost history; with Joi Lin in his arms, he thought about the future. Until recently, he hadn't known how lonely he really was. Joi Lin filled a void he hadn't known existed. Their life together was so right, so natural, that he knew he would never let her go.

Early the next morning, Joi Lin visited Sid Roque. The housekeeper let her in and she found Sid was in the rocking chair in the nursery, holding Sydny Ellen.

"Good morning, Sid," she said, taking a seat next to him and touching his arm.

He looked at her and smiled sadly.

"I wanted to stop by and check on you. You know the police caught Ellysa's murderer."

He nodded. "Yes, Lieutenant Hollis called and told me the whole story."

"It wasn't anything Ellysa did," Joi Lin said. "Rusty wasn't even after Ellysa. In his sick mind, he thought Sydny Ellen was the source of DDL's problems."

"My God." Sid sighed. "It's all such a terrible tragedy, Joi Lin. If I had only known, I would have convinced Ellysa to continue Spheres's advertising campaign. I guess she was so consumed with the baby she didn't think to mention it to me. I would have fired Lucille Ritter in a heartbeat." A tear threatened to spill down the corner of his eye, and he turned his head away before Joi Lin could see it.

"Please let me know if there is anything I can do to help you," she offered.

She sat with him for a while, but there wasn't much more she could say. Only time would heal his pain. When she left, he was still in the rocking chair, holding Sydny Ellen.

From Sid's house, Joi Lin drove to DDL to tell Betsy what had transpired. Betsy had already arrived and was trying to decide whether to cross the police's roped-off area.

"Holy shit!" Betsy exclaimed as Joi Lin hurried up the sidewalk. "What the hell happened here?"

They crossed under the tape and went into the agency. Joi Lin explained what her relationship was to Alan Ainsley Anderson and everything that had happened over the past twenty-four hours.

"Poor Derian," Betsy said over and over. "She loved Rusty so much. Sometimes you just never know about people. Frogs! How weird!"

At that moment Frank arrived, followed by Tartella. Frank walked over and put his arm around Joi Lin, squeezing her shoulders. Betsy stared at them with a look of surprise on her face.

"Oh, there's one other thing I forgot to tell you, Betsy," Joi Lin said apologetically. "Frank and I are sort of— friends."

"We may have started out as friends," Frank corrected her with an affectionate smile, "but we're much more than that now."

Betsy looked from one to the other and then over at Tartella.

"Hi, my name's Betsy," she said with an impish smile. "You wanta be friends?"

After Frank and Tartella had surveyed the crime scene,

they left. Joi Lin and Betsy decided that the best way to handle the news of Derian's death was to hold an all-agency meeting that afternoon and they began telephoning the models.

They were so engrossed in their calls that they didn't notice the flash of brilliant color squeeze through a crack in Derian's office doorway into the reception area.

At that moment Tiffany flounced into the agency, slamming the door behind her. "Hey, what's with the barricade?" she asked, popping her gum. She sat down on the edge of Betsy's desk and proceeded to straighten her panty hose.

Joi Lin broke the news to her, and to Joi Lin's shock Tiffany murmured a few obligatory words of sympathy and then narcissistically launched into questions of how Derian's death would affect her and her career.

"I know it's an awful situation," Tiffany said, straightening her blouse and staring at her reflection in the window-pane. "But what about my bookings? I can't afford to lose any of my accounts."

Joi Lin felt herself doing a slow burn. How could Tiffany think about herself at a time like this? Didn't it matter to her that five people were dead? She started to tell Tiffany exactly what she thought of her when the telephone rang and she stopped to answer it.

While Joi Lin spoke on the telephone, Tiffany impatiently wandered around the room, nosing through booking sheets and billings on the desks, observing her reflection in all available shiny surfaces. She casually glanced down at the floor and noticed a spot of color.

"Eeekk," Tiffany squealed in disgust. "Doesn't anyone ever clean around here?"

Joi Lin, engrossed in her conversation, looked up just as Tiffany was bending over for a closer look.

"No!" Joi Lin screamed, dropping the phone as she saw the tiny frog. "Don't touch it!"

But at that moment, Tiffany lifted her foot and crushed the frog.

"I think it was some sort of weird roach," she told Joi

Lin, oblivious to the danger. "You know, you guys really oughta keep it cleaner in here!"

Joi Lin and Betsy looked at each other and burst out laughing.

"Are you guys laughing at me?" Tiffany asked insecurely, making a quick check of her appearance in the reflection of the window.

Later that day at the models meeting, Joi Lin told the models about what had happened to Derian and the plans to close the agency.

"But why do you have to close DDL?" Julie asked. "Why can't you and Betsy run it?"

"Yes, why not?" five or six other models chimed in.

"I—I'm a bookkeeper, not a booker," Joi Lin stammered. "What do I know about running an agency?"

"You can learn," Misha said. "You'd be great."

"We'll help you," Linda called from the back of the room. "We don't want to close DDL and go to other agencies. We're a family here, we want to stay together."

Joi Lin was quiet. It had never occurred to her that the models would want to keep the agency open. The truth was, she loved the fashion business and the models.

"I think we should take a vote," Misha called out. "All in favor of backing Joi Lin and Betsy to run DDL say aye."

"Wait a minute," Tiffany protested from the back of the room. "What if some of my accounts don't want to book me because of the stigma attached to DDL? I mean I have my image to think about."

"Tiffany, for once in your life, shut up," Leatrice said dryly.

"Aye," the rest of the models shouted in unison.

DDL's doors stayed open.

Two weeks after Ellysa's death, Sid sat behind her desk, his eyes traveling over the sleek wood and settling on her picture. In his grief, Sid had decided that the most important things in his life were his baby daughter, and making Ellysa's dream of Spheres being the number-one trend-setting boutique in Los Angeles and Beverly Hills a reality. The first step in his plan was his arrival at Spheres before it opened. Then he studied the accounting books and was appalled at what he found.

The boutique was floundering. In the sportswear department, no one was buying new merchandise or even getting the merchandise already stocked on the floor. The pool needed cleaning, and several of the male exercise instructors and masseurs had quit. Mrs. Ritter had hired inexperienced instructors and masseuses in an effort to save money with disastrous results. Now none of the Beverly Hills matrons wanted to use the facilities. Mrs. Ritter had fired Mr. Paul, the manager of the couture department, and the department was in a turmoil. No one was handling the position of fashion coordinator.

His first decision was to fire Lucille Ritter and he called her into the office.

"Mrs. Ritter," he began as tactfully as possible, "I want to thank you for all the help and support you've given Spheres."

"Oh, you're welcome, Mr. Roque," Lucille said, bobbing her head.

"I've gone over the situation here and I've come to some hard decisions, but decisions nonetheless that have to be made if Spheres is going to continue to grow."

Lucille was silent. An alarm was going off in her head and she waited for him to continue. Her bad eye started to twitch and water.

"I'm going to take over the management of Spheres," he told her. "I'll make sure you get a generous severance, but we won't be needing you any longer."

"What!" Lucille exclaimed, half standing, her fists clenched at her sides. "What! After all I've done?"

All you've done, Sid thought to himself. Maybe it wasn't fair, but he couldn't help think that Ellysa might have lived had Mrs. Ritter not cut Spheres's advertising program. She had no way of knowing that, of course, but still every time he looked at her he was reminded of that fact.

"I appreciate everything you've done, but I'm going to take over," Sid repeated firmly. "Call it therapy if you will."

Lucille was silent; she didn't know what to say. How could she argue if the man wanted to manage his own company?

"Of course, if you'd like to remain on in your former position, you're welcome to," Sid added generously. He didn't want her working for him, but he felt it was unfair to let her go with no other prospects.

Lucille tossed her head back and summoned all her pride. The last thing she was going to do was take charity. "I don't think that will be necessary, Mr. Roque," she said haughtily. "Xenon down the street has been begging me to work for them."

"If that's what you want," Sid said quickly without an argument. Getting rid of her was easier than he had anticipated.

With Mrs. Ritter's departure, Sid was still left without a fashion coordinator so he called Joi Lin for advice.

"Let me think for a moment," she said, racking her brain. Then a thought came to her. "I know the perfect person!" she exclaimed excitedly. "She's a former model. Her name is Charis."

"Charis?" Sid repeated the name.

"Yes, she would be perfect!" Joi Lin enthused. Joi Lin knew Charis's modeling career was over and she suspected that in the past two weeks, Charis had finally realized it herself. The position of fashion coordinator at Spheres was a prestigious one, and she hoped that Charis would be interested.

Joi Lin arrived at the Polo Lounge at the Beverly Hills Hotel for her lunch date with Charis. As she walked through the doorway, she spotted Charis, and to her surprise she saw Sid sitting with Chi Chi Von Wittsburg at a table beyond. Sid saw her and waved. Waving in return, she made her way to Charis's table.

They ordered salads and iced tea.

"How have things been going at DDL?" Charis asked. She hadn't been back to the agency since Derian's death.

"Really well, actually," Joi Lin answered. "Our accounts for the most part have continued to book through us despite everything that's happened. I've also had Betsy making cold calls and sending out the headshot book to prospective clients. I think everything is working out."

The waiter brought their lunch, and Charis continued the conversation. "I've heard from some of the other models that you have a new love in your life," she said with a smile. "Is this something permanent?"

Joi Lin blushed, but her face lit up. "It looks like it. Frank asked me to marry him last night," she confided, her face glowing with happiness.

"I'm so happy for you," Charis exclaimed, giving Joi Lin a warm hug.

"Life works out in strange ways, huh," Joi Lin said. "If Rusty hadn't murdered Alan, then I would never have met Frank. Life is such a matter of timing."

"You're right," Charis reflected. "I've spent the past few weeks coming to terms with my faltering modeling career. Derian's death has taught me about the fragility of life and the importance of timing. I know now that it's time to move on to another stage in my life."

Joi Lin listened without speaking.

"I'm so sorry about my last meeting with Derian," Charis continued regretfully. "I've wished so many times that there was some way I could turn back the clock and change it."

"Don't hold it against yourself, Charis," Joi Lin said, giving her a reassuring hug. "I think Derian knew your anger was only temporary. You two had been friends for too long. She knew that you had stuck by her for years and that loyalty was what really counted with her. She knew she needed to make some changes, but she wanted what was best for you, too. If there's one thing we can learn from Derian, it was her strength and determination to keep trying."

Charis nodded. "Now I just have to find another career."

"I have a suggestion," Joi Lin said.

"What's that?"

"Spheres is looking for a new fashion coordinator and I recommended you. Think about it, no more competing with modelettes, no more insecurities about your appearance. You'd be the boss!"

Charis thought for a moment. "I think I might like that."

"You know, Charis," Joi Lin said, signaling the waiter for their check, "leaving your modeling career isn't an ending, it's a beginning."

They paid the check and started for the exit. Sid had just finished his lunch with Chi Chi and he met them at the door.

"Sid," Joi Lin said, "I'd like you to meet Charis. She's the woman I told you about."

If Sid recognized Charis from the Spheres fashion show, he didn't mention it and neither did Charis.

"I understand you're looking for a new fashion coordinator at Spheres," Charis said, picking up on Joi Lin's cue. "I'm very interested in the position."

"Good," Sid said, escorting the two women through the doorway. "Let's set up a meeting to discuss it."

Chi Chi Von Wittsburg watched Sid, Joi Lin, and Charis leave together from the number-one booth in the lounge. She signaled to Emilio to bring her a telephone. Sid had told her everything, and she couldn't wait until she got home to start dialing her friends with the entire DDL story of twisted jealousy, deep love, and heart-wrenching insecurities in the world of the sleek, the chic, and the dead.